THE HUNTED

A Life and Death Adventure

Colleen Flanagan

First published 2025 by Colleen Flanagan

Produced by Independent Ink
independentink.com.au

Cover design by Peter Flanagan
Edited by Michele Perry
Internal design by Independent Ink
Typeset in 12/17 pt Adobe Garamond Pro by Post Pre-press Group, Brisbane
Map on page v by Peter Flanagan
Cover image: 811948/Pixabay

ISBN 978-1-7640990-0-4 (paperback)
ISBN 978-1-7640990-1-1 (epub)
ISBN 978-1-7640990-2-8 (kindle)

for Peter

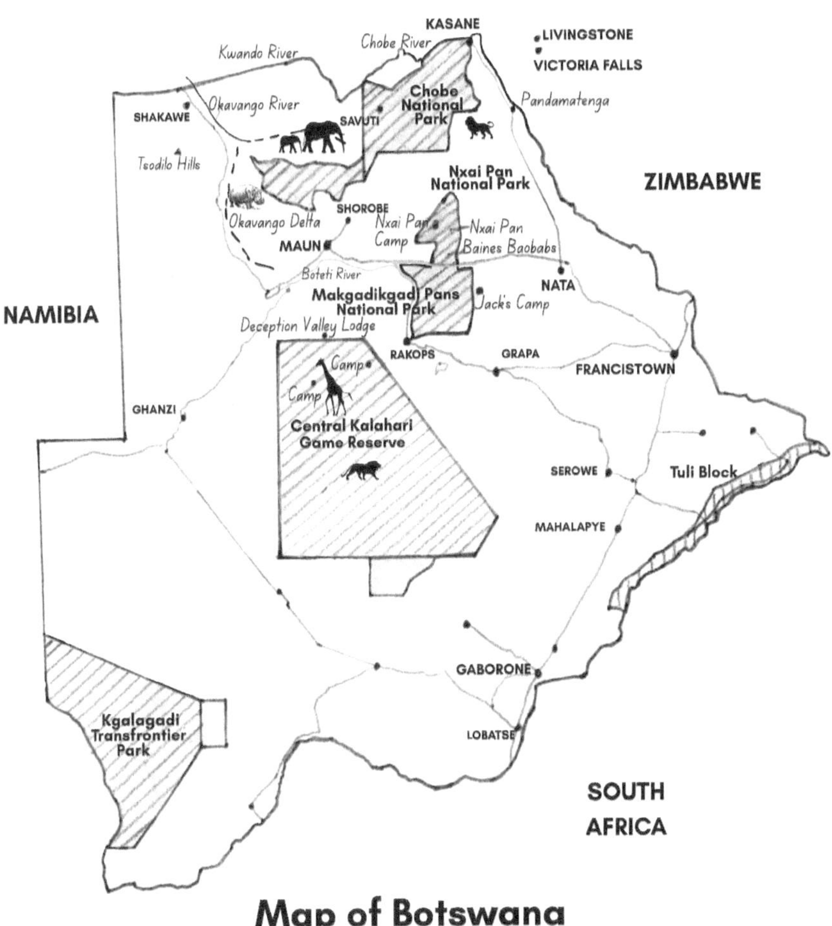

Map of Botswana

Dorset

I sat in my favourite chair facing the afternoon sunshine. Cobwebs of hazy golden light sifted through the window, warming my coat and soothing my tired old bones. I let out a gruff purr as the silence creased over me.

She stepped into the room; the bright-red nail polish on her toes looked like little drops of blood on the glossy white tiles. Her eyes were framed with red circles, and flakes of mascara sat on her cheeks. Her hands fidgeted with her sweater, pulling the edges into tight little balls. Her dress flowed over her, and I imagined it slipping off to pool on the floor. Her bright-blue eyes rooted around the room, reaching into all the corners and chasing over the furniture. At last, she spied me, and with tears welling in her eyes, she sat on the floor, her fingers laced through my thick fur.

'What's wrong with him tonight, Dorset? Why is he so furious with me?' Her voice trembled.

I stretched out my paw towards her hand.

She jumped a little from the touch, as though she forgot I sat beside her. She looked startled, and I began to worry. Then she wrung her hands nervously, to dig her nails into the soft flesh of her palms. Blood knitted through her jumper, but I doubt she cared. We sat together while the sun dipped closer to the horizon, our shadows growing long across the floor.

Heavy footsteps on the stairs broke the serenity of the afternoon.

She cowered closer to me, trying to make herself invisible, so if he came in, he might see only me. Perhaps his anger would dissolve if he saw me sitting so contentedly.

But that didn't happen.

'You crazy bitch. How did I endure your changing moods for so long? You belong in an insane asylum. Get out of my house, witch, and if I ever catch you lurking in the corners again, so help me, I won't be held responsible for my actions. You spend more time with that damn cat than you ever did with me.'

She crumpled at his words, like someone had sucked out all her breath. She turned towards me, and I saw the terror in her sky-blue eyes. As she struggled to stand, she glanced in my direction. Her hand trailed across my head, softer than a butterfly, and I feared I may never see her again.

CHAPTER 1

Australia

Bella stood on the foreshore, staring into the hollowness of the sky. It had been a week since that night, but still, the memories clustered about her. The sun slanted behind her, digging into her shoulder blades; beads of sweat trickled down her back. The rays – so thick with remorse you could cut through them with a knife – trailed low over the ocean.

Bella tried to catch at snippets of her married life. *Where did it go so horribly wrong?* Bradley had been too overpowering for her gentle nature. Bella's anxiety twisted inside her. She had tried several times to apologise, but Bradley refused to speak with her. He even wouldn't allow her to visit her cat. *Dorset must be fretting for me by now,* she worried. His tolerance for having to deal with her depression and anxiety now floated out of reach.

The air back in her stark motel room, across the street from the beach, had stifled her. The lingering reminder of previous forgotten guests laced permanently into the threadbare wallpaper. Bella had needed to breathe in the salty tang of the ocean.

She ran barefoot along the beach; her dress clinging between her thighs. She thought she could outrun the bubbles of resentment that bounced off her husband, but she couldn't. The loneliness shadowed her everywhere.

Strolling to the water's edge, Bella let the pull of the waves suck around her ankles. Strands of seagrass nibbled against her toes. She shivered when a slight breeze floating over the water tugged at her dress.

Day twelve of living without a husband dawned cool and overcast. Bella sat on the rock wall overlooking the ocean, reading the text message from Tissa, for the hundredth time: *Please meet me for coffee, so much to tell you.* The ten words cut into Bella.

Light rain skimmed off the water. The weather seeped into Bella, her head ached, and the chill clung to her bones. Craving to touch reality, if only to remind herself that she existed, Bella decided to go to the trendy café in the middle of town, to meet Tissa. She needed to confront her face to face, to hear her confess as to why she threw away ten years of friendship to sleep with Bradley. The one person Bella imagined would never betray her was now in love with her husband. Bella cringed at the thought of Tissa in the home she once shared so passionately with Bradley. The idea of her best friend running her crimson fingernails over Bradley's naked body, the immaculate Italian leather furniture and Dorset curdled into her heart … she shook her head to rid herself of the thoughts. And then she took a deep breath and peeled herself away from the calming essence of the ocean and headed to the café.

Bella fidgeted with her napkin as she waited for Tissa to join her. She ignored the curious stares from the men in the room as she raked the back of her hand across her cheeks to wipe away the tears that refused to leave her. Tissa kept Bella waiting for over fifteen minutes. Bella tried to gather the courage to leave the café and forget Tissa had stolen her husband, but her nerves were stretched too tight across the table.

Tissa waltzed in, weaving around the tables. Lingering traces of Chanel No. 5 chased after her. She was a vision of perfection, and a twinge of panic knotted in Bella. She seldom made an effort with her appearance; yet another contentious issue Bradley found fault with. Her tousled hair cascaded down her back in untidy whorls, and she wore the same dress she had left home in. The small tear at the hemline grew by the hour as Bella scrunched it into a ball to dry away her tears.

'You look adorable,' Tissa trilled shriller than a canary in the crowded room. The kiss she tried to plant on Bella's cheek dangled in mid-air, sliding down onto the table where it lay waiting for some sign of recognition.

'Liar, I look and feel like shit,' Bella whispered into the room that held a hint of coffee and cinnamon. She doubted they held a single thing in common now, apart from her husband. Bella let her silence infuse through the café.

'Did I tell you Brad and I are going to the Premier's Ball? Everyone will be there. It's the highlight on the calendar. Such fun.'

Bella remained silent, staring at a small crease in the tablecloth.

Tissa laughed. 'Did you say something? Anyway, Brad's buying me that gorgeous Marina Rinaldi evening gown for the ball. It's so divine.'

Bella's heart crumpled around the edges. Tissa didn't even seem to notice how her words were like blades cutting into Bella.

Tissa kept babbling. 'Sorry. Do you want another coffee? My shout. It's great to catch up. Brad's taking me to dinner at—'

Bella stood up, and without drinking any of the tepid tea, or mumbling any clichés to Tissa, she left the café. A smile caught at Bella, with the realisation of never seeing her again coated through her.

Weeks floated by, following the ebb and flow of the tides. The finality of her divorce cut her to shreds. Bella had spent her whole life lost in cobwebs of doubt, and now she had to find a reason to live. Her husband had crushed her confidence but not her spirit. All her unhappiness was sewn through Dorset's fur. She felt his aura floating around her, willing her to be safe and happy.

The walls in her motel room inched closer by the day, they were hemming her in. Bella went outside to stand in the middle of the empty carpark. She faced west, trailing her fingers through a heavy sea fog. Breathing in to clear her mind of rubble, everything became crystal clear for Bella. She remembered a safari to Zimbabwe with Bradley. She loved it, surrounded by lions, but Bradley hated the flies and dust. Maybe that had been the beginning of the end of her marriage. She wanted to set herself free from Bradley, Tissa, and her clinging insecurities.

She did a small amount of research about the African country that held all her dreams, but in the end chose Botswana. The name resonated with dewdrops falling from an acacia tree. It magically wove its way into her heart. She could already smell the sands of the Kalahari, gritty and welcoming.

Perhaps that had always been her problem. She had been born in the wrong country. Never feeling at peace in Australia, Bella wanted to believe Botswana held the serenity she had been craving.

And so, Bella booked a one-way ticket to Maun, spending the days until the flight there more nervous than an impala tiptoeing in the long grass. Maun, a town in the northern part of Botswana, was nestled at the bottom of the Okavango Delta. She thought its dusty streets and isolation were the perfect location for her to lose herself and discover some purpose in life.

Bella sat in the taxi to the airport. Tears had crawled down her cheeks when she whispered goodbye to her mother and sister – the family that didn't want her. Did they stop to wonder at the grey shadow passing over them? Did her ex-husband wake up, reach over to touch her shoulder, wondering why a stranger lay next to him?

Bella placed her fingers on the cold surface of the taxi window. She felt certain her spirit touched the family she was leaving behind, even if it lasted for one fleeting second in their lives. She prayed for them to stay safe, and now no longer a part of their lives, they could find happiness.

Bella felt the tug of Dorset, deep in her soul. A vision, or was it a dream that floated in front of her eyes? Dorset was sleeping in his favourite chair. His whiskers twitched as though a bad dream itched at him. She raised her hand to let her finger stroke his soft fur, trying to reassure him. In her mind, he relaxed at her touch. She could almost sense Dorset's rumbling sigh, and when he opened his eyes to stare at her there was moisture glistening on his cheek. Or were they her tears? His purr hummed through her body, making Bella tremble with the realisation that she would never hold him again. Then the vision disappeared and all she could see was the highway and vehicles weaving in and out of the heavy traffic. Her tears rolled down her cheeks.

Dorset

I woke with a start. Something touched my fur, maybe a fly. Now I was wide-awake, I swore I saw the indent of a finger in my soft coat. I was convinced it was she. I hadn't seen her for a few weeks, and without her, my days were never-ending. She and I shared a closeness I didn't expect from a human. When she gazed into my eyes, it felt like she saw inside me.

In the last year or maybe two, she had been unwell. Not sick with the flu, but sick like she had lost her motivation to live. The sunshine had left her luminous eyes. She dragged her feet as though she failed to recognise these familiar rooms. She retreated into a different world. She seldom went outside into the garden to pick the flowers like she used to. She would let me play with the petals when they fell on the table, but not anymore.

I used to lie close beside her, letting her gather solace in my purrs while she stroked my silky grey coat. I didn't understand why people laughed at her kindness. She had such a gentle nature, not like the other lady he brought into my life.

The sun clawed at the window, and a tremor rumbled through my body. I felt Bella sitting near me, telling me she was going away and to be brave. I saw the tears falling from her eyes and felt a tug in my heart. I let out a soft purr to let her know I loved her too. It was the last time I ever purred. Tears touched my cheek, and when I detected her drifting further from me, I ceased to be of this world. My spirit followed her to keep her safe.

CHAPTER 2

Africa

The flight to Johannesburg passed in a blur of tiny bottles of Merlot. Bella booked into the City Lodge Hotel for her first night on African soil. Sleep stayed out of reach, so she scrambled out of bed before the sun could warm her sterile hotel room. She dressed in a rush, not bothering to comb the knots from her hair. Her cherry-coloured jumper draped in folds over her dress. Her boots hid grains of sand from solitary meanders along the beach beside her former home. A gritty reminder of her broken marriage.

Bella ignored the inquisitive glances from all the men as she sat waiting for her next flight. The Air Botswana plane to Maun may have shown a touch of tardiness about leaving on time, but with a great rush down the runway, Bella was at last airborne. The plane flew out of Johannesburg, slicing through fluffy white clouds into an iridescent blue sky. She stared down through the haze onto a patchwork of roads, farms and small houses that blinked bright jewels of colour in the warm sunshine. Rivers that – like her – hesitated about which way to go, snarled as confused snakes through the parched landscape.

Bella looked out of the window when the plane began its descent. Maun was bigger than the picture she had created in her mind. It spread out to hug the desert landscape. The Thamalakane River twined along one edge of the town, a ribbon of blue guarded by sycamore figs and mopane trees. Tiny houses sprinkled without much thought in the sand. Their yards were the colour of dried corn. Tar roads stretched their tentacles low to the ground before they disappeared into the fizzy heat. Traffic ravelled together, then slunk away in some bizarre jam-tin dance. The sun glistened off windscreens to bounce back into the sky.

The aircraft bounced with a heavy thud onto the runway, shaking on impact as though it had got a fright. Bella watched the terminal building fly past the tiny window, while the pilot brought the plane to a shuddering halt at the end of the runway.

The terminal, a low two-storey brick building, crouched like a dung beetle in the billowy mist. The heat ricocheted off the tarmac as everyone straggled down the stairs. Bella removed her jumper, tying it around her waist; sweat beaded down her back. She joined a long queue of fellow passengers meandering across the tarmac towards the terminal.

They were baking in the scorching sun; their shoes sticking on the hot bitumen while they waited to enter the immigration office. About twenty minutes later, Bella entered the airconditioned interior, glad at last to be out of the glare of the sun. She leant up against the grimy wall while waiting for her turn at the top of the queue.

Bella shuffled along, pushing her suitcase with a grubby boot to where a sign stated: *NON RESIDENTS*. At last, she reached the immigration official. He didn't even glance at her before taking out his rubber stamp to seal an ink smudge in her passport. He added his initials to the blue smudge before waving Bella away. She was now free to officially enter Botswana. Bella picked up her small suitcase, ducked under the sign saying: *Nothing to Declare*, and spilled out into the busy airport lounge.

Bella stood so still; her breath caught when the realisation that she had no idea about what to do with her life in Maun hit her. All the planning had led up to this moment. She shivered, clutching her handbag while a sea of fellow travellers jostled against her.

Bella chose to look carefree and in control of a life she had spent scratching the surface of. She strode with feigned confidence towards the glass entrance doors. Once out into the heat, she sighed, soaking up the surroundings like a sponge. The dusty-blue sky melted over her as she mentally embraced the township of Maun, in fact, the whole of Africa.

She felt at peace here, even after venturing a mere five metres from the terminal building. Tiny stalls in bright oranges and greens sold everything from cold drinks to haircuts. The stalls leant against mopane trees, so clients didn't have to wait in the sun. A bougainvillea curled through an acacia tree; its red flowers fell to carpet the sandy footpath.

She had forgotten how friendly the people were in Africa. Everyone who passed her greeted her with a 'Dumela Mma.' Their grins lit up their faces. The women wore dresses with swirls in every colour of the rainbow. Their hair was cornrowed and braided, with vibrant beads jangling around their faces and down their backs. Breathing in the air held hints of pine, honey, coffee beans – from the café across the road – and happiness.

CHAPTER 3

A café, swaying in the distance, rippled like a mirage in the afternoon heat. Hunger nibbled at her, so she walked towards it. A few curio shops fanned out beside her. Bella wove around wooden giraffes, elephants, and stacks of bright material that spilled out from the curio shops, to tempt the passing trade. She struggled with her bag in the thick sand at the side of the road, trying not to snag her legs on the thorny bushes growing at random in the hot sun.

The crowded café, aptly called the Dusty Donkey, defied the sand that clung to it. Bella stamped her boots and wandered into the noisy interior. The acrid punch of coffee mingled with the lighter tones of bacon frying and bread being toasted. She managed to squeeze into a small table at the rear next to the kitchen.

The waitress appeared, to help Bella push her bag under the table. She handed Bella a tatty menu with coffee stains blurring some of the words. 'Dumela Mma, what can I get you to drink?' She pulled out a pen that had been twisted into her long hair and started writing the table number in a small notebook.

Bella's throat felt rough with sand, and an icy beer sounded tempting, but she found herself answering, 'Dumela. A Coke Lite, no ice, thanks.' Now didn't seem the appropriate time to start drinking. She advised herself to stay alert to find some sort of accommodation for the night.

'Do you want more time deciding on your lunch, Mma?'

'No, I'll have the Caesar salad without the bacon, thank you.'

While she sat squashed between the kitchen and a display cabinet, Bella let the atmosphere twirl over her. She sipped on the chilled Coke and pushed bits of lettuce across her plate. Pieces of conversation blended into her; snippets of lives she would never be part of. For some strange reason, Bella felt at home here, although she knew no one.

Leaving the café, she hesitated about which direction to go in. Bella turned right; her hand shielded her eyes from the bright sunshine. Her sturdy boots sank into the soft sand as she stumbled down the tattered edges of the road.

In minutes, a tired, beat-up taxi pulled up next to her. A young lad leant out of the driver's window. 'Dumela Mma, I take you somewhere?' he shouted above the noise of the traffic, donkeys and people.

'Err yes.' Bella's anxiety stitched into her. 'Dumela. Can you take me to a lodge or hotel where I might be able to spend the night?'

'Of course, Mma. Please, I'll take you somewhere nice. How are you? You have arrived on the plane just now.' He jumped out of the car in a millisecond to toss her bag without a lot of care into the boot. The young driver then ushered Bella into the rear seat, slamming the door so hard the hinges groaned.

She collapsed into the sticky vinyl; a strong odour of sweat, stale beer and cheap perfume teased against the driver's minty aftershave. He kept up a steady stream of conversation, explaining about the town and where all the shops were. He gave Bella no time to answer his questions before more words tumbled from his mouth.

He drove, almost at a snail's pace, through the busy streets of bustling downtown Maun. People dressed in bright-coloured clothing dazzled in a hazy afternoon, their footsteps heavy in the sand. They shopped at the busy Choppies Supermarket, retail shops and market stalls.

Her adroit driver seemed to be creating alternate roads. He zigzagged around people and other cars, waving and smiling to them as he negotiated the labyrinth. 'I take you to the best lodge in all of Botswana. My brother is the head waiter there. He'll look after you, Mma,' The taxi driver yelled above the noise.

'Thank you,' was all Bella could muster. She didn't have the energy to question him about the distance they were driving, so she relaxed into her seat to watch Africa glide past the window.

It seemed hours to her strung-out body when at last he turned off the main road onto a sandy track overrun by a jumble of trees. After greeting the security man, a boom gate swung open, and they drove into the parking lot of the Island Safari Lodge. The lodge sat close to the Thamalakane River and settled in a grove of twisted trees with branches snaking in all directions.

Bella took mere minutes to settle into her little cabin by the river. The cabin, rendered the colour of winter grass, sat in lush gardens. Its thatched roof hung low, forming an eave. Two giraffes made of wrought-iron clung to the wall beside the heavy timber door. The cool interior spread through the dimness, and it took Bella a moment to adjust to the gloom. A strong smell of disinfectant and beeswax curled into her nostrils. Two beds were made up with crisp linen and fluffy throws depicting African wildlife draped across the doonas. Although old and fusty, the large shower room sparkled with cleanliness.

Once unpacked and freshened up, Bella retraced her steps along the cobbled paths meandering through giant trees; their branches straining towards the sun. Vervet monkeys played in the foliage. They stared down at her through the dappled light. The main lodge wore the same faded winter grass colour as her cabin. Its thatch dipped low to shade the interior. One side opened out to the weather, where heavy mahogany chairs sat at random around an open fire and the bar area.

Bella strolled across a paved terrace to the wooden tables and chairs placed with care to give expansive views across the river. On the far side, cattle were making their way to the water's edge for their afternoon drink. The serenity of the scene wrapped through Bella.

She ordered a chardonnay, and while waiting for it, Bella let her mind flow in time to the currents eddying in the river. She knew she should be making decisions, but for now, she let the peace fold into her, to take away her anxiety. Bella sipped the wine, not wanting to make a spectacle of herself at the moment.

Finishing her second chardonnay, she pulled herself up from the table. Maybe a walk alone by the river would clear her head. A few people gathered by the railing to gaze at something in the water. Bella turned towards the river, and to her surprise, a hippo bobbed against the currents. Her first wildlife encounter in Botswana. She leant over the rail to watch while the hippo wallowed in the shallow water. He also appeared to be on his own.

The hippo gave Bella a boost to her wilted confidence. When she had booked in at the reception, she saw that they ran safaris each day into the Moremi Game Reserve. How soothing would it be to watch a lion, to hear their whispers and touch their love? She left the hippo to wander back to the reception desk. Before Bella found the chance to reconsider, she had booked a ticket.

The pretty girl at the reception told her the safari left at five-thirty the next morning and didn't return until late the same day. Also, there would be a briefing after dinner to meet the guide. At last, with some sort of plan, even if it was for one day, the tightness that stitched inside Bella began to evaporate. Wandering through the lodge, she let the traces of a smile spread across her face.

CHAPTER 4

At the door to her cabin, a small scrawny cat stretched and yawned. His light-sandy-grey coat looked dishevelled, and his tawny eyes pierced into Bella's heart. She crouched down, stretching out her hand to try and coax him over.

His warning hiss touched her, lighter than a feather; however, she ignored his feigned attempt to scare her away. Bella crept closer, listening to his soft miaow.

The cat crawled from beneath the bush. His eyes glinted, and the incandescent flints mesmerised Bella. She saw deep into his soul, and a calmness spread through her. When the cat reached her outstretched arm, she trailed her fingers across his coat. Burrs and small twigs from the bush snagged in his fur. He relaxed while Bella tried to disentangle them from his soft coat. He even let out a gruff purr as though unused to kindness.

The instant their heartbeats aligned to the same rhythm, Bella knew the cat had been waiting for her.

'*Hallo, hoekom is so a deurmekaar roos praat aan a wilde kat?*' The loud throaty voice broke into the silence. He frightened her furry friend, who scampered further under the bush.

'Excuse me?' Bella stood to dust the burrs from her loose-fitting dress. She caught a glimpse of his outline silhouetted against the red glow of the setting sun. Bella scrunched up her eyes to get a better look at the unwelcome visitor.

With the speed of a cat, he went to stand beside her. 'Sorry, I thought you were South African. I'm supposed to be meeting a group of them tonight to discuss the trip to Moremi tomorrow.' He towered over Bella, standing so close she smelt his aftershave, and the scent of the bush permeated around him. His long, wavy, pitch-black hair rippled over his head as it danced towards his collar. His eyes were the exact colour of dark chocolate oozing over marshmallows. When he smiled, his teeth glowed brilliant white against his tan. His safari shirt strained across his muscles.

He was perhaps the most handsome man on the planet. He wore his sexuality like a badge, but his arrogance draped over him thicker than a Turkish rug.

Bella wondered why arrogant men gravitated towards her. She backed away from him, memories of her divorce festering in her heart. 'What did you say to me?' She bristled under his intense stare.

'I asked why such a dishevelled rose is talking to a wild cat?'

'I find the cat more charming, so excuse me, I'm going into my room.'

'A rose with thorns. Now, this is a combination that intrigues me.'

'Don't flatter yourself.'

'By the way, the cat you are patting is an African wildcat.'

Bella almost choked on his words. 'Of course, it's a wild cat,' she retorted, thinking he had stated the bloody obvious. She then laughed and turned; her hand brushed his well-toned biceps as she nudged past him. After slamming her cabin door shut, Bella leant against its comforting surface, her breaths heavy and disturbing.

She changed into a clean dress the colour of the ocean at dawn, then tugged on her canary-yellow oversized jumper before pulling on her black scuffed boots. She ran her fingers through her hair, letting it cascade down her back. The cooling evening air wafted across her shoulders as she made her way to the bar for dinner and a drink.

Dingo

Night fell as fast as a blink to chase away the light. I sat shivering under the bush where she had found me. I felt safe from other predators if I stayed close to the cabin during the day. At night, I usually went hunting behind the lodge where there were plenty of mice to be found. I had lived on my own for such a long time now, so when she touched me, I almost forgot how to purr.

I guess she was the reason I chose this cabin. When she looked into my eyes, I got the sensation of a gentler soul entering my body. It caused my heart to flutter wildly. The man she spoke to had killed my mama. My brother and I had maybe drifted past one season old. Mamma told us to hide while she went hunting. We coiled into each other under a thick bush, knowing the night held a hint of frost. Mamma ran from us, and her attention was caught for an instant by the noise of a dog barking.

She didn't see the car. He drove straight into Mamma. She lay broken in the sand. Her blood was already pooling outside her body. We ran to Mamma, and I looked into the man's eyes, where tears glistened. Her spirit lifted, leaving her body, and as her last breath escaped, a quietness fell over us. The silence floated beside me, shadowing my every movement.

We had never killed anything by ourselves. We weren't old enough. Following a lot of near misses, we started catching moths or grasshoppers. Those meagre offerings never satisfied our hunger. My brother was smaller than me and too weak to stay. One day, he lay down close to me and never stirred again. His little body grew wintry beside me, no matter how much I tried to keep him warm. His paws turned to ice, and he became stiff. His eyes stared at me,

but I knew he wasn't looking at me. After my brother left me alone,
I scraped by without a friend in the world, until today.

CHAPTER 5

When Bern stared at the slammed door, he knew with certainty that his life would never be the same again. He ambled into the bar to order a beer. Soon, Bern found himself lost in her amazing eyes and glorious hair. His mind was so clogged with the numerous preparations and details for the safari tomorrow that at first, her beauty blind-sided him, as though someone had squeezed the blood from his heart.

When she had stood to glare at him, all he wanted to do was to kiss her. Her thick liquorice-coloured hair had tumbled in disarray about her face and down her back; her eyes like brilliant sapphires had glistened in the late afternoon sunshine. Her flawless skin held the faint tinge of a sun-kissed tan. She even seemed oblivious to her beauty. And while Bern had caught a flicker of interest chase across her face when he stood close to her, completely adrift in her eyes, those eyes showed a tinge of guilt. He was convinced some bastard had fucked up her life.

His mind wouldn't let her go. She was so different to the other women he had been with. And he couldn't help but contemplate that maybe this woman would make his relocation from South Africa to Botswana worthwhile. This could be the beginning of a new start, away from one-night stands and over-possessive females. Bern's thoughts, as usual, then turned to his parents. They had the perfect loving relationship. Bern wanted that for himself.

Bern ordered another beer. He couldn't stop daydreaming about the woman with deep-blue eyes and the haunted look that clouded them. *She better not stay in her room all night*, he mused, sipping his beer. He had to get to know her, to chase away the demons following her.

Bella, so used to being invisible, got a shock when he peeled himself off a barstool to saunter over to her.

'My name is Bern; may I buy you a drink?' His deep, melodic voice filled the room.

'No, thank you, I don't accept drinks from people I'm not interested in meeting.' The words sounded rude, but Bern's closeness unravelled Bella. She went to the opposite end of the bar, trying to quell unwanted sensations that sprang inside her.

Bella squeezed on a barstool between two fat male patrons. His quizzical smile in the mirror behind the bar reflected towards her as he returned to his seat at the other end of the room. She doubted anyone had ever said no to him.

The bartender came over immediately. 'Good evening, Mma. What can I get you?'

'A glass of chardonnay, thank you.'

The two men resumed talking, leaning across her as though she didn't exist. Their conversations about the tourist industry twisted into her, tangling with her cluttered musings.

Bella ordered another glass of wine, carrying it to a table by the door. She then watched on as the handsome man found a table closer to the bar. Two giggling ladies who should have known better joined him. The ladies swooned, fluttering eyelashes and glimpses of bosom.

Bella chose to be on her own. Getting close to people always ended in grief.

A light breeze trickled in through the open door, bringing with it that pungent fish scent of the river. Lights strung up in the gnarled branches of the trees brought a magical glow over the terrace towards the swimming pool.

Bella ordered the pan-fried fish with vegetables, already thinking of her new furry friend. An uneasy sensation tingled down her spine. Turning slightly, pretending to glance around the room, Bella's gaze trailed across to where Bern sat. He winked at her! *The audacity of the man*, Bella mused. *Why did he do that, when he's already having dinner with those two ladies?* Heat suffused Bella's body. She turned away from him, breathing deeply, unsure why these sensations welled inside her. She tried to regain her equilibrium by gazing across the river.

Bella refused the offer of another wine. It wouldn't do, to appear drunk when meeting her fellow travelling companions for a briefing in the conference room after dinner. They were to meet the guide for tomorrow's safari.

She wrapped the fish in a serviette, placing it in the secret corners of her oversized handbag. The cat wasn't under the bush, so Bella left his meal tucked under a branch, safe from the prying eyes of the monkeys.

CHAPTER 6

The evening air tingled with the tangy scent of wild rosemary, and a fog teased across the river. The stars waltzed in the sky, glistening along the Milky Way. Why did everything appear more alive, more vibrant, and more romantic in this corner of Botswana, Bella contemplated.

She started dancing as she wandered along the cobblestone paths. It seemed a lifetime ago that she'd felt this happy with her life, but that serendipitous moment didn't last. Bern was standing at a desk; behind him was a banner depicting Moremi Game Reserve.

Why did it take her addled brain so long to tweak to the fact he would be the one guiding the trip tomorrow? If she hadn't been so absorbed in her small world, she might have comprehended sooner; he had mentioned that he was going to meet a group of South Africans to discuss the Moremi safari. Bella tried to ignore the glances of the other guests. She collapsed into an empty seat at the rear of the small room.

The others seemed relaxed with each other as they sat chatting together in Afrikaans. An older couple with their two sons were in the front row. The closeness of the family tugged at Bella's memory. The two thirty-something giggling ladies from dinner zeroed in on Bern. They ignored his attempts to get them to sit down. Bella tried to look invisible as she squirmed in the chair.

'Please, sit down, so we can make a start. I'm sure no one wants to be here all night,' Bern said to the group as they milled about.

The two women pouted at Bern before settling in the second row.

'Thank you for sparing a few minutes to come here tonight for the briefing. Because it's an early start tomorrow, I'd like to get most of the formalities over with the night before.'

His hypnotic rich voice could tempt lilac-breasted rollers from their nests, but Bella's heart remained frozen after her failed marriage.

'My name is Bern de Villiers, and I will be your guide tomorrow. I appreciate most of you are more comfortable speaking Afrikaans, but for the sake of our Australian guest, I'll be speaking in English.'

Chairs scraped and twisted on the hard surface of the floor. The group turned to stare at the outsider sitting behind them.

'Thank you for thinking of me.' Bella's whispered words landed with a trickle on the floor.

'Kabo will be accompanying us. You'll meet him tomorrow. He's a local boy with a vast knowledge of the bush and the animals. Apart from his excellent tracking skills, Kabo organises all the meals for the duration of our trip.'

Bella was momentarily distracted by the family at the front. The mother was trying to shush her sons, who were busy sharing some joke on their phones. It was obvious the sons weren't as excited as their parents were about the trip tomorrow.

Bern seemed unperturbed, as he barely glanced in their direction. 'First of all, the safety of my guests is my top priority. We're travelling in an open vehicle, and this means I don't, at any time, want you to put any part of your anatomy outside of the vehicle. Please, no leaning out to get a better photograph or a closer look at the animals. These animals are wild, they aren't from a zoo, so they can be unpredictable and dangerous. If we're lucky enough to find lions, and I'm almost positive we will, please remain as quiet as possible. No screaming, especially from the ladies …'

Such an infuriating man, Bella wanted to scream at him.

'… and no sudden movements. Don't, under any circumstances, stand up in the vehicle, unless I deem it safe for you to do so. We make three stops during the day. One for morning tea, one for lunch and the last stop is for sundowners. I plan to arrive back at the lodge in the evening. These stops are a chance for you to stretch your legs and use the bush toilet if you need to.' He paused, stared at Bella, then took a sip of water. 'I understand five-thirty will be an early start for most of you, but anyone who isn't dressed and beside my vehicle, by at least five-twenty might be spending their day here. Do I make myself clear? I'm not waiting for anyone. Are there any questions?'

'My knee isn't as young as it used to be. Will it be difficult for me to climb into the rear of the vehicle?' the older man enquired.

'It's not so difficult, Adem. If you're finding it an effort, you're welcome to sit in the front with me, and Kabo won't mind sitting up the back with the others.'

'Ooh, may I sit in the front with you too?' one of the giggling ladies cooed.

'Afraid not, Sylvia, I'm certain with your athletic legs you'll have no trouble climbing into the back. Which reminds me …' Bern stared unashamedly at Bella. 'We haven't been introduced to each other. May I suggest we start in the front row and tell everyone our name, where we come from and a brief reason why we are on safari in Botswana? I'll go first. I used to be the head guide at the Londolozi Game Reserve in South Africa. I needed a change and had connections with different tour operators in Maun, so I moved to Botswana. I freelance for a few of the larger companies, doing a lot of trips into the Chobe Game Reserve, and also the Central Kalahari. I love being a guide here, the scenery is breathtaking, and the wildlife encounters leave you in awe. Now, we can start in the front row.'

The gentleman stood, his hand reaching for his wife's shoulder. His face twitched with pain, and a wheeze escaped through his clenched teeth. He shifted the weight off his bad leg, rubbing his hand down his hip. His fingers reached up to run through his thick grey hair, leaving it standing straight up. 'My name is Adem. I'm sixty-five years old, and we're on our first trip to Botswana, although we live not far from the border in Mafikeng. Sitting next to me is my wife, Bibi. I better not tell you her age. Women are a bit secretive about sharing how old they are, although Bibi has seen almost ten less summers than me.'

Bibi laughed, slapping him playfully on his chubby rear end.

'We're travelling with our sons Adriaan and Rylond. They finished their schooling, and we're doing this trip as a celebration of their hard years of study. They're growing up, and all they dream about now is their girlfriends, not their parents. Thank you.' Adem sat down in his chair, grimacing. He stretched his leg out, rubbing his thigh. He gave his boys a pat across their cheeks; they moaned appropriately before turning their attention once more to their phones.

The time came for the giggling ladies to make their speeches.

The over-bleached blonde one stood up. 'Hallo, my name is Sylvia. I'm from Cape Town. I, not so long ago, found myself single, so now I'm ready to mingle.' She gave Bern a mischievous smile followed by a seductive wink. 'I work as a receptionist for a law firm and have never been on a safari.' Sylvia sat down, showing way too much of her athletic thigh.

Her friend stood, reaching for the chair in front of her, to stop herself from falling. Her hair glistened with the colour of autumn leaves on a windy day. She had it scrunched into a band at the top of her head. Her ponytail bounced with a life of its own across her back. She wore a low-cut frock, and her voluptuous bosoms heaved from the effort of standing up. 'My name is Lou; I'm Sylvia's best friend from our school days. I'm supposed to keep all her confidences, but don't mind gossiping. I live in Cape Town also, and like Syl, this is my first safari to Botswana. I did one other safari in Kruger National Park, so I'm eager to see how Botswana stacks up against Kruger.' She bent over seductively, her breasts straining against her dress.

Bern's eyes skimmed past Lou towards Bella.

Bella's turn to speak became her worst nightmare. All of a sudden, her mouth tasted grittier than the winds blowing sand over the Kalahari. Anxiety crowded into her, so she sprang to her feet. 'Shit,' she muttered when the chair fell with a bang on the terracotta tiles.

Bern appeared beside her in a heartbeat, setting the chair to its upright position.

Bella hadn't realised such a muscled man could move so fast

if he set his mind to it. He stared, for a second too long into her eyes, unnerving her. His annoying wink dragged Bella back to the present.

'Take as long as you need, beautiful, I'm willing to wait all night for you.' His whisper floated across her cheek.

The flippant remark annoyed her. 'Hello, my name is Bella Winter. I come from Australia, and this is my third visit to Africa. I've also been to Morocco, Kenya and Zimbabwe. I came to Botswana because the name sounds sweeter than summer rain in the desert, thank you.' Bella sat down to let their stares flood through her.

She didn't listen to the rest of Bern's waffle, too engrossed with dusky daydreams snatching at her. Bern finished speaking; chairs scraped as they made ready to leave. Adem and Bibi left first. Adem struggled a bit with his leg. Bibi reached for his elbow; to offer a bit of support. Bella hesitated until they were out the door. Rylond and Adriaan thanked Bern then mooched behind their parents, staring into their phones.

Sylvia and Lou made a beeline for Bern, almost knocking each other over in their haste to talk to him. Bella took their enthusiasm as a cue to make a hurried exit into the inky night. A chill chased across the river when Bella threaded along the cobbled paths that led to her cabin. Her speech fiasco mortified her, and so did the way Bern had stared at her while he set the chair upright. Bella's heart had somersaulted when she looked at him.

She checked on her little friend. He curled himself up in a tight ball, as though he too begged to be invisible. Bella reached out to him, listening to his soft miaow. He crept closer, allowing Bella to give his fur a gentle pat. It was obviously enough contact for one day because, in a twinkle, he disappeared into the night.

Swirls of mist soon absorbed him, and she hoped he stayed safe. Emotions pinged through Bella; she couldn't hold onto them. The day had been long and eventful, so she sought some solitude by closing the door, locking it against the world.

Dingo

I ate her small offering, but hunger stayed in my belly. She radiated kindness, I could touch it drifting about her. I had lived without a care for a long time now, and I was reluctant to reach out to her. I left her because I had to start my night-time routine.

My territory embraced a large area from the river to the surrounding bush. The edge of the mopane trees to the right was as far as I went in that direction. The last edge of my territory had become a bit vague. It used to be the edge of a waterhole until the water went away. Another cat lived there, and already he had picked a few fights with me. It became the one area I had to be cautious of. I checked my territory then went to sit next to a hollowed-out tree. I crouched more silent than the wind echoing off the leaves.

I spotted a small rat leaving the safety of his home. He didn't smell any threat, so I followed him like a shadow, biding my time. I pounced, my teeth circling him by the throat. His little feet kicked, trying to gain purchase on my stomach, but my strength soon overpowered him. I bit down hard, to taste his warm blood. His little legs beat slower as his spirit left him. I ate in a rush, fretting about attracting other predators.

I licked the blood from my paws and face before I retraced my steps to my bush outside her cabin.

CHAPTER 7

Bern stared at Bella as she made a hasty exit. He didn't want to be rude to Sylvia or Lou. His mind was too full of conflicting sensations, to absorb their inane questions about tomorrow. He wanted to follow Bella, to wrap her in his arms, to alleviate the hurt in her troubled eyes, but she had disappeared into the night with the speed of a cheetah chasing its prey.

He finished answering Lou's question about suitable attire to wear tomorrow and declined their offer of a drink, before he went out to his vehicle. He drove to his home in Maun; his mind was a jumbled mess of conflicting emotions. And he wasn't looking forward to the inevitable confrontation that waited for him there.

Bern didn't enjoy doing one-day safaris; however, he was impatient for tomorrow to begin. He had all day to get to know Bella a bit better, and with any luck, she might change her mind about him.

A breeze off the Thamalakane River was drifting over his house when he pulled into the driveway. Every light in his house was blinking nervously. 'Shit,' Bern mumbled to himself when he walked up his front steps.

At four-thirty, when the beeps flowed into her dreams, Bella relished the fact her first full day in Botswana had begun. The heat of the shower dissipated the tension weaving in her muscles. She pulled on clean but crumpled safari trousers and a shirt, before lacing up her sturdy boots. She twined her hair into a messy braid and let it hang below her right breast. Bella checked her camera bag, making sure the batteries were charged, before picking up her handbag and hat. She then closed the door behind her, bending to pat the cat's fat belly; his gravelly miaow reached into her soul. His night-time hunt must have been a success.

The sun hadn't yet peeped above the horizon when Bella wandered to the front of the main lodge where the vehicle waited. The pale sky blushed pink, lighting up the eastern sky to chase the last of the stars into hiding. The new dawn crystalised so perfectly, making Bella appreciate that anything might be possible today.

Unfortunately, she arrived first. Bern was deep in conversation with another guy, whom she guessed to be Kabo. A few of the kitchen staff began loading up the Toyota Landcruiser Safari vehicle with food and beverages. Bella turned to make a swift exit into the lodge to wait for the others until Bern spotted her.

'Hallo, Bella, keen to make a start, or are you keen to talk to me.'

She thought him an odious man. Thankfully, she was saved from answering him by the arrival of Sylvia and Lou.

Sylvia pounced on Bern, almost knocking him over. '*Ooh goeie oggend—*'

'Sylvia, please speak in English, for Bella's sake,' Bern cut into her gushing words.

'Sorry.' She pouted at Bella then ignored her as she turned back to Bern, putting her hand on his arm. 'You look good enough to eat, at this unholy hour. God, I'm never out of bed until noon if I'm on holidays. I'm certain my lipstick is smudged; I failed to see my reflection in the bathroom mirror. Couldn't they install brighter lights?' Sylvia spun around. 'Am I presentable enough to go on safari?'

Bern gave a half-smile. 'You'll do, now get yourselves settled in the seats while we wait for the others.'

Adem and Bibi arrived a few minutes later. Adem struggled with the steps into the back of the Landcruiser. He refused all offers of help to clamber over the awkward sides of the vehicle. He fell into his seat, a cry of pain escaping from his lips. Adriaan and Rylond straggled up the rear, both with their heads down peering into the screens of their phones.

Bibi sighed. 'My boys are at that rebellious age where they no longer listen to their parents. It would be a shame if they missed the beauty of Botswana, by texting their girlfriends all day.' Bibi's words floated to no one in particular.

'I'm sure the pull of scenery and wildlife will distract them enough to forget about their phones,' Bella acknowledged her with a smile.

There were three rows of seats, each with spaces for three people in the rear of the converted Landcruiser bakkie. The seats staggered up with the last row teetering over the tailgate of the vehicle. A canvas canopy covered the seating area, providing a modicum of shade from the sting of the sun.

Adem, Bibi and Adriaan settled into the front row. Sylvia and

Lou spread out in the middle row; looking miffed they didn't take the front seat when they had the opportunity. Rylond and Bella climbed into the seat at the rear of the vehicle.

'Is everyone ready?' Bern shouted above the noise of the motor, seemingly not expecting a reply. He swung into the driver's seat, slammed the door and the safari began.

Bern signed the necessary paperwork at the gate. He drove over the rough track leading from the lodge to the main road. He eased into the sparse morning traffic, speeding up once he hit the tar road heading in a north-easterly direction.

Bella soaked up the surroundings as Africa floated passed her, waiting to alleviate the tension she always carried between her shoulder blades. Little farm holdings glided past, and small children danced in the sand while they tended to the cattle and goats. They used sticks, longer than they were tall, to keep the stock from straying onto the road. Bern kept braking, to avoid having the hapless animals end up as roadkill.

He slowed his vehicle on the outskirts of a village where a sign stuck on a pole told them they were about to enter Shorobe. Children ran about in circles as they waited for another day of school to begin. The women opened up their small shops in preparation for the day's trade. Old men stood huddled in groups while they exchanged gossip, sharing tales of times that were fading into a murky past.

They bounced over the last of the tar at the edge of the village. The farm holdings soon disappeared into the dust flying from the tyres. Every time another vehicle passed them on this forlorn stretch of gravelled road, everyone was coated in a thick layer of grit. It laced around the excited group, settling in their eyes and hair.

Bern and Kabo were in relative luxury in the front of the vehicle, chatting away to each other. Trees sped past, to wave their branches in a greeting before waiting for another layer of dust.

They stopped again briefly after the village at the Mawana Veterinary Control Gate. Bern had a few words to a sour-looking man, who grumbled as he waved the vehicle through.

Bella could feel the tension starting to ease the niggling headache she always carried. Africa was once again spinning its way into her heart. The suddenness of her divorce and betrayal of her best friend still rankled, but for some reason, the honesty of Botswana surrounded her with peace. She wanted to capture every second of this adventure, knowing that something magical was about to happen to her.

CHAPTER 8

Once civilisation winked in the rear-view mirror, they started to spot a few animals. Bella glimpsed a giraffe in a wrinkle of mist, but it disappeared before she could alert anyone. As they rounded a slight bend, Bern skidded to a stop to avoid hitting a small herd of elephants ambling in the middle of the road. The babies trotted aimlessly, their tiny trunks waving like windmills. Their mothers and aunts trumpeted noisily, shaking their heads at the vehicle, then they ushered the little ones into the forest.

'Did you see the elephants, Rylond?' Adem exclaimed in a harsh, loud voice, drawing the wrath of Bern.

Rylond responded, taking his eyes off the tiny screen in his hand. 'See what, Pop?'

'Never mind, son. Please look at the scenery and not your phone, for at least today,' Adem said in a more subdued tone.

Everyone was on alert, trying to spot the next animal.

Sylvia gushed at Bern when she saw a herd of impala. Bern ignored her, clearly too interested in keeping his eyes facing the front of the vehicle, appearing to be alert for anything else darting out onto the road.

An hour later, Bern pulled the vehicle to a stop at the impressive South Gate entrance to the Moremi Game Reserve. Two butter-cream-rendered buildings sat on either side of the road, one for the ranger's office and the other for toilet facilities. A tall, thatched gable roof joined both the buildings together.

The ladies sprang down from the vehicle in an obvious hurry to use the bathroom. Bella queued up last in the line and waited a little impatiently for Sylvia and Lou to re-apply their make-up and exchange gossip about Bern.

When Bella left the ladies, she almost bumped into Bern leaning against a post. He looked like he had all the time in the world. 'Sorry, am I holding everyone up?' Bella tried to sidestep around him to return to the vehicle.

'Never. You can hold me up anytime, but for now, we better join the others.'

She ignored his remark and climbed back into her seat.

'If you're ready, let's continue.' Bern settled himself in the front of the vehicle.

Why does he have to single me out, Bella wondered. She wished he'd turn his attention to Sylvia or Lou and leave her alone.

Not long after they entered the park, Bern pulled off the track next to a waterhole. Several hippos wallowed in the shallows, and their grunts were loud against the shrill call of the black-collared barbets. Kabo jumped out of the vehicle to set up the table for morning tea. While Bella waited, she reached for her camera, hoping to take some photos, to etch every experience into her memory.

The sun climbed high in a cloudless sky and diffused a warm glow across the land. They watched a saddle-billed stork tiptoe in the currents at the edge of the water. His long, skinny legs appeared too fragile to hold up his weight, and his bright-red beak glistened in the morning sunshine.

Once Kabo had called them over, Bella ordered an Amarula and hot chocolate. She had tasted one eons ago in Zimbabwe with her ex-husband and loved the mellowness of it. She picked up a pecan nut biscuit and went to lean against the vehicle, where the view of the waterhole stretched in front of her.

The others clustered about in small groups. Adem and Bibi chatted to their sons who had left their phones in the vehicle. Sylvia and Lou cornered Bern and asked him ridiculous questions such as, 'Where are you hiding your gun?' or 'Have you ever killed anything?'

Bella relaxed momentarily, happy to be away from them. Depressing images of that other African trip knotted in her. She then regretted ordering the Amarula and hot chocolate; it carried too many splinters of blissful times of a life expected to last forever. The envelope holding her divorce papers flashed into her brain. Bella stamped her boots to get rid of them, before tossing the last of her drink on the ground.

Bella soon found herself lost in another painful memory. She got a fright when Bern's hand brushed her arm. The touch sent ripples of fire through her body. She felt confused at having his tanned muscular body so close. Bella took a step away, trying to regain her composure. 'I'm sorry, did you say something?' she blurted out in a voice tinged with anxiety.

'I'm trying to understand why a stunning lady carries such a haunted look in her amazing eyes?'

'That, Bern, is none of your business.' Bella turned, going over to Kabo with her empty cup. 'Thank you for the drink, Kabo.' She climbed into the vehicle, needing to steady the trembling in her body and to take a few more photographs.

Bern continued to weave along the soft sandy tracks, keeping an eye out for anything interesting. The vehicle bounced over the rough terrain and around a marsh in an area called Xini. He hugged the tree line; the vehicle chugging at the slow pace through the sand.

All of a sudden, Bella spotted two lionesses lying low under a tree. She called in a voice a whisker above the noise of the engine for Bern to stop.

He braked abruptly, causing everyone to lurch forward, a mere twenty metres from the lionesses.

The others scrambled for cameras or phones to take photos; their excitement bubbled over.

Bern urged everyone to be quiet. His soft voice floated above them. 'This is part of the Xini pride. It's quite a sizable pride, with two black-maned lions, six females and three almost fully grown cubs. One of these females is the grandmother of the pride, and we guess she's about sixteen years old. This is a fair age for a lion in the wild. We recently discovered the lioness on your right gave birth to two cubs. The cubs may be close by because Seagal – another guide – saw them here last week. If you're all agreeable, we might sit tight for a few minutes to see what happens.'

'Where are the other lions?' Adem enquired.

'As a rule, prides split up during the daylight hours to rest. They start calling to each other when the sun starts to dip and a chill drapes over them. After they're reunited, they should in all likelihood prepare for their night-time hunt. These two stay with the cubs. They're protective of their young and guard them during the first few months of the cub's lives. Oh, by the way, nice spotting, Bella.'

After sitting for twenty minutes, without much activity, the female stood. She stretched out her front paws, digging her toes into the soft sand. She watched the leaves and twigs on her coat fall to the ground. She glared at the vehicle before turning her tawny eyes towards a bush. Her low growl whispered across the ground. Two cubs emerged, scrunching at their shadows before they trotted over to the lionesses. The cubs rubbed heads with their mother, who lay down in the sand with a gentle thud, sending dust motes to float in the air.

Bella sat enthralled until Rylond spoke with the rudeness of youth, 'Can we go and find buffalos now, Bern?'

'Ja, if we're able to locate any. Are you all ready to leave the lions?'

There were various mumbles of agreement from everyone except Bella.

'You right to go, Bella?' Bern asked.

'No, but if no one else wants to stay with the cubs, I guess we can go.' Bella's words caught in her throat.

CHAPTER 9

Bella turned to watch the lionesses and cubs disappear in the dust. They meandered around ancient elephant trails, the vehicle swaying in rhythm to the soft sandy tracks. Bern drove through mopane forests where elephants brushed up against the trees, stripping the branches of their leaves before they plodded along for a drink at the many waterholes. Zebras dazzled as they danced out on the plains, and a lone wildebeest kept pace with them. They saw at least a gazillion impala tiptoeing with nervous energy in the short honey-coloured grass, their coats quivering in the warm sunlight.

Bern stopped in a clearing overlooking a waterhole, a perfect spot to pause for lunch. Sylvia, Lou and Bella were in a hurry to pee, so they asked Kabo what tree offered the best privacy. He checked out various spots before deciding on a large termite mound about ten metres from the vehicle. Both Sylvia and Lou went together, while Bella jumped from one leg to the other. At last, her turn came. She crouched low, scrunching her trousers and knickers into a ball to try not to let urine drip on her trousers or pool under her boots.

When she finished peeing and was about to stand, Bern strode towards her. 'What the heck are you doing?' she cried, pulling up her trousers.

'Stand still and shut up.' Bern's determined response startled her.

Bella zipped up her trousers before straightening her shirt. 'Did you get a good look?'

'Not as good as I might have liked, but there's a lion ten metres from where you were crouched. The long grass covered him, but now he's sitting up watching us.' Bern's voice held a cadence of urgency.

Bella stood frozen in the moment; her boots weighed heavy in the sand.

Bern positioned his powerful body right in front of her, with his hand resting on her waist. His closeness unnerved Bella, and she felt certain he sensed her erratic heartbeats thump against his muscled back.

'Now keep close to me while we step away from the termite mound, and don't make any sudden movements that may alarm him. I want him to lose interest in us. I recognise this lion, and he's never shown aggression towards humans. He might have been perplexed, though, as to why you were daring to undress in front of him.'

Bern's soothing words calmed Bella. She glanced at the lion, noticing with admiration his magnificent face. His dark luxuriant mane was flecked with burrs from where he slept in the long grass. A few scars etched across his nose, and one of his ears frayed at the edges. 'He's gorgeous,' Bella murmured.

They inched around the termite mound.

Bern guided Bella towards the vehicle, his fingers trailing across her waist softer than a butterfly's wing. The touch was electrifying as it sizzled over her. The length of his body, a mere whisker from her, made Bella tremble like snowflakes fluttering to the ground. She breathed in the musky smell of his aftershave. Her breasts rubbed against his muscled back, and she was embarrassed at the idea of having his body melded against hers.

The lion kept his eyes on their every move. He didn't stand or try to approach. If Bella panicked, she knew he'd have chased her swifter than an echo bouncing off the trees. Bella returned the lion's stare, but she felt no fear; she was certain he meant her no harm.

They reached the relative safety of the vehicle. The rest of the group appeared to be sitting fearful in the vehicle while Kabo finished stacking the lunch paraphernalia under the last row of seats.

Bern seemed unable to free his fingers from Bella's back. He moved closer, drawing her into a hug he clearly was reluctant to pull away from. They stood behind the vehicle, well away from the others.

Bella shook and snatched at tears falling down her cheeks, but these reactions weren't from the lion. She found herself on fire with Bern's touch and his closeness. It seemed a lifetime ago since Bella touched the warmth of another human, and she shivered from the sensations swelling up inside her. She sensed Bern misinterpreted her trembling as shock from the close encounter with the lion. She would be mortified if he knew being next to him had made her shiver.

'Are you all right?' he whispered in Bella's ear while his hands kept teasing her waist.

'Of course I am, thank you. That amazing experience will stay with me forever.'

Bern helped Bella into the vehicle, a perplexed expression clouding his face. His deep-brown eyes seared through hers. 'You, my adorable Bella, are quite the enigma, aren't you?'

She let his flirtatious remark fall to the ground unanswered. She thought it might be better to ignore him completely.

'Oh, you were so brave, Bern. You didn't look the tiniest bit afraid. Imagine if it happened to us, Lou. I couldn't stay as still as you did, Bella, especially with having Bern so close,' Sylvia exclaimed, obviously trying to get Bern's attention.

'The lion, in all likelihood, was more afraid of us, Sylvia. Always show them respect, and don't make any sudden movements if they're close.' Bern climbed into the front of the vehicle. 'Now, if you're ready, let's find another location to stop for lunch, and with luck, no lions will be lying close by. Bella, are you certain you are okay?'

'I'm fine, thank you, Bern.' A touch of wistfulness blurred her words.

Bern sat in the driver's seat, gripping the steering wheel. Bella had turned his world upside down. She was the first woman he had ever taken on a game drive that didn't freak-out about being so close to a lion. He had wanted to protect her, but she seemed unfazed by the whole ordeal. He'd been anxious to start this safari with Bella as his guest, now he didn't want today to end. He couldn't think straight. He had to remain professional, but his heart skipped a beat when he had hugged her.

'You okay, Bern?' Kabo's words brought Bern back to the present.

'Sorry, Kabo. Bella's reaction to the lion has confused me. She didn't seem at all scared.'

'Maybe it's just your undeniable charm, with the ladies, that's put her at ease.'

Bern laughed. 'I don't think she's even noticed me. We better get a move on and find some other place for lunch.' He started the engine.

'What about the ancient baobab. It's more out in the open,' Kabo suggested, with a frown creasing his face.

'Good idea,' Bern replied.

CHAPTER 10

Bern drove a few kilometres north through a mopane forest. The trees stood eerily quiet. Bella stared at them. It seemed to her that the withered skeletons of the long-dead branches were reaching for leaves that were no longer there. The heat of the sun had turned the bark a pale grey. It reminded her of a cemetery for the forgotten, until a kaleidoscope of butterflies, disturbed by the noise of the Landcruiser, fluttered wildly as they tried to escape the vehicle. They were like flakes of snow flapping against the breeze.

Bella reached for her camera to capture the moment.

Ten minutes later, Bern parked the vehicle out in the open, next to an enormous baobab. These ancient trees lived for centuries and carried legends deep within their bark.

Bella experienced a warmth of belonging when Adem, Bibi, Sylvia and Lou came over to where she stood waiting for Kabo to prepare lunch. They took it in turns to hug her and enquire if her nerves had settled. 'Thank you for your concern. I'm a lot better now.'

Sylvia, however, spoilt the moment by saying, 'You're quite the little minx, Bella, love. I bet you spotted the lion as soon as we stopped and sent Lou and me off first, so when your turn came, you acted all helpless in front of Bern.'

'Of course, Sylvia, I planned it all, well before we left the lodge this morning. I wanted to put the whole group in danger. Any excuse for Bern to wrap his arm around me.' Bella rolled her eyes.

'You're asking me to wrap my arms around you again, hey Bella, and there's not a lion in sight. I'm happy to oblige, once we return to the lodge.'

Bella hadn't seen Bern approach, and his words sliced through the air. 'No, thank you, Bern, although Sylvia might be a more eager participant.' She turned away; her spine tingled when she went over to where Kabo had set up lunch.

The table groaned under the weight of the delicious food. The others, already lined up, were piling delicious meats and salads onto their plates.

'Plate for you, Bella?' Kabo asked while he wiped a plate with his towel before handing it to her. 'Help yourself to springbok, kudu or ostrich slices, along with my favourite chicken wings. There's a pasta salad, cauliflower, mango and chickpea salad and also a potato salad. The fresh bread is at the other end of the table. Take what you want and sit down with the others. I'll bring the wine or beer for you in a minute.'

Kabo knew how to set a lunch table, and hunger gnawed at Bella. She skipped the meats, going straight for the salads and a slice of bread, taking her full plate over to the table and chairs Kabo had set up alongside the baobab tree. White linen cascaded over the table, where sparkling wine goblets and crystal glasses nestled next to the shiny silverware.

Adem stood, flinching from the obvious effort. He came over to pull a chair out for her.

'Thank you, Adem, it's nice to see some gentlemen still exist in our fast-paced world,' Bella replied, sitting down next to Rylond.

Kabo came with the drinks, and Bella chose the chardonnay, while Rylond opted for a beer.

Bern and Kabo were the last to fill their plates, and she silently begged for Kabo to take the vacant seat at the head of the table next to her.

Bern, however, sidestepped him to manoeuvre his lean body down beside Bella. 'This has been quite the day for you, Bella.' He began to shovel the salad into his mouth. 'You're quite extraordinary. You showed no panic whatsoever being faced with a lion watching you at such close quarters. Anyone else might have panicked and made the situation even more dangerous. But all you could do was whisper to me about how majestic he looked.' Bern's soothing words simmered low over the table, curling towards Bella. He continued eating his salad while staring into her eyes, waiting for an answer.

'I've loved lions, or any other cat for that matter, for as long as my memory stretches. I gaze into their eyes, and it's like I'm looking at myself. I read their minds, touch their pain or share their joy. The lion we saw today never intended to harm me. I could never be anywhere there are no cats, and of course, that includes lions. It's the main reason I'm in such an amazing country. The other reason I'm here is because … well, I don't want to talk about it at the moment …' Bella let her words trail away.

'One day, Bella, I want you to tell me all about yourself. I can tell someone has hurt you but now isn't the time. Let's enjoy the lunch.'

Bella turned away from Bern. 'How are you enjoying the trip with your parents, Rylond?' she asked him, trying to start up a conversation.

'It's okay, but I'm missing my girlfriend. She's the reason why I'm always on my phone,' Rylond answered with a dreamy smile on his young face.

'Your girlfriend is going to be waiting for you. Now is a special moment for your parents. They understand you're growing up too fast and will be leaving home soon. For your mama and papa, your trip here is a memory to be treasured long after you're off and settled with a family of your own.' Bella didn't want to give him a lecture, only once she began talking, she didn't have the willpower to stop.

Rylond blushed. 'Sorry,' he mumbled, stuffing the phone in his pocket. 'I s'pose you're right. I'll get Adriaan to do the same. Thank you.'

'Rylond, you're going to be fine; your parents have raised two special lads.'

After lunch, Bern wandered over to where Bella stood alone by the vehicle. 'Have dinner with me tonight, please, Bella.'

'No, I'm afraid that's not possible.' Tears stung at Bella's eyes.

He reached for her arm, standing so close to her that she counted the long eyelashes fringing his eyes.

Bella caught her breath in anticipation of his lips tasting hers, but he released his grip as his breath teased her hair.

'Maybe not tonight, but I'll hold onto a glimmer of hope that you'll say yes one day, Bella.' Bern stepped away when Lou's long fingernails dug into his arm. Her heavy bosoms heaved against the tight constraints of her shirt.

'Well, look at the two of you getting cosy, but there are others here seeking your attention, Bern.' She sounded miffed, and Bella failed to understand why.

'He's all yours,' Bella snapped before climbing into the vehicle. She turned to face Bern; his expression was quizzical. Bella put it down to the fact no other female ever wanted to say no to him.

She smiled at Rylond when he joined her in the back seat. Both he and Adriaan had stowed their phones in their bags. Adriaan was even chatting to his parents in the front row of the vehicle.

Bella couldn't quite believe Bern was flirting with her. It wasn't professional of him. She didn't for one moment think he wanted to have dinner with her. He didn't even know her. The hurtful words Bradley had said to her had crushed her confidence. Bradley had showered her with compliments when they first met, but his feelings for her had been shallower than a puddle. She wasn't going to make that mistake again.

Bern climbed into the driver's seat. 'Hope you enjoyed your lunch and got enough to eat. If you're ready, we can continue driving down to the South Gate.' He started the engine. 'Let's locate those buffalos now, Rylond.' He reversed the vehicle to begin the slow journey the way they came.

He knew he should be concentrating on all his clients, but Bella's face kept filling his vision. He didn't know her travel arrangements. Most tourists spent only two nights at each place. Bella could be gone from his life, forever, if he didn't do something.

That was why he was so persistent about having dinner with her. But in his arrogant way, he might have scared her off.

About ten minutes later, Kabo touched Bern's arm and pointed to the west. Bern pressed hard on the brakes bringing the vehicle to an abrupt stop. There was an almost fully-grown leopard cub frolicking in the long grass, swaying in time to a flurry of wind. She didn't appear perturbed about the intrusion into her life as she wove a path through the long grass.

Bern followed her until she disappeared into a thicket. 'Eh, what a good sighting, not many people see a leopard on their first visit here. Ready to go?'

'Yes, thank you, Bern,' everyone muttered.

Once they left the leopard, Bella sat quietly, flicking through the photos she had taken of the leopard cub. A smile teased her lips. She couldn't quite believe that she had spent a small piece of her time with a leopard. She desperately wanted to share this moment with someone, but there was no one who cared enough. Bradley certainly wouldn't, and her mother and sister didn't even know where she was. Bella put her camera down and soaked up the scenery drifting past her.

CHAPTER 11

They continued driving through Xini. Most of the group were on the lookout for buffalo. Everyone except for Bella; she was always searching for lions, or any of the other African cats.

In a sudden jolt, Bern turned the vehicle towards a waterhole, changing direction. He spooked a small herd of zebras that wandered down for a drink. They took flight, leaving drops of water to glisten in the late afternoon sunshine. Bella recognised the area from earlier; it was near where they saw the two lionesses with the cubs. It took Bern a few minutes to find the lions. The noise of the engine woke the two females; they raised their heads to glance at the vehicle. Slumber soon overtook them again, and they settled down to continue daydreaming.

'Thank you, Bern.' Bella stared awestruck at the little group. She detected a closeness with them and touched their warmth draping over her.

'You're welcome, Bella, and your smile is reward enough for me.' Bern's words floated over to her. 'But I'm sorry we can't stay longer, as it's a long drive to the lodge. So, if you're ready, Bella, we'll leave them in peace.'

'Yes, of course,' she replied with a slight catch in her voice.

Sylvia and Lou turned towards Bella.

'Well, princess, you've had quite the day. When we first met Bern, we thought we'd have some fun with him, then you entered the room. Maybe next time we go on safari we'll make sure you're not on the guest list.' Sylvia laughed. Her voice hardly touched Bella, over the noise of the engine.

'Sorry, I didn't mean to spoil your fun. The main reason I came on this safari was for the big cats: the lions.'

Rylond gave both the girls a crooked smile as he flicked his thick blonde fringe out of his eyes. He then turned to Bella and gave her the thumbs up; it seemed they had bonded a little since lunch.

Bella let her gaze drift over the scrubby bushes. The sun arced its way towards the far horizon, taking with it a pinch of heat. All of a sudden, a small herd of buffalo appeared in a rumple of dust. She nudged Rylond and pointed him in the right direction.

'Bern, over there to your right, it's a buffalo,' an excited Rylond called.

Bern stopped the vehicle, and they watched the buffalo make slow progress through the short grass. All their heads faced down while they grazed. They didn't pause to appreciate the beauty in their world, now the sun had started to dip low in the sky.

'Good spotting, Rylond. At last, you've seen your buffalo.'

Rylond picked up his camera to take a few quick photos. Their dusty bulk silhouetted against the waning sun made for a perfect shot. Bern explained that they called these groups 'dagga boys.' Old buffalos ousted from the herd, to spend their twilight years roaming around gloomier than old men and almost as cantankerous.

'Thank you, Bern.' Rylond tucked away his camera; a smile spread across his face.

They didn't stay long with the buffalo because Bern and Kabo were discussing the best location to stop for sundowners.

Bern drove the vehicle into a small clearing backing onto a leadwood forest. They faced due west, and the red ball of the sun blushed crimson before it dissolved into the landscape.

Bella jumped from the vehicle. She wandered over to where Bibi and Adem stood gazing at the sunset.

Bibi chatted about the amazing day and the sightings they shared. Bella praised Adem for his strong determination to refuse to give in and sit in the front of the vehicle with Bern. He managed with a painful limp to climb in and out of the vehicle without any complaints.

'It's been such a wonderful day with Bibi and my boys, the discomfort is of no importance. We're going to keep this trip in our hearts for many years to come. I'm grateful to you too, Bella; I don't know what you said to Rylond. Now my boys have at last ditched those infernal phones and are starting to chat to their old papa.'

'I'm confident it was nothing I said, and I'm happy you're enjoying your safari.'

They watched Kabo set up a table laden with wine, spirits, beer and soft drinks.

Bern helped him prepare a selection of snacks to enjoy with their drinks.

Kabo then enquired, ladies first, what they desired for sundowner drinks. Sylvia and Lou opted for a gin and tonic; Bibi asked for red wine; while Bella chose a chardonnay. The ladies chatted about life away from the safari. Well, at least Sylvia and Lou did; Bella stood on the edge of the circle and let their words swim over her.

As the evening faded and glasses were filled again, Lou smiled at Bella. In a sugar-sweet voice, she asked, 'So, what's the mysterious Bella doing here in the wilds of Africa? It sounds such an unusual destination for an Australian to venture to.'

'Why do you say such a thing? Except for the animals and eucalyptus trees, Australia is similar to this part of Africa, so why not come here.'

'Yes, but is there a special man in your life, someone pining for you at home?'

'No, sorry to disappoint you, Lou, no one knows I'm here, and if they did, I suspect they wouldn't care.' Bella felt a slight twinge of anxiety.

'I don't believe you. You must have someone waiting for you in Australia?' Lou persisted.

'There used to be one man in my life, my husband. I met him during a star-filled night at the opera. He swept me off my feet, then swept me out into a night frostier than the moon to start living with my best friend.' Bella knew she had said too much, damning the bloody wine. Their probing questions speared into her heart, bringing with it too many memories. Bella excused herself a little too abruptly to return to the vehicle.

Bern stood with his back to the setting sun, busy texting someone. 'Hallo, Bella, are you looking for me? I'm letting the lodge know what time we'll be arriving back.'

'I don't care what you're doing. I came over here to breathe in the twilight. I don't understand why the air always smells better at dawn and dusk.'

'Because at dawn, it's fresh and eager, and at dusk, it's full of all the scents it collected throughout the day,' a philosophical Bern answered.

Maybe it was the wine, but Bella thawed a little bit at his words. 'I see in your eyes you love your job.'

'Ja, of course I do. I'm a lot happier in the bush. I hate being confined in town. I'm like a caged lion waiting to return to the wild. Also, if I didn't stand in for another guide today, I may never have met the enigmatic Bella. Please join me for dinner tonight?'

'I'm sorry, Bern, I'm the last person you should be contemplating getting involved with. I came here to escape my demons, not to search for new ones.' Bella's words floated against the twilight.

Bern took one step towards her. His arms encircled Bella, crushing her against his muscled chest as he went to kiss her.

Bella took a deep breath; his closeness unnerved her. Even the sound of hyenas close by didn't disturb them. She then stumbled, unsure of why his kiss took her by surprise, but he tightened his embrace.

His kisses intensified. He had been flirting with her all day, still, Bella quivered when his hands explored her body. His tongue eased her trembling lips apart. The deep, hungry kiss chased the chill from Bella's heart, and to her shame, she moved her body even tighter into him.

The hyenas' cackling became louder, but still, Bern persisted in kissing Bella.

'Ahem, excuse me, Boss.' Kabo coughed, startling the couple.

They sprang apart, breathing like they had finished running a marathon.

Bella gripped the vehicle to stop herself from falling.

'Ag man, what are you doing?' Bern growled thickly.

The noise of the hyenas was now an echo.

'I'm starting to pack up now, and Sylvia is beginning to wonder if a lion didn't eat you both. You better go and reassure her, Bella.'

Without glancing at Bern, Bella edged away from the vehicle, and on shaky legs, she returned to the others.

They were finishing up the last of their drinks when she wandered over to them. 'Sorry, I wanted to go and pee in rather a hurry. Did I miss anything?' She was thankful the night covered her embarrassment.

'Where's Bern?' Sylvia's voice held a touch of annoyance.

'I've not the faintest idea where he went. He showed me what termite mound to pee behind.' The lie rolled off her tongue, but she would have been mortified if Sylvia or Lou found out Bern had kissed her with such passion that it left her breathless.

While Kabo finished stashing the gear in the vehicle, Bern wandered over to where they stood. His eyes sought out Bella's, fixing them with a penetrating stare she soon became lost in. Bella silently thanked Kabo for bringing her back to reality. She wouldn't make the same mistake twice.

She climbed into the vehicle, trying to forget her weakness at falling into Bern's embrace. She had arrived in Botswana one day ago, and already she had kissed the first guide that crossed her path. For all she knew, Bern could have a wife or girlfriend at home, waiting for him.

The rest of the trip to the lodge passed in a blur.

When Bella jumped down from the vehicle, Bern's hand reached for her arm. 'Have dinner with me tonight, please, Bella?' His soothing voice melted over her.

'I don't think that's a good idea, I'm sorry.' How easy would it be to fall under his spell and say yes; Bella wanted to. But she felt tired, stressed out and maybe a little jet-lagged. She shivered, but not from the cool breeze teasing her. She needed space between them.

Bella didn't want to waver under his apparent charms. She reached into the vehicle to retrieve her camera bag before the night swallowed her.

Bern waited for a moment, to see if she would come back – she didn't.

Kabo came over to him. 'Don't tell me a female is not falling under your spell?' He chuckled as he started to unload the vehicle.

'I must be getting old or losing my touch. She's refused to have dinner with me.' Bern answered, helping Kabo with the unpacking. 'There's something about Bella, though. She's unlike any other female I've ever met. I want to learn all about her and chase away the demons that seem to be following her.' He replied wistfully.

'Man, you've got it bad. Come on, let the staff collect these. I'll buy you a beer.'

'Thanks for the offer, maybe another time. I'll let you get back to your family. I might try and apologise to Bella.' Bern opened the cooler box and pulled out a few slices of kudu.

CHAPTER 12

Bella checked on her little friend – at least she could count on him not to faze her. Crouching low, she saw his intense amber eyes watching her every move. He had been clearly waiting for her. His miaow turned into a yawn before he stretched his paws into the soft earth. Bella reached out to let him smell her scent, to allow him to familiarise himself with her. He sniffed her fingers for a long time before fear obviously left him and he crawled onto her lap. He began purring while her fingers stroked his head. At least he seemed a bit more relaxed in her company now.

She forgot to bring him an offering of food and began to feel guilty when a deep voice startled her.

'If he's hungry, give him this.' Bern stepped beside her in an instant, holding out the kudu slices. His legs brushed Bella's back, and the heat twirled through her body.

The cat hissed, baring his teeth at Bern. The hairs down his spine stood to attention. He let out a low growl, warning Bern not to come any closer.

'Hand me the meat, please, then go away. My little friend

seems agitated with you.'

'Come to the bar after you finish feeding him. I want to apologise for my rudeness, and I think you owe me a drink, for bringing some food for the cat.'

'All right, but please go.'

When Bern's footsteps faded, the cat settled a bit. He snatched the meat from Bella's hand, carrying it to his bush to devour.

'You ought to show some respect to the person who gives you a meal,' she chided but didn't blame him.

Bern possessed the knack of being the most infuriating man she had ever met.

Bella then retreated into her cabin and tried to calm the butterflies scattered in her stomach before she saw Bern again. She stood in the bathroom gripping onto the sink, trying to regain some composure. Without making any effort to change or unravel the knots through her hair, she left the cabin to retrace her steps to the dining room.

Bella saw Bern a second after she entered the bar. He sat at the far end of the room, talking to Lou. She had a smug triumphant look on her face. She'd somehow managed to find the energy to dash into the shower, redo her make-up and brush her hair, before squeezing into a dress the colour of burnt oranges. It covered her like a second skin, showing off her impressive breasts.

When Bella turned to run into the night, Bern caught her eye. He peeled himself off the barstool, muttering something to Lou before he ambled over.

'Sorry to interrupt your cosy chat with Lou, I'm leaving. Her eyes are pleading with me to leave the two of you alone.' Bella trembled when Bern's hand touched her arm. 'I'm going,' she choked out in a voice no louder than the currents that looped in the river.

'Now you're by my side, Bella, you're not going anywhere. Let me buy you a drink.'

Bella glanced over to Lou who raised her glass in a salute before turning away.

Bern slid his arm around Bella, and with a practised grace, he ushered her out of the bar. They sat at a table overlooking the river. The faint scent of gardenias living in confusion near the dining room teased against them. It mingled with Bern's aftershave and Bella's perfume. Lights in the gnarled branches of the trees sprinkled like rain over them. Bella sensed she could get lost in the moment here, everything pulsated with romance and a luminosity lingered over the cobblestones.

Bern went to pick some gardenias, bringing them back to Bella.

'Thank you, they're beautiful,' Bella said, her fingers stroking the petals.

'Sorry if I made you feel uncomfortable on the game drive. It was never my intention to upset you.'

Bella huffed. 'Apology accepted.' She could see a softer side to Bern, which suited him better than his overbearing side.

Bern ordered drinks, and they sat studying the dinner menus while they waited.

After the waiter had poured their wine, Bern asked. 'What would you like for dinner?'

'I didn't know I agreed to eat dinner with you. I owe you one drink and that's all.'

'Well, you must eat somewhere, so it may as well be here with me. Why are you being prickly? You're alone for dinner, and I'm also alone. It's logical that we eat together.'

He's got a point, Bella confessed to herself, *and how much trouble can I get into over a meal?* 'I'll have the sugar-bean salad with feta, thank you.'

'The kudu steak with rice and vegetables, thank you, Ngaka.' Bern sounded pleased with himself.

Bella then let her gaze shift across the river. The crescent moon shimmered behind an opaque cloud in an otherwise clear night. 'So, Bern, what made you decide to become a guide? Or has your interest always been in wildlife?' Bella had to deflect the conversation away from herself.

'I spent most of my childhood holidays in the bush, in the Hluhluwe-Imfolozi Game Reserve. My father was a professor at the University of Kwazulu-Natal in Durban, and we always seemed to be on holidays. The best memories I keep from my childhood are the holidays we had in the game reserves. I love the bush, hate cities, too much concrete and pollution.'

Bella nodded and relaxed slightly. Bern was showing a softer side to his personality, and it suited him.

'My mother is Italian. If we weren't in the bush, we spent our holidays ambling the narrow streets of Florence, soaking up the history. Not a bad life for my brother and me. Mama taught me passion and a zest for loving this life we have. And they never hid their feelings for each other from us.' Bern beamed at her.

'How lucky you are.' Bella took a sip of her wine.

'Why?' His brow furrowed.

'To grow up in such a loving family. I wish I had … never mind. Tell me about how you came to be a guide?' Bella changed the subject. Her private life shouldn't be shared with a stranger, especially one she wouldn't see again.

'Well, I first studied to become a vet, but being enclosed in a practice in the city set my teeth on edge. So after I qualified, I did a Professional Guide Course, then I took up a position in one of the exclusive Lodges in Sabi Sands in South Africa.' He seemed proud of himself.

Bella had to admit, 'I envy you. It must be amazing to spend so much time in the bush surrounded by the animals, and of course the lions.'

Shaking his head, he replied, 'Enough about me, tell me your story.'

Bella went to straightening the offending curls escaping from her braid to coil in disarray down her back, until Bern caught her wrist.

He held her hand for a few seconds and brought it to his lips so he could kiss the softness of her palm. 'You're perfect exactly the way you are. It's a complete waste of effort to straighten yourself up on my account.' His words trickled through her.

The meals arrived, saving Bella from answering his personal questions about why she travelled to Africa alone. All of Bella's energy went into concentrating on her salad. Once she finished eating, retreating to the cabin was her best option.

Bella wasn't used to having all the attention focused on her. Bern's closeness overwhelmed her. Even her ex-husband never radiated the magnetism Bern did. It confused Bella, but he looked to be enjoying her discomfort as his eyes devoured her. With all her concentration focused on eating her meal, she hadn't heard Bern order another round of drinks until a chilled glass of chardonnay appeared on the table.

'Now, please tell me the "Bella life story," and why you're travelling alone. If you were mine, I'd never let you stray too far from me.'

For some reason, Bella had to share her life with this stranger. 'I naïvely assumed my marriage was full of happiness in Australia, until my husband threw me out one night so he could take my best friend into our bed. I guess they're happy, but I'm passed caring anymore. After my brother died, my father lost his desire to live. I failed to reach the shadowy corner he had retreated into. My mother never wanted me, so she went out of her way to ignore me. After Dad died, Mum and my sister shut me out of their lives.'

Bern reached for her trembling fingers. He held her sweaty hand in his strong, warm grip. A look of sadness darkened his eyes, and Bella was uncertain of how to react.

She removed her hand, and a sting of coldness fussed around her fingers – gone was the warmth of Bern's touch.

Bella sighed. 'There was no one left in Australia who loved or cared about me, so I wanted to go somewhere where happiness always found me: Africa. The choice to come to Botswana started as a fanciful notion, but I loved it from the moment I stepped off the plane. Now, my best friend is a stray cat.' She paused to sip on her chardonnay and gather her thoughts. 'I seem to hold an uncanny knack of turning people away from me. You might be better off if you concentrated on the ladies who swoon over you, like Sylvia or Lou.' Bella finished the painful monologue, wondering why Bern wouldn't stop staring at her with those incredible eyes.

'I'm not interested in Sylvia or Lou, although I'm interested in you.'

To change the subject, she asked, 'Do you take all the safari trips from here, or are there other guides to share the load?'

'No. I sometimes do the occasional trip from here. I'm based in Maun, freelancing with the major safari companies there. Seagal, who always works out of here, phoned in sick and asked me to fill in. Seagal is a great friend of mine; I agreed to do it for him. As a rule, I would prefer not to do safaris for one day, but I must admit I wouldn't have missed out on this trip for all the elephants in Chobe. I owe Seagal a beer next time I catch up with him.'

Bella finished her salad and gulped down the last of the wine. 'I better go … I want to leave food out for Dingo. Thank you for dinner.'

'God, you already named that scrawny cat.' Bern looked bewildered.

'Of course, I can't keep calling him *cat*, and I think the name suits him. It's a small keepsake from Australia.' Bella stood, gathering up the gardenias, ready to flee.

Bern took a step towards her, drawing her into him. 'Bella, you take my breath away. Your connection with the wildlife, and in particular the cats, seems to run through your veins. You seem to be able to read their minds and recognise their characters and dreams. The cat you befriended is a full-blooded African wildcat. He was born under the stars wild and free, but I find you sitting with him on your lap in what, one day? It's a rare gift and one you ought to cherish. The close call with the lion today didn't faze you at all. It was almost surreal, I can't explain it, but the lion seemed to relax with you standing so near him.'

'Oh, sorry; Dingo is an actual breed of wild cat? I thought you were being a smart-arse yesterday calling him a "wild cat." I've loved cats my entire life; they became my friends while I weathered the minefield of growing up. My father gave me a book about a lion, and I carried that book with me everywhere. The book started my passion for lions and Africa. I always relied on our family cats, at least they remained faithful to me, unlike my family or friends.'

They reached her cabin, and Bella's nerves stretched way too taut. She sensed Bern listening to her heart beating in tune with his. Bern's nearness flooded over her like waves on an isolated beach. Stalling for time, Bella crouched down, wanting to touch Dingo's soft coat, but he wasn't under the bush. She stood up in a panic and brushed the leaves from her trousers. 'Good night, Bern. Thank you for the amazing game drive and the dinner.' She opened the door and went to step inside, but Bern reached out to her.

'Not so fast,' he murmured in Bella's ear, his breath mingling with her hair. He turned her around, pressing her spine into the door jamb. His lips were then already teasing hers.

Bella didn't hesitate – perhaps it was the wine or the fact she hadn't been held by a man for such a long time.

Bern grabbed her around her waist and lifted her up.

Her legs straddled his waist.

Bern then carried Bella into the room, kicking the door shut with his foot.

They lay on the bed, tangled together. Bern's lips trailed a line across her body. His hands roamed all over her. The burning intensity of her desire for Bern shocked her. She had only just met him, one day ago, and now she was tumbling about in bed with him.

They didn't have Kabo to interrupt them now.

Bern stood and the bed sighed when his weight lifted off it. With the speed of a springbok, he peeled off his clothes then leant down to undo the buttons of Bella's shirt and the zip of her trousers. His touch on her bare skin inflamed her desire for him, and she followed his lead as he explored and devoured her body.

They lay for a long while afterwards, the sweat of their bodies merged with the iridescent light threading a path into the room.

Bern propped himself up on his elbow to stare down at Bella. A slow smile spread across his face. 'Bella.' Bern's voice shook with raw emotion. 'I think I may be …'

'Maybe what?' Bella stared up at him. Her rash decision to sleep with him was already starting to niggle.

'Nothing. I'm glad you went on the safari today.'

Bella didn't have an answer, so she reached up to kiss him.

Dawn snatched at the window; suffused light blinked between the curtains. The scent of gardenias still clung to the walls. They fell asleep, snuggled in each other's arms. For the first time in many years, Bella hadn't succumbed to the nightmares that always sought out her dreams.

The beeping of a phone roused them both. 'Shit, it's mine,' Bern mumbled. He kissed Bella before struggling out of the bed. He rummaged for his trousers lying discarded on the floor, reaching for his phone. 'Ja. Can't you get someone else? I'm kinda busy right now, and I'm booked for Chobe on Sunday.'

Silence filled the air, draping over Bella. She wanted the dawn to retreat back into Zimbabwe, so she could curl into Bern's arms for a few more minutes.

'All right, give me an hour.' He tossed the phone onto the bed and turned to Bella with disappointment clouding his eyes. 'This is not how I expected our morning to go. One of the guides rostered on to take a three-day trip to the Central Kalahari pulled out. His wife gave birth to their first child last night. Unfortunately, I have to fill in for him. I'm sorry, Bella, duty calls.'

He stooped down to kiss her.

Bella luxuriated in the heat of his body.

'Join me in the shower. We can save on water, eh,' Bern suggested.

She smiled up at him and watched him as he sauntered into the bathroom.

However, the sounds of the water splashing on the tiles brought Bella's world crashing into reality. In the remote light of the morning, she tried not to think about what a fool she had been. Even so, she ached to have his fingers dance across her bare skin.

She crawled out of bed, determined not to follow Bern, but for some reason her footsteps betrayed her. Her toes reached the cold tiles of the bathroom. She hesitated for a moment, and then Bern's phone beeped again.

Bella glanced at it pulsating with life on the dishevelled sheets. The phone announced *LAN* on the tiny screen. The happy photo stung her, with the bite of a jack jumper ant. With the backdrop of a waterhole, Bern stood with his arm around a petite Asian lady. Both smiled from the tiny screen; a loving couple out enjoying themselves. Her nerves blistered; she should have foreseen this. She then questioned why Bern didn't return to Maun last night? Why did he stay here to turn her fragile world upside down?

Bella fumbled on the floor for her clothes, dragging them on. She picked up the phone to carry it into the bathroom. 'This is for you.' She threw the phone at him.

'What the hell, Bella.' He scrambled for the phone as it fell into the steamy atmosphere of the shower.

'I think your girlfriend's wondering why you didn't go home last night.'

'Bella, wait.'

Bella stormed out of the bathroom and the cabin, slamming the door shut with a deafening bang.

The leaves fluttered from the small bush where Dingo hid.

The cat stared at her, reading her mind.

'Sorry, little one,' she said, crouching low to pat him.

Dingo's paw reached out to touch Bella in comfort. He looked hungry, making her feel a twinge of guilt. She could hear Bern still in the bathroom, so she quickly went back into her cabin to retrieve some food she'd saved for Dingo.

Dingo purred once his meal was in front of him, but then his happy mood seemed to swirl away in the glimmers of dawn. He growled low, devouring the small offering. His hunger snatched away his gentle nature.

Bern was desperately trying to dry himself with the miniscule bath towel. Water pooled at his feet and dripped down his body. This situation with Lan was already bringing him to breaking point, but he couldn't finish things with her at the moment. The lion-poaching racket was too fresh in all the guides' minds. He heard Bella come back inside.

'Hey, Bella …' He called, but she had already left. *Fucking hell, can my life get any more complicated.* His rule of never sleeping with one of his clients had been broken.

During their dinner last night, Bern had no intention of spending the night with Bella, although God knows he wanted to. He could tell she was in a fragile state, and he had decided he would take it slow with her. But after the sad story about her childhood and the bastard husband throwing her out, his heart melted. One hug wouldn't do any harm, but once Bella relaxed into him, Bern's plans to 'take it slow' flew out the window.

Bern pulled on his grubby safari clothes. He left Bella's cabin. The scrawny cat glowered at him. 'Don't look at me like that.' Bern lectured him. 'Did you see which way Bella went?'

Dingo turned away and ran off towards the main lodge.

Bern walked down the path towards the river.

Bella ran in the opposite direction of the main lodge, towards the camping ground. Her tenuous hold on sanity might shatter if Bern found her. She arrived in Botswana two nights ago and had already slept with the first man who crossed her path. *What an idiot I've been*, she scolded herself. She blamed the wine during dinner, and the magical atmosphere of the lodge, but she couldn't lay all the guilt there.

To her shame and dismay, Bella had practically begged him to make love to her. How he must be laughing now? *Damn, damn, damn you to hell*, she shouted soundlessly at Bern; tears already flowing down her cheeks.

She was leaning over the railing, trying to disappear into the murky water when Bern found her. He appeared to have dressed in a hurry. His shirt was damp from where he tried to dry himself in haste, his curly hair uncombed and dripping water onto his collar.

'Bella, please let me explain, it's not what you think.'

'Go to hell and leave me alone. Every person I ever loved has rejected me. They cast me aside like I'm a piece of garbage, without any concerns at all about me. And now you waltz into my life. God, why did I fall into bed with you? What was I thinking? I've never jumped into bed with a stranger. I'm guessing you do it all the time, though. Go and gossip with your mates about me, then return to your girlfriend Lan. Please don't come near me or touch me ever again.' Bella was hysterical by this stage; her world had broken into tiny pieces. She saw Sylvia and Lou, along with a few of the other guests from the lodge starting to gather.

'I'm leaving, but believe me, what we have is not over by a long shot. For Christ's sake, Bella, I think we can have something special. From the moment I first saw you, crouched down with that bloody cat, I knew you were—'

'Sorry to interrupt. Now, why am I supposed to believe you? If Lan means nothing to you, why do you have her picture on your phone? It's plain, even to a dim-wit like me, you two are close. Please go.' Bella started to cry, and when Bern tried to comfort her, she pushed him away. Glaring at him through eyes misted with tears, she saw the heartache etched in his face.

'One day, I'll tell you the truth, Bella. Please believe me, I'd rather swim in crocodile-infested rivers than hurt you. All I'm asking for is a few weeks. If you walk away now, it's like I'm losing part of myself. Please, Bella, trust me.'

How could she trust herself with this man? Bella glanced at Bern; the probing look he gave her pierced into her soul. She turned from him; on shaky legs, she went to where Sylvia and Lou stood.

Sylvia and Lou enfolded Bella in their arms, supporting her to the cabin. They came inside to settle her on the same bed she had shared with Bern not too long ago.

Sylvia sat beside Bella, holding her hand while she cried. Lou handed her a tissue, then busied herself making tea.

Bella scrunched up into a little ball and wept. She felt destined to live a life loving people who never cared enough about whether she lived or died.

'Why didn't you leave Bern to us, sweetie?' Lou handed Bella a cup of steaming Rooibos. 'We saw straight away he was out for a bit of fun, and both Sylvia and I are experts in the field of men. Believe me, we're bigger players than Bern ever dreams to be.'

'She's right, honey,' Sylvia joined in. 'Lou and I made a bet about who bedded him first. I'm convinced he fancied me until you showed up. As soon as he saw you, we both knew he never looked at us the way he looked at you.'

'You're such a gentle person, and men find those characteristics alluring. Harden up a little, Bella, take a piece of Syl and Lou with you, so if you come across him again, kick him in the balls for the three of us.'

Bella laughed at her words and then rolled over, pulling herself up to sit on the edge of the bed. 'Thank you for the talk and the tea. I appreciate your kindness, although I could use a shot of whiskey in the tea.'

'Now, you're talking, princess. Sylvia and I have a plane to catch in a few hours. Let's straighten you up a bit and wander over to the bar to drown our sorrows.'

They were perched up on barstools, laughing at something Sylvia said.

Bella looked up to see Bern walking towards reception, and as soon as she caught his eye, he paused. Her breath caught in her throat.

He started coming over to them until Lou stopped him in his tracks by saying in a voice edged with enough chill to freeze the Dead Sea, 'Bye, Bern, it's not safe for you to come over here. I'm confident you won't be able to handle all three of us at once.

Till next time.' She raised her glass at him, a smile etched on her attractive face.

'This isn't over by a long shot, Bella,' he uttered, his hand light on Bella's arm.

The touch sent sparks coursing through her body. It made her heart beat erratically. 'Please take your hand off me. I'm sure Lan doesn't want to hear about your escapades when she thinks you're working.'

Bern bent to kiss Bella. He nodded his goodbyes to Sylvia and Lou. 'You haven't heard the last of me.' He then turned; his footsteps sounded hollow on the polished floor. The glare coming off the river soon swallowed him.

Bella tried to ignore the emotions swirling inside her, but it felt like a small piece of her heart had left with Bern.

Bella sat chatting with Sylvia and Lou until the taxi came to take them to Maun for their afternoon flight to Cape Town. She had misjudged their flirtatious antics. They were, in fact, nice ladies out for a bit of fun while they took a break from their hectic jobs.

Bella went out with them into the warm sunshine, and they hugged each other goodbye. They invited Bella to visit with them in Cape Town, an offer she promised to hold them to.

Loneliness then fell over Bella, thicker than storm clouds gathering at dawn. She couldn't believe her stupidity at falling into bed with Bern. She pictured him driving into Maun, with those emotions he imagined he carried for her trickling out of his mind, like leaves falling to the ground during a cold winter.

But he laced all over her in her hair, clothes and on her skin. His fingers chased an electrifying path across her body, and she burnt at the memories of the intimacy they had shared. Bella smelt of him, his manly scent and his aftershave. She returned to her cabin to check up on Dingo. He was coiled in a tight ball, and she didn't have the heart to disturb his dreams. Let him chase spurfowls in his sleep.

Bella went into the room; grateful the cleaners had cleared away the clutter and straightened out the bed. They'd removed all traces of last night's escapades. She stripped off her clothes and threw them on the bed before going into the bathroom. While waiting for the hot water to heat up, she stared into the mirror, thinking perhaps she had changed after a night of passion. The same face full of insecurities peered at her. The steam coming from the shower made her reflection blur and slide down the smooth surface of the glass.

Bella scrubbed all traces of Bern off her body. The confines of the room haunted her. Everything about it now reminded her of Bern. His smile, his touch, the way his eyes wrinkled when laughter reached them, and heaven help her, his tanned muscular body.

Images of her ex-husband swam inside her brain. Bella thought he had loved her, but his love had turned into a string of lies, and now Bern was trying to waltz into her life. She was not ready to be hurt again. Sylvia and Lou almost begged Bern to bed them. Why did he zero in on her?

Bella went to the main lodge, and without a hint of guilt, she went straight to the bar. She ordered a bottle of St Louis Lager, anything to make her forget about Bern.

CHAPTER 13

Bern walked away from Bella, with a heavy heart. He had some serious explaining to do before she forgave him. But she had to forgive him; he refused to believe she never wanted to see him again. Bern had waltzed through most of his adult life without a care about the women he slept with. He found it easy because most of the women he met threw themselves at him. Although he wasn't the womaniser most people considered him to be.

Bern believed in a strict code of conduct. He didn't sleep with anyone he took out on safari. Bella was the first one he crossed that hidden line with, but she was so different from anyone he had ever met. She appeared prickly, aloof, and frightened someone could be interested in her. Looking for a lasting relationship hadn't appeared on Bern's radar the instant he laid eyes on her, it simply happened, like a streak of lightning. He found her squatting on the ground, trying to coax a scrawny cat out from the bushes beside her room, without realising how fierce those little creatures were. They were born wild, and as a rule, they stayed wild. However, Bella sat on the ground patting the little scrap.

Standing to dust leaves and twigs off her dress, she had glared at Bern, and his whole life changed in that split second. She was so unaware of how gorgeous she was, and Bern found those qualities endearing. Although, getting her to see he wasn't a complete bastard might prove difficult. He had a lot happening in his life at the moment. But he was confident of winning Bella's trust, and with any luck, something more.

While on the safari yesterday, it had stunned him how calm she stayed being faced with the lion. Bern knew they were in no danger from the lion at that particular moment. All he longed to do was enfold her in his arms, to protect her. Bern's fascination with lions had begun at a young age, knocking about game reserves with his brother. And from what he gleaned from Bella last night, she also shared the same passion for the big cats.

But right now, Bern was the angriest he had ever been. *Bloody Lan for texting me. This whole sordid thing with her should have been over by now.* He had reached the point where he found it frustratingly difficult to keep up the pretence of liking her. It would be harder now he'd met Bella. He was optimistic, though, that another few more weeks with Lan would give him the answers to prove her involvement in the lion-poaching that had started up in Botswana. He didn't want to tell Bella about his suspicions, for fear it could expose her to danger.

He tried to steady his beating heart as he picked up his mobile and made the call. However, when she answered, he couldn't stop himself from yelling, 'I told you never to call me at work, Lan. What's so fucking important it couldn't wait until I got home?'

'I'm sorry, honey,' her irritating accent droned down the connection. 'I phoned the office. You didn't come home last night. I was worried about you.'

The only person she worried about was herself. Bern went along with her irritating babble. 'Some mechanical issue with my vehicle, so I had to spend the night here. It's fixed now, and I'm on my way home.'

'Thank God you're all right. I'm a bit upset. I was told you were going to Kalahari tomorrow. What happened to the Chobe safari?'

'Why all the sudden interest in my work, Lan?' Bern knew her interest always peaked when he did the Chobe run.

'Sorry, lover, I miss you.'

Sometimes he longed for the solitude of being able to breathe. He tried to sound interested, but his mind floated elsewhere at the moment. Bern craved the space to concentrate on his safari and for a few days forget the troublesome Lan, who had squeezed her way into his home. Bella twirled all over him, and her touch on his body burnt into his soul. Although these sensations he felt whenever he gazed into her incredible eyes or touched her skin drove him crazy, he knew these feelings he had for her would last forever.

CHAPTER 14

Lan's life had begun to unravel into the sands of the Kalahari ever since she flew into the dustbowl called Maun. The dust seeped into her, pawing at her body. It rained over her hair, eyes and clothes, and with the humidity, it clung to her skin, no matter how many times she showered and scrubbed to be rid of it.

Maun stifled her, and if she didn't love Johan with all her heart, she might have been on the first flight out of Maun. Lan wanted to spend more time with Johan, but he was too busy liaising with Nguyen in Vietnam. He travelled to Vietnam every month and always returned in a foul mood. The fact he did business with Nguyen brought a blast of ice to Lan's heart.

Her sister Mai told her the bitter stories about Nguyen. How he would invite whores to his bed. He would then slit their throats from one perfect ear to the other, so he could get the gratification he craved. She also told her he had arranged for his parents to be murdered, simply because they failed to bail him out of jail.

And now, Lan bubbled with annoyance about Bern not coming home last night and the change in plans, that she flew out of the house in a temper. She stood on the footpath for about one minute until a taxi pulled up.

'Take me to Riley's quick,' she spat at the poor driver, ignoring his attempts to be polite.

Riley's Hotel was situated in the centre of town, backed onto the Thamalakane River. The reason Lan liked Riley's was because the instant you entered through the reception area, you were in a little tropical paradise that reminded her of Vietnam. And not one speck of dust sprinkled over her. The bar area had large windows that opened out onto the lawns, towards the swimming pool and river beyond.

A noisy group of Italian tourists had taken over one corner of the dining room. Lan scowled at them as she squeezed past to get to the bar. She ordered a St Louis Lager and carried it over to an empty table on the verandah. She hoped the Italians would shut up. She took a few deep breaths; the beer traced a path down her throat. Lost in fragments of her childhood, Lan reflected on her life.

She was the youngest of nine children, born into a dirty world of poverty. Her mother, weary of being pregnant, lay on a mat one day, closed her eyes and never woke again. Her father, always drunk, became lost with the passing of Ma. He stared at his growing brood like they came from a different planet. Her family lived in a crumbling high-rise in the Ancient Town area of Hoi An. She spent her childhood trotting behind her siblings, scrabbling for food or money. Her eldest sister, Mai, always came for Lan when the sky fell, and shadows lengthened along the streets. Mai sang in a low, soothing voice while they criss-crossed along the streets to home. Lan enjoyed these fleeting moments, with Mai making a fuss of her. For a brief time, she could forget their poverty.

Lan ordered another beer. Memories of Mai's death still festered inside her.

Mai worked in a brothel and fell victim to the drugs that swam through the seedy rooms. Her face soon took on a hollowed ghostly look, and she scratched at pus-filled sores on her skinny arms and legs until blood started to pool. One day, Mai never came home. Weeks later, the police fished her body out of the Thu Bồn River; she was bloated and smelling of rotting seaweed. The next day, Lan's brother Thuan took Lan to work at the same brothel.

Lan stumbled to the bar for her third beer. She sat overlooking the swimming pool, still lost in her musings. Sipping on her beer, Lan settled into her chair. The main reason she came to Botswana was because she had fallen in love with Johan, one of the punters at the brothel.

Lan had every second of their meeting seared into her psyche. She took a long gulp of the beer, remembering their first night together.

His tall, well-toned frame filled the room, and his suit smelt of crisp dongs. Lan had led him with feigned modesty to her room. When they were both naked, Lan had straddled him. She'd lowered herself onto him, sensing his urgency. She'd gyrated her body to match his rhythm. Pleasure had stained his face. When he smiled, Lan had fallen in love with him.

He soon became one of Lan's regulars, and over time he began to trust her. On one of his visits, he told Lan he led the African connection to a lion-poaching racket between Botswana and Vietnam.

Draining the last of her beer, Lan stayed in the cobwebs of her memories.

She couldn't contain her excitement about the illegal poaching

Johan seemed to be involved in. She saw it as a way to get the hell out of Vietnam and spend quality time with Johan. Three of her brothers – Thuan, Duc and Chinh – also needed to get out of Vietnam, after a run-in with the law.

Following sex one night, she had mentioned her plan to Johan. Lan had told him about the trouble her brothers were in and of their desire to leave the slum they had called home. Johan said her brothers would be an asset in Botswana. He needed some men to camp out in the reserves to be ready at a moment's notice to slaughter lions.

The noisy crowd of Italian tourists brought Lan back to the present. Her simmering rage against Bern still lingered, the alcohol did little to soothe her.

CHAPTER 15

Bern climbed into his Toyota Landcruiser. Before he stuck the key in the ignition, he punched some numbers on his phone.

Seagal answered on the third ring. 'How's it going?'

'Not good, I'm bloody pissed at the moment, but I've a favour to ask of you.'

'Okay, my friend, how can I help?'

'I met a stunning Australian woman by the name of Bella Winter.'

'So why are you asking for my help?' Seagal's deep laugh spread down the connection.

'Ag, man, I'm serious. I met her two nights ago, and I think I'm in love with her. I never pictured it happening to me, but it did. There's one snag, though.'

'What is it?'

'She found out about Lan and wants nothing to do with me. Man, she's so unaware of the effect she's having on me. Christ, she befriended an African wildcat in one day, without realising how feral they are. And then during the safari yesterday and our break for lunch, Bella went behind a termite mound, and about ten metres away, a lion sat up to watch her. I thought this was my chance to go in and protect her, making her fall for me, you know the drill, heroic guide saves a petrified lady from the jaws of a lion. She didn't appear to be the slightest bit worried. All she could do was whisper to me how exquisite the lion looked, and that we had disturbed its dreams. I'm determined to do whatever it takes to wipe away a troubled past she seems to be escaping from.'

'Wow, you have it bad, my friend.'

'She's the one for me, and here's where you come in. I'm off to Deception Valley tomorrow, so please keep an eye on her for me. Make sure she stays safe and happy. Bella's staying at the Island Safari Lodge, so it won't be too hard a job for you to do. Also, you might put in a good word about me. Tell her what a great catch I am.'

'Sure, Bern, I'll take care of your lovely lady till you get back, eh.'

'Thanks, mate, I owe you one.' Bern pushed the end call button on his phone, tossed it onto the seat and drove out of the lodge.

At the junction of the tar road, Bern turned south, easing into the morning traffic. As he drove along the familiar roads towards his home, he let his mind wander to that God-awful day when one of the lions in Chobe ceased to exist.

After Bern first relocated from South Africa to Botswana with a company called Bush Ways, Seagal became his boss. He was a legend in these parts, yet Bern found him to be a humble unassuming guy. In no time at all, they had formed a strong friendship.

Seagal's passion for the wildlife and the preservation of the animals matched Bern's. Both men shared a deep love for the cats, and in particular the lions. Seagal introduced Bern to the Ihaha pride in Chobe, and all the guides kept a close watch on them.

The pride used to be made up of three lions, eight lionesses and now two cubs. The lions were magnificent creatures with thick black manes. The guides named them Kagiso, Tan and Neo. If Bern ever got his hands on the people who butchered Neo, he would do to them what they did to that lion. Poachers. The lot of them should have been rounded up and tortured before being shot between the eyes.

Bern knew the Vietnamese had shifted some of their operations from South Africa into Botswana. The rangers had cracked down with the full weight of the law in South Africa, with more surveillance operations and arrests being made almost daily. And so, with too much focus on South Africa, the poachers had moved north into Botswana.

Seagal, Steven and Bern were desperately trying to stop the Botswana racket, halting the trade in lion bones. Sadly, they believed one of their own was relaying information to the Vietnamese. If only they could figure out who the low-life was. And heaven help the bastard when they caught up with him.

As Bern neared the outskirts of Maun, he slowed down. He lived on the edge of town on the banks of the Thamalakane River. His home was a modern two-storey house with wide verandas and a large open-plan kitchen, dining and lounge. It had three bedrooms and two bathrooms, somewhat of a luxury for dusty sprawling Maun, but Bern loved it, mainly because the back deck overlooked the river. A perfect retreat for a frosty beer when he returned home after his safaris.

He dreaded Lan being at home. He wasn't in the mood to be nice today. Thankfully, luck favoured him. The house rattled with emptiness. Bern stripped off his dirty safari shirt and trousers, pulling on a clean pair of shorts and a Springbok's T-shirt. He piled a heap of washing into the machine and turned it on before going into the kitchen.

Taking an icy bottle of St Louis beer out of the fridge, Bern retraced his steps onto the deck. Bella filled his mind. Everywhere he looked, her brilliant-blue eyes followed him. He longed to be the one to take away the sorrow etched across her face. He had only met her one day ago, and already he had started to romanticise about a future with her.

Bern stared out over the water, where goats and cattle wandered down for a drink. The view of the river always calmed him down, but for some reason, a niggling sensation of dread coiled in his chest.

Lion

My brothers and I got the fright of our lives that day. The vehicle approached close to us, but we didn't take any notice. The first bang alarmed us; a deafening noise pierced into our eardrums. The sand kicked up at our paws, and we smelt the fear. We turned to run up the slight slope into the forest until a second bang recoiled in our ears. My brother and I took off faster than the wind, despite the heat that draped over our coats.

Our brother didn't follow us, so we turned to see why, and our world crumbled, crashing down around us. Our brother lay on the ground, trying to get up. He raised his head to peer at us, and a darkness clouded in his eyes. The humans watched from the safety of their vehicle, and one of them pointed a gun in our direction.

We hesitated about what to do because our brother led the pride. We were perplexed as to why he didn't follow us. When we started to go to help him, another shot rang out. It teased the sand at our front paws, and the noise stayed inside our ears. We stopped, frightened by the noise. We paused, eager for our brother to tell us what to do.

Our brother then called to us. The feeble whisper barely touched us, so perhaps we dreamt it. He raised his head for the last time, looked at us with faraway eyes then fell to the ground.

The humans jumped out of the vehicle, and using all their strength, they dragged our brother to it. They heaved him up and over the rear section of the vehicle. He disappeared from our sight, but we knew he lay in the vehicle. They threw dirty rags into the back, covering our brother. All the men jumped into the vehicle to drive off.

We trailed behind the vehicle, never letting it out of sight, as though we stalked a kudu. At the edge of our territory, they kept driving. We had never been to the other side of the acacia tree, so we sat in the hot sand. We believed they would bring him back. We waited patiently, staring down the sandy tracks, and into the bushes.

We sat close to the acacia tree for seven sunsets, yet we saw no sign of our brother. The females of our pride became restless; they kept calling to us for guidance. We had lost our way without our brother telling us what to do. Hunger gripped us, but we ignored it. Our coats lost their sheen and draped in folds over our bones. Our eyes lost their gloss while we sat in grief, mourning for our brother.

The oldest of the females came to us on the eighth sunrise. She called to us, sharing her sorrow at the loss of our leader. She urged us to fight again for the sake of the pride. We dithered about leaving the acacia tree, because it was here that we last had a connection with our brother.

Hunger and the desire to keep the rest of our family together urged us on. We turned our backs on the tree. My brother and I limped with an unsteady step: our paws heavy on the sand. We turned west to follow the female. We were too weak to hunt, so the females went out during the night and killed a male impala.

They carried the offering to us, and we ate hungrily. Bit by bit, we have clawed our way to full strength. Without our brother, we are now leading the pride. He is always in our hearts; we carry him with us each day. Every time we pass the acacia tree, we pause to remember that once our brother walked by our sides.

CHAPTER 16

Lan stretched, running her fingers through her long hair. She wanted another beer but thought better of it. She knew she couldn't afford to get on Bern's bad side, so she had to control her temper when she went home a bit later. It was vital Lan went with him on the Chobe safari. She was stressing out, though, as she was desperate to spot a lion and get the information to her brothers who were camped illegally in Chobe.

She glared at the Italians before she tried Thuan's mobile number and held her breath until he answered. 'What the hell are you three up to?' Lan yelled into her mobile.

The Italians, having quietened down, turned to stare at her.

'Nothing, Lan. We're having a break for three days. It's hell out here in the reserve – hot – and wild animals scare us all the time. We didn't hear from you, so we went into town for a rest. We needed to restock our food and beer supplies, anyway.'

'Are you keeping a low profile? Please don't do anything stupid in town. You're working for me. I don't want to have to bail you out of jail because you were doing something illegal.'

'No, of course not, Lan. We're not drawing any attention. We won't let you down. Are you flying up on the weekend for the safari?'

'Yes. I need to stay sweet with Bern. We had a bit of a tiff earlier. I have to grovel to say I'm sorry.'

'Not a problem for you, Lan, you're used to getting men to be putty in your hands.'

'Fuck off.' Lan hit the end call button, fuming with her life at the moment.

Half an hour later, Lan tossed a few pula on the bar. She shoved her way past the Italians on her way out into the hot afternoon sunshine. The heat ricocheted off the footpath. It seeped into her short polyester dress. Lan squirmed; beads of sweat tickled down her spine and thighs, making her dress wilt against her body. She hailed a taxi and climbed into the backseat, grateful to be out of the hot sun at last. The stickiness of the vinyl seat clung to her dress and bare legs.

On the drive to Bern's house, Lan remembered how easy it had been to wriggle her way into Bern's life. She had had a meeting with a guy at a bar in Kasane to discuss the failure of her recent trip to locate lions in Chobe. He told her, if she didn't get the necessary information on the whereabouts of the lions, Johan would search for someone else to take over from her. Lan knew the unsaid words between them. She knew too much for them to let her live.

He had pointed to two guys deep in conversation at the bar, saying the taller of the two was Bern de Villiers, an experienced guide. All she had to do was wheedle her way into his life, to get him to take her on safaris to find lions. It had all sounded too easy.

Lan had trotted up to the bar, thinking what a good-looking specimen this 'Bern' was. She melted into his eyes before shaking away the sensations. She had given her heart to Johan. Lan then had shed a few tears and spun a story about being dumped by her boyfriend and getting the sack. She needed to get to Maun to apply for another job.

Bern was wary, at first, but the other guy talked him into letting Lan stay at his house. One hour later, Lan sat squashed in an overcrowded bus heading for Maun. Bern's spare set of house keys were in her bag.

Lan was pulled back to the present when the taxi driver pulled to a sudden stop in front of Bern's house. She paid the correct pula and slammed the car door without bothering to thank the driver.

She saw Bern's Landcruiser in the drive. Thank God, he was home; now she had to rein in her burgeoning temper. Lan let herself in, and the house took a breath as if it waited for someone other than her to enter. She guessed Bern to be out on the deck. The sound of her sandals slapped against the timber floors, bouncing off the leather lounge and walls. Several African tribal rugs hugging the floor did little to muffle the noise. The double glass doors to the deck were open and a gentle breeze ruffled Lan's hair. She made her way into the glare of the sun.

Bern slouched on a deck chair, staring out towards the river. He didn't even stir when she trotted up to him. He looked to be a million miles away.

'Hi, honey, I'm happy you're home. Can I get you another beer, I'm having one?' She leant over to kiss the top of his head.

'No thanks, I'm fine.'

His curt answer annoyed her. Taking a deep breath, Lan curled up on his lap. His body reeked of cheap motel soap and expensive perfume. Lan didn't believe his story about car trouble. She clenched her nails into her fists to stop herself screaming at him. She knew he had spent last night with some tart he'd met on safari.

A shiver chased down Lan's spine, which had nothing to do with the breeze off the river. If Bern got too attached to someone else, she could forget about him taking her on any more safaris, and Johan wouldn't be pleased. She knew she had to watch Bern more closely from now on. She was in the right frame of mind to use someone as a punching bag. 'How was the safari? Were the people nice, and did you find any lions for them to look at?'

'Please, Lan, I'm not in the mood for idle chatter.' Bern pushed her off his lap.

Lan went into the kitchen, pulling a can of beer from the fridge before going onto the deck to talk to Bern again. 'Sorry, lover, I was worried about you. I got a bit hysterical. I'm not happy if you go away from me, even for one night. I get frightened in this big house all alone.'

'Drop it, Lan, I'm trying to get ready for my safari tomorrow. It's going to be a dawn start, and I'm not in the mood to start an argument with you.'

The harshness of his voice alarmed her. Bern was evidently preoccupied with someone.

He stood with the grace of a cheetah and walked through the lounge and down the stairs.

Lan could then hear him in the laundry, taking clothes out of the washer and piling them into the dryer.

Bern's footsteps sounded hollow on the stairs, and she guessed he was headed for the bedroom. Time to make her move and get in his good books, the only way she knew how.

Lan started undressing the moment she left the verandah. When she entered the bedroom, the air drifted across her naked body.

He had his back to the door, busy packing a duffel bag for the trip tomorrow. Lan approached Bern. She placed her hands on his muscular back. Bern's body tensed at her touch. He let out a deep impatient sigh, and for one awful moment she held her breath. His indifference washed over her. Bern turned to face her. His kiss, full of exasperation, was evident. His day-old stubble chaffed like sandpaper on her lips. Tossing his bag on the floor, Bern unzipped his fly. It lasted mere seconds, and his roughness grazed her. She already felt the bruises starting to crawl across her skin.

Without saying a word, he peeled off the rest of his clothes and went into the bathroom. She gritted her teeth, determined to give him a bit of space. Although, she was getting anxious about the whole situation. More so if he had met some bitch on the bloody safari.

Bern turned the hot water tap to full, letting the steam curl across his body. His anger at what had happened with Lan coiled through the steam. Christ, he was sick and tired of her cheap sex and nauseating voice. He longed to go back to the time when Lan didn't occupy space in his house. His parents had raised him to respect women. His guilt at using Lan needled deep inside him. Still, if she was involved in the poaching, it was better to keep her close, even more so now that they thought one of their own was involved.

Wearing one of Bern's shirts, Lan lay across the bed, clearly waiting for him to come out of the shower. 'I'm looking forward to the trip with you to Chobe. It will be good for us. We can get away from here for a while.' Her voice grated across the steamy atmosphere of the room.

'Yeah, okay, Lan. I'm a bit preoccupied with the trip tomorrow, and if it's all right with you, I'll finish my packing. If you're looking for something useful to do, please iron the shirt you're wearing. I want it for the trip.'

'Glad to help, lover.' Lan took off the freshly laundered shirt. She sauntered naked past him, sashaying slightly so he got a good view of her perfect breasts and trim arse.

Bern, however, didn't glance at her, his mind already clouded with thoughts of Bella.

Lan was waiting for Bern downstairs, shirt now ironed. 'How about a date night?' she suggested, handing Bern the shirt. 'We can go to Riley's for a drink. Maybe romantic dinner later.'

'Yeah, whatever, Lan,' Bern answered, a little too terse for her liking; however, a smile tugged at Lan as she watched him fold the shirt. She thought back to the first time they had sex.

After three months of living with Bern, they had fallen into a convenient, if strained, relationship. At first, Bern had never approached her for sex; he showed no interest in her whatsoever. However, Johan kept insisting that Lan get closer to Bern. And she knew what he meant, so to please him, she swallowed her pride and approached him one night.

After that, it had been easy to take over his bedroom. Fortunately for her, Bern knew how to please a woman, and she had enjoyed their romps in bed. Lan didn't for one moment think Bern carried any romantic notions about her, but she needed him. Bern had become her meal ticket, and she would watch him with the tenacity of a hawk looking for prey, to make sure no other woman entered his life.

CHAPTER 17

Bella was on her second chardonnay when a guy came in. He ambled over to where she sat. He perched himself up on the stool next to her. The bartender came over, and the guy ordered a Coke. Bella wondered why the men in Botswana chose to sit next to her. There were plenty of other empty stools, so why one close to her. She wasn't anything special. And besides, Bella longed to be alone, and with gloomy determination, drink herself into forgetting all about Bern.

'Dumela, my name is Seagal, may I buy you a refill?'

The name sounded familiar to Bella; hadn't Bern mentioned a friend called Seagal? Maybe Seagal was a common name in Botswana. 'Sure, why not,' she replied. *What can it hurt*, she thought, *maybe he can also help take my mind off Bern.*

Seagal's tall frame sat with ease on the small barstool. He looked to be on the wrong side of fifty. His black, wrinkled hair was now flecked with silvery-grey strands, as was his close-cropped beard. Laughter crinkled through his eyes, which were the colour of roasted coffee beans ready to be ground. His broad shoulders contradicted slim hips narrowly touching his stone-washed jeans, where a belt tugged taut to emphasise his narrow waist. His hands were the size of small dinner plates, and he wore a wedding ring – at least he didn't hide the fact he had a partner. His sandalwood deodorant failed to hide the earthy tang that sifted around him.

His long fingers scratched at his beard. 'Please tell me your name. I don't want to share a drink with a stranger with no name.'

'Sorry.' She held out her hand. 'I'm Bella Winter. It's nice to meet you, Seagal.'

They then chatted about Australia and Botswana, comparing weather and lifestyle.

Seagal finished his Coke, switching to a beer, and Bella ordered another chardonnay. 'You're not friends with Bern de Villiers are you?'

'I am.' Seagal's dry, melodic voice surrounded her. 'I've known Bern for a while now, and he's a great guy, for a South African that is. I believe him to be one of my closest friends.'

'I might disagree with you about that, Seagal. I met the guy two days ago, and I find him to be an arrogant, overbearing man.'

'So be it, Bella, although you may change your mind once you get to understand him a bit better.'

'I doubt it. Enough about Bern, tell me about yourself. What is the Seagal story?'

'I'm a safari guide from Etsha, originally, but now my wife and I live in Maun. I've been cutting back on work a bit of late – my wife was tired of me not being at home to help with our children and grandchildren, eh? I do the daytrips out of here now.'

'Sounds like a nice life you've carved out for yourself.' Bella warmed to Seagal.

'Yes … but getting back to Bern, he's been a great help to me. He stepped up to take over my longer-term safaris, giving me extra free time. He holds a unique wonder for the job and a connection to my land, which normally comes from someone born here.'

'You make him sound almost saintly, but he has covered me, thicker than a rash since I met him. His live-in girlfriend must be very understanding, because he blatantly flirted with me on the safari I did with him yesterday. I doubt he gave her a guilty thought all day.'

'Ag, about that, Bella, it's a long story … and one I better let Bern explain to you. May I get you another drink, and perhaps you might join me for lunch?' Seagal offered.

'I should pass on the drink, although I'd love to join you for lunch.' Although Bella felt nervous talking to strangers, she didn't hesitate about agreeing to join Seagal for lunch. She found something soothing and caring about him. A kind of gentleness whirled near him, making her relax in his company, and his deep love for Botswana and the wildlife evidently pulsed through him.

Over lunch, Seagal's storytelling about the numerous safaris he had been on seeped into Bella. She loved listening to his deep, rich voice reminisce about the animals. Like Bern, he too professed a profound love for the big cats.

'I envy you spending so much of your life with lions. I've loved the animal for as long as I can remember. During my childhood, the only friends I kept turned out to be the cats living in our house. I loved spending time with them. I followed the poor things everywhere, lay beside them while they slept and chased dragonflies with them. If they went and hid from me, I always cried.

Sorry, I'm positive you're not interested in my ramblings. I've had too much wine. Now you must think me a complete loop.' The embarrassing after-effects of Bella's night with Bern had begun to haunt her. She tried to make a graceful exit, having made a fool of herself with such a gentle man. 'Thank you for lunch, Seagal, I might see you sometime. I'm unsure about what I'm doing, but I'll be staying here for another few days at least.'

When Bella stood to go, she felt Seagal's large hand on her arm. 'Please stay for a moment, you're upset. Let me buy you a coffee.'

Tears welled in Bella's eyes, and she wiped them away. 'Thank you, I could do with a good cup of tea at the moment.'

Seagal called the waitress over. He ordered a strong coffee for himself and a cup of Rooibos for Bella. 'You have a gentle nature, Bella. I can almost touch it. It's the way your eyes light up every time you talk about your childhood days spent with your cats. Cats are intuitive; they bond with similar creatures. It is a rare gift; promise me, never be embarrassed about your love of cats. You say you're unclear about what to do, now you're in Botswana; I may have a solution for you.'

'What in the world could I possibly do for you? I'm happy to do anything, but all I'm good at is making a fool of myself with the first guide I meet and stuffing up my marriage in Australia.' Bella had no idea about how to begin helping Seagal.

'I doubt you've ever heard about the illegal trade in lion bones.'

Bella choked on her tea at the mere utterance of those words. 'What! God no, don't they only poach elephants or rhinos? Horrific as that is. What on earth possesses someone to be cruel enough to kill lions?'

'It's a bad world out there, Bella.' Seagal held his emotions deep in his eyes. Even the mention of it clearly caused him pain. 'It used to be a problem for the South Africans, but now Vietnamese thugs are moving some of their operations into Botswana. Not too long ago, a lion lost its life by a poacher's bullet. It happened in Chobe, and the male led the large Ihaha pride. The three impressive brothers ruled a large section of the reserve, until one day, boom, poor Neo succumbed to the greed of poachers. It left a terrible gap in the pride.'

Bella gasped. 'That's the cruellest thing I've ever heard. How can people do that to living, breathing animals? What happened to the rest of the pride?' She had tears in her eyes.

'Kagiso and Tan mourned the loss of their brother for a long time. They lost a lot of weight, and all the guides worried about the unity of the pride. We're keeping a close eye on them because another slaughter could mean a new male takes over. If that happens, it doesn't bode well for the young cubs.'

Bella's tea sat on the table, lukewarm and alone. She fiddled with her hands, listening to the shocking story Seagal told. She wanted to be doing something to help; however, she felt at a loss about what to do exactly. 'I received a healthy settlement with my divorce. I'm keen to give you some to assist with fighting the poachers. Apart from the money, I don't know how to help you.'

'Bern told me about your gentle connection with lions. You showed no fear when confronted with one while you went on the safari yesterday, and I must say you impressed him with your reactions.'

Bella couldn't believe Bern had gossiped about her already; it stung her already frazzled nerves. 'I always sensed a connection with cats. I think my spirit travelled freely from human to feline in all my previous lives, and naturally, now I'm in this life, certain catlike characteristics filtered through to me. God, the cats I lived with during my childhood later became my friends, but that unhappy story is way too distressing to recall.'

'Sorry to hear about your past, Bella, but you may well be the one we're looking for, to help us in our fight against poachers.'

Bella felt a sliver of excitement enter her. 'Tell me what you want me to do, and if I'm able to assist in any small way, I'm all yours.'

Seagal smiled widely. 'The poaching racket is done out of Chobe, although it's vital we figure out who the top players are. We're looking for someone to be based in Kasane full-time. The town is way up in the north-eastern corner of Botswana. Your job, for the moment, would be to keep an eye and ear out at the lodges and the safari companies. You might be able to pick up on something out of the ordinary. A good friend of mine up there is on the lookout for a person to liaise between the tourists and operators. It may be the perfect cover for you. He owns P.A.W. Safaris. There are a few good guides up there. With the workload of driving in and out of Chobe for full-day trips, or being away for longer safaris, it doesn't give them a lot of time to be on the ground, eh.'

Bella's whole body tingled. This could be the reason Botswana had jumped out at her when she was deciding to change her life. Lions had always been a passion for her, now she could actually be doing something to help them.

'Bern is convinced Lan is involved somehow, but he's having a bit of trouble trying to prove it, at the moment. He doesn't want her getting suspicious of him, so he's pretending to care for her because if she is involved, she is guaranteed to lead us to the ones in charge.'

Bella's eyes narrowed. 'So, what you're trying to tell me is that Bern isn't a bad guy after all.' She smiled.

'Nice to see you smile, Bella. Never endanger your life, so no heroics, please. All you should do for now is report to me … and Bern, if you're ever happy to talk to him again. He would kill me if anything happened to you, and man I'm getting too old to find myself on his bad side.'

'I'm still embarrassed and hurt about how I let Bern into my life.' Bella bit her lower lip. 'I don't want to complicate things any further between Bern and Lan. Moving to Kasane to help you fight poachers, though, could be the reason I'm here.'

'Thank you, Bella, I'll call my mate Steven and arrange for you to go up there to meet him.'

Bella breathed in the gardenia scented air. It's been a long time since she felt this happy. Although she was devastated at the time, Bradley had done her a favour by divorcing her. She couldn't ever imagine going back to that troubled life she had in Australia.

CHAPTER 18

After speaking with Seagal, Bella felt energised for the first time in a long time. She found him to be such a sweet man; his honesty when he told her how much he cared about the plight of the animals was written in the lines creasing his face.

Bella took Seagal to her cabin, hoping to introduce him to Dingo. The cat had curled himself into a ball under the bush. As soon as Bella bent down, he woke up, no doubt blinking away the leftover traces of his dreams. He snatched at the fish she brought, devouring it greedily. Hunger clearly nibbled at his empty belly; he had to eat in a rush, always fearful of other predators.

With his meal over, he allowed Bella to pat his soft fur. He peeped up at Seagal, though he didn't appear frightened of him.

'You sure do have a way with animals, Bella. Dingo isn't a domestic cat; yet here is the little chap eating out of your hand. Bern's right, you're one of a kind.'

'It's nothing, Seagal. Besides, I guess the little guy felt a tiny bit lost. He was searching for someone to be kind to him. He sees you as a friend also, because he refuses to be civil with Bern. Whenever he comes near, Dingo growls and hisses at him.'

'I'll tell you a little story about Bern, one he may share with you at some time, but I think you should know it now.'

'I'm never seeing Bern again, so you better tell me the story.' Bella invited Seagal in and made him a cup of coffee. She made another cup of tea for herself.

They carried them outside to sit in the chairs with views over the river.

Dingo wandered over to curl up under Bella's chair.

'Well … about six months ago …' Seagal's deep voice trailed off the water. 'As Bern drove into the lodge carpark, the barking of the owner's dog distracted him. He swerved to miss it, and I'm sorry to say, he ran over an African wildcat.'

'Oh no, how awful. Poor Bern.'

'It was the first time I ever saw Bern cry. I know it affected him rather badly. He's a true animal lover, and it's not in his nature to harm anything; except, sometimes horrible accidents do happen. Two kittens were mewing there also. They scampered off before Bern could grab them.'

'I do feel sorry for Bern. What a shock for him to kill an animal, although that doesn't make me change my mind about him. I went through an awful time with my divorce, and the fact my husband betrayed me with my best friend … I won't allow myself to be hurt again, even if his relationship with Lan is just for show.'

'You may change your mind about him one day, but it's not my decision to make. I told you the story because of your little friend Dingo. He may well be one of the kittens who lost his mother on that night.'

Bella nodded. 'There's another thing I want to discuss with you, Seagal. I've been worrying about Dingo ever since you mentioned moving to Kasane. Would it be possible to take the cat with me? I think he depends on my gifts of food, and if I'm not here, he'll be all alone again, with no one else to care for him.'

Dingo let out a gruff miaow.

'It's almost impossible to introduce a wild cat to another territory, but I'm convinced with your connection to the little guy, it may well be feasible. You better find some accommodation out of town a bit. I don't imagine Dingo is a city fella. I'll assist in any way possible, and you can count on Bern to help.'

She felt her face flush. 'Please don't mention me to Bern. I'm trying to fade with a little dignity out of his life; I made such a fool of myself with him already. I'm positive he'll struggle to remember my name by tomorrow.'

'No comment.' Seagal stood and stretched. 'I better be leaving now. I'll be in touch with you after I speak to Steven.'

'Thank you for the talk and your kindness. I appreciate it more than you imagine.' Bella reached up to hug him. She then accompanied him to his vehicle and waved goodbye as he pulled out of the carpark.

When Bella returned to her cabin, she made herself a cup of tea and curled up on the bed. She longed for the solitude to think; Seagal's words bounced inside her head. It horrified her to learn that certain people went out of their way to kill lions for their bones. With her limited knowledge, all bones were the same, so why not kill a few worthless people instead of endangered lions?

Bella liked the sound of Kasane, notably for its isolation from Maun. However, her breath caught, snatching against her ribcage, knowing Bern lived in Maun, a few kilometres away. His so-called relationship with Lan bothered her, even if it was 'fake.' On his phone, the photo showed a happy couple. Bern must be sleeping with Lan, and if he was, she wanted nothing more to do with him. If only she could turn back the clock and not make the disastrous lapse of judgement by going on the safari yesterday. She feared the decision she made then changed the destiny of her life forever, no matter what she did to try and stop it.

Even if Steven had already found someone else to help him, Bella loved the idea of moving to Kasane. By her searches on the internet, Kasane looked picturesque, hugging the Chobe River and within easy distance of the Chobe National Park.

She picked up her laptop and sat cross-legged on the bed, typing into the search engine properties for sale in Kasane. A few sites came up, and she chose one at random. There weren't a lot of properties for sale in the picturesque town, although Bella did discover one backing onto the Chobe River. It looked to be on the edge of town, but close enough to walk to the shops and supermarkets.

The African-inspired dwelling sat on a large plot of land encased by a sturdy fence. By the pictures on the website, it looked to be rendered blockwork painted the colour of biscuits baking in the oven. Its thatched roof draped over the windows. A substantial timber verandah reached out to the river, perfect for sundowners. A huge sparkling swimming pool graced one side of the verandah. It looked to be pure heaven, somewhere to retreat to, somewhere to find herself.

Without hesitation, Bella contacted the agent, Karyn Watson. She told her of her interest in the property.

'I wonder if it might be possible to fly up tomorrow to view the house,' she asked.

Karyn sounded excited someone showed an interest. 'This is great news, Bella. The property is spectacular, right on the banks of the Chobe River. It was built two years ago. The owners were fastidious about the style and landscaping. They are relocating to Gaborone, hence the sale.'

'Sounds perfect.' Bella beamed with joy.

'Let me know your flight arrangements, and I'll meet you at the airport.' Karyn's enthusiasm soothed over Bella.

She phoned Seagal to tell him about the house and her intentions to fly up tomorrow to view it. 'Do you know the name of any vets in Maun?' If she moved and took Dingo with her, she should discuss some options with a vet first.

'My cousin is a vet. I can give you his number.'

Bella phoned the vet surgery; she mentioned Seagal's name and why she wanted an appointment. The vet found a free spot for her in his bookings later that day. Bella sighed with happiness at how everything seemed to be falling into place.

Bella tried without success to straighten her creased trousers and shirt before reaching for her bag. She went to the reception office to order a taxi. The hot sun streamed through the leaves of a mopane tree to seep into Bella.

Twenty minutes later, she climbed into the taxi, wound the window down and gave the driver the address of the vet surgery. The air shifted over her when the taxi edged onto the main road to speed up towards the town centre. The driver dropped Bella off at the entrance to the surgery. Counting out the correct pula, she thanked him and made her way into the reception area.

The vet appeared to be a carbon copy of Seagal. He knew all about her because Seagal phoned him to fill him in about the cat. 'Seagal called you "the cat lady," mma. How are you and how can I help you?'

Bella found him easy to talk to, and his eyes radiated the same kindness his cousin did.

She explained how she intended to shift Dingo from Maun to Kasane and wondered if he might be able to tell her what the best options were. They chatted for about half an hour, and she left the surgery more at peace with her decision.

Her life was falling neatly together now; she would be out of Maun and off Bern's radar. Bella wanted to stay in town for a while to do a bit of shopping. Then she planned to find a hotel close by, to celebrate the making of decisions on her own. Decisions that would change her life forever.

'Can you please tell me the name of a good hotel that's not too noisy?' Bella asked the receptionist.

'I always recommend Riley's, and it's not too far away.'

'Thank you.' Before her drink, Bella went to the airport to arrange her flight for the next day.

Now reassured about Dingo's move, a drink and a cooling atmosphere to sit beckoned. Bella waved down a taxi.

She found Riley's to be a little oasis in hot dusty Maun. The gardens exuded lushness, and the bar area looked inviting. Bella ordered a glass of the aptly named Serendipity Pinot Noir.

Once her wine arrived, Bella sat at a table. She overlooked the swimming pool, letting the African air caress her into a sense of belonging she had never experienced before. Sipping her second glass of wine, Bella pondered that now might be the time to start living her life, lost in Botswana. Her main focus would be to help stop the lion-poaching. Bella breathed in deep, savouring the moment.

When she opened her eyes, her fragile world crashed into reality.

CHAPTER 19

The dusty colour of the evening started to coat the sky when Bern wandered into Riley's with his girlfriend Lan on his arm. She melded her body against him, standing close enough to be his shadow. Lan stared with unashamed adoration into his eyes and laughed at something he whispered to her.

Bella tried to disappear into the corner. She hoped the sultry evening air covered her, and they were too engrossed in each other to look in her direction. Being invisible always worked for Bella in the past, but not tonight.

Seconds after they entered the bar, Bern's eyes showered over Bella. She shook herself free from his penetrating stare. Lan then glared in Bella's direction. The look she gave her radiated with hostility. There was a remoteness about Lan, and the coldness of it sent an icy shiver through Bella.

She reached for her handbag, ready to make a hurried strategic exit. Instead of going past them, she turned the other way to a door situated on the far side of the room. She threaded her way through the bar, cursing her decision to come to Riley's. The sun, half-hidden in the horizon, bathed the carpark in a warm glow. She went out into the waning heat to wave down a taxi. Bella hoped the wait wouldn't be long, although she couldn't imagine Bern would follow her. His girlfriend looked furious, and even with Bern's blatant charms, she doubted he could soothe her ruffled feathers.

The taxi skidded to a stop as Bella ran over to it.

The driver jumped out of the car to open the door. 'Dumela Mma. Where do you want to go?'

'Dumela. The Island Safari Lodge, thank you.' Bella scrambled into the back. Her phone beeped. She thought it might be from Karyn, so she reached into her oversized handbag. To her dismay, the message came from Bern.

Bella, please let me explain. Can I come visit you tonight?
Bella punched in *NO.*
I am leaving for the Kalahari tomorrow, please Bella.
Again, NO.
Bella switched off her phone. She couldn't think about Bern at the moment. From where she sat, the two of them looked like any other loving couple, which was at odds with what Seagal told her, about Bern only *pretending* to care for her. Bella was too distraught to think about why Bern spent the night with her and not Lan. Flashes of her ex-husband and his philandering ways with scant regard for her still rankle inside her.

Bella arrived back at the lodge and headed straight to her cabin. She dumped her bags on the bed then retraced her steps to the dining room. She ordered a salad and a glass of chardonnay. Bella took her usual table by one of the doors. It overlooked the terrace that led down to the river. A small herd of cattle were making their way home, trailing in single-file along a worn-out dusty track in the fading light.

Bella's mind buzzed as she pushed pieces of food in a never-ending circle on her plate. She couldn't understand the conflicting sensations swirling through her body ever since that passionate night with Bern. The sensible thing to do was to forget all about him.

She hardly touched her meal before ordering another drink. The dining room overflowed with noisy German tourists laughing and having a good time. Their laughter kept reminding Bella of her loneliness.

She sought solitude and tranquillity, if only for a minute, and found a secluded spot on the terrace, overlooking the river. The spicy scent of warm gardenias toasted in the breeze floated over her, seeping into her soul.

Bella felt the heat of Bern's presence, way before his deep voice floated to her.

'Hallo, Bella, please, I must talk to you, stay with me for a minute.'

Bella struggled to stand, in an attempt to flee. 'I'm in no state to deal with you at the moment, please leave me alone, Bern.'

'Don't rush off. I can see the hurt in your eyes.' Bern put his arm out to stop Bella.

She sidestepped away from him, breathing deeply. 'Of course, I'm hurt. You used me. I don't understand your relationship with Lan. Why spend the night with me when she is waiting for you at home? Or don't you care?'

'It's complicated at the moment … but never doubt my feelings for you.' Bern scraped his fingers through his thick hair. 'Please—'

Bella cut him off. 'Don't lie to me. The ink isn't even dry on my divorce papers. My husband uttered the same words to me that you are now, every time he came home from spending the night with someone else. You must forgive me if I'm having trouble believing you.' She started to shake. She had to get away from him, but her feet were lumps of lead on the cobblestones.

Bern took a step closer to her. 'Not all men are monsters, Bella. I promise I'm not like your ex-husband. I know he hurt you, but you must learn to trust again.'

Bella shook her head. 'How can I trust you? I only met you five minutes ago. All this talk about Lan and lion-poaching. How do I sift out what is real?' Bella had a sudden urge to vomit. She swallowed down the bile rising in her throat. 'Go back to your cosy dinner.'

'I'll go, as soon as I know you're all right.' Bern had the saddest look on his face. 'When you didn't answer any of my text messages, I imagined something awful happening to you. You're all alone in a foreign country, and I saw how upset you were. Please, Bella, I wanted to make sure you are safe.'

'Ha! I'm perfectly safe thank you. Return to your *complicated relationship* with Lan, and without a backward glance, leave me alone.' Bella moved away, but Bern stepped closer.

His fingers were light on Bella's arm; his breath catching in her hair. His arms circled her waist as his kisses lingered over her lips. Bern's expertise took all her inhibitions away. He used his tongue to delve into the hidden corners of her mouth. He moved a few centimetres away when her fingers rippled down his back. The quizzical expression on his face and his mesmerising eyes held Bella spellbound. He smiled; his teeth flashed white in the moonlight. He winked at her before he folded Bella in his powerful embrace.

His words were a curl above a whisper, 'I think I'm falling for you, Bella.' His lips melted into hers.

Bern was so clearly aware of his sexuality, and Bella was too self-conscious of hers. She felt captive under a magical spell. She moved even closer against his muscled torso in an attempt to luxuriate in the heat radiating off him.

He went to pick her up, but the movement caused them to stumble against the table. It sent the empty glass of wine crashing on the paved stones of the terrace.

'Shit,' he murmured.

Thankfully, the noise brought Bella back to reality. She scolded herself, thinking she should free herself from him. But Bern's body was close enough for her to get marooned in his heartbeat. So, she stepped away, trying to distance herself from him. 'Why are you doing this to me, Bern? I don't hold a good track record with people. Everyone who ever said they loved me has left me in less time than it takes for an ant to cough. You're no different to any of them. The main reason you find me intriguing is because I refuse to swoon at your feet like all the other females do. Please leave me alone, return to Lan, she's your girlfriend, not me.' Bella ran from him, her boots loud on the rough pathway. And when she heard his footsteps getting louder, she reckoned on making it to the room before he caught up.

However, Bern finally caught up with her as she fumbled to open the door.

She dropped her keys, startled by Bern's closeness.

'Please, Bella, listen to me. I promise I won't touch you again tonight, although that's all I dream of doing. I'm leaving for the Central Kalahari tomorrow, and the phone reception down there is sometimes a bit hit-and-miss.'

The look in his eyes made Bella blush with unwanted emotions.

'I couldn't go without telling you that Lan means nothing to me – never has, never will.'

Bella's lower lip quivered. 'They are mere words, which seem to fall out of your mouth so effortlessly. You know nothing about me. Maybe you started with no attraction towards Lan, but it's clear, even to someone as slow as me that you do now. What tale did you spin to her about leaving Riley's? You'll need your saccharine-coated words for an apology to her. Enjoy your trip to the Kalahari. Goodnight, Bern.' She turned on her heels.

Bern touched her arm, lightly. 'One day, you'll see that all I want is to make you happy, I just … can't leave Lan right now. Please, Bella, trust me when I say I love you.'

Bella turned to face him. 'Like I said a moment ago, I heard the same words from my ex-husband, and he didn't mean it either. The words slide out of your mouth without a concern about their impact, and I won't let myself be hurt again. Now go, please.' Bella opened the door, went inside and leant against its reassuring surface.

She shut out the night and Bern, her emotions swimming wildly inside her.

His footsteps disappeared into the cobblestones, but she waited inside a full five minutes before she opened the door. The night shook itself free of him, but his presence lingered near her.

CHAPTER 20

Bern climbed into his vehicle. He sat behind the wheel for a full ten minutes, lost in his thoughts. His simmering emotions for Bella were too powerful to ignore. His whole life changed in that split second he first laid eyes on her. He thought his future to be all planned out. He'd imagined meeting his kindred spirit for such a long time now, but in his dreams, it never happened like this. He longed for the romantic connection his parents had.

The trouble was, now Bella had found out about his *so-called* relationship with Lan, she wanted nothing to do with him. He liked a challenge, though, and the one he had now was trying to convince Bella he wasn't such a bad person after all.

Bern edged his vehicle into the busy night traffic, for the slow drive into Maun and the feisty Lan.

He doubted the welcome numbness of sleep would find him tonight. Bella kept crashing around in his mind. It had been a mistake to visit her. When he saw her sitting all alone at Riley's, his heart contracted. He longed to go to her, to touch her and to know she was all right. He gave Lan a feeble excuse about leaving his sunglasses at the lodge, so their cosy dinner at Riley's had to be postponed. He hailed a taxi to take her home. The belligerent Lan clearly didn't believe any of the lie he said, but he didn't care about her anymore. Before meeting Bella, being with Lan twisted into a fractured relationship. Now he found it tedious.

He wanted to meet the ex-husband who hurt Bella. He would be happy to wring his bloody neck and watch him suffer the same way he made Bella suffer. His chest tightened as though someone punched him. If only Bella knew the effect she had on him. He wanted to comfort her. But the moment her body melted against him, all notions of keeping it platonic, flew with the swish of a fish eagle across the river. He lacked his usual self-control around Bella. If he wasn't with her, he longed for her, and if he was, he worried about doing or saying something to frighten her away.

Earlier in the afternoon, Bern phoned Seagal to ask him how it went with Bella. He didn't get a lot out of him. All Seagal would say was that Bella impressed him, and he saw why Bern fell for her. She had a gentleness and an uncanny gift with cats, both wild and tame. Seagal said she was keen to help in the fight against poaching, but he refused to say anything else on the subject. Seagal promised to take care of Bella, to make sure she stayed safe, out of harm's way and happy. Now Bern would be worrying all the time, until these criminals were behind bars, or better yet, they were stampeded by an angry herd of elephants.

Bern knew he had to calm down before he saw Lan again. He drove past the entrance to his home and across the river to the Maun Lodge. A beer might take the edge off his frustration. He couldn't think straight and yearned for the day Bella could find a place in her heart for him.

Bern arrived home a tick passed nine-thirty. He wished for Lan to already be in bed, but the house lit up brighter than a bloody Christmas tree. Now he faced another tongue-lashing from a possessive Lan.

He remembered with regret the day he met Lan. He had been at the Old House Lodge in Kasane, talking to Steven about the heinous crime of lion-poaching. Steven owned the safari company P.A.W. Safaris and had vented his rage about the senseless slaughter of elephants and lions. They were on their third Lion Lager when Lan had trotted up to them. She had begun to cry and spun a farcical story about a jilted love affair and the need to get to Maun. Steven, a soft touch, suggested they help. Bern agreed with reluctance, and before he could sneeze, Lan had moved into his house.

Now, sitting in his car outside his brightly lit home, he groaned and clenched his fists in anger before taking a deep breath and getting out.

Then as soon as he walked in the front door, Lan sprang up from the lounge, startling him.

'Where the hell have you been?' She picked up her empty coffee cup and threw it at Bern. He moved out of the way, and the cup shattered on the floor. 'It doesn't take a couple of hours to drive from here to lodge, then home again. You went to visit her, didn't you, the cow you saw at Riley's. Tell me the truth, you *đồ khốn*.' Lan's words coiled through the house before dispersing in the light currents drifting off the river.

'See who? You're being paranoid, honey. I went to get my sunglasses and bumped into an old guiding buddy from South Africa. We had a beer to catch up.'

'Liar, I smell her white, greasy scent from here; she's all over you. I catch her near you again, I'll scratch her eyes right off her pinched, little face. What do you see in her, she's as ugly as a baby baboon. You're mine; you never disrespect me again. Don't forget my words, lover boy. Never dump me in a restaurant again. I was humiliated.' Lan sounded hysterical.

'How can I ever forget about you, Lan; you keep reminding me all the time. I apologised then, so don't make me apologise again.' He sighed.

'That bitch better watch out.'

Bern could tell Lan itched for a fight, her fists clenched, and her lips curled tightly.

'Drop it,' he said forcefully. 'Can you even hear how crazed you sound? I'm not about to start an argument with you. I'm off to the Kalahari tomorrow for a few days, then we're doing the Chobe safari together. Let's leave it for now, and by Sunday, we'll have forgotten all about it.'

Lan's breath was heavy in the still air as the tension slapped against Bern.

He forced a loving smile. 'I'm having a shower before going to bed. Better clean up the mess. That's the third cup you've broken this week.'

Lan stayed unusually quiet.

Bern dropped a perfunctory kiss on the top of Lan's head before going to the bedroom. He then stripped off his clothes. They did smell of Bella; no wonder Lan got her knickers in a knot. He went into the bathroom and couldn't help but remember the sensual moments he had spent with Bella. He turned off the hot tap, to let the frigid blast of cold water take the heat from his body.

Bern might have slept at some time during the night, but for most of the hours before dawn, he lay flat on his back staring up at the ceiling. As soon as the first shades of dawn coiled through the blinds, he jumped out of bed and dressed in a hurry. He finished packing and left the house without waking up Lan.

CHAPTER 21

Somewhere in the middle of Chobe National Park, Thuan, Duc and Chinh were well and truly drunk on the beers they had purchased in Kasane. Dusk was fast approaching, and Thuan knew it was time to move. He climbed into their vehicle; Duc and Chinh squashed into the front seat beside him. He had to find another isolated location to set up camp. His mind, thick with alcohol, hindered his ability to steer the vehicle over the rough terrain. His bleary eyes were clouded in fuzz.

The bush circled them, waving branches, more menacing than witches from long-forgotten grim fairy tales. The pale evening light faded; it turned the sky a dove colour grey.

Thuan, however, didn't switch the headlights on, for fear someone might find them. The safari vehicles wouldn't be driving this late, but with several camping grounds in the area, he wanted to be careful. The light from their headlights piercing through the trees could alert the rangers or other campers of their presence.

Thuan veered around trees and burrows in an almost circular direction. He tried to navigate over the unforgiving ground.

He squeezed through two Zambezi teak trees; their low-hanging branches scratched the side of the vehicle when he swerved to avoid a large termite mound. Thuan tried to regain control of the steering wheel.

All of a sudden, an elephant loomed right in front of the vehicle.

Thuan skidded to a stop, and both Chinh and Duc fell forward, hitting their heads on the dashboard. They rubbed their heads before swearing at Thuan.

The three men from the crowded streets of Hoi An knew nothing about elephants and how unpredictable they got if provoked. If only they understood, bull elephants could display extremely aggressive behaviour, the brothers might have shown more caution.

Duc and Chinh stared wide-eyed with terror, as Thuan jumped out of the vehicle.

The alcohol dulled his brain. It gave him the false impression he could outwit an elephant. Thuan raised his arms at the animal, waving them in circles, expecting to chase it away. Thuan didn't comprehend the gravity of the situation. He wondered why this elephant didn't merge back into the forest. That ignorance turned out to be his fatal error.

Elephant

I was annoyed that this vehicle had disrupted my evening ritual. I shook my head at it; my ears flapped in the wind scattering dust. The sound of my anger reverberated off the trees, bouncing around the vehicle, louder than thunder. I stood so still I became part of the landscape. My heavy, long tusks almost scraped my knees. The vehicle started going backwards, and the rear tyres spun in the soft sand, wedging it in a vice-like grip. The vehicle showed no signs of moving in any direction. My mood was always placid, but tonight I was uncharacteristically angry. I raised my trunk high to sniff out the reason for the intrusion. I smelt the fear coming from the vehicle.

I spread my ears wide, not flapping them to cool my body. I glared at the human who was waving his skinny arms in never-ending circles at me. My foul mood spread through the forest as my testosterone levels soared off the chart. I scraped up the sand with my right foot, pawing the ground and squashing some ants. I wished the human would dissolve into the leaves blowing across my hide. The human yelled in a voice that wouldn't disperse further than the termite mound.

I gave the human a chance to evaporate, but he stood firm. Now, with fury boiling inside me, I bent my head low and charged. I could see his surprise at the speed of my attack. The sharp snap of bones breaking reached me as my tusk pierced into the human's chest, impaling him. I heard gurgling sounds as blood gushed from the human. It plopped syrupy on the ground, to pool a deep red in the white sand. A hiss of wind escaped from the human then nothing.

I raised my head, wondering why the human still dangled from my tusk. The human's legs twitched in the slight breeze. I shook my head, trying to free my tusk from the dangling human.

The human cleaved into two gory halves, one side landing on the ground with a deep thump. The other side of the human flew off to crash against the termite mound. When I freed myself, I backed up. Now, my sights were set on the vehicle. Two other humans cowered in the front seat; the smell of their urine permeated the air. I charged towards them, and with one almighty push with my tusk, I flipped the vehicle onto its side. The sound of glass splintered, and metal being squashed filled the night with a prolonged death knell.

Satisfied I had inflicted enough damage for one night, I backed away from the vehicle. Shifting my stance, I sniffed the air again before continuing my stroll down the steep slope towards the edge of the river. I washed my tusks in the water and watched the last traces of the human sprinkle through the strong currents. I drank deeply of the cooling water before returning to the forest to feed.

CHAPTER 22

Duc couldn't tear his eyes away from the grizzly scene. A haze of death spread through him, as spirits swirled. He screamed, as did Chinh; their voices caught in the leaves to float into the night. Both the brothers listened to that final gasp of shock as Thuan's life flowed into the ether of dusk.

Duc and Chinh lay for what seemed to be hours but was perhaps mere minutes in the front of the vehicle. The tusk of the elephant had missed Duc by millimetres. They lay huddled together, their tears mingling.

There didn't appear to be any major injuries to both of them, only a few bumps and cuts from the front windscreen when it rained over them.

They moved their bodies until a spine-tingling sound, like the ghostly squealing of children being tortured, entered them. It sent the fear of God to bubble inside Duc. He peered over the dashboard, too petrified to blink. Revulsion gripped him. It turned his stomach to water. His eyes bulged, making it impossible to blink.

The two brothers were forced to look on at the horror. Panic nibbled at Duc's eyes.

A pack of over twenty African-painted dogs danced over the two halves of Thuan. Their squabbling minced through the night air. They ripped the gory remains of Thuan into a hundred pieces.

Duc and Chinh crouched in the vehicle, listening to the tearing of their brother's flesh and the crunching of his bones. The dogs seemed to be making a sport of it. They carried bits of Thuan in and out of the bushes, their bickering swirled through the brothers. All of a sudden, the dogs fell silent, their rounded fluffy ears twitching against the breeze. The mist of night soon swallowed the dogs

Duc and Cinch stayed more silent than a barn owl in flight, unable to console each other. Duc quaked in terror, and his teeth refused to stop shivering.

The air was coated with the heaviness of death; the leaves refused to stir in the wispy air. Duc felt a nervousness cover him, then a deafening roar.

The sound of lions calling shook the ground. It sent shock-waves to bubble over the ground. Duc's bowels simmered when he sensed the lions tracked closer. A brittle light sifted down, doing little to alleviate the loss Duc felt. He watched with revulsion while two enormous lions tracked towards his brother … and him.

Lion

The elephant and the painted dogs disturbed the harmony in our territory. Sensing death flowed through the leaves while a spirit journeyed to the afterlife, we went to investigate. We left the females of our pride to continue the search for kudu.

My brother and I loomed large on the scene; our enormous paws padded over the ground like we wore shoes made of guineafowl feathers. Our nostrils flared as we bared our teeth to sniff at the blood. There would be nothing left for us to scavenge a meal here tonight. My brother and I knew, from other kills, greedy painted dogs rarely left enough for other predators to feast on. The smell of the blood caused our empty stomachs to grumble.

My brother growled. The sound reverberated through the air. It ricocheted off the termite mound into the night.

We padded over to the vehicle, where the humans crouched. We smelt the fear from inside. It was the same smell filtered from impalas before they were eaten. We breathed in with mouths wide; our long, razor-sharp teeth glinted in the pale moonlight. The scent of human sweat, pungent in the air.

My brother and I recognised all too well the brutality of man because we had witnessed the death of our brother. We still got caught in our memories when we passed the acacia tree, the last place we saw our brother. Our growls rumbled, swirling around the termite mound. It scared a pair of squirrels huddled deep in their burrow attempting to get a bit of sleep. Cautious of the inhumanity of humans, we turned our backs on the overturned vehicle to disappear into the night. We smelt kudu nearby, as well as the scent of the females. The night was still dark enough to make a kill.

CHAPTER 23

Chinh wanted their ghastly night to be over. Dawn stayed a lifetime away, and insanity already leached into his soul. All ideas of being there to shoot lions floated away with Thuan's blood.

Chinh didn't stir at all during those long murky hours. The sounds of the African bush cascaded over him, ghostly echoes to shake away his dreams while he waited for dawn. The first wrinkles of light creased into the eastern sky and clawed at him. Chinh nudged Duc awake before struggling out of the vehicle. He stretched his tight muscles so he could stand. The morning air tingled with a hint of frost. The stillness of death floated into him.

Duc stood beside him, and for once he kept his mouth shut.

Chinh scratched at his hair while he assessed the surroundings. Duc helped him search the ground for traces of Thuan, except there didn't appear to be enough left of him to bury. They gathered together what remained, shovelling sand over the blood. Duc stacked branches and three smooth stones on top. A last reminder their brother shared a life with them for the briefest of moments.

There didn't appear to be a lot of damage to the vehicle, except for the broken side window and windscreen. The passenger door was in no mood to ever open again. It crumpled at odd angles into the seat, ripping the vinyl. The vehicle had toppled onto the termite mound from the force of the elephant's temper. Chinh tied one end of a length of rope through the windows, and the other end Duc twined around a nearby tree. Chinh pushed with all his strength against the side of the vehicle, while Duc pulled on the rope. The vehicle started to sway, and once they gained momentum, the car plopped onto its wheels. Duc retrieved the rope, and he climbed into the vehicle.

Chinh drove, and after a few false starts, the vehicle inched forward in the soft sand. The sight of so much carnage began to fester then fade in the rear-view mirror. Chinh slammed his foot down hard on the accelerator. He drove in a southerly direction. He didn't notice the difficulty in his haste to leave the park.

A torturous couple of hours later, Chinh yelled above the drone of the vehicle, scaring Duc. Chinh had reached the tar road. He turned left and didn't stop until the Pandamatenga border crossing, into Zimbabwe, came into view.

Chinh left the vehicle on the side of the road and picked up his bag. Duc grabbed his bag and the bag containing their guns. They both sauntered up to the customs office. The two men pooled together the money Lan had given them to buy supplies. Chinh used most of it to bribe the officials, thankful Zimbabwe turned a blind eye to corruption. Safely across the border, they hitched a ride into Victoria Falls. Neither of them bothered about retrieving their mobile phones from the vehicle. Chinh didn't pause to consider the mess he had left Lan with, nor did he care. She possessed enough street savvy to look after herself from now on.

CHAPTER 24

Johan's temper sparked alarmingly. The sixteen-and-a-half-hour flight from Johannesburg to Vietnam exacerbated his already foul mood. He sat opposite his boss. He could almost touch the flints of annoyance darting into him. Nguyen's stature was made even smaller by the mahogany desk taking up most of the room in his opulent office.

'You and your insane idea, with that whore and her brothers, is starting to scrape into my brain. The responsibility for the lack of lion bones had to fall on someone.' Nguyen spat the words across the table. 'I demand results immediately, or someone's head will be floating without a body in the nearest river.' He stood stretching his arms above his head and arching his back.

Johan could hear the crink of bones as he sat squirming in his chair.

Nguyen looked out the floor-to-ceiling windows to where the smog clouded over the Ancient Town towards the harbour, his fingers massaging his temples.

'I'll get the results you want boss. Leave it with me.' Johan was already planning how Lan would take the blame for this debacle.

As Johan left Nguyen's office building, he was accosted by two Americans. Both men appeared to be in their early thirties. One had a bony frame that hardly touched his grimy shirt or trousers. The sun had already turned his fair skin to the colour of cooked lobsters. He had long hair a shade deeper than carrots after harvesting, hung in straggles down his back.

By contrast, the other one had olive skin that showed no sign of sunburn. His body seemed to have been muscular at some stage, but now beer and fatty food rendered him flabby. He wore his long, thick black hair in a plait down his broad back, and his bushy beard whorled in on itself to form matted dreadlocks. His clothes were also creased from overuse and smelt of body odour. A scowl marred his chiselled face, like the world owed him something.

They pushed Johan against a wall. The lanky one with red stringy hair held a knife to Johan's throat. The stockier one demanded money. Johan, furious after his meeting, punched the one with the beard in the face and slipped the knife from the red-headed one, who had the strength of a jellyfish.

After the scuffle, Johan detected a coldness about the men. Could these two be the answer to his problems with Lan and her stupid brothers, he questioned. 'How about I buy you a beer?' he asked them. 'No hard feelings, or do you want me to call the police?'

'We'll take the beer.'

Over a few beers at a nearby tavern, Johan felt the tension from his meeting with Nguyen start to evaporate.

After introductions, Johan said, 'So, tell me why you two low-lifes are skulking around Hoi An, and don't fucking lie to me. I'm in the right frame of mind to make your life hell.'

'Hey, man, no need to be like that. I go by Ly, and he goes by Mason.' The Asian-looking one spoke. 'Me and Mason met at school in Detroit, Michigan. Schools are for the nerds. We began stealing autos at thirteen, doing drugs at fourteen and robbing jewellery stores at sixteen.'

'Quite the enterprising young lads from Detroit.'

'Yeah, whatever, smart-arse. Three months … or was it four … we were high on drugs. It must have been a bad mix. We met some skanky chick at a disco. She was all over us, then when we wanted more, she got all uppity with us. Then we read in the papers she was murdered.' Ly sniggered. 'We didn't want to hang around, if you get the idea.'

Johan nodded. 'Sure, continue.'

'I'm half-Vietnamese, so I figured we would come here. We fenced some of the jewellery we stole, bought our plane tickets and here we are. We figured to lie low for a couple of months, before going back to the States.'

Johan let a smile spread across his face. He was positive they could do a better job than the annoying Lan and her incompetent brothers. 'I've another scenario for you to consider. How about flying to Botswana.'

'Fucking never heard of it. Is this a con?' Mason went to stand.

'Sit down, moron. Botswana's in Africa. I run a poaching ring between here and there. All you have to do is shoot a couple of lions, tell my man in Botswana and that's it.'

'Holy shit. Are you fucking pulling my leg?'

'Do I look like I'm kidding?' Johan leered at them. 'What do you say?'

'Fucking yes,' they answered together.

Johan arranged for them to fly into Lusaka in Zambia, where he organised a private charter plane to take them into Kasane in Botswana. The African connection would meet them in Kasane and make all the arrangements from there, including the supply of two Ruger SR9C pistols.

Mason and Ly's meeting in a hot steamy Kasane proved fruitful. They soon found themselves on another charter plane heading for Maun. The two men booked to go on a three-day safari into the Central Kalahari where they were to shoot a lion.

Johan arranged for three of his men to already be camped at the Passarge Campsites in the Central Kalahari Game Reserve. Two of the men would bring their wives. The third man would play the part of safari guide while the others pretended they were tourists. Johan knew the authorities were cracking down hard on poaching, and a group of men camping out in the parks was a red flag to the rangers. Johan arranged for Mason and Ly to join Bern's group.

If Mason and Ly killed a lion, they would get in touch with one of the men and tell him the location of the carcass. They would handle the shipment of the bones to Vietnam. Johan also didn't mind who else got shot, as long as there were dead lions by the end of the trip.

CHAPTER 25

Bern drove along the streets towards the Sedia Riverside Hotel. He watched an unspoiled day begin to waken in Maun. The hotel, situated on the outskirts of town, was where he would meet the guests he was escorting on the three-day safari to Deception Valley, in the Central Kalahari Game Reserve. The group consisted of two couples from South Africa and two guys from America. The ever-affable Brighton would be joining him on the trip to help with the cooking and tending to the campsite. Bern loved the emptiness of the Central Kalahari. He craved some peace at the moment to take his mind off Bella.

The Sedia sat with the grace of an old lady in thick sand one hundred metres from the main road. Bern bumped over the rough track, noticing that Brighton waited patiently with a big smile on his rugged face. Brighton leant against their Toyota Landcruiser safari vehicle, which had a fully laden trailer hitched to the towbar. The trailer held all the supplies and camping equipment they required for the next three days.

'How's it going, man, you a bit late this morning, eh, a busy night with the girlfriend?' Brighton greeted him.

'Ja, you know me too well.' Bern saw no reason to go into any details about his complicated love life at the moment. The arrival of the guests saved him from making any comment.

After introductions and Bern's spiel about safety in the vehicle and around the campsites, they were ready to start. Everyone found a spot in the rear of the vehicle, and Brighton and Bern climbed into the front. He loved this moment of anticipation, before a safari. He was at his happiest in the bush, showing excited visitors the beauty and spirituality of Botswana. There was nowhere else in the world that tugged at your heartstrings more than being surrounded by wildlife and immersed in nature. Bern sensed that Bella felt the same as he did, but he pushed that thought aside for the time being. He needed to focus on his small group and ensure they had the best time possible.

He nodded to Brighton, then started the engine.

Maun yawned and stretched with a hint of possibility and excitement. People already began opening up the myriad stalls fringing both sides of the tar road leading out of town. Goats and dogs mooched about, dodging the traffic, seasoned warriors on the never-ending hunt for food. Shops began to open for another busy day. When the last of the shops, businesses, traffic and people disappeared in the rear-view mirror, Bern picked up speed. Maun disappeared under a cloud of sand, to await their return.

About half an hour later, Bern's tired body heaved a sigh of relief. He turned right off the main highway into the tiny village of Makalamabedi. He stopped for a moment to stretch his legs and have a chat with one of the locals, and then he climbed back into the vehicle, dreading that the tar road crumbled into dust.

Now started the challenging straight and narrow track, bumping along the side of the veterinary cordon fence. The whole of the single-lane track consisted of thick clinging sand, and it took all of Bern's skill to push the vehicle and trailer through it. It was, without a doubt, the most boring stretch of track in all of Botswana. His guests had stopped their eager chatting and were nodding off to sleep, heavy with the hazy heat that covered them.

About halfway along the road, Bern pulled the vehicle off to one side to allow his guests to stretch their legs, use the bush toilet and eat some of the morning tea Brighton had prepared. The group finished their coffee, and with some trepidation, a few used the nearest tree for a toilet stop. They jumped in the vehicle for the final push on this challenging stretch of road.

The sun had journeyed past its zenith by the time they arrived at the Matswere Gate, the entrance to the Central Kalahari Game Reserve. Bern went into the office to sign the necessary paperwork, while Brighton set up lunch under the shady branches of a sausage tree.

When Bern left the office, he saw everyone piling their plates with cold meats, salads, and bread. They sat at the table to chat and enjoy the meal. The warden at the office told Bern that one other safari company booked a site at the Passarge Campsites, whereas Bern's group was staying in Deception Valley. With luck, they might cross paths somewhere in the vastness of the Kalahari, to share news of possible lion sightings.

The flat plains of Deception Valley were covered in short wheat-coloured grass stretching in all directions. It faded into the ancient

mists of time, where small emerald-green shrubs clung to the sand. Kalahari apple trees and graceful acacias dotted the landscape, giving shade when the sun sizzled, liquifying the air.

The plains overflowed with all of the grazing animals. Herds of springbok, oryx and giraffe gambolled and played, sensing that the heavy heat had chased the predators away to shelter in the shade. Bat-eared foxes frolicked close to their dens, and jackals forever wove a path through the grass.

The two couples appeared thrilled with all the sightings. They took lots of photos each time they stopped. Their enthusiasm soon washed over Bern, taking away the tightness. It left him with a mellow calmness.

There were six campsites in Deception Valley. Bern nudged his vehicle up the slight rise away from the endless plains. He turned left off the main track towards campsite number two. The other five campsites remained empty, so the whole of the Central Kalahari would be theirs to explore.

Brighton and Bern unpacked the trailer, throwing tents and chairs onto the ground under a shady tree. The campsite included two circular timber structures that remained open to the elements. A crude bucket-shower sat rusting in one, while the other housed a drop toilet. Bees buzzed incessantly in both structures. Bern made a start on pitching the tents while Brighton set up the table and chairs, giving their guests somewhere shady to sit while they waited for their canvas homes to be ready.

The two couples from South Africa – Pieter and Yolandi, and Willem and Janel – chattered to each other, while Mason and Ly (the two Americans) stood a little apart, deep in conversation. They didn't appear interested in socialising with the others. Mason carried a satellite phone and was in constant contact with someone.

Once the three tents were nestled under the trees, all the guests began to settle into their homes for the next three nights. Bern and Brighton pitched their tent a little further away. At three-thirty, Brighton called everyone over to the table. He made coffee and opened a packet of ginger-crisp biscuits for them to eat while they waited for the afternoon game drive. Mason and Ly preferred to have a couple of ice-cold St Louis Lagers. They took their beers to the other side of the camp, well away from the others.

Bern glanced over to where they stood. A blast of frigid air seemed to blow around their boots. Both men looked like they hadn't slept in weeks or changed their clothes. Body odour and grime curled around them. Bern went over to talk to the men, trying to gauge the main reason they chose to come on safari. He received mumbled replies from both Mason and Ly, but he knew with a tight twist of trepidation they were up to no good.

He relayed his misgivings to Brighton, saying to be on alert for anything not quite right.

On their afternoon game drive, they saw a smattering of the grazing animals and a few jackals. Lions were on the top of everyone's *must-see* list; however, Bern, conscious of the poaching going on in the Kalahari in recent weeks, hoped the lions proved hard to find.

CHAPTER 26

Dawn started with a slight hesitation the next day. A sooty fog hovered over the landscape, to dampen the mood of Bern's little group. The grazing animals that never let any visitors down proved hard to locate on their game drives. The emptiness of the Kalahari swallowed them as though the rest of the world ceased to exist. The ghostly atmosphere lasted all day, and Mason and Ly looked twitchy and were annoying the two couples.

Bern failed to understand why they never crossed paths with the other safari company either. Usually, guides were in constant contact with each other about sightings. Maybe this group was keeping west of the Passarge Campsites.

They returned to camp in the evening of the second day, watching dark clouds coat the horizon, to cluster together with the promise of a storm. Bern caught a nuance of friction sizzle within the group, made worse by the hint of bad weather.

Lightning flashed and thunder rumbled low against the clouds. Light rain fell during most of the night but failed to dampen the sand. The group emerged from their tents on the last full day a little crestfallen. Bern knew finding lions would break the tension that was forming between the two couples and Mason and Ly.

The morning held a wraithlike fuzz floating close to the ground. Willem and Pieter spoke with Bern. They had opted not to do the early morning game drive, preferring to rest in the camp with their wives and Brighton.

Both Mason and Ly tossed camera bags into the safari vehicle. Bern wondered about this because neither of them showed any interest in taking photos. He didn't ask them any questions, but a twinge of apprehension looped inside him.

Mason and Ly climbed into the second row of the vehicle. Both men remained adamant about seeing lions, so Bern drove to Sunday Waterhole. Lions had been calling during the night and into the hours stealing towards dawn, so he knew the direction they were in. He drove his vehicle around the camelthorn trees huddled together on one side of the waterhole. Two male lions lay close to the water's edge. One of the males had several porcupine quills stuck in his paw and chest. His brother stayed close to keep him safe.

Before Bern reached for his satellite phone to alert the rangers, he twisted around to the two men. What Bern saw sent a shiver of ice to pierce into his heart.

Mason stood clumsily, in the second row of seats, with a pistol aimed at the lions.

'What the fuck,' Bern yelled. He pressed down hard on the accelerator and turned the steering wheel to the left.

The sudden change in direction threw Mason off balance. He fired a shot at the lions. The bullet soared high catching in the branch of one of the camelthorn trees, out of reach of the intended targets. Mason struggled to regain his balance; his hands stabbing in the air. The momentum made him stumble, dropping his pistol out of the vehicle.

Bern pressed hard on the brake; Ly fell forward, knocking himself out on the steel bar of the seat in front of him. He slumped low into his seat; blood already began to dribble from a cut on his forehead.

Mason somersaulted out of the vehicle, to land with a thud in the compacted sand. He sprang to his feet, but Bern was one step ahead of him. He seized Mason in his strong grip, and punched him with force in the face, breaking a few teeth. Bern, too furious to care, punched him again. Mason reeled from the impact and aimed a punch at Bern. But Bern sidestepped the smaller man. He gripped onto his wrist, twisting his arm at an awkward angle until his ulna snapped.

Mason screamed, writhing in agony. He slumped to the ground, clutching his broken arm.

Bern picked up the pistol and stowed it in the front glove compartment. He rummaged in Ly's camera bag, retrieving another gun and the satellite phone from it, storing them with Mason's gun. He then took a length of rope from under the front seat and tied up the hands and legs of both Ly and Mason. He picked up Mason, grateful he weighed less than a baby wildebeest, and tossed him into the second row of seats.

Mason shivered, yelling expletives at Bern, who ignored him.

Ly began to stir. He mumbled incoherently, 'What the fuck hit me?'

Bern punched him hard; his nose shattered, causing him to sprawl across the seat.

'You fucking moron. I'll bloody kill you,' Ly swore at Bern.

'What the hell do the two of you think you're doing? You idiots are heading straight to jail!' Bern yelled at both men.

'Fuck you,' Mason slurred, watching another tooth fall out of his mouth. 'You bloody broke my arm, and you can't prove anything, you prick. Untie us, man.'

'No way in hell! Now, shut up both of you. I'm in the right frame of mind to dump you out in the middle of the Kalahari and watch how long it takes before a lion or hyena gets to you.'

Bern then drove to their camp, frustration thrumming inside him. He tried to calm his seething temper by relaxing into the emptiness of the Kalahari.

When they arrived back, he immediately briefed Brighton about what happened at the waterhole.

'They must be working for someone. They're too stupid to think for themselves. Maybe the other campers in the Passarge Campsites were in on it too. I'll let the authorities know, at the gate and also when I take them to the police station,' Bern advised.

'Terrible business, but I think you're right.' Brighton clenched his fists into balls, swearing under his breath. He strode well away from the others to seemingly try and control his rage.

Bern had figured Mason and Ly carried traces of evil about them; however, he hadn't suspected they carried guns and were itching to slaughter a lion. He couldn't understand how they thought their sketchy plan would work, and he worried things might have deteriorated at a deadlier pace, especially for him. He considered both Mason and Ly twitched with a craziness making them stupid enough to kill anything that moved, solely for the sport of it.

He told the others what transpired, while Brighton made cups of coffee for the ladies.

Willem and Pieter decided to go with Bern to help him with Mason and Ly, who remained forlorn in the vehicle.

Bern couldn't let go of the rage swirling inside him on the eighty-kilometre drive into Rakops, the nearest town to the Central Kalahari Game Reserve. It took them well over an hour on the unforgiving tracks, and this time, Bern didn't mind because each bump rendered cries of agony from both Ly and Mason.

Bern drove straight to the police station, which was nestled in one of the back streets in the dusty sleepy town. He strode into the building that smelt of disinfectant, going straight up to the desk.

Another hour dragged by while he gave his statement to the police.

Two skinny officers, with their hats pulled low, dragged Mason and Ly into the holding cells. Let the authorities deal with them now; Bern didn't intend to have anything to do with either man ever again. The penalty for poaching in Botswana was severe. Mason and Ly were liable to languish in jail for a long time and wouldn't remember the reason for their incarceration once they were released. He phoned Seagal to tell him what happened, saying all the guides should be on full alert now.

They arrived at the campsite ready for a late lunch. Bern thanked Willem and Pieter for coming with him to Rakops and for their patience and understanding. Both couples weren't interested in doing their afternoon game drive, but Bern said it could take their mind off the horrors of the morning. Also, he planned to check and see if the two lions remained at Sunday Waterhole, so he could relay their whereabouts to the vets who would deal with the injured lion.

The lions rested from the heat under a scrappy camelthorn tree.

Bern made the necessary phone calls, knowing the rangers and vets would do the rest.

Everyone stayed up late on the last night. They huddled close to the fire while Bern told them the frightening details of the events at the waterhole earlier in the day. A sense of foreboding surged through his body. He realised the poaching of lions in Botswana had only begun.

Once they were all zipped up in their tents, Bern lay on his back staring into a blackness so complete it took his breath away. He chatted with Brighton until three in the morning. Brighton fell asleep midway into one of his sentences, snoring softly. Bern envied him because the emptiness that came with a dreamless sleep eluded him. In the luminous spell before dawn started to chase the night, Bern's mind returned to Bella. He longed to lose himself in her embrace, to take away the turmoil unravelling inside him.

CHAPTER 27

The last day of the safari dawned clear and cool. The heavy mizzle from yesterday vanished, leaving a sky so blue you were soon adrift in it. Bern folded his exhaustion to the hidden corners of his mind. He had to stay clear-headed for a day that stretched longer than shadows at sunrise. He encouraged the two couples to get up earlier than usual because Brighton and he wanted to make an early start on packing up the camp.

They struggled out of their tents, and with a hint of chill clutching at the air, they rushed to the fire. Brighton served them steaming cups of coffee and gave them buttermilk rusks to quell their hunger. Bern urged them into the vehicle; he wanted to take them on one last drive. He thought an incredible cat sighting might make them forget about the disaster of yesterday.

Bern reckoned if he started a bit earlier, he might find the lions that had disturbed their sleep during the night. Their calls came from the plains, so he nosed the vehicle out of the thicket of trees beside their campsite, turning right at the junction of the track. He dipped down to the flat, endless plains, starkly empty at this hour of the morning. The sky held a hint of raspberry red as the sun hid behind a bank of clouds low on the horizon. Bern imagined the two couples were freezing in the open back of the vehicle, but he believed that if he found the lions, they'd forget all about the frosty dew covering them. The first morning rays of golden sunlight did little to warm their bodies.

As Bern drove towards Deception Pans, he spotted three cheetahs. The female cheetah was with her two sub-adult cubs, who also turned their faces towards the east. The cubs were now at an age where she could start leaving them for longer periods. It was almost time for the cubs to fend for themselves.

Bern was confident that with such an awesome sighting, the two couples would all but forget their search for lions and the events of yesterday. Cheetahs were such a rare treat for anyone nowadays. Bern picked up his camera from the front seat to take photos of the three cheetahs. He wished Bella was with him. He wanted to share all these incredible moments with her.

Bern's guests were so excited by the cheetahs.

'This is amazing. Who needs to see lions, when you can see these animals,' Pieter said.

The others all agreed. They stayed watching the cheetahs for over an hour. The mother led her cubs off the sandy tracks to shelter in the small shrubs growing at the edge of the road. A herd of springbok had caught her eye.

Brighton had most of the gear stowed in the trailer in readiness for the long drive to Maun. Bern helped him with loading the final pieces of equipment into the trailer, hitched it up, and they were ready to leave. The two couples climbed up into the vehicle, sharing their stories about the cheetah sighting.

The drive to Maun mirrored the tedium of the drive down,

and once Brighton and Bern finished talking about the botched poaching attempt, politics, family, and the price of petrol, a quietness settled over them. Bern's chaotic ramblings returned to Mason and Ly. *What the hell possessed them to do such a harebrained act*, he pondered. Even to their addled brains, they must have known they were never going to succeed. No way would Bern allow another lion to be slaughtered on his watch. He yearned for the trip to be over with; except he had guests to take care of.

CHAPTER 28

The day after Bern left for his safari to the Central Kalahari, Bella flew to Kasane, approximately 300 kilometres north-east of Maun. Karyn, a tall, willowy blonde wearing a smart crisp uniform met her at the airport. The bright unforgiving sunshine hung over Bella.

Karyn pushed her oversized sunglasses onto her head. 'It's nice to meet you.' She held out her hand in greeting. Her long champagne-coloured hair cascaded down her back in waves of gold, sparkling in the dazzling heat bouncing off the carpark. Her pale skin kissed by the sun glowed a light-bronze shade. It made her big green eyes glitter, and given they were fringed with the longest of lashes, they would make the most fastidious of giraffes envious.

Karyn chatted about the property as they made their way to her Nissan Pathfinder. She took Bella on a tour of Kasane, before showing her the property. The delightful town enchanted Bella from the moment she saw it, and she felt at home here, like she never did in Australia. Kasane appeared smaller than the sprawling streets Maun overflowed with, and Bella loved it. The town followed the flow of the Chobe River, with most of the lodges dipping their toes into the cooling waters. The street thronged with people in bright-coloured clothes going about their business, either shopping, out for lunch or merely catching up with friends.

With the tour of the town over, Karyn drove to the property. It settled in a lush plot of land to the west of the main town centre and also nudged the border of the Chobe National Park. A family of bushbuck wandered past, nibbling at the short, sweet grass. Bella loved the house the moment she set eyes on it. It looked perfect, perhaps a little large for one person, but she could always get help with the cleaning if it got too much for her.

'What do you think of it?' Karyn enquired.

They wandered out onto the verandah to admire the view.

'I love it! How do we make this happen?' Bella was too excited to wait any longer.

'Great, we'll drive to the Chobe Safari Lodge for lunch, and I'll run all the details by you.'

In a few minutes, they had arrived at the impressive entrance to the lodge. Chobe Safari Lodge perched high above the river with expansive views across to Namibia's Caprivi Strip. They found a table on the deck that overlooked the river. The serenity enfolded Bella, and the stress she kept holding onto could float away on the lazy currents of the river. Karyn ordered two glasses of chardonnay.

Karyn told Bella she was born in Dublin and met her husband Mike, a Londoner, while she worked as a waitress in a bar in Soho. Love blossomed at first sight for both of them, and they married within three months of first meeting each other.

Mike, a trainee pilot, moved to Maun to get his flying hours up, by ferrying guests to the remote lodges. He loved the lifestyle in Africa, and after he married Karyn, they both moved to Kasane to live. Mike, now a pilot for Air Botswana, loved his job. They had no intention of ever returning to chilly grey Europe.

Bella and Karyn sipped on their second chardonnay while waiting for their lunch.

'Tell me a bit about yourself, Bella?' Karyn enquired.

Bella started to wring her hands together. 'Not a happy story, I'm afraid. Married, divorced, husband is now living with my ex-best friend. After my brother and father died …' Bella reached for the napkin. 'My mother and sister disowned me. I guess they're happy now I'm no longer in their lives. I came to Africa because it's the one place in the world where I'm able to breathe. I'm trying to draw the frayed pieces of my life together. This house sounds perfect for me to start living again.' She wiped her mouth with the napkin.

'I'm certain of that. Sorry your past has put you through a rough patch of late. Always look forward, never back, is the motto I live by.'

They chatted about everything and nothing, an easy friendship flowing between them.

Karyn had to go to the office to do the paperwork for the sale. She said it could take a few hours to finalise. She would email Bella all the necessary paperwork to look at. If she felt certain about her decision to purchase the house, Bella could sign the weighty documents and direct debit a small chunk of the divorce money into the real estate's bank account.

Karyn drove Bella to the airport, hugged her then climbed into her vehicle to drive to her office.

Excitement bubbled inside Bella when the plane touched down in Maun. She phoned Seagal to tell him the news. He said he was about to drive to the Island Safari Lodge to meet the guests about the safari to Moremi tomorrow and didn't mind giving her a lift.

'It's good to see you looking so happy,' Seagal greeted Bella.

'Yes … for the first time in a long time, I am! So, if there's anything you want me to do to help you with the lion-poaching, please tell me.'

'Thank you. You're a lifesaver. I've already been in touch with Steven, and he's looking forward to meeting you. I can give you his mobile number.' By this stage, Seagal pulled into the carpark of the lodge.

'Thank you for the lift, Seagal, I'm happy to help you, but please don't mention to Bern about me moving. I don't want anything to do with him.'

'That's a shame, Bella. Bern is one of the good guys. But I respect your wishes, even though I think you're making a mistake where Bern is concerned.'

'Thank you.' Bella reached up to kiss him on the cheek before she went to the cabin to get her laptop.

Bella went to her favourite table by the river. There were no messages from Karyn, so she ordered a glass of wine and soon found herself lost in the tranquillity of the afternoon.

However, the sense of peace didn't last long. Fear gripped Bella; her breaths fluctuated wildly.

Lan stood over her with a scowl on her face. 'What the fuck are you doing. Coming onto my boyfriend?' she screeched. 'I swear I'll kill you if you don't leave him alone.'

How did one person get to be so angry, Bella questioned. Her heart clenched. She stared up at Lan. 'I'm not interested in your boyfriend. He's all yours.' Bella tried not to let the quiver in her voice take over. She shivered, but not from the coolness blowing off the river. The hurtful words Lan spat at Bella grated across her.

'Don't mess with me. You don't know who you're dealing with. You should be terrified. I've squashed bigger rats than you. And I'd do it again, with pleasure. Bern came home the other night reeking of your perfume. You were all over him. Don't lie to me,' she yelled, and her erratic behaviour soon drew a crowd.

Bella wanted to disappear to her cabin, to be as far away from Lan as possible. When she stood up to leave, Lan punched her in the face. Bella reeled backwards mostly from fright, but also because it bloody well hurt. She fell onto the table, sending the glass and laptop crashing to the ground. The fall took the wind out of her, and Bella already sensed the bruises had begun to creep across her back. She struggled up, wincing from the pain that stripped through her body. Unsure of what to do, Bella saw Seagal running towards them.

'Ag, for God's sake, Lan, leave her alone. Bella's done nothing to you.' His voice, calm and decisive, defused the situation. He gripped Lan in a vice-like grip, bringing a painful yelp from her.

'I never thought you'd stoop to such violence. What's wrong with you?' Seagal ushered Lan out of the lodge, his fingers gripping into her elbow.

The staff rushed over to offer any assistance or to enquire about phoning a doctor. Bella told them a doctor wouldn't be necessary. She thanked them for their kindness.

The bartender handed her another glass of wine. 'On the house, mma.'

'Thank you. If you don't mind, I might take it to my cabin to drink.'

'No problem at all, I can carry it to your cabin for you.'

The waiter tucked his hand under her arm, to help relieve some of the pain. Bella clutched her laptop to her chest. She limped; soreness was already searing her body. Now she was sorry for Bern, getting mixed up with that crazy, violent person. Bella tasted fear, and Lan's detachment swirled about her. Kasane sounded like the perfect answer to distance herself from Bern, so Lan had no excuse to get jealous and attack Bella again.

Once in the room, Bella sat on the bed, shaking uncontrollably. No one had ever assaulted her, and the ordeal was terrifying. Lan had a sinister side, and Bella feared that she would fight fiercer than a wildcat if someone came between her and Bern.

When her hands finally stopped shaking, having finished the 'on the house' wine, Bella made a strong cup of Rooibos. Her lip had swollen badly; the blood was already a sticky scab. She feared it might be difficult to drink tea or eat for a while. Bella suspected a bruise had already started to stain the side of her face, and her back now throbbed to the same tempo as her heartbeat. She stripped off her clothes, stumbling into the shower, letting the hot water steam over her, to alleviate the pain and blur Lan from her troubled thoughts.

'Lan, what were you thinking? Hitting Bella like a demented person, you could have hurt her. You're lucky she's only going to nurse a few bruises and a sore back for a while.' Seagal shoved Lan into her vehicle, slammed the door and told her never to go near Bella again.

'I'll fight for my man! Tell that slimy bitch to stay away from Bern,' she spat at him, putting her foot down hard on the accelerator. The tyres spun in the loose gravel in her attempt to hurry out of the carpark.

Lan bristled with annoyance at Bern, the bitch Bella, and her brothers. Her world was tumbling apart at the moment. Bern was way too obsessed with the slutty tart; she hadn't been able to reach her brothers for days; and Johan was annoyed with her for not getting any results.

God, now Lan had to grovel to Bern because she wanted him to take her to Kasane in a few days. She hoped Seagal didn't text Bern to tell him about how she warned off the bitch Bella. Those two were as thick as thieves. If Bern found out, the Chobe safari could be down the toilet. Lan fumed about her brothers' lack of conscience, so they better not stuff up another lead. She should have let them rot in a Vietnamese prison cell and not save their sorry arses by bringing them to Botswana with her. If she didn't hear from her brothers and things kept spiralling out of reach, she might have to kill a bloody lion herself. Lan chose not to trust anyone anymore and take care of herself for a change.

Bern had another two nights away. It gave her plenty of hours to stew about her sorry life. She tried to ring Thuan again, but it went to voice mail. 'Where the fuck are they?' She threw the phone across the bed. It ricocheted off, landing with a loud thud on the tiled floor. 'Shit,' she shouted. Her body splintered with pent-up rage. She stormed into the kitchen, to get a beer out of the fridge. She carried it out onto the deck.

While she sipped on the cooling amber liquid, she tried to calm down. Her mind raced like an out-of-control kaleidoscope. It was vital for Lan to get a grip before Bern came home. Johan was depending on her, and she wasn't going to let him down.

Lan still felt the froth of annoyance the next morning. She stormed into the kitchen to make a cup of coffee. While the water boiled, she stared out of the window. Even the air tasted heavy with trepidation. She poured the boiling water into her cup, stirring in three heaped teaspoons of Frisco Instant Coffee. She picked up the cup to carry it outside.

Loud banging on the front door alarmed her. The cup fell, shattering wisps of steam to curl close to the floor. 'Shit!' she yelped, feeling the sting of heat catch at her bare legs. Her mood mellowed when she opened the front door and saw Johan standing there. 'I am so happy you're here,' Lan said, stretching up to kiss him.

Johan pushed past her. 'Where the fuck are your bloody brothers?' He seemed to be barely able to control his fury.

'I haven't heard from them for days. I keep trying.' Lan began to whimper.

'If we don't locate them soon, you might have to kill a bloody lion yourself. I figure you know your way around a gun; therefore, killing a lion shouldn't be too difficult. You've already shot a man, for Christ's sake,' Johan hissed at her. 'We must make a kill in the next few days, sweetheart, or you might be swinging from an acacia tree. Now work your magic on the dim-witted Bern and get me some results from the fucking Chobe trip.' Johan clenched his fists.

Lan flinched in readiness for a punch, but Johan kept his fists at his sides. He glared at her with hatred, storming out of the house in a terrifying rage.

The door slammed shut.

Its finality brought a sense of loneliness to Lan. She understood that without her errant brothers, her job became a little bit harder.

Lan had scared off the ugly bitch Bella, and now, with her out of the way, she had to crawl into being Bern's centre of attention once more. Chobe was beginning to be a headache biting into Lan. They needed to find lions, or she might have to kill Johan or even Bern, if things unravelled. Killing again to save her own life brought a shudder of pleasure to twirl through her.

Lan made herself another cup of coffee and took this one out onto the deck. Staring into the emptiness of the azure sky, she evoked every second of how she sent the brothel owner to hell.

It was the day before Johan came to take them to Botswana.

Her boss had kept her a prisoner at the brothel. And so, she asked to see him. Sweat had beaded on his upper lip. He'd smiled; his little yellow teeth hanging like broken bits of china. He told her she would never get out. Lan almost gagged at those cruel words. Standing at the foot of the bed, his smirk reached down to her.

She had stretched; her arms behind her head, arching her body in a sexual pose. She undid her blouse, and loosened the bra strap, to expose her breasts towards him. All of her nerve-endings had buzzed with excitement. Lan reached between the pillows to touch the reassuring smoothness of her pistol. She wriggled her arse, letting her skirt sidle up. It revealed the fact she didn't wear any panties. Lan had begged him to do her. He'd licked his lips with his slippery tongue in anticipation of sticking it into Lan. She'd already saw a bulge had formed inside his trousers.

When Lan's fingers stroked the pistol, her body quivered, so she relaxed into her arousal. She ran her tongue over her lips, the gun aimed at his callous heart. The instant he figured out Lan's murderous intent, he begged for his miserable life. Lan had just smiled. She held the power, and at last, she knew how to use it. She clutched the pistol with a strong firm grip.

'Please don't shoot me.' He'd mewled louder than a kitten.

A wet stain had seeped down his trousers. It brought with it a strong smell of urine. Lan, too caught up in the pleasure of the moment, squeezed the trigger. She surrendered to the effects of her orgasm. A pool of blood from a gory hole in his chest started to drip onto the shabby carpet.

Standing on the deck with her cooling cup of coffee, Lan now smiled at the memories as heat saturated her body.

CHAPTER 29

Bella stayed in her room, fearful of venturing too far. Her lip and cheek were bruised and swollen from the whack Lan had given her. For someone so slight, Lan sure knew how to pack a punch. Bella's back coloured to a watery purple, the indent of the side of the table now etched into her skin. The staff at the lodge kept Bella supplied with food and alcohol and sat with her, chatting about their day after their shifts had ended. Karyn emailed the details of the contract. Bella grazed the surface of the lengthy document, before promptly signing it.

Unfortunately, the timeline for finalising the paperwork could take about four weeks. Karyn said that if Bella preferred, she could arrange for her to rent the house until she officially owned it. The arrangement sounded blissful to Bella. She would stay another two nights at the lodge, and with any luck, Dingo should be ready for the trip by then. Seagal told Bella he had warned Lan not to visit her again, and Bern, busy with his safaris, had in all likelihood forgotten she existed. Bella sent a text message to Seagal, telling him about her plans. He sent his reply at once. He had spoken to

Steven yesterday. Steven was keen to meet Bella after she settled into her new home.

Bern arrived at the Sedia Riverside Hotel in the early afternoon. He shouted lunch for his guests, to apologise for the unfortunate turn of events the day before when Mason and Ly attempted to slaughter a lion. He led them through the cool, molasses-infused reception, out onto the raised teak deck where an enormous jacaranda tree shaded the area. The two couples eased into the hypnotic rhythm of Africa. They soon forgot all about the attempted poaching and focused on the highlights of their trip. Bern wished both couples all the best and encouraged them to make a return visit to Botswana.

Bern had left his vehicle parked under a large jacaranda tree. Lilac flowers and tiny emerald leaves covered his vehicle in a splatter pattern. The floral blanket did little to reduce the baking-hot temperature inside the vehicle. Before he started the engine, Bern phoned his father. He always discussed difficulties with him. Arno had a logical mind, and this helped Bern to get things in perspective. He felt a lot better after the chat with his father.

He drove to his home at a steady pace, dreading the fact Lan occupied every space between its walls. Her staccato voice, and her erratic temper jarred across his mind.

He had a mountain of work to do before the flight tomorrow. Bern liked more of a gap between safaris, but this time it couldn't be helped. All the guides worked well with one another, and Bern knew he too might have a favour to ask of them one day.

He pulled into the drive, noticing all the windows opened to the breeze. He let out an indignant sigh, slamming the car door.

Lan's sandals were loud on the timber floor in the kitchen, so he made his way upstairs to the kitchen.

She sashayed from the bench to the fridge, busy tossing ingredients into bowls or saucepans.

'Hallo, Lan, I'm home from the Kalahari.'

'Oh, lover, I'm happy you're home. Did you have a good trip? I've prepared your favourite meal tonight. Can I get you a beer?' Lan seemed to stumble over the words; her voice sounded shaky with guilt. She reached up to kiss him.

God, what could be wrong now, Bern feared. He couldn't shake a twist of dread that knotted across his shoulders, and he wondered at the cause. 'I'm having a shower first before I drink my beer on the deck.' He turned away from her to go downstairs to the bedroom.

He then tossed his clothes on the unmade bed and went into the bathroom. He let the hot water stream over his head and down his tired body, in an attempt to alleviate his troubled mind.

Several minutes later, Lan had discarded her clothes on the bathroom floor and entered the shower. Her fingers traced down his spine.

Bern froze at her touch. 'Not now, Lan, there's too much on my mind at the moment … with getting ready for the trip tomorrow.' He cringed at the notion of having sex with Lan. He longed for the serenity he used to find in his house.

Lan stormed out of the shower, dried herself and dressed quickly, then headed upstairs.

Bern heard her clanging dishes in the kitchen. He reached for a towel and wrapped it around his waist. His phone rang. 'Ag, Seagal, howzit man?' he said.

'Good. I'm proud of the way you handled yourself down in the

Kalahari. A bullet between the eyes is too good for those idiots.'

'Ja, that's one trip I don't want to repeat. I'm glad to be home. After I pile my clothes into the washing machine, I'm going to visit Bella.'

'Not a good idea,' Seagal said. A touch of anxiety edged his voice.

'Why ever not, I won't mention it to Lan. I'll spin her a story and tell her I'm catching up with you.'

'Leave Bella be. Visit her after you return from Chobe.'

'You're starting to worry me, man. I'll do what I bloody well, please. Bella's the only one to chase the irritation coursing through me at the moment. Talk to you later.'

Bern finished dressing and called out to Lan on his way to the front door, 'I'm off to see Seagal about Chobe.' The lie came easily to his lips.

'Okay, lover, try not to be late; I prepared a big night for us.'

'Lekker, see you later.'

Bern pulled into the carpark of the lodge. He was surprised to see Seagal's Landcruiser there. They hadn't actually arranged to meet; so what the heck was he doing here?

Seagal was in the bar. He looked worried. 'Before you go, I want to tell you something, and flying into a rage won't help the situation and might upset Bella.'

'Ag man, you're scaring me. Has something happened to Bella?' Bern squeezed his hands into tight balls.

'Lan visited her, and in typical Lan fashion, she vented her fury. She hit Bella hard, making her fall against the table. No bones are broken, although she's nursing a few bruises and her lip is swollen.'

Bern started to go to Bella's cabin until Seagal touched his arm. 'For Christ's sake man, calm down, eh? Don't go to her with this anger bubbling inside you. Bella's all right, the staff here are taking good care of her. You may make it worse if you go to her in a temper.'

'Sorry, my broer, I'm going to check for myself if she's okay.'

'Well, I'm coming with you.'

Both men strode across the terrace towards Bella's cabin.

Seagal knocked on the door. 'Hey, Bella, can I come in? Are you all right?'

Bella opened the door, but when her eyes met Bern's, she tried to close it again. 'Shit, Seagal, why did you tell him?'

Bern jammed his foot in the door. 'It's not Seagal's fault. I want to see for myself how you are. I'm not here to pressure you … please, Bella.'

She opened the door to let both men in.

Bern went to embrace her, and she flinched at his touch. He loosened his grip but persisted in keeping his fingers massaging her waist. 'Liefie, let me look at your face?'

Bella recoiled; he could see the fear in her eyes.

He gasped, taking a step away to stare at her bruised swollen lip.

Bella almost stumbled when he took his arm from her waist. With an intimate touch, he lifted her shirt. The light from the bathroom seeped into the murky interior of the room. It showed the bruises across Bella's back. She pulled her shirt down, covering the bruises.

'Ag, if I knew how to take away the pain Lan caused you, I would do it in a heartbeat. It'll be impossible to control my temper with her.'

'Don't be annoyed with Lan. I'd be upset also if my boyfriend kissed other women. Please, Bern, don't make a big deal out of this. Lan has a dangerous, cold nature, I don't want to give her any reason to get jealous again.' Bella's voice shook.

'It hurts me that you're in this state. I'm cancelling my trip.'

'I don't imagine that's going to wash with Lan. I'm happy here at the lodge, and you're taking Lan to Chobe tomorrow.'

'We better leave now to let Bella rest,' Seagal said, trying to usher Bern from the room. 'Lan may get suspicious if you're away too long, and now you know what she's capable of, don't upset her any further.'

'Seagal's right, please go,' Bella pleaded.

As much as Bern didn't want to leave her, he knew it was the right thing to do in that moment, so he dragged himself away.

'This is all my fault. Lan is becoming unpredictable,' Bern said as he leant against his vehicle.

'I'm more certain of Lan's involvement in the poaching. The way she reacted to the situation with Bella unsettled me. There's something unstable about her. Something cruel,' Seagal admitted.

'I think that's an understatement. It's imperative we figure out who she's working for. I better get home. Lan mustn't know I came here.'

CHAPTER 30

Bern tried to rein in his temper on the drive home, his fingers aching from gripping the steering wheel so tight. He wound the window down to breathe in the spiciness of evening. Even Steven seemed optimistic they were getting closer to finding out who was involved in the poaching racket.

Bern drove up to his house, parking his Landcruiser in the driveway. He threw his keys on the table, by the front door, before continuing into the kitchen. Lan had her back to him while she cut up salad ingredients on the bench. The window where she stood overlooked the garden towards the river beyond. He sighed deeply, trying to quell his muddled emotions. He touched his fingertips on her slim waist before kissing her on the top of her head.

She swung around, her lips hard against his. 'So, you missed me, lover?' Her voice shredded the evening sky.

'Ja, but now I'll check on my washing. You return to cooking the special meal you promised. I'm getting a beer and will be in my usual spot.'

'Dinner is almost done; I'll serve it on the deck. We can gaze at the stars.'

'Ja, sounds great.' Bern took his beer from the fridge and padded to the laundry to remove his clothes from the washer. He piled them into the dryer, slamming the door and setting the timer for one hour. A mountain of paperwork waited for him to do in preparation for tomorrow, and he longed for a dreamless sleep to forget all about Lan and the poaching.

Lan had set the table with a crisp tablecloth depicting African animals, and Bern's best dinner set. She'd positioned candles along the centre of the table and on the handrails.

He wasn't in the mood for romance either, not with Lan anyway. He tried to steer the conversation away from personal matters to their trip tomorrow. 'Have you finished packing?' he asked when Lan set a bowl of bobotie in front of him, along with a bowl of crisp green salad.

'Of course; I'm ready. It's been ages since we went on safari together. I want to spot the lions you always talk about.' Lan settled herself in the chair opposite him. The candlelight threw an unfavourable shadow across her face. It gave her a sinister appearance.

'I'm confident of being able to locate the lions. I spoke to Steven, and he mentioned some of the guides said they were in the area, and if they are, I'll find them. I didn't think you liked me talking about lions all the time, though. You yawn with boredom every time I mention them.'

'Course not, sweetie. I love seeing them sleeping, like they're already in heaven.'

'Where did that bit of poetic speech come from?'

'I guess I missed you. It makes me sentimental. I'd hate it if you weren't here.'

'Now you're making me choke on my food … enough talking and more eating.' He scraped the last of the bobotie into his mouth. 'Can you get me another beer, if you're going into the kitchen, please?' Bern moved away from the table.

'Sure, lover.' Lan picked up the dirty dishes to carry them into the kitchen. She returned with his beer and one for herself. She sat on his lap and kissed him before taking a mouthful of the beer. Lan's hand moved over Bern's groin. 'We go to bedroom?'

'In a bit, Lan. I need to finish packing, call Brighton to make sure he's ready for the trip tomorrow, and do a quick run-through of my clients. I have to make a start preparing some sort of itinerary for the next few days in Chobe.' Bern tried to keep the fury from fogging his voice.

'Sounds like you'll be busy till midnight. Please wake me if I'm asleep. I'm always hot and ready for you, lover. I'll finish my beer in kitchen while I wash the dishes.'

He didn't bother to answer her as he picked up his beer.

In the serenity of his office, he breathed in the spiciness of the sage growing in the garden.

Over dinner, Bern had told Lan about the attempted poaching in the Kalahari. He wanted to gauge her reaction. Lan had looked sufficiently shocked. She didn't 'seem' to know anything about it, but he still wasn't sure. Maybe there were two groups of poachers working in Botswana. It was a puzzle, but he was too tired to deal with it now. He would speak to Seagal when he got back from Chobe.

Bern then busied himself with phoning Brighton and catching

up on paperwork. He kept an ear out for signs Lan had gone down to the bedroom. Although Bern's body ached with tiredness, he refused to go to bed until he knew Lan was asleep.

He faced another sleepless night. Bella's beauty suffused his body. He took full responsibility for Lan's actions, and it pierced deep into his heart that he was to blame for what she had done to Bella. With Lan fading out of the picture, he made a promise to himself, to spend the rest of his life ensuring Bella stayed safe and happy.

He finally pushed himself up from his desk at two, knowing full well his alarm would shrill at five.

He fell into bed alongside a sleeping Lan, except slumber didn't find him. His mind was filled with images of Bella's injuries. The alarm shredded the pre-dawn sky. Bern groggily leant over to turn it off. He thought for a moment the scent of the Kalahari filled the space until Lan reached over to kiss him. He groaned, turning away from her.

'Ooh, you look good enough to eat, lover, all tousled from sleep.' Lan's voice scraped off the walls. She reached out to Bern, her hands touching his groin. 'We have time for a quickie?'

'No, Lan, we have a flight to catch. I'm meeting my clients the minute we land. Now, get out of bed and into the shower. I hardly slept last night. And today is going to be an extra-long one.'

Lan fiddled in the bathroom, having a shower and putting on her make-up. Her mind pinged in erratic circles since Johan's visit the other day. Last night, Bern had told her about the trouble with those Americans in the Kalahari. She knew nothing about it. She had phoned Johan to see what was going on, but he sidestepped her questions. Her brothers still hadn't returned any of the myriad of calls she had sent them, and her life was spinning out of control. Lan needed to relieve some pent-up sexual tension. She left her clothes in the bathroom.

Bern had his back to her.

'Come, lover, please. Leave the packing for a bit.' Her hands roaming all over his body.

'I already told you, I'm not in the mood, now get dressed,' Bern said sternly.

Lan screamed silently at Bern, Johan, her brothers and the whole of fucking Botswana. She started putting on her safari clothes, thinking how Bern was always the same before every safari. She fumbled with her shirt. 'Shit.' One of the buttons flew off to land beside Bern's feet. She bent to pick it up. 'I know you're anxious about the safari going well. I promise to be good.' Lan needed to calm down. They had to find lions on this bloody safari. Johan was counting on her.

Lan finished dressing and brushed out her hair, tying it in a ponytail. She left Bern to have his shower in peace. She picked up her bag and dumped it by the front door before going into the kitchen to make herself a cup of green tea to settle her nerves.

Bern changed into his safari clothes. He carried his bag to the front door, placing it next to Lan's bag. 'I'll finish drinking this, then we have to leave,' Bern said, stirring his coffee.

'Ooh, lover, you're the sexiest man in all Botswana in safari uniform. There better be no single females on trip. I'll fight them off you,' Lan quipped.

'You'll do no such thing. I've already told you a hundred times, that if you're on a safari with me, we are professional. Our private life is to remain separate. Do I make myself clear?'

'Yes, boss,' a sassy Lan replied. She had no intention of letting him get close to any other female, no matter what threats Bern yelled at her. She needed Bern's whole attention on her and finding lions.

Bern left his vehicle with a friend; he didn't trust the security at the airport. He took the luggage out of the vehicle and spoke to his mate before giving him the car keys. The airport terminal was clogged with people at such an early hour. Bern and Lan joined a long queue of travellers waiting for their turn at the counter. Brighton waved a greeting to them. He stood several people closer to the counter talking with another guide.

Once they received their boarding passes, Bern went down the road to the Dusty Donkey Café to order three takeaway coffees.

'Anything else I can help you with.' The waitress smiled.

'No, thanks.' Bern's mind was already on the safari.

Carrying the hot coffees, Bern strolled into the busy terminal, dodging people and luggage. Lan and Brighton were already sitting in the crowded departure lounge, so he joined them there. He handed out two of the coffees as he sat down in the vacant chair next to Brighton.

'Hey, thanks, man,' Brighton said, taking the coffee.

'Ja, I needed something to keep me awake,' Bern admitted.

They finished their coffees moments before the intercom announced their flight.

Bern, Brighton and Lan threw their empty cups into the bin, then went out into the hot morning sunshine frizzing off the ground. They joined the line of fellow passengers snaking across the tarmac to the waiting Air Botswana aeroplane.

CHAPTER 31

The sun streamed in through the opened curtains on Bella's last full day of living at the Island Safari Lodge. She found it hard to believe how her life had changed in such a short time. She now had a purpose to her life. Since being here, she had started making her own choices. A couple of them may have bordered on an irrational need to touch another person. That was why she naively slept with the way-too attractive Bern. She didn't blame anyone apart from herself for that moment of weakness.

Anxiety persisted to knot in her stomach about the trip to Kasane tomorrow. She had a slight twinge of unease about how Dingo would manage with the trip, and the upheaval of having his life turned upside down. Bella had asked Seagal to get Steven to organise a group of men to construct a huge enclosed area towards the side of her house. The perfect haven for the cat to familiarise himself with his new surroundings. Once Bella felt sure he was confident in his enclosure, she aimed to reintroduce him into the wild. Dingo should never become a house-bound cat, he was born wild and deserved to live with the wind combing off his fur and in harmony with his world. The vet had given Bella tablets to give to Dingo before the flight the next day. They were to keep him calm, and with a lot of luck, he should sleep for the duration of the trip.

She went along the now familiar path to the dining room for breakfast. Her bruises were a bluish-purple shade, and her back was tender to the touch, but she needed to feel the sun on her. Too bad if the other guests stared, speculating about how she acquired the swollen lip and bruises.

Bella's heart skipped a beat when she sat down at her usual table. Her breath tightened in her chest as though someone she loved had left her. A shadow passed in front of the sun, although there were no clouds in a sky the colour of blue ice. Bella wondered why these sensations floated through her. She sat gazing across the river to the horizon, noticing a plane arc before it turned in a north-easterly direction on its way to Kasane. Bella experienced the loss of something deep in her heart as she watched the plane disappear into the haze.

Her gaze floated across the river. Daydreams about life in Kasane shifted through her. Bella saw Lan's tormented spirit wrinkling inside her. Her whole body coiled tighter than a martial eagle waiting to swoop on its prey, and Bella suspected she never relaxed. Bella still felt fragile from her husband's dalliances and the harshness with which he dumped her. She foolishly imagined his love would last a lifetime, and his rejection left her broken and alone. Bella had to forget the sensations of belonging whenever she looked at Bern.

Bella arrived back at her cabin to finish packing, her heart feeling heavy, and apprehension coiling after her. She arrived in Botswana such a short time ago and already sensed the start of something magical. Bella didn't recognise the person she was now to the haunted one who bumped around life in Australia.

Before Bella went inside, she knelt to check on Dingo. 'Tomorrow is going to be a long difficult day, little one,' she warned him.

His little body twitched in a deep sleep, so she left him to his dreams. Her unease about him coping with the turmoil tomorrow still bothered her. When she touched Dingo, Bella felt Dorset's purrs rumble through her. She knew Dingo's wild spirit and Dorset's gentle nature were protecting her. Her life was now entwined through Dingo.

CHAPTER 32

The flight from Maun droned through clear blue skies. It touched down with a light thud on the tarmac at Kasane International Airport. Bern, engrossed with his daydreams about Bella for most of the trip, refused another cup of coffee from the gorgeous flight attendant who kept trying to catch his eye. For once, Lan kept her distance. She preferred to stare out of the window for the whole flight.

Once inside the airport, they waited with the other passengers to retrieve their luggage.

Bern, Lan and Brighton then strode out into the bright glare of the morning sunshine.

Steven was slouched against the door of the safari vehicle smoking a cigarette. His bright Hawaiian shirt seemed an odd choice for an African sojourn. He stretched his arms high in the air, exposing his fat stomach, before ambling over to meet them, smiling broadly. He picked up Lan's bag and tossed it into the vehicle along with Bern's and Brighton's.

'Dumela, Bern, Brighton, Lan, looking forward to the safari, eh?' Steven greeted the three of them.

'Ja, thanks, Steven, I'm a bit tired from the trip in the Central Kalahari, and the dramas with the poachers.'

'Nasty business, eh? You handled the situation like a pro. Did they give you any indication about who they were working for?'

'No. I want the buggers to rot in jail. That trip is best forgotten; let me concentrate on this one. Don't worry, I'll be good to go, once I meet the next lot of clients.'

'They're ready and waiting at the Chobe Safari Lodge, sipping gin and tonics, I suspect. There are five of them, and they're all from London. It's their first trip to Africa, so I guess all you need to do is show them a dung beetle, and they'll be impressed.'

'Ja, if only that was the case. First-timers to Africa are the most demanding on safari, but I always try my best.'

'That's the mettle, Bern,' Steven said as he manoeuvred into the traffic heading towards the town centre. He parked in the carpark of the lodge, and the four of them entered the cavernous interior. Their fully laden safari vehicle and trailer was already parked outside the imposing front doors.

Bern loved the décor and coolness of the Chobe Safari Lodge. It sat in a prime position on the banks of the Chobe River. He had yet to stay there, preferring the cosiness of the Old House if he stayed overnight. Lan kept pestering him about how she fancied booking in at the lodge, but Bern continued pretending he didn't hear her. They ambled past the reception desk and curio shop and out onto the timber deck and bar area. Bern was in a hurry to meet up with the guests he was about to be sharing his life with for the next four nights.

As Steven predicted, they were all propped up at the bar

sipping their gin and tonics. The two couples appeared to be in their mid-fifties, and a single lady about Bern's age sat with them.

Lan went to stand beside Bern, her arms circling his waist. He disentangled himself, scowled at her and then introduced himself to his guests. 'Hallo, my name is Bern de Villiers, and I'll be your guide for the next few days. This is Brighton and Lan. Brighton is in charge of setting up the camp and cooking your meals et cetera. Please don't hesitate to ask Lan for assistance with more personal matters regarding camp life. So, if there are any questions about the camp set-up or the food, Brighton or Lan are the people to speak to. If there are any other questions, please don't hesitate to talk to me.'

With the pleasantries of introductions over, and once everyone finished their drinks, Bern ushered them to the vehicle. It was nearing eleven o'clock and he aimed for their camp to be set up well before lunch, allowing Brighton enough time to prepare the meal. Bern planned to give his guests the space to relax and familiarise themselves with the novelty of camp life before they ventured out on their afternoon game drive.

'Fuck, Lan, do you mind keeping it professional while we're on safari? No coming up to me and acting all jealous every time I talk to the guests,' Bern hissed in Lan's ear once the others had wandered out to the vehicle.

'Okay, lover. The white bitch better not get close. You know how jealous I get.'

'Give it a rest, Lan, be grateful you're here. One more false move, and I'm putting you on the first flight back to Maun.'

'Sorry. I'm a bit stressed at the moment. I don't like being out in the bush. And I saw the way that woman looked at you. You're my boyfriend.'

'Drop this ridiculous act, Lan,' Bern warned before storming away; he could hear Lan's boots echoing behind him.

'Well, if we are all ready, let's go. It's about five kilometres to the Chobe National Park, and we can do a slow game drive on the way to our campsite. With a bit of luck, lions may be sleeping under a tree somewhere.'

Once they turned off the tar road onto the familiar sandy tracks, Bern breathed a sigh of relief. He was where he longed to be, surrounded by the bush and wildlife. They lurched over the uneven tracks, threading their way through the thick undergrowth.

Bern soon spotted an old male giraffe, his gangly legs almost graceful as he paused in front of the vehicle. Bern stopped and turned off the engine.

A quietness settled over them all.

Everyone delved into their belongings for their camera or phone to capture the moment.

Bern explained that the male giraffe could grow to a height of six metres, and their blue tongues were almost fifty centimetres long.

The giraffe reached up to remove the pods from a camelthorn tree, twining his tongue around the pods.

'If you're finished taking photos, we'll continue.'

Bern drove down a slight bank towards the Chobe River. The river stretched in both directions, flat and wide. A smattering of game tiptoed near the river at such a late hour of the morning. Most of the animals seek a reprieve from the heat of the day. A few hippos lay close to the bank, ignoring the crackle of the sun.

Bern followed the flow of the river. He stopped next to two crocodiles sunning themselves on the bank. Once the click of the cameras died down, he continued driving close to the river for several kilometres. He turned away from the water to climb up the steep bank into the forest before heading to their designated campsite.

The campsite was nestled in a grove of trees with the nearest neighbours about 500 metres away. The small group climbed out of the vehicle. They stretched; nerves all clearly caught in their throats. They glanced at their surroundings, seemingly not quite believing how remote the area looked.

There weren't the usual signs that designated a camping site, and the isolated patch of ground they stood on was to be their home for the next few nights. A herd of impala wandered close to them; their black eyes stared at the humans. There were murmurs of concern from the guests. It always shocked first timers visiting Africa to understand that campsites usually were hidden under a tin sign nailed to a tree. There were no fences, and wild animals often shifted through camp in the dead of night. Bern's words about never leaving their tents during the night-time hours always appeared to bring more apprehension to the guests' frazzled nerves.

Each tent came with its own en-suite attached to the rear, complete with a flushing toilet. Brighton began unpacking the trailer. The tables and chairs were the first items to come out. Brighton set them up under a tree before taking wood out of the trailer to start a fire. He then placed the kettle over the grate. Minutes later, the water started to boil. Soon, the small group stood in the shade of the sausage tree, sipping their coffees and munching on Brighton's homemade biscuits.

Lan stood to one side watching Bern and Brighton set up the campsite, a scowl on her face. *Why the hell is Bern sharing a tent with that idiot Brighton, so far away on the other side of the camping ground.* Lan could hear the rest of the group chatting and laughing together. She wanted to scream the leaves off the trees.

She fumed, realising she and Nancy (the single lady) were meant to share a tent. God, now, Nancy's prattle about the wonders of Africa were about to bore her into a raging fit. *Damn you, Bern,* Lan scolded. She wondered why he was always so annoying on the safaris they did together.

She then consoled herself that if they spotted lions, all the suffering of being in the wilderness away from her creature comforts could be worth the itchiness and heat she had to endure. Lan hated being out in the bush. She shivered with disgust at the strangeness of Botswana. She yearned for the concrete jungle of the larger cities. Lan revolved in a world surrounded by a life that teemed with people, not sky and empty voids.

Lan and Nancy were sitting on their bunk beds in their tent.

'I guess you're used to being in the wilderness. I'm afraid I'm a bit nervous,' Nancy admitted.

'Whatever. Please, be quiet,' Lan beseeched her.

'Lunch is ready,' Brighton's voice cut into the tension in Lan and Nancy's tent.

They went to head to where he had set up the dining table under the spreading jackalberry tree.

The table groaned under the weight of all the food, wine and beer bottles. It looked delicious, and Lan's mouth watered. She had skipped breakfast.

After lunch, Brighton cleared away the plates and glasses, carrying them to the trailer to wash.

'It might be a good idea to rest for a couple of hours, before our afternoon game drive,' Bern suggested as he carried the leftover salads to the trailer.

Lan tried to corner Bern until he threw her a tea towel. 'Please go and help Brighton with the dishes.' He turned away to help Nancy fix a problem with her camera.

Lan's sullen mood bubbled over, and she wanted to shout obscenities at everybody. *The bitch better not get too close.* Her temper was at boiling point. She slammed the dishes onto the table, breaking a cup. 'Shit,' she muttered as she stormed into her tent.

At three-thirty, Brighton roused everyone out for coffee and cake. Once they finished their drinks, he urged them into the vehicle for their afternoon game drive.

Bern drove towards the river while twilight began to coat the brilliant blue sky with whiskers of grey. Nowhere else in the world compared to sitting next to the Chobe River, watching the blood-red ball of the sun float towards the horizon, he thought. Sometimes hundreds of elephants left the forest to drink and swim in the cooling waters of the river.

The elephants, thankfully, didn't let him down on their game drive.

The guests watched on as the tiny calves trot into the river with no fear at all about the depth of the water. A few were swallowed up by the strong currents until their mothers swam beside them. Soon, little trunks twisted out of the depths to curl on their mother's stomachs.

Bern parked the vehicle a safe distance away from the elephants and let the scene speak for itself. There were no words to describe the incredible sight anyway. He let the view fold over his guests, without him talking all the time.

When night fell, Bern started the engine to head to camp.

Everyone thanked him for the amazing first day of their safari.

Everyone, except Lan. 'Can we go back now, I have to pee,' was all she could muster.

With his guests safely at camp, Brighton donned on his bartender cap. He poured out drinks, ushering them to the fire where the chairs he set up circled close to the flames. He left them to finish preparing their dinner.

Bern sat with them, trying to get them to talk about their reasons for coming to Africa. He was attempting to gauge what they preferred to see and what experiences they expected from their first visit to Africa. He sipped on his coffee, chatting to them while he waited for Brighton to serve dinner.

He made his way to the head of the table, and Nancy sat down next to him on his left. This meant a clearly cranky Lan flounced to a seat at the far end of the table after the husband of one of the couples sat down on the other side of Bern. Happy with the seating arrangements, Bern commenced a conversation with Nancy. Lan glared sparks of fire at both of them.

After an hour or so, the long day and tension of Lan's presence caught up with Bern. He tried to stifle his yawns; tiredness dug into him. He sighed with relief when his guests didn't want to stay up late to chat around the fire. The sound of hyenas close by was enough reason to scatter everyone back to their tents.

Bern and Brighton did the washing up, securing the rubbish in the trailer before retiring to their tent for the night. The hyenas were soon joined by the roar of lions, but their calls teased over the ground no louder than the wind sifting in the trees. Bern listened to the sounds of the night, lulling him into a deep dreamless sleep.

CHAPTER 33

The morning of her departure from Maun crystallised into a perfect day. Bella didn't get much sleep because an uninvited twinge of regret bubbled away in her, at the idea of never seeing Bern again. However, she told herself that she had to respect his relationship with Lan, even though he said Lan meant nothing to him. She had started an exciting but scary chapter in her life and happiness melted through her.

Bella sensed a tug in her heart at leaving the lodge. All of the staff treated her like she was part of their family; however, she never intended to stay there for the rest of her life.

Bella ground up the prescribed dose of tablets for Dingo, disguising it in a piece of fish. She went outside, praying Dingo returned from his night-time hunt.

He sat under the bush with a perplexed look on his small face. Bella gave him his breakfast. He sniffed at it; his nose wrinkled. *It must be the metallic tang of the tablet*, she thought, holding her breath. He glanced up at her before he wolfed down the meal. The vet had told her what adverse signs to be aware of, so she sat on the ground to monitor his progress. He licked his paw to clean his face.

A few minutes later, his little paw fell to the ground, refusing to obey orders. Dingo gave Bella a worried look before his eyes fluttered closed. He toppled over onto the grass, and she saw that his little chest swayed with breath. Bella picked him up and settled him in his carry bag.

She then picked up her bag and Dingo's carry case, to make one final trip to the main lodge. All the staff came out to bid her well. She hugged each of them, thanking them for their kindness and the friendship they showered over her. She promised to return to visit with them whenever she could.

Seagal had offered to drive Bella to the airport, and she saw him waiting in the carpark.

'They gave you a heartfelt farewell, eh? These folk care about you, Bella, which should tell you something. I've never seen them go to so much trouble for anyone.' He stowed her suitcase in the boot and the cat's carry case on the rear seat before both he and Bella settled into the car, and off Seagal drove.

The airport terminal hummed with chaos. Seagal was wonderful helping Bella with the cat and her luggage. The flight attendant soon came to stow Dingo. Mike, Karyn's husband, happened to be the pilot on this trip, and he said the cat would be welcome to sit in the cockpit with him. Bella found her allotted seat and collapsed into it.

The flight touched down on a cushion of air. Bella retrieved her luggage and Dingo from a smiling Mike. She thanked him for his kindness, promising to buy him a beer. Bella squinted when the brightness of the sun nibbled at her eyes.

Karyn stepped out of her vehicle, looking gorgeous and smiling, her teeth brilliant-white against the red of her lipstick. The sunshine bounced off her golden hair. They hugged before going to her vehicle, tucked in beside an open safari truck.

Once they were settled, Karyn's curiosity got the better of her. 'What happened to you? That looks to be the remains of a nasty bruise on your face?'

'Wait till you see my opponent, although I'll leave my sorry story for another day.' Bella was too excited about being here to worry about Lan.

It didn't take them long to drive to her house by the river.

'I'm so excited you're here at last. I think we're going to have a lot of fun together. Mike suggested we invite you around for dinner tonight, but I assumed you might prefer to stay with your little mate to make sure he's all right. I left a lentil stew for you in the fridge, along with a good bottle of chardonnay. Here's some chicken for Dingo's lunch. We can always catch up once you are settled in.'

'Thank you for arranging everything for me, Karyn, I owe you one. And as soon as I'm confident Dingo is okay, I promise to buy both you and Mike dinner. I want to thank him for taking care of my little friend on the flight up.'

'It was his pleasure. He's the nicest guy I know; I'm lucky he's mine, and now I'm making it my mission to find a friend for you.'

Bella shook her head. 'No way, I hold such a bad track record where men are concerned, I'm going to stay single ... at least until the ink dries on my divorce papers. I already made a fool of myself with a guy, after being in Botswana for less than one day.'

'Ooh, now that's a story we'll save for another time, intriguing though it sounds,' she said as she pulled into the driveway.

When Karyn turned the engine off, Bella jumped out of the vehicle, anxious to settle the cat into his new home. The enclosure Steven's mates constructed took over a huge chunk of land to the side of the house. It looked to be the perfect spot for Dingo to start living the life he deserved. Bella was convinced Dingo would love it here and forgive her, once he got over the initial shock of being uprooted from his previous home.

Karyn handed over the keys, hugged Bella, and with a promise to catch up soon, she disappeared down the driveway.

Bella carried the cat basket over to a sturdy gate with a set of keys dangling from a padlock. Bella placed the cat basket on the ground inside the enclosure. She closed the gate behind her.

Once inside, Bella tipped the chicken into Dingo's bowl.

He began to stir, raising his head and blinking a few times up at her. He clearly found the effort too much, so he plopped down onto his pillow. His legs then shook, and his paws tried to catch the air.

Bella patted him to reassure him that if he trusted her, everything was going to be all right.

Ten minutes later, an almost fully alert Dingo peered at his strange new world before jumping a little shakily from his cage and wobbling over to the food. He sniffed it, turning away from the bowl, to return to Bella, who sat cross-legged on the ground. When he sat on her lap and started to purr, she had a tear in her eye. She knew instinctively that Dingo had forgiven her.

Dingo

I could sense a tightness brewing in her. Her fingers stroked my head. I hissed, not because I wanted to be without her, but because a few dragonflies had settled in my stomach. Once I saw the worried look on her face, my gentler spirit – Dorset – took over. I began purring in an attempt to allay her fears. I stayed close to her.

We watched the sun chase shadows on the ground, lengthening grey fingers coiled low and long. I suffered no adverse reactions to the dreamless slumber and the shift to this alien ground. I prowled with confidence, sniffing and marking out my territory. Satisfied with exploring, I returned to the bowl where the smell of chicken caused my stomach to grumble.

CHAPTER 34

Dingo's eyes pierced into Bella after he finished his meal. Satisfied he would never leave her; Bella went to explore her new home. She wandered through the rooms, her boots echoing on the polished concrete floors. Stained timber rafters held the thatch in the high-pitched ceiling. Thankfully, the house came with furniture, which reminded Bella of an African resort.

She strolled out onto the verandah. The sweet fragrant scent of gardenias permeated the air. Their ramshackle branches arced towards the ground, heavy with blooms. The sturdy cane outdoor furniture looked luxurious, and the sparkling swimming pool glistened gold in the failing light of sunset. The railing at the edge of the verandah was a jumble of twigs that twined together in a messy hug. Bella leant against it, letting her gaze stretch across the currents of the Chobe River. She sighed, relishing the fact that at last, she was home.

Bella retraced her steps into the kitchen. Karyn had arranged everything, down to stocking the refrigerator with food and alcohol. She reheated Karyn's homemade stew, poured a glass of wine, and carried it out onto the verandah.

Bella stayed outside until mist laced off the water to send a shiver to her bare arms. Carrying her luggage into the main bedroom, she unpacked a few toiletries. Bella then let the fog of steam in the shower cleanse away painful memories. She pulled on boxer shorts and a T-shirt, crawling under the crisp white sheets.

At some stage, she had to purchase a vehicle, although that could wait for a few days. Choppies Supermarket was a short distance away, if she required anything. Her mind buzzed with things she ought to be doing, but for now, Bella luxuriated in the fact that she belonged here.

CHAPTER 35

Bern relaxed into the gentle rhythm of Chobe; all his guests seemed to be getting on except for Lan, and he overlooked her irritating behaviour. On their first full day of game-driving, Bern spotted a leopard deep in the shade of a woolly caper bush. A perfect camouflage for his dappled coat. Bern stopped the vehicle, pointing his guests in the right direction. Most of the time, leopards were a bit shy if a vehicle approached; but this fellow seemed quite content to have his photo taken.

Lions had been vocal deep into the first night of their trip. The sounds resonated further south in the park where there were no tracks. As Bern drove to camp late on the second night, a herd of well over 1000 buffalos silhouetted against the backdrop of the setting sun. They were making their way across the water to the islands that held fast in the river. Cape buffalo were a dangerous and unpredictable animal, so Bern manoeuvred through them with care. It was a spectacular sight that seeped into his guests to remain with them forever.

Once they returned to the campsite, Brighton served drinks. They took them over to the chairs he set up by the fire. Bern made himself a strong cup of coffee and sat with them, explaining the behaviour of buffalos and why they were so dangerous to humans.

His phone beeped, splitting the air, so he excused himself to take a call from Steven.

Steven explained to him that a couple of Vietnamese tourists straggled into his office. They were staying in Botswana for a couple of nights, and from the brochures they waved at him, he guessed they fancied a visit to Chobe.

'I'm having a hell of a time trying to figure out what they want to do. Their bloody grasp of the English language is non-existent. I wonder if you might spare Lan. I want to use her as an interpreter. Andy has already agreed to take them out. He offered to drive into the park to collect her at first light in the morning.'

Bern let out a sigh of relief at such welcome information.

'Thought you'd be glad to get rid of Lan for a while, eh.'

'Ja. Sure, mate, Lan will be happy to oblige. I can drive halfway out of the park during our morning game drive to meet up with Andy.'

'Thanks, Bern, I owe you a beer.' Steven ended the call.

Bern smiled at Nancy when he passed her on his way to talk to Lan. A blush stained Nancy's cheeks as she stared after him.

Bern then turned to Lan. 'Steven asked if you wouldn't mind going to Kasane tomorrow and joining Andy and a couple of Vietnamese for a short safari.'

Lan's expression lit up with anger. 'Why the fuck do I have to do that? I want to stay with you.'

'You're being childish, Lan. A few nights, I'm positive you can handle it. I presumed you'd be glad not having to make small talk with my guests; you're not taking the trouble to get to know them now.'

'Fine, I'll do the bloody job. But I'm not happy about it.'

Bern wasn't happy about it either. Steven was a mate, so he felt he had to agree. There was no point in getting angry with him, though. Bern had wanted to keep Lan close, in case they did come across the lions, to see how she reacted. Lan's temper had been spiralling out of control the last few days, and he was certain she was about to crack. Hopefully, this safari she was doing for Steven with the Vietnamese would calm her down. He was fed up with her tantrums and wanted to send her packing to the hole where he found her – but now wasn't the time.

Lan fumed the next morning, grumpier than ever. She spent a sleepless night stewing over the fact Bern asked her to leave.

'Why are you leaving so suddenly?' Nancy almost whispered.

'Shut up. Don't talk to me.' She then flew out of the tent, tripping over the ground sheet. 'Shit,' she yelled to no one in particular. She threw her bag into the vehicle, ignoring the stares of the English guests. 'Rot in hell.' Lan was beyond caring if they heard her or not. She snatched a coffee out of Brighton's hand. Standing beside the fire, she glared at everyone.

Drinking their first cup of coffee for the day, the two couples remarked on how vocal the lions had been during the night. Bern told them the lions were moving closer to the river to follow the buffalo, and with luck, they should find them today or tomorrow.

'Shit,' Lan mumbled. *Now, with me gone, they're sure to find the bloody lions.* Lan had imagined it would be so easy, leaving her poverty-riddled childhood in Vietnam to spot lions. All she had to do was go on safaris, see lions, phone Johan, tell him where the lions were – end of her involvement. But none of that turned out the way she had expected it to. *Steven better have a rock-solid scheme worked out, or it may well be another wasted trip*, Lan considered. Johan's patience was already like wrinkled paper burning on a fire. Steven did his best; however, with Nguyen baying for blood, whatever he had in mind for her to do, better work.

They meandered along the river towards the main entrance soaking up the incredible scenery. Bern, anxious to be rid of Lan, didn't want his guests to miss out on another amazing sighting. He kept to a steady pace by the riverbank, searching for game. Pods of hippos wallowed in the shallow waters as they argued about territories.

He saw Andy's vehicle speeding towards him, so he slowed down to wait for it. 'Howzit going?' Bern greeted Andy.

'Eh, good. How are you?' Andy turned to the guests in the rear of the vehicle. 'Good morning, I hope this fella is looking after you?'

There were murmurs of agreement from the happy group.

Lan climbed down, picked up her suitcase and strolled over to Andy. She threw her bag into the Toyota Hilux then turned back towards Bern.

He waved to her. 'Bye, Lan, enjoy your next safari, see you around,' he called over the noise of the engine.

Lan waved back at Bern, a scowl scratching across her face. She returned to Andy's vehicle and climbed into the front seat. He did a swift U-turn on the soft sand of the riverbank.

Bern turned away from the river to continue his search for lions further south in the park. They had about an hour until he stopped for the morning tea Brighton prepared. He intended to locate the Ihaha pride to check up on how they were faring. He relaxed into the drive; now with Lan gone, tranquillity washed over him.

Bern searched for about an hour, with no luck. He then drove high up onto the riverbank to Serondela Picnic Spot. Several concrete tables and chairs were scattered throughout the picnic ground, lining the bank with spectacular views across the river. The public toilet facilities made it perfect for a morning tea break.

They had finished their coffee and cake when Bern took a detour. He drove down to the river towards Kabulabula. Another pride of lions called this part of Chobe home. He saw no sign of the lions, however, but they did find herds of elephants and buffalo. So without sighting the lions, everyone seemed pleased with the game drive.

When they returned back to camp for lunch, Brighton had set up the table a little way from the tents under a shady tree. He placed all the dishes of food on a long trestle table. After a quick wash, everyone piled a plate with food. On a separate table, wine, beer and spirits stood waiting for the guests. Bern sidestepped the alcohol. When working, he stuck with strong cups of coffee.

Nancy sat next to Bern. 'So, what's a good-looking guy such as yourself doing out in the African bush? Is there a Mrs Bern somewhere?'

'No, not at the moment, but I live in hope,' Bern replied, thinking of Bella.

'Lucky girl.' Nancy picked up her wine to toast Bern. A smile spread across her face.

That same afternoon, Bern found the lions. They turned left instead of the usual right at the end of the track to the campsite. He drove inland away from the river, and at last, luck favoured him.

An hour later, he spotted the two magnificent males who lead the Ihaha pride. They lay right in the middle of the track, so Bern swerved up a rough bank to avoid hitting them. No one minded the sudden jolt of the vehicle; they were all too excited at seeing lions. He stayed with them for over an hour; it seemed no one wanted to move. They soon relaxed into the sublime peacefulness of watching the sleeping cats.

Driving back to camp, the crimson dusk coated the vehicle softer than a rainbow. A happy group of clients greeted Brighton, relaying their lion sighting to him. There remained one full day of game-viewing left, and hopefully, the pride would stay in the area, now the huge herd of buffalo had ambled from the river to the tree line.

<h1 align="center">CHAPTER 36</h1>

Andy dropped Lan off at Steven's office before continuing to the Coffee Buzz for lunch.

She strode into the small dusty room, fuming with annoyance. Instead of the Vietnamese clients she expected to see, Johan was sitting across the desk from Steven.

'Lover!' Lan said, brightening. 'Why are you here?'

'Nguyen's breathing down our necks. We'll get to that in a bit. I know why you haven't heard from your worthless brothers.' His voice, low and menacing, bounced around the small office.

Lan took in a sharp breath of anxiety mixed with fury; *yes, where the hell are they?*

'Two of them are across the border in Zimbabwe. They're trying to fleece the tourists in Victoria Falls, and true to form, making a nuisance of themselves. No one has seen or heard from the third brother. I'm guessing he's up to no good somewhere deep in the hidden corners of corrupt Zimbabwe.'

Lan breathed a sigh of relief; at least they were all right, because she worried they had met with foul play. However, she bristled with a pent-up rage that they left her here alone to face the music with Johan. 'It's good to see you, Johan, I miss you if you're not here.'

'Not now, Lan, there's business to do first. If we fail to come up with lion bones soon, we'll both be gazing down the wrong end of an AK 47. Steven gave us one of his safari vehicles and a tent. We're driving into Chobe National Park ourselves to find the fucking lions. Do you possess any idea from the pretty boy you sleep with where the hell they are?'

'Lions roared last two nights. Bern says they're further south, away from the river. There are good areas to camp illegally. Most legal camps are near the river.'

'Great, now get your pert little arse out of here and settled in the vehicle. We're leaving in a minute; I have to sort out a few things with Steven first.'

Lan huffed but left the men. She then waited in the hot vehicle, stewing over the news of her brothers.

Eventually, Johan strolled out of the office and climbed into the vehicle. He gave her a quick kiss before he settled in the driver's seat.

Then he drove along the tar road towards the turn-off to Chobe National Park.

Lan sensed Johan's annoyance with her.

'So, you reckon the lions are in the south?' Johan's voice was edged with bitterness.

'Yeah, Bern kept telling the clients that. They roared during the night. I guess he figured where they are. We have to keep out of designated camping spots, if we don't want to be found.'

'Nguyen's angrier than ever; he's obsessed with the bloody bones. If this trip doesn't yield at least one lion, we're going into hiding. Although, I'm convinced if we hide at the top of a volcano in the middle of the Congo, his bloodthirsty henchmen will sniff us out.'

'You worry a lot, lover, but I've got a gun. How hard is it to shoot lion?' Lan replied, smugly.

'I'm carrying a weapon also, and you better be right,' Johan countered.

A tremor chased down Lan's spine, listening to Johan speak those chilling words. He didn't sound like the lover she had met in Hoi An. *This trip better be productive*, she worried, *or I might well end up food for the lions.*

They were entering the park illegally, so they bypassed the main Sedudu Gate, preferring the quieter Nantanga turn-off. It drifted into the somnolent phase of the afternoon, heavy with heat, and the drowsy animals preferred to tug in the shade, too weary to eat. Lan knew the legal campsites to be a long way away, yet she urged Johan to be careful – they couldn't afford to attract attention. Lan gave him detailed directions. She tried to remember all of Bern's driving routes, but Chobe's indiscernible tracks looked like an angry nest of snakes.

About two hours later, Lan directed Johan to pull off the main track. They struggled over the rough ground for a few kilometres until she told him to pull into a small grove of trees, where they would pitch their tent for the night. It looked isolated enough for them to hide there. The sun waltzed towards the horizon. It took with it some of the heat as they finished putting up the tent and blowing up the air mattress.

They had an hour until darkness crept over them, and visibility dwindled with the sun. Lan ached to have Johan's naked body beside hers. She approached him, reaching for his hand to lead him into the tent.

'I'm not in the mood.' Johan's voice sounded gruff.

Lan ignored his protests. After she kissed him and undid his belt, Johan groaned, pushing Lan onto the air mattress. 'I love you, Johan,' she hummed; her body shook with pleasure. She nestled into him, twisting her fingers in his hand, satisfied at last. Sex with Johan differed from sex with Bern. Bern was rarely rough with her and was always in a hurry for it to be over. It seemed his mind floated elsewhere, even more so since Bella had arrived on the scene.

Their wild romp on the air mattress left Lan experiencing a calmness spread through her body. She savoured the fact that deep down in her heart, Johan wavered a heartbeat away from proposing to her. He understood her grim childhood and how she worked in the brothel, but he didn't care. The life she always dreamt of was going to be hers. With Johan's wealth and tenacity, they could go to every country Lan had always dreamt about, yet she yearned to live in dust-free America, away from the whisper of a lion.

Johan lit a fire and heated some of the food Steven supplied for them. Lan opened a couple of bottles of beer to wash their meal down with. They sat staring into the licks of flame; Lan was lost somewhere between apprehension and excitement. The light from the fire permeated like pin-pricks through the thick air.

Lan worried someone might spot their illegal camp, so after they finished their beers, they doused the fire with water, covering it with sand to extinguish the flames. They used their torchlights to help pierce the gloom. The stars blinked bashfully in the sky a million miles away. The moon, sulking from last night's orbit, remained out of sight for another hour or so.

Lan and Johan stayed in their tent, listening for the lions to make any noise on such a bleak night. Lan lay on the bed too overwrought to even contemplate having sex again. The small lamp in their tent tossed a pale yellow shadow across the canvas. They seemed to float on the air mattress, a cloud in a starless night.

At last, the sounds of lions roaring rumbled low over the ground towards their tent. Johan turned off the lamp and unzipped the tent, treading silently. Lan shone her torch, failing to see anything other than ghostly trees in the beam of light. Johan and Lan tripped over tree roots, almost hidden in the fading light.

The lions roared again. The noise, almost deafening on a still night, reverberated through them. Johan drove in the direction Lan figured the roars came from. They wove around bushes, termite mounds and warthog burrows.

And tonight was to be their lucky night.

When Johan swerved to avoid a tree, its branches scratching the vehicle, six lionesses loomed large in the headlights. Their eyes reflected back at them.

Johan switched off the lights, letting the blackness swallow them. They pulled their night-vision goggles on and fumbled for their guns. Their world became eerily green. The lions' bodies and iridescent green shimmer in the night. Both Johan and Lan aimed their guns at the lions.

However, before they had a chance to squeeze the trigger, the lions disappeared in a gauze of green.

Lion

We paused, holding a sigh. The males were calling to us. Their growls bounced off the sand, low to the ground. They had been following the buffalo closer to the river. We were on our way to meet up with the males. Our two sisters were already at the river, looking after the two cubs. Our pride hadn't eaten for several days, and hunger chased us tonight.

The suddenness of the vehicle stopping in front of us caused us to hesitate for half a breath. This vehicle stood in the way. Our aunt, the oldest female in the pride, gave the signal. We took off; the wind rustled through the leaves, and soon the bush absorbed us. In no time at all, we were with the males, planning how we would chase down an old buffalo.

CHAPTER 37

'Shit,' Johan swore under his breath, staring at the retreating lionesses. He slipped the vehicle into reverse to avoid hitting the tree. They pitched sideways into a painted dog den. 'Shit!' he yelled again. Pressing hard on the accelerator, he reversed the vehicle.

'Hurry, you'll lose them!' Lan shouted at him, but it did little to fix the problem.

The lionesses vanished, and they could be anywhere by now.

Johan's city driving skills were being tested. It took several attempts for him to right the vehicle. By then neither Johan nor Lan knew what direction the lions disappeared into. The emptiness of Chobe alarmed them; now the murky gloom of night shrouded them thicker than a cloak.

'What the bloody hell do we do now?' Johan's words scrambled through the vehicle, beating against the windows.

Nguyen had given Johan a dire ultimatum: if they didn't kill a lion in the next two nights, their blood would be a stain on the river. Johan didn't tell Lan this piece of information. He thought it best to keep a few things to himself, in case he had to placate Nguyen's burgeoning temper.

With a sinking heart, Johan comprehended the lions' roars growing fainter and fainter until only a sigh murmured through the trees. A silence, coated with dust, sucked the breath from the night. There was no use searching for the lions; they were probably in Savute by now, and they can't afford to get lost out here in the wilderness.

Johan drove with care to their camp, not speaking to Lan again, in case his temper simmered to the surface. His hands itched to tighten around her neck and squeeze the life from her.

Back at camp, the air in their tent buzzed against the canvas.

He eventually fell into a tortured sleep deep in the centre of the Chobe Game Reserve.

Dingo

I listened for her footsteps coming to greet me. She bent to pat me, and I saw a swirl of trepidation in her. She handed me some raw chicken, and because hunger gnawed at me, I snatched it from her. She sat down in the dewy grass to watch me eat; concern scratched at her. After my meal, I crawled onto her lap to reassure her that I was happy in my new home and that I would never leave her. My purrs stitched into her as she stroked my fur.

CHAPTER 38

Bella woke from a dreamless sleep to a brilliant clear morning. She imagined anxiety would clutch at her all alone in an unfamiliar house, but she felt so relaxed here.

Bella stayed with Dingo for several hours until hunger and the sound of her mobile brought her to the present. Setting Dingo on the ground, she let herself out of the enclosure to run inside.

Bella picked up her phone.

'Hi,' Karyn said. 'Just wanted to know how your first night in the house went. Also, is Dingo settling into his new home?'

'Great, and yes, Dingo seems happy. If you're free today, how about lunch at the Chobe Safari Lodge, my treat.'

'Sounds great, meet you there at noon.' Karyn ended the call.

Instead of walking everywhere, Bella decided to purchase a car. She searched on the internet, finding a car sales yard located in the middle of town. The over-friendly salesman told her they had a Toyota RAV4 for sale at a good price.

Bella arrived at the Chobe Safari Lodge fifteen minutes before noon, to beat the lunch-time rush and get a good table that overlooked the river. The waiter came with the menu and a wine list. She ordered a bottle of the Thelema Mountain Sauvignon Blanc.

Karyn strolled in about five minutes later, looking stunning. Her forest-green eyes lit up when she spied Bella waving at her. 'Hello, you,' she said, sitting down. 'You look wonderful and happy.'

'Yes, I'm happy for the first time in a long while. I already ordered a wine, hope you like sauvignon blanc?'

'If it's cold and wet, I'm fine with it,' she replied. 'To us and a lasting friendship.'

They toasted each other.

'I wonder if I might borrow Mike one day to advise me about a vehicle I'm considering purchasing. I get a clutch of anxiety talking to car salesmen.'

'Sure, he'll be happy to help you. He's not working today. I'll text him the details, and he can go with you this afternoon, if that's okay?'

'That's great, thank you. I'd be lost without your friendship.' Bella beamed at her.

'You do know you're easy to like, and I'm positive everyone you meet says the same thing.'

Bella fiddled with her wine glass. 'Not really. I was never one to collect friendships. And after I married Brad, it was a whirlwind of functions, always fleetingly meeting people, but not getting to know them.' She took a sip of wine.

'That sounds sad. I'm certain Botswana will hold happier memories for you.' Karyn reached across the table and squeezed Bella's hand.

Once the meals arrived and they were on their second glass of wine, Karyn asked, 'About the story you started telling me about … with a mystery man … I want all the details, please.'

'Ooh, I forgot I mention that embarrassing subject. Do you know a safari guide called Bern de Villiers?'

Karyn choked on her sip of wine. 'My God, Bella, him?'

'Afraid so. What an idiot I am. I blame it on drinking too much wine and jet lag. I went on a safari my first day in Botswana, and he happened to be the guide.' Bella pushed bits of food around her plate.

'Lucky you! He's delightfully yummy, and if I was single, not ecstatic about being married to the wonderful Mike, I might be giving you a run for your money with the gorgeous Bern.'

'You're welcome to him. It's a mystery why he focused his attention on me. A couple of swooning ladies on the trip kept vying for his attention all day. For some reason, which I can't understand, he zeroed in on me.'

'Really!' Karyn's eyes widened. 'Makes sense to me. He's gorgeous, you're beautiful, you'd make the perfect couple. I thought he was a confirmed bachelor, but if anyone could get him interested in an actual relationship, I bet you could.'

Bella frowned. 'Not so fast, I'm not sure I believe him. There's a girl, called Lan, living with him. Bern says it's nothing and to trust him. But … after what I've been through with my ex, I'm a bit wary of men.' Bella shook her head. 'Stupid, stupid. I can't believe how easily I fell into bed with him.'

'I can.' Karyn smiled cheekily. 'It's funny, though, Mike never mentioned they're in a romantic relationship. And another thing … I once saw Bern and Lan having lunch here, must have been after a safari. But they never spoke to each other. Bern looked preoccupied, and Lan looked like she was ready to explode. How about I invite him over for dinner one night when he's in Kasane, and you be there. It may allow you to talk it through with him, with Mike and I there to support you.'

Bella sucked in a breath of surprise. 'How do you know Bern? I didn't think your paths would ever cross. He's a guide, you work in real estate, and Mike's a pilot.'

'Botswana's a small country. Every white expat here knows about every other white expat. Mike met Bern a while ago. He piloted him to and from some of the lodges, and they formed an immediate friendship.' She paused to take another sip of wine. 'He drinks at the Old House in town after his safaris in Chobe, and if Mike is home, we often catch up for a boozy night with him there. If you don't like the dinner scenario, how about the four of us meet there for drinks?'

'Steady on, Karyn, I'm not sure I even like him.'

'Of course you do, what's not to like?' Her green eyes twinkled.

'Lan, she frightens me. She's the one who punched me in the face, and I get a sneaky suspicion she's not the sharing kind.'

'Ooh, how awful, what happened?' Karyn's eyes flashed with concern.

'I saw them together at Riley's, and they looked like any other romantic couple. Bern was laughing, and Lan was snuggled up to him. Then Bern spotted me. He stared at me with those eyes that could absorb the stars, ignoring the words Lan was whispering to him. I dashed towards the exit, hoping to avoid them. Lan caught Bern looking at me, and she looked furious. Bern followed me back to the lodge, and I'm mortified to tell you … it got a bit hot and heavy between us.'

'See, you do like him.' Karyn winked at her.

'No.' Bella then finished telling Karyn about her brush with Lan, finishing with, 'I don't need to come between them again, although I do pity Bern. Lan's a dangerous and mentally detached person.'

'You poor pet, the sooner he dumps her, the better off we'll all be.'

After Karyn rushed to work, Bella sat gazing across the Chobe River, lost in the tranquillity rippling inside her. Sipping on the last of the wine, she waited for Mike.

Mike picked Bella up half an hour later.

'How are you settling in, Bella?'

'Fine, thank you. Your gorgeous wife is wonderful, with all the help she has given me.'

'Yeah, Karyn's the best. Now, let's go buy you a RAV4. Dad was a mechanic for Jaguar, so some of his knowledge has filtered down to me.'

They went to the caryard where Mike took over the negotiations.

'You can see she's in tip-top condition. We look after all our vehicles here. Another couple are interested, but please take it for a test drive. You won't be disappointed.' The slick salesman fussed around them.

Once they arrived back at the office, Mike agreed it did run well. 'You're not planning on driving it off-road, are you? I doubt it would handle a trip into Chobe. Other than that, it's a good buy.'

With the formalities over, Bella became the proud owner of a shiny white RAV4, with one small dent in the bumper.

She kissed Mike on the cheek. 'Thank you for your help. I owe you and Karyn a beer. She mentioned the Old House, let me know what night you're free, and I promise to buy you a dinner.'

'Thanks, Bella, that's a date. We can pay for ourselves, though; you owe us nothing. Karyn likes you, and I'm always available to help a beautiful lady in distress.' Mike smiled.

Bella then happily drove her new car home. Before going inside, she went to check up on Dingo. He appeared to have no ill effects from his trip and was roaming about in his huge enclosure as though he had always been there. She took some food out of the fridge and refilled his food bowl.

Dingo

I ran up to her, rubbing against her leg to let her know I had forgiven her. I was beginning to feel strong, but the enclosure stifled me. I wanted to explore my surroundings and live wild. Her bright-blue eyes watched my every move. I felt she was fearful I'd run away. My softer spirit had connected with her. I knew she sensed a gentleness as my purrs radiated into her soul. I wanted her to open my enclosure and trust that she knew I'd never leave her.

CHAPTER 39

The next morning fizzed with the promise of heat to come. The cloudless sky dazzled when Lan and Johan unzipped their tent. They stayed hidden all day, out of reach of prying eyes. Chobe National Park was a gigantic unspoilt wilderness, there were countless areas where lions could hide for weeks without detection by humans.

They laid low all day, staying in the tent. Lan had begun to fret. Johan's fury was visible to even a mongoose family he chased out of the campsite with a broom.

'Do you want another beer?' They were the first words Lan spoke during lunch.

Johan remained silent, he just kept fiddling with his glass.

Lan felt the gulf between them now wider than the Chobe River. She longed for the lions to return tonight, so they could make a kill and return to civilisation. A ghostly mist covered them on the second night and threads of grey stitched through the tent and into her soul.

Lan refused to sleep. She waited for any kind of sign from the lions to show they were close by.

Lion

My pride was gathered several kilometres away closer to the river. We had been trailing a herd of buffalo that meandered towards the water. Two of the lionesses were sheltered in the bush, looking after the cubs. The buffalo paused at the river's edge, feasting on the sweet grass growing there. My brother and I motioned for two of the lionesses to approach from the front, downwind of the herd. We stayed out of sight; the other four lionesses crouched low in the long grass at the back of the herd. We bided our time; patience was always with us if we wanted to make a kill.

An old bull lingered too long eating the grass. He became separated from the main herd. This was our opportunity. The two lionesses started running to the old bull. He saw them too late to make a hasty retreat back to the herd. The other four lionesses sprang from the grass to help the others. Two of them jumped on his back, while another two reached for his hind legs. We had to be careful of the horns; we didn't want to get injured. This old bull still had plenty of fight left in him. My brother and I joined the lionesses. I went to the head, my front paws ripping into the soft flesh around the buffalo's neck.

He soon fell to his knees, a sure sign we were going to win this battle. The buffalo was no match for us, and his spirit lifted into the air. My brother and I ate first before the females joined us. The cubs were the last to come scratching for the leftovers. We ate in a hurry, with no table manners, wary of drawing the attention of hyenas.

Light began swirling on the horizon, sending creases of heat to warn us that another steamy day had gathered. We left the carcass to go up the slope away from the river and into the forest. A woolly caper bush offered meagre shade from the relentless heat of the sun. My pride tangled together, sharing our shadows. A long drowsy sleep crept over us. We had no desire to travel any further than the river for a few days.

CHAPTER 40

As soon as dusk reached down to them, Lan and Johan jumped into the vehicle. Lan's nerves scattered after her. Searching for the lions remained a futile attempt, but staying in the tent meant the friction that bubbled between Lan and Johan could boil over. She had eavesdropped on Johan's phone call earlier. He had to be talking to Nguyen. Piecing together the one-sided conversation, she realised how serious their predicament had become.

She shook like leaves in a summer storm. 'Please, Johan, tell me everything will be all right.'

Johan's eyes grew dark. 'I can't do that. We're in serious fucking trouble. Pull yourself together. We need to find the fucking lions tonight. Don't keep staring at me.'

'Yes, Johan. I'll look for lions.' Lan's breath held in the air for a few moments before disappearing. She turned her attention to the passing landscape. The trees slapped against the side of the vehicle. The headlights pierced the gloom, but all they saw were a few kudu, a small herd of impala and a lone bull elephant. 'I can't peer into the bush. It's getting darker. Where is the moon?' Lan's eyes hurt from staring into the darkness.

Johan kept driving, and with no clear direction about which way they ought to be heading, he chugged through the thick sand.

Following a fruitless two hours of driving in ever-increasing circles, Lan suggested they return to their campsite. The only noises in the bush came from the whoops of hyenas, and they were as useless to them as flippers on a giraffe.

'You're right. This is fucking hopeless.' Johan's words dripped with ice.

'We might hear lions later. Bern says they hunt at night. It'll be okay, Johan.' Lan tried to sound upbeat, but her heart wasn't in it.

'Lan, lions don't roar when they're hunting. Can't you even get that right?'

Lan looked down at her toes. 'Sorry, Johan. I'll try harder.'

The minute they arrived at camp, Johan's voice smacked against Lan. 'I can't believe I ever agreed to your reckless scheme of bringing you and your brothers over here. You've been nothing but trouble from day one.'

'I tried hard, Johan. Not a lot of lions in Africa.' Lan shivered, even though the night was sticky with heat.

'My two-year-old daughter could do a better job than you. Shit, what the fuck do I tell Nguyen now. Rest assured, my sweet Lan, you're taking full responsibility for this debacle.'

The coldness of his words sliced into Lan. She clenched her teeth and made a low droning noise, trying to stop the hatred coming from him. Her mind clouded thicker than a thunderstorm, but all she heard was the part about a daughter. 'You're married? You don't act married. Why didn't you tell me before,' Lan cried; this couldn't be happening to her.

'Ja, of course I'm married. Fuck, you didn't think I'd be

interested in a piece of trash like you. You're a whore and will always be a whore. And don't get me started on your fucking brothers. They disappeared at the first sign of trouble.'

Rage filled Lan's head. 'You heap of shit, leading me on. I think you fancied life with me, but you're married.'

Johan's eyes shot daggers at her. 'Grow up, Lan, shit happens. Let's get tonight over with. And then I never want to have anything more to do with you again. I'll give you a head start before I get in contact with Nguyen. After that, you're on your own, and heaven help you if that despot finds you.'

'You can't leave me here all alone.' Fear froze in Lan's veins. 'What would I do, where would I go?'

'I don't give a shit,' Johan snarled. 'Now get out of the vehicle!'

Lan crawled into the tent, trying to escape reality. Johan followed her; sighs of trepidation edged out of him. Hot tears stung Lan's eyes, and she sought the space to gather pieces of her tumultuous life together. She curled into a tight ball on the edge of the mattress before reaching into her handbag to stroke the cool sexiness of her pistol. She drew a certain amount of comfort from knowing her weapon sat within easy reach, if Johan chose to throw her out of the tent, or worse still, if he decided to shoot her to appease Nguyen.

Johan lay flat on his back, staring into the pitch-blackness of nothing.

Neither spoke; the air frizzed throughout the confines of the small tent, teasing both of them.

Lan's mind frayed as though someone ran a carving fork through her head. *How can this be happening to me*, she contemplated as she let the tears come.

Once she had no more tears left, she glanced at her watch, it was nine o'clock – she knew she wouldn't be able to sleep. Her heart crusted over like it had been burnt; she couldn't wait for morning. She snatched up her bag, clutching it close to her chest. 'I'm going to pee.'

Johan snored softly; the noise hung in the still air.

She fumbled her way off the mattress, until her fingers found the zip of the tent. She fell out the canvas door, after catching her foot in the zip. 'Shit,' she said, trying to regain her balance on the uneven ground.

Lan went to the back of the tent, pulled her trousers down and peed on the sand. She saw nothing as she stood to gaze into a night blacker than an elephant's shadow. Lan now wished she had remembered to get her night-vision goggles from the vehicle. She slung her handbag over her shoulder, her fingers light against the canvas.

She stumbled back to the front of the tent, touching the open flap. She then searched in her bag until her fingers laced around her pistol. She knew what to do before Johan had the chance to kill her, to keep in sweet with Nguyen. Johan had become her enemy. She dared not wait any longer.

The prick had a wife and a kid. He never intended to be with her. He stank the same as all the other punters in the brothel; he had used her. Hatred simmered inside her. Lan cradled the pistol in her hands, to let her warmth take away the coolness of the metal.

The soft snoring from Johan saturated the air.

Lan's eyes stared into an abyss, covering her in a black treacle fug. She smiled, realising Johan's watch ticked away his last seconds in this mortal world. The luminescent face shone in the darkness, tiny green stars in a glass of ink. She aimed at the watch, and taking her time, savouring the moment, she squeezed the trigger.

Johan gurgled his last breath. The noise of the gun reverberated off the forest, a harsh sound in an otherwise serene night.

She scrabbled about for the lamp and flicked it on, laughing when she saw the bullet had left a hole in his chest. His eyes now closed in a sleep that would last for infinity. Blood was already seeping onto the mattress.

Lan had to work fast; she couldn't afford to leave his body in the tent all night. She bent down and clasped both of his ankles in an attempt to get him into the vehicle. *God, he weighs a ton.* She pulled with all her strength, her muscles stretching and aching alarmingly. She dragged the dead weight of Johan through the zippered opening, manhandling him as far as her tired body allowed. She gasped, breathing hard from the effort.

Finally, she collapsed on the ground, letting the stillness cover her until a piercing noise started getting louder with each heartbeat. She jumped up and ran to the vehicle, breathing hard.

Unlocking the door, she fell into the driver's seat, slamming the door behind her. Lan shook with adrenalin and sexual excitement after killing Johan. The deafening noises scraped across the ground. She pushed the lock down, though she questioned why she believed locking herself in gave her any sort of protection.

The noise resonated from right outside the vehicle.

Lan's fingers curled across the seat; she picked up her night-vision goggles, and then her screams filled the night. She was petrified by what she saw.

Four hyenas bickered on top of Johan, whooping and eating, the sound of bones crunching shattered the air louder than thunder. Drool and Johan's blood dripped from their powerful jaws. His body was being ripped to shreds.

Lan stuffed tissues in her ears to try and block out the

frightening sounds. For the first time in her life, Lan touched fear. She vomited all over the front seat until her stomach brought up bile; still, the horror of the night crept through her, flowing into her heart.

Lan endured endless hours of frenzied feeding and squabbling from the hyenas. She realised it was pointless to drive away. She couldn't abandon the campsite. She had to pack up the tent to return it to Steven. Also, the tracks in Chobe were a sheer terror at night. She needed the sun to help guide her to the main road.

Ripping off her goggles, she scrunched into a tight ball to warm her freezing body with the heat of her vomit. She stayed in the same position, stuck in her nightmare until the morning rays stretched a path between the grove of trees to her campsite.

Lan uncurled herself, gagging when the smell of stale vomit overwhelmed her. She peeped out of the window. Nothing remained of Johan, save for the tattered reminders of clothes, his watch, and a lot of blood. Bizarrely, she saw no bones at all. *Where did they disappeared to?* Lan shook herself. She tried to forget the horrendous scenes of the night. Johan would have killed her, with no remorse. She saw the hatred in his eyes and his hands impatient to strangle her because she kept all his dirty secrets. God, Bern's softer nature had begun to rub off on her. She told herself to toughen up if she was to survive this ordeal.

Lan reached for one of the water bottles they kept in the vehicle and a towel belonging to Johan. She tried cleaning off the vomit from the front seat and the floor. She then made a small fire. The licks of flame teased into the pre-dawn dew. Pulling out the mattress from the tent, she let the air out before tossing it on the fire. It caught light the moment the fingers of flame touched it and soon became a raging inferno. Lan didn't expect anyone to be wandering about at this hour of the morning to see the flames dancing high in the air.

Next, she threw her soiled clothes into the flames and shovelled the remains of Johan on top of her clothes. Then she sat on the ground, watching the licks of flame, until the fire sputtered into the sand. She covered the ashes with water and sand, dragging leaves and branches to disguise the scene of the bloodbath. Finally, she dismantled the tent, folding it into a bundle. Picking up the tent poles and tent, she stowed them in the vehicle, along with their kitchen equipment. With nothing left to do, she changed into clean clothes.

She took a moment to inhale deeply and ponder on her shattered life. She had loved Johan. How could she have killed him? Her brothers had gone. Steven would be angry with her. Bern was always angry with her. Hoi An seemed a million miles away. Lan shook her maudlin thoughts away.

Lan jumped into the driver's seat, started the engine then turned to make sure she hadn't left anything to incriminate her. The campsite looked disturbed; however, Lan didn't think it so unusual. Perhaps it was a lion kill, and those happened almost every day in the wild.

She watched the spurfowls and starlings start fussing on the ground, kicking up the sand. They pecked and squabbled in the ashes cleaning up Lan's mess. She then began the tedious job of driving in a southerly direction. The terrain became so treacherous, she had to keep stopping to avoid warthog burrows, elephants and trees crowding in on her. A couple of hours later, she bounced onto the tar road and turned left towards Kasane.

CHAPTER 41

Bern felt sick on the last morning of his safari in Chobe. A gunshot late into the night disturbed his dreams. He thought poachers had found a lion and butchered it. His guests also woke up, frightened by the noise. They became upset, fearing their lives might be in danger from gun-toting bandits.

Bern explained to them that the sound of the shot came from a long way away, and it could have been from a poacher's gun, not bandits. He told them how lions were being killed for their bones; a racket that probably began somewhere in Asia. His guests expressed how shocked and distressed by the news they were and started their last game drive, in such an astonishing but deadly part of the world, in quiet contemplation.

Bern drove towards the river. He tried to lighten the sticky atmosphere hanging over the vehicle. He believed a sighting of one of the many herds of elephants in the area might do the trick. Elephants were creatures of habit and never deviated from their routine. Bern was confident of finding them splashing in the water, eager to greet a new morning.

He drove two kilometres until his eye caught something unusual by the bank of the river. He reached for his binoculars, and adjusted the focus, squinting his eyes to block out the morning sunshine. He picked up a shape lying close to the water – a buffalo carcass, and it looked fresh. He pointed it out to his guests, telling them the Ihaha pride of lions had made a kill. His optimism grew, knowing the pride may be somewhere close. He concentrated all of his attention towards the thickets lining the slight rise away from the river.

They scanned the undergrowth, all reminders of the gunshot in the night forgotten. Bern spotted the males first; they laid low under a small bush, clearly hoping the sun's rays stayed out of reach. He nosed the vehicle towards them, trusting the rangers didn't drive by and catch him off-road. He wanted to see if the females were with the males because it meant the poachers had missed their target.

He turned off the engine, and a calmness settled in the air. He reached again for his binoculars, training them towards the low bushes. He wanted to see if the rest of the pride were scattered there. All of a sudden, a tail flicked in the air. Holding his breath, he counted the eight females and two cubs. They sheltered further up the bank, with their fat bellies turned towards the sky.

Bern breathed a sigh of relief, although the direction of the gunshot last night mystified him. It came from the same direction where the sounds of hyenas pierced through the night. It puzzled him; yet he wouldn't dwell on it now. His guests came first, and now he was content because his precious lions were safe, for at least another day.

He continued the game drive following the ebb and flow of the Chobe River. Bern then turned inland where huge numbers of buffalo, their bodies coated in ochre mud, snorted and scuffed in the sprinkling shade of a few acacia trees. They ignored the sharp thorns as they caught at their shadows, trying to gather respite from the fierce sun. Bern edged around the trees near their camp, stopping when a leopard stepped in front of the vehicle.

All things considered, since Lan left for her private safari, he started enjoying himself with his small group of Londoners. He had grown weary of the merry-go-round dance he kept doing with Lan. And he knew with certainty that Lan had something to do with the gunshot last night. So, he planned on discussing it with Steven when he saw him later.

CHAPTER 42

Driving along the tar road, Lan shook all her guilt out the window. Gone were the lingering misgivings about shooting Johan. She felt no remorse; in fact, she rather enjoyed the whole experience, apart from the hellish ordeal of the hyenas. The bastard had every intention to do away with her, except she had outsmarted him. How childish was she to ever imagine that love could blossom between the two of them? He had used her from the first moment she met him. She happily killed two worthless men; men who threatened her survival. She pondered whether her heart froze when Johan rejected her, or did her complete lack of empathy start that first night in the brothel? Whatever it was, she didn't care.

She drove into town, straight to Steven's office. He sat at his desk, holding the phone away from his ear; a scowl spread across his face. His crumpled shirt, festooned with pink flamingos, had coffee stains blurring the bright pattern. Lan understood by Steven's body language that Nguyen screamed obscenities from the other end of the connection. She sat down opposite him, and a tight wad of panic knitted in her belly. She then made a zero with her thumb and index finger and mouthed the word 'lions.'

Steven's fingers trembled when he relayed the sorry news to Nguyen.

Nguyen's anger buzzed inside the room, but she had tried her best. With Nguyen's limited knowledge of lions, he wouldn't be able to grasp the difficulties they faced over here. Lan wasn't dumb; she knew Nguyen hungered to blame someone, to splatter their blood for the perceived incompetence. Lan had to be certain she didn't end up with a bullet through her heart.

Steven finished his conversation with Nguyen, and then his fingers flicked in the air before he flexed his palms hard on the desk. He scowled at Lan. 'This is not what I expected from you, Lan. I heard reports of a gunshot last night. Now you're telling me *no* lions were killed.'

Lan smirked. 'You're right, Steven. We got close first night. There were six in front of us. Johan hit a ditch. They escaped. He got the car out of ditch. We searched for hours.' She started tapping her feet; the sound echoed across the floor.

'So where's Johan now?' Steven studied her intently. 'Please tell me you left him at your campsite, and the reason you're here is to pick up more supplies.'

'Yeah, I left Johan.' Lan stuck her nose in the air.' He's not chasing lions, or anything, ever again.'

'Bloody hell, Lan, what did you do?' He glared at her. Beads of sweat formed across his brow and top lip.

'I save my own life. Johan was going to kill me. No one will find the body, maybe four fat hyenas. If I were you, Steven, I'd keep this information to yourself,' Lan advised, narrowing her eyes. She continued to tap her feet, louder now.

'I'm in this up to my eyebrows, sweetheart! Trust me, I won't be gossiping about last night's killing. We better come up with something soon. I'm positive Nguyen is getting ready to send a truckload of thugs over here to sort out the problem.' He stood up abruptly and pulled his shirt over his protruding belly. 'Now, get out of my office, I don't want anyone seeing the two of us together. I better try to come up with a strategy and bloody soon.' He bit his lower lip and wiped the sweat from his brow with a dirty handkerchief. 'Go and get ready to meet Bern, and for God's sake be nice. The bastard still might prove useful to us.'

'Yeah, I know what I need to do to keep Bern happy. You keep your mouth shut. I'm not going to stuff this up,' Lan threw at him as she flounced out of the office.

Lan stumbled along beside the road, swearing at the fact there wasn't even a footpath. She was glad Steven's office was close to the Old House Lodge. She went straight into the reception area to book a room for the night. She hated the staleness and cheapness of the lodge. For some reason, Bern loved it, so she gritted her teeth and kept telling herself it was for one night.

Lan went into the room, tossing her bag on the bed before stripping off her clothes. The hot, steamy atmosphere of the shower soon washed away any misgivings she had about shooting Johan. Bits of vomit stuck to her hair. Lan reached for the shampoo, squirting most of it over her head. She lathered it up, trying to remove all traces of last night. Smelling of rose and geranium oil, not vomit, and in fresh clothes, she decided she needed a drink. Her room drowned her in sweat, making her dress cling between her thighs. She strolled over to the open bar area overlooking the Chobe River, where a warm breeze teased the air.

Lan ordered a beer, found a table by the river and let her mind drift to Johan. How did she get to be so detached? She carried no twinge of regret at what she had done to Johan. Her tough upbringing hardened her heart. Her mother died when she was young, and her father cared more about drinking than caring for her or her siblings. The death of her sister Mai broke her. Mai had been her only sibling to show her kindness.

No one should be forced to work in a brothel. The things I've seen there. They must have robbed me of empathy. She naively thought that Johan loved her – *how stupid was that.* With her brothers gone, Lan felt empty. She ordered another beer, the first one empty on the table. She would wait to see what Steven came up with. If they actually killed a lion, it would satisfy Nguyen and get her some much needed money to leave Botswana and go … *fuck, where can I go.* She downed her second beer and ordered another. She stared through the trees to the river, but she didn't see the beauty there.

Lion

My brother and I quenched our thirst at a small puddle beside the river. The lionesses had left us to seek shelter deeper in the forest. The water tasted warm from the sun, so we curled our lips to catch a slight breeze. Our paws scrunched the sand as we retraced our footsteps back up the slight rise from the river. We plopped on the ground under a shady bush; a fog of lethargy draped over us. My brother and I sought out the meagre shade, impatient for the sun to lose its tussle with the horizon and ooze into the landscape. We smelt herds of impala and kudu lingering in the forest, eating their way through the undergrowth. The sound of buffalos scratching together against the branches of trees reached us, but we were in no mood to eat.

CHAPTER 43

They had a successful morning of game-viewing. When Bern drove back to camp, Brighton had already stowed the tents in the trailer. He had set up the dining table under the trees, where a mottled shade sprinkled over them, giving a bit of relief from the hot sun. Brighton then prepared a delicious chicken pie with salad for lunch. A broad smile etched his face as he greeted everyone. He served the meal out and made sure everyone had a full glass of wine, beer or a soft drink.

Bern made himself a cup of coffee and sank into the seat at the head of the table. Everyone showered praise on him for his excellent tracking skills, and for Brighton with how wonderful the food tasted and his always-cheery disposition.

Bern and Brighton finished packing up the campsite. The red-necked spurfowls moved into their site. They and the cape starlings busied themselves pecking at the leftover crumbs Brighton sprinkled over the ground. Soon, all that remained were their footprints to show that for a brief moment in time, memories of this special part of Botswana had trailed into their hearts.

A quietness settled over them on the trip out of Chobe. They spent the time gazing into the bush, searching for animals, and Bern hoped they were dreaming about their next visit to Africa.

Bern drove with extra care, making the trip to the lodge a game-drive. They came across the Ihaha pride again, seeing only the two males.

He then turned away from the river for the last time, driving up the steep bank. He followed age-old tracks, weaving and ducking in and out of the trees. Some of the tracks were so narrow the branches etched cobweb lines down the sides of the vehicle.

The sun was inching closer to the horizon, when he pulled the vehicle with the heavy trailer stuck fast to the towbar, out onto the tar road. He then picked up speed, now the vehicle had freed itself from lurching along the soft tracks.

He turned into the carpark of the Chobe Safari Lodge, the final destination for his guests.

Brighton helped them carry their luggage into the reception.

Bern farewelled them, thanking them for their enthusiasm and easy-going manner.

Bern and Brighton accepted, with grace, the tips being snuck into their palms when they shook hands with the men.

The two couples wandered off into the lodge, so Nancy approached Bern. 'Now, technically you're not my guide anymore, so do you fancy a drink in the bar and a cosy dinner later?' Her voice quivered with obvious nerves. She then gave him an eyeful of her enormous breasts as her fingers laced through the top button of her shirt.

'Sorry, Nancy, I'm still working, and don't forget about my girlfriend waiting for me.'

'Ouch, sorry, I didn't think you meant it. She's one lucky lady to land such a gorgeous guy. Here's my card, if it doesn't work out with her,' Nancy said, handing over her card and lingering her hand in Bern's.

Bern smiled brightly at her. 'Thank you, I trust you enjoyed your trip and start making plans to return to Africa sometime in the future.'

Nancy then reached up to Bern, about to kiss him on the mouth, but he turned his head so her lips lightly brushed his cheek.

'Goodbye, Nancy,' he said before climbing into the vehicle, where Brighton sat laughing his head off.

'Eh, man, you get all the girls, you lucky bastard ... must be the uniform. Maybe on the next trip, I can be the guide and you the cook, then I might get lucky with the ladies.'

'You're welcome to the ladies, Brighton. I've a special one in mind for myself and haven't the energy or the inclination to go looking for someone else.'

Brighton screwed up his face. 'I thought you were tiring of Lan. Did she crawl in to warm your cold heart? I imagined you to be the eternal bachelor, always with a different woman on your arm.'

'I never mentioned any names. Be patient.' He gave a lopsided grin.

Bern drove the vehicle and trailer to the side of Steven's office building. He nosed it in beside Steven's beat-up Landcruiser. Steven's capable staff then took over, doing the tedious job of unpacking and cleaning all of the equipment ready for the next safari.

Bern said goodbye to Brighton before striding into the office for a word with Steven about how the trip went.

As soon as Steven greeted him, he said, 'Lan's back; she said everything went well with the Vietnamese. I reckon she missed you, though.'

'Yeah, I bet. Did you hear about the gunshot last night?'

'Nasty business. Lan told me about the gunshot too. Scared the pants off the Vietnamese, eh.' Steven laughed.

'Let me know if you hear anything. I received a text message from Lan. She booked us a room at the Old House for tonight. So, I'm heading over there now. I'm beat, back-to-back safaris take their toll, or I'm getting too old for the job now.'

'You'll be guiding in your eighties, man. You love it. It's in your blood! Now, get out of here … go to that dazzling lady of yours, eh.'

'Thanks, Steven, I'll be in touch.'

Bern picked up his bag and nodded to Steven before leaving the office. He dreaded seeing Lan again. He didn't want to fight with her tonight. Bern was impatient to return to Maun to visit Bella. Perhaps she had missed him a little bit.

He shifted hands with his luggage, as he went into the bar area. He spotted Lan perched up on a high barstool overlooking the river. Several beer bottles stood empty on her table, and that meant one of two things. She was either tanked or had met up with someone for a drink, although that seemed unlikely. Lan kept to herself; she had a closed demeanour about her. The Vietnamese from the trip might have offered to buy her a beer. Better yet, if she drank alone, and judging by the number of empty bottles on the table, she would soon be passed out, saving him the trouble of having to talk to her.

He wandered over to the table and threw his bag under her seat. 'Hallo, Lan, Steven tells me your trip with the guys from Vietnam went well.'

'Sswhat,' she slurred, evidently trying to focus her bleary eyes on him.

'That's enough drinks for you tonight. Do you want dinner or are you too drunk to eat?'

'Hello, lover, God you look sexy.' She lurched, swaying when her sandals slapped against the timber floor.

Bern wrapped his arm around her before picking up his bag to guide her out of the bar.

Thank heavens their room was the first one off the bar area, because Lan was sliding out of his arms. Bern opened their door, noticing Lan's crap sprinkled throughout the small room. Her luggage and junk were strewn across the bed, and a trail of discarded clothes lay on the floor leading to the bathroom. Wet towels were thrown into a heap on the bathroom floor.

Bern pulled her luggage off the bed, pushing Lan down onto the soft doona. She lay there with clear lust in her eyes, her hair fanned out across the pillow. Lan reached for Bern, trying to hug him, but she passed out without getting a chance to kiss him. Bern climbed off the bed, throwing a blanket across her.

He changed into a clean pair of jeans and a crumpled linen shirt before checking on Lan, but she snored louder than an old bull elephant. She wouldn't be waking up anytime soon. Going straight to the bar, he ordered a bottle of St Louis Lager, carrying it over to the same table Lan had occupied. The waiter had already been to clear it of her empty bottles.

Bern loved the quirkiness of Kasane and the Old House. It sat alongside the Chobe River. He always stayed there, ever since he moved from South Africa and felt at home in the familiar surroundings. He was thinking about selling his house in Maun and moving here permanently. He found his home too full of the harshness of Lan, and the serenity dissolved with her. Bern longed for a fresh start, now he dreamt about a life with Bella. He finished his first beer and ordered another, along with the pan-fried kingklip fish, chips, and salad for dinner.

He wondered what went wrong with Lan's trip; she hardly drank any more than two beers. Lan was always flinty and in control; perhaps the trip she finished with the Vietnamese didn't go as well as Steven mentioned. Still, it didn't concern him, whether she was drunk or sober.

Bern was too impatient to be in Maun to visit with Bella. His flight left at ten in the morning, so with luck, he could drive out to the Island Safari Lodge tomorrow afternoon. He hoped Bella had forgotten the evilness Lan inflicted on her. Her gentle nature should never be touched by violence. He would do everything in his power to make sure Lan never went near Bella again.

CHAPTER 44

Lan woke with a head that thumped in time to a heavy metal band. She struggled out of bed to run into the bathroom, reaching the toilet bowl in time to vomit. In her fuzzy state, she forgot about Bern in the shower until he turned off the tap.

He reached over her to get a towel. 'Not too well, eh Lan?' he said in a voice loud enough to interrupt dreams.

'Shut the fuck up,' she whispered, leaning over the toilet bowl again.

Bern reached into his bag, pulled out a couple of aspirin, filled a glass with water and handed it to Lan.

She accepted it with a grateful nod, downing the tablets in one gulp. She crawled into the bedroom to lie down.

'Don't forget, we're flying home soon. Are you having any breakfast?' Bern asked.

'No, leave me alone, go eat breakfast. And *don't* slam door. I'll be okay soon, ready for the flight home.'

Bern pulled on his jeans and a faded shirt, leaving Lan to nurse her hangover.

Bern headed across to the bar where a continental breakfast looked inviting along a low-height wall. He ordered poached eggs on toast from the waiter, before going over to the self-service table and pouring himself a strong cup of coffee. His footsteps were hollow in the emptiness of the bar area.

Bern always woke up when dawn clawed at the horizon on safari and found the habit hard to kick when in civilisation. He didn't mind, though, because he loved the smell of dawn. Everything was crisp, making you think anything could be possible. He finished his first coffee and strolled over to get another when his meal arrived. The waiter set it on the table with a flourish. 'Thank you,' Bern said. He didn't mind at all about Lan staying in their room, but he did speculate why the usually-in-control Lan managed to drink herself into a stupor.

Bern finished his breakfast and another cup of coffee. He stood from the table and threw his napkin over his empty plate. He nodded a greeting to a couple who had wandered in for breakfast.

When he entered the room, he found Lan sitting on the bed, looking forlorn. 'I've never seen you drunk. I spoke to Steven, and he said the trip went well. What happened?'

Lan turned her head up at him; her eyes were blood-shot. 'Nothing; trip was a blast. Went according to plan, no dramas. I missed you, though. Beer helped to numb mind. Guess I drank too much.'

Bern gave a half-smile. 'Not to worry. Finish packing; our pick-up is arriving soon to take us to the airport, and I promised Steven I'd call in before we left. You can sleep at home.'

Lan slept through the flight to Maun, only waking when the plane landed heavily onto the runway. They retrieved their bags; the heat covered them as soon as they went out into the hot sunshine. Lan shielded her eyes against the glare. She reached into her bag for a pair of sunglasses.

Bern's vehicle waited for him in the carpark. Thanking his friend, Bern took the car keys. He ushered a shaky Lan to the vehicle and stowed the luggage in the boot.

Once they arrived home, Lan went straight to the bedroom. 'Please don't disturb me. My head's still spinning. Need sleep.'

'Okay, Lan, you rest,' Bern said. 'I have to go into town to check in with the office anyway. With luck, you'll be more human after a sleep.'

Bern never intended to go into the office.

Once in the car, he turned left at the end of his driveway, towards the Island Safari Lodge. He drove into the carpark and parked beside Seagal's vehicle. He then strode towards Bella's cabin, when Seagal stopped him.

'She's not here, Bern.'

'What do you mean? Please tell me she's in Maun doing some shopping.'

'No, she moved out of the lodge.'

Bern's eyes narrowed. 'Now you're starting to piss me off. She's not on a plane to Australia and reconciling with that ridiculous ex-husband of hers, is she?'

'No, of course not. Bella sees Botswana as her home now. I promised I wouldn't say anything, but you're going to find out sooner or later. Come join me for a beer on the terrace and I'll tell you where she is.'

Sipping on their beers, Seagal told him the story. 'Well, she never planned to live in the lodge forever, she had to leave here at some time, eh? During our lunch the other day, I told her about the lion-poaching racket; she was horrified. Bella asked what she could do to help stop such heinous acts. I felt sorry for her and wanted to help. I mentioned Steven being on the lookout for someone to liaise with the tour operators. I said he lived in Kasane, way up north. She jumped at the chance to distance herself from you and Lan, now she knows what Lan is capable of. Lan scared the hell out of her! She found a house for sale, bought it and is now living there.'

'God, I bloody left Kasane a few hours ago.' Bern gritted his teeth. 'Why didn't you tell me sooner, we're supposed to be friends?'

'We are, but Bella asked me not to mention it to you. She's already moved to Kasane, so I'm sure she won't mind me telling you now.'

Bern was livid. 'Fuck you. How do I explain to Lan I want to go there straightaway?'

Seagal looked at him with compassion. 'You don't! Give Bella space for a while and call her instead. Maybe she's starting to miss your undeniable charms by now.' He chuckled.

Bern sighed. 'A phone call to her isn't what I dreamt of when coming here to visit Bella. Steven isn't about to put her in any danger, is he?' He questioned.

'Of course not. Steven's one of the good guys.' Seagal shuffled his feet. 'All Bella has to do is see if she notices anything unusual while she's out and about. It's giving her a reason to believe she's doing something to stop this craziness eh.'

'Give me her address.' His words were harsher than he intended.

'It's the least you can do.' He shouldn't be angry with Seagal, but hell he was frustrated.

'Sure, no problem.' Seagal reached into his pocket for his phone.

Bern frowned. 'What about the scrawny cat? I refuse to believe she abandoned him.'

'No, it's not in Bella's nature to abandon a cat. She took him with her, and by all accounts, the little chap is settling into his new environment.'

'Of course she took him with her, that's my Bella and why I love her.'

'Call her, man.' Seagal stood, putting his large hand on Bern's shoulder. 'I have to return to my office to chase the never-ending trail of paperwork waiting for me.'

CHAPTER 45

Dawn oozed into another perfect day. The call of the fish eagle floated off the trees before curling across the river. It sounded even better than kookaburras laughing in the sunshine.

Bella phoned Steven to arrange a time to visit him. He told her Bern had an appointment with him at nine about some safari business, but she was welcome to visit him after Bern left. Bella held a clutch of guilt about not mentioning to Bern she had bought a house in Kasane. She failed to chase away the nagging doubts twining in her stomach.

If the meeting with Steven went well, she'd text Bern to tell him. She knew Bern worked with Steven against the vile poaching of lion bones, therefore they should be working together to share information.

Bella drove to Steven's office at ten in the morning. The heat sizzled, and she didn't wish to appear all sweaty and flustered meeting him.

Steven looked to be a man in his late fifties. His crinkly black hair held a hint of grey at the edges. He was short, and in his younger years, he might have been wiry. Age and lack of exercise had accumulated into a paunch around his middle. He wore an outlandish shirt, more suited for a Hawaiian holiday than the African bush. It hung in folds over his shoulders and stretched disturbingly across his waist. His face crumpled, showing the effects of too much alcohol. This was a shame, because his strong facial features now crept towards his chin. His no doubt once-clear chocolate eyes were circled with red rims, and he kept rubbing them with a handkerchief.

However, his smile appeared forced when he greeted her. And she had to shake off an uneasy feeling when she offered her hand to him, reminding herself that Seagal held him in great esteem.

'Hello, Bella, nice to meet you at last.' He had a firm hand-shake, crushing Bella's fingers in his bear-sized hand. An alpha male trying to prove his strength and authority over her.

'Nice to meet you, Steven. Seagal's told me all about you. He regards you as a friend, and this is all the recommendation I require.' Bella smiled at him, sinking into the seat he held out, a twist of panic continued to waft across her heart. 'I'm at a loss about what to do to help out. All you have to do is say the word, and I'll do whatever you ask of me. I'm ready to write you out a large cheque to cover the hidden expenses I'm sure you deal with on a day-to-day basis.'

'Thank you, Bella, it all helps in our fight against such insidious crimes. I guess all you should do at the moment is spend your days in town, talking to people, getting them to relax in your company. The folk here are angrier than we are with the lion poaching happening in their national park.' He sat back in his chair. 'They get a lot of kickback with the money and trade from the tourists.

All the visitors who come to Chobe have lions at the top of their *must-see* animal list. So, they're loath to consider another lion could be taken from them. I guess your job for the moment would be to keep your ears open. If you think something sounds suspicious, or you get a bad vibe about someone, come and report it to me. Please don't involve yourself in any unsafe situations. Seagal already warned me about putting you in danger, and man I'm too old now to get into an argument with him.'

'It all sounds a bit too easy. What if people are reluctant to talk to me? Are you sure there's nothing else I can do to help you out?' Bella enquired.

'This is fine for a start. We don't know who or what we're dealing with. Any feedback from you, no matter how trivial you think it sounds, may help us stop these criminals.'

The phone on his desk rang, a shrill sound in the small office. It startled Bella.

Steven picked it up. He frowned, putting his hand over the mouthpiece. 'That's all for the moment, Bella. I'm always here if you want a chat or any questions answered, but now I must take the call in private. Thank you for coming.'

'Ooh sorry.' Bella went to stand up. 'I'll be in touch.' She picked up her handbag. 'Thank you.' Bella shook Steven's outstretched hand. She closed the door behind her and found that she had relaxed more after her talk with Steven. He seemed genuinely concerned about the plight of the lions. She all but forgot about her first impression of him.

Bella was meeting up with Karyn and Mike for lunch at the Old House. They told her they loved it, and Bella admitted to being smitten when she entered the bar area. Its décor appeared rustic and homey. Bella eased into the cosy atmosphere. She ordered a bottle of chardonnay, carrying it over to an empty table large enough for three. Sitting down to wait, she soaked up the surroundings, staring out through the trees to glimpses of the Chobe River.

They sauntered towards her arm-in-arm about ten minutes later, and their closeness caught at Bella for a moment. She remembered the loving shared times with her ex-husband and realised she may never have the same intimacy with someone ever again. 'Hello, don't you two look gorgeous.'

Both Karyn and Mike dropped a kiss on Bella's cheek before they sat down.

Mike poured out three glasses of wine. They chatted companionably, while they dithered about what to eat for lunch.

'I saw Bern in here last night, and before you ask, no I didn't mention your name. He sat at a table having a drink and dinner alone,' Mike mentioned.

'Wonder what happened to Lan, not that it's any of my business.' Bella took a sip of wine.

'Well, he seemed happy and not missing her at all, so I didn't ask. I had popped in to buy a bottle of wine to take home for dinner last night.'

Karyn put a hand on his arm. 'Now, Mike, the next time you meet him, ask him about his relationship with Lan. See if it's serious, but don't mention Bella or me.'

Mike beamed at her. 'Righto, love, consider it done.'

'Hey, I don't know about that,' Bella said.

'I know it's difficult for you. Your divorce has left you shattered. But wouldn't it be better to know if he liked you or if he was being a cheat?' Karyn asked, reaching over to put her hand on top of Bella's.

'I guess so.' Bella tried to smile but squeezed her lips together instead.

They finished off the spicy mushroom pizza in silence. Bella felt so relaxed with Karyn and Mike, they felt like the family she had always craved. After lunch, Bella drove into the carpark of Choppies Supermarket. She wandered up and down the aisles, tossing items into her trolley and chatting with the locals. She found a trip to the supermarket was a special occasion and a chance to gossip.

CHAPTER 46

Bern punched in Bella's number. He held his breath until she answered.

'Hello, Bern, why are you ringing me?'

'Seagal told me you had moved to Kasane.'

'What!' Bella gasped. 'He was supposed to keep that a secret.'

'After I flew back from Kasane, I went to the Island Safari Lodge to visit you. Seagal met me to tell me you had moved there. He thought you wouldn't mind. Christ, I left a few hours ago, I could've visited you. Damn it, Bella, I'm in … never mind.' Bern held back from saying too much to scare her even further away.

'Goodbye, Bern.'

'No, please wait …' Bern pleaded. 'Seagal told me you took the cat with you … How's the little fella adapting to his new home?' He attempted to change the subject.

'He's doing well. Dingo took about a day to settle in, and he's happy now. I think I'll start leaving the gate to his enclosure open. He has a wild spirit, and though I worry about him, I don't wish to tame him. The trouble is, I'd be lost if I didn't have a cat in my life to fuss over and talk to.'

Bern's heart flipped. 'You're welcome to fuss over me, if you like?'

'I'm pretty sure that's what Lan is for. Goodbye, Bern.'

'No wait …'

But she already ended the call.

Bern's frustration boiled over; all he thought about was returning from Kasane to visit Bella. He damned Seagal for not telling him sooner, before climbing into his vehicle to drive to his house where the irascible Lan lived.

Bern expected Lan to be asleep; however, she lay naked on the bed, staring up at him, with a grin that held more lust than mirth. 'Shit,' he mumbled, noticing the look in her eyes.

'Come to me, lover.' Her voice jarred in the tranquil room.

'Not now, Lan, I'm busy,' Bern tossed at her. He went into the bathroom, slamming the door behind him.

Bern changed into shorts and an old Kruger T-shirt, then headed upstairs to the kitchen.

He took a beer out onto his deck, musing over how to come up with a plausible excuse as to why he had to return to Kasane at once. He punched in Seagal's numbers on his phone, checking Lan remained in the bedroom. 'You owe me, man. I'm making up a bogus safari to Chobe. If Lan phones, can you verify my story.'

'Okay, no problem, eh.' Seagal ended the call.

Bern smiled in anticipation of seeing Bella again.

An hour later, Lan came out to curl up on his lap. She reached up to kiss him until Bern stopped her. 'I've got a bit of bad news to tell you first. A guide has another bout of malaria, and I agreed to fill in for him. I'm flying to Kasane at first light in the morning.'

Lan scowled. 'They should ask someone else. You've been working so hard lately.'

'Everyone else is busy. It's for two nights, not two years.'

'Can I go too?' Lan thought if she went, they might find a lion for her to shoot.

'Not this time, sorry. I'll be doing a safari to Moremi; you can come with me then.' Bern sighed.

Lan screwed up her face. 'Great.' She then smirked. 'I'll tidy up the house while you are gone and go shopping at the mall. I want to buy a pretty dress.'

'Sounds like you'll be too busy to miss me.' Bern pushed Lan off his lap. He left her on the deck to make a start on his packing.

Bella knew she ended the call with Bern a little too abruptly. She found to her dismay she was missing him. However, she understood Bern was only intrigued because she kept pushing him away. Usually, women clambered to be near him. Even though Lan frightened her, Bella had to respect their relationship, whatever that was.

The house closed in around her, everywhere she looked, Bern's incredible eyes followed her. She needed to breathe so went into town. She enjoyed the stroll along the busy footpaths. There never seemed to be a moment when President Avenue didn't teem with foot traffic.

Bella left the house in such a hurry, she forgot to wear her hat. The sun's rays scorched into her thick hair, making it a jumbled sweaty mess. By the time she reached Chobe Safari Lodge, Bella was sweltering. She turned off the footpath to wander into its welcoming interior, thinking the only reason she went there was to buy a hat. Somehow, though, she bypassed the curio shop to wander over to the bar.

After ordering a Lion Lager, she carried it over to the table on the edge of the deck. She never tired of gazing across the dazzling Chobe River, where boats oscillated to the same tempo as the currents.

After finishing the beer, and with a bit of self-control, she declined the offer of another. Bella then wandered around the curio shop and bought the first hat she saw. It had a wide brim with the Chobe Safari Lodge logo on it. Now, wearing a hat, she went out into the sunshine to finish her walk.

Along the way, Bella bumped into Karyn.

'Got to fly, I'm already late for a client. Join us for dinner tomorrow night at the Old House. Mike should be home from his flying jaunt by then,' Karyn suggested.

'Sure, sounds great,' Bella replied before Karyn dashed to her vehicle. She then strolled past Choppies and the Chobe Marina Lodge. Heat and dust bounced off the footpath twirling around her legs. Bella stopped at one of the many craft stalls that lined busy President Avenue. She dithered about purchasing a colourful tablecloth. Finally, she settled on one with bright giraffes and zebras woven into the coarse fabric. It was too hot to continue her walk, so Bella turned around and headed for home.

True to form, Bella was running late for dinner with Karyn and Mike. She had spent all day in the garden taming the overgrown gardenias. Trying to look presentable, she pulled an oversized sweater the colour of storm clouds over her grubby dress. Bella's boots held a hint of mud from the garden, but they would have to do. She applied a light dusting of foundation over her face, finishing the look with several coats of mascara to emphasise her eyelashes and bring out the deep blue of her eyes. She tried to comb her tousled hair, but in the end, she dragged most of it up into an untidy mess and fastened it with a clip. She thought the lighting on the verandah of the Old House would be fuzzy enough to hide the fact she looked similar to her wild gardenias.

A cool breeze tugged at her jumper as she stood at the edge of the bar area.

Karyn approached her, a worried look in her stunning eyes. 'Hi, glad you went to so much trouble getting ready.'

'Sorry, the hours flew by, and I ran out of the energy to change. I'm going to pretend the haze, swirling around the lights, will cover my untidiness, and I'm not here to impress anyone,' Bella assured her.

Karyn then put a hand on her arm. 'Never mind, even unkempt you look amazing. A word of warning, though, we have another guest for dinner, and please, don't blame me. Mike invited him. He met Bern at the airport in Kasane this afternoon. Unfortunately, he let slip that he was having dinner with you at the Old House. Mike mentioned it to me on the drive here. I'm sorry.'

Bella glanced around nervously.

Bern stood to stare at her.

'Shit, may I go now,' Bella pleaded with Karyn.

'Maybe a bit late to do that. Don't worry, Mike and I are here. If you feel uncomfortable, we'll say we have to leave.'

Standing beside the table, Bella tried to untangle her hair, with fingers that wouldn't stop shaking.

'You look stunning,' Bern said with a wry smile across his face.

'Liar, I came straight from gardening.' Bella collapsed into the seat he pulled out for her. 'Why are you here? You're supposed to be in Maun. Is Lan with you?'

'No, Lan isn't here. I missed your gorgeous smile and your deep-blue eyes. After Mike mentioned the three of you going out for dinner, I thought I'd tag along. I hate odd numbers, particularly if a beautiful lady is involved. I jumped at the chance to be your date, to equal out the numbers.'

Bella frowned. 'I didn't ask you for a date, thank you. Why don't you wander over to the bar where those two females are making eyes at you?'

'Too late, I ordered a bottle of the sparkling brut; I'm in the mood to celebrate.' He signalled to the waiter to bring the bottle, an ice bucket, and four champagne flutes.

When Bern finished filling the glasses, he proposed a toast. 'To good friends, happy memories, and of course my gorgeous, grubby Bella.' He winked at her.

Bella refused to try and clean herself up. She glanced at her hand holding the wine glass, noticing the grime under her fingernails. *God, why did I leave home without having a shower*, she scolded herself. Bella gulped down the first few mouthfuls of the sparkling brut.

Now, the alcohol had hit her throat, she wished she had taken a break from gardening to eat lunch. She found having Bern in such close proximity made her tremble. His quizzical stare with those wonderful eyes unravelled her. She glanced up at him over the rim of her glass, and his wink made Bella's heart cascade into a million pieces. She wriggled in the chair, turning away from him, letting her gaze fall on the moonlight shining through the trees to the surface of the river.

Dinner passed in a blur. Bern was the attentive and caring date Bella hadn't expected, and true to form, she drank one glass of wine too many. She then switched over to water halfway through the main course. At one stage, Karyn and Bella excused themselves to go to the toilet.

'You're more fidgety than a fish out of water. Bern didn't seem like he was pining for Lan. Perhaps their relationship is what Bern says. I think he has genuine feelings for you. His eyes never leave your face.'

'He scares me more than anything. My husband kept telling me he loved me, and that turned out to be a lie. Everyone I ever loved has either died, divorced me, or disowned me. I was a mess before leaving Australia, and I don't carry enough strength to go to that foggy corner again. Bern's girlfriend is a bit possessive, if I'm not mistaken. I don't think she's ready to share him. He could be toying with me because I'm not falling under his spell,' Bella confided.

'I think you have him all wrong,' Karyn remarked. 'I don't have the time to debate it with you now. We better go before they send a search party to look for us.'

They wandered into the dining area.

Bern ordered coffee for himself, Karyn and Mike, and a Rooibos for Bella.

After they finished the drinks, Karyn and Mike stood to leave.

Bella struggled to her feet, crashing the chair to the floor.

Bern jumped up to set the chair upright. 'Please stay.'

'You'll be fine, love,' Karyn whispered.

After they left, Bern's charisma covered her, tightening her breath and sending a shiver to chase across her lonely heart. He stood so close, Bella's shadow blended over him. Minutes ceased to exist as her world tilted ever so slightly off-centre. She held out a hand to shake Bern's. 'Thank you for dinner, I better be going home to feed the cat.'

'Not so fast, you're in no state to drive. What sort of gentleman do you think I am, if I allowed you to go home by yourself? Let me drive you.' He wrapped his arm around her, ushering her out of the dining area.

Bella told him the address. She then closed her eyes as she listened to Bern's rich melodic voice flow through the vehicle, softer than a kitten's paw. The heat of their bodies radiated in the tight confines, drawing them closer. Bella was caught up in a spell that wove a magic path into her heart.

He pulled into the drive switching off the engine, breaking the spell.

Bella shook the sensations aside. 'Thank you for the ride, I'll phone for a taxi to take you to the Old House.'

'If it's all right with you, I want to check how Dingo is. It's the vet in me coming out. I'll take a professional look at him, if you don't mind.'

'You never showed any interest in him before. Let me get some food. The enclosure is over there, I'll be a minute.' Bella went into the kitchen, breathing deeply. Why did he insist on staying? She took a piece of chicken from the fridge and went out into the night.

Bern had opened the gate to let himself in. He sat on the ground nursing Dingo.

'Traitor,' Bella admonished as she emptied the food into his bowl.

'You've done a remarkable job with him, Bella. He has adapted well, considering such turmoil to his young life.'

'Yes, I think he likes it here as much as I do.'

Dingo jumped from Bern's lap to wander over to his meal.

That was their cue to leave.

Bern stood close enough for her to catch a hint of his aftershave. It carried a whisper of blood oranges and patchouli. He bent to kiss Bella, and at first, she tried to resist. His expertise at getting females lost in his spell, however, took away all her inhibitions. Her arms reached up to him, drawing him even closer to her body.

Bern then picked Bella up to carry her into the bedroom, where a cobalt-blue light of late evening trailed its way across the bed.

He took his time undressing her, his touch electrifying. Bella was impatient to have him lying naked beside her. Her hands danced all over him as she trailed her fingers over his rippling muscles and bare skin. The bed sighed when they tumbled into the soft doona; it was as though they had come home.

Bern was the consummate lover, and Bella never imagined being anywhere else but in his arms. The heat of their bodies soon thawed the chill coming off the river. Bella quivered when Bern let out a soft groan, easing his body from hers. He enfolded Bella in his warm embrace, his hands laced through her tousled hair.

'Did you say you loved me a moment ago?' A triumphant smile spread across his face.

'I doubt it.'

'I know what you said, liefie, and I'm holding onto this

information until you admit it to me again. I've all the patience in the world when it comes to you.'

Bella wriggled out of his embrace. In the bathroom, she splashed her face with cold water. Bern's presence overpowered her; he filled every secret corner of her. She longed to be with him, yet those persistent reservations about his sincerity bristled through her. It would be so easy to fall in love with him, however, Lan kept buzzing in Bella's head. She was dangerous, and they seemed to be in a relationship of sorts.

Bern followed Bella into the bathroom; his lips teased her neck. 'You take my breath away, with your glorious hair and captivating eyes.'

She coloured at his words. No one, not even her ex-husband, ever showered compliments over her.

'Love yourself, Bella. You're an incredible woman. Please find it in your heart to let go of your past. Believe what I'm saying to you. Be the person I already know you are.'

'That is easier said than done … my past trails inside me every day. It never allows me to be happy.'

Bern dragged on his clothes. 'Dress in something warm,' he advised, kissing Bella on the lips.

She reached for an old favourite tracksuit.

They stopped at the fridge for a couple of beers, before going out onto the verandah. Fireflies glowed in the trees across the river as though someone had strung up party lights.

'Your house here is stunning, although it requires a man – like me – to make it a home. You are the love of my life, Bella, and I never want to be anywhere other than right here beside you.

You may not believe me, but it's the truth. I'll keep telling you I love you until you believe me, then every day for the rest of my life. I know things were difficult for you in Australia. Whatever happened to you there, makes you the person you are today.'

Bella fussed over a frayed edge on her tracksuit. 'You say those words so easily. I'm nothing special, just someone trying to begin my life again after a broken marriage.'

'All of the suffering you endured has turned you into a caring, sensitive, funny person. If you could see yourself as everyone you meet does. Take Karyn and Mike, you met them a couple of days ago, and the three of you are already firm friends. Trust me, people never seek your company because they pity you. They do this because they care. You hold a rare gift; one I'll treasure forever. I'm always going to be grateful you chose to be with me.' Bern beamed at her.

Bella nibbled on her lower lip. 'I don't remember saying I chose you; but thank you for your kind words. There's a caring side to you under all that arrogance.' Bella tore her eyes away from Bern; she couldn't tell whether he was being sincere or flippant. She gazed across the river at the twinkling lights of a lodge in the Caprivi Strip, a long finger of land in the north-eastern part of Namibia. She jumped when Bern touched her arm. It was like a bolt of electricity through her body. She desperately wanted to believe him.

Bern kissed her cheek. 'I've told Mama and Papa all about you. They're dying to meet you. Perhaps we could fly down to Cape Town to visit with them.'

She shook her head. 'You're moving too fast. My divorce still wrinkles. I don't know if I'm ready yet.'

Bern took her in his arms. 'I'll give you all the time you need.'

They finished off the beers; neither had the urge to break the enchantment creasing over them.

They fell asleep during those translucent hours before dawn.

Bella only stirred when a cool fog whipped off the river. The sun, being tardy, stayed behind a bank of clouds sweeping low in the eastern sky.

Her movement woke Bern. He stretched lazily, shivering in the cool air. 'Keep me warm woman,' he pleaded, snuggling close.

'Come inside, let me make you a cup of coffee.' Bella offered out her hand and took him into the kitchen. Her mind was clicking faster than a woodpecker looking for insects. Bradley never had this softer, caring side that Bern seemed to have. Bradley had only been interested in showing her off to his rich circle of friends. She had always been hesitant around men. Bradley had been the first man she had let into the metaphorical box she always retreated into when life overwhelmed her – and look how that turned out. She wanted to trust in Bern's sincerity, but she needed to shake Bradley from her life first.

CHAPTER 47

While they were having breakfast on the verandah, watching the changing colours of the river, Bern suggested a game-drive into Chobe National Park.

'Great, my own personal guide. Thank you, Bern, I've been wanting to go there ever since I arrived here.'

'I phoned a mate who lives here, and he's coming by with a proper 4WD for us to use. You can't expect your pretend SUV to make it over the rough tracks.'

Bella's eyes went wide. 'Please, you're insulting Raven, if she can handle the Choppies' carpark, she'll skim through driving around Chobe.'

'My God, you named the bloody vehicle.' Bern chuckled.

She ignored his retort while they waited for the 'proper 4WD'.

Twenty minutes later, the vehicle arrived.

Bella packed a picnic lunch, putting it in the vehicle, along with a chilled bottle of chardonnay and a few beers.

Bern drove to the impressive Sedudu Entrance Gates, where he went in to pay the park fees. He chatted with the game-warden about possible lion sightings. The warden told him another guide found a mating pair of lions not far inland from Serondela Picnic Ground.

The Chobe River looked spectacular, a ribbon of blue against a backdrop of ochre-coloured sand, with spreading acacia trees and baobabs dotted about. Elephants wandered down to the river to beat the heat of the late morning. Giraffes dotted beside the river. Hippos grunted and argued in the shallow water. A few of them waddled out to plop on the hot sand. The sun turned their hides a peppery red colour.

Bern drove inland from the river. He told Bella to keep an eye out for the lions. 'I better start teaching you how to spot animals, if you're to be of any use to me. First of all, clear your mind of clutter. Next, don't make the mistake of looking at your surroundings, see through the landscape, not *at* it. Always separate the animals from the bush, and don't look at it as a whole picture. Trees, bushes and grass only sway with the wind. If there is a movement not following the flow of the wind, it should be investigated. Also, lions and other predators are flat-out during the hottest parts of the day, making them difficult to spot. So be watchful for a tail flick or a paw in the air swatting a fly.'

'Well, maybe these are the two lions you're looking for, underneath the camelthorn tree?' Bella smiled, pointing to the left of the vehicle.

'See, you're a natural. It's because you're being taught by the best guide in Botswana. You're a fast learner and have a good eye, Bella.' Bern pulled to a stop.

The two lions sheltered in the shade, obviously trying to stay out of sight and out of the hot sun. They also looked annoyed someone had intruded into their romantic rendezvous.

Bern, always the experienced guide, commenced explaining more about lions. The mating habits, family structures, the role of the male, the having and tending of the cubs and everything in between. 'Lions are lazy cats. They spend hours a day catching dreams and the occasional fly humming too close. If you're lucky enough to come across a mating pair, you're almost guaranteed they'll remain in the same area for several days.' Bern's deep voice caressed over Bella.

The male stood, turning his head towards them. He glared deep into Bella's soul. His amber eyes stared quizzically at her, seemingly sensing her gentle nature. Although a few battle scars traced across his face, he clearly hadn't touched many seasons on his coat. His mane, thick and luxuriant, cascaded over his head. His partner appeared older. She obviously remembered the rigours of mating and appeared a little bored with the whole procedure.

Bella would never tire of watching lions, and they watched these two all alone, without the interruption of any other vehicles. She thanked Bern for his patience in letting her watch the lions for as long as she wanted.

'It's my absolute pleasure to bring you here. Please don't thank me. Your smile and your eyes misting with tears is all I need. I'm confident we're going to spend a million other days exactly like this one.'

Bella almost believed his words when she looked into his eyes, trying to find some cynicism there.

He reversed away from the lions and bypassed the Serondela Picnic Ground, saying too many annoying monkeys harassed people there. He then drove towards Kabulabula and through the dry sandy riverbed across to the island.

Bella set out the picnic food on the bonnet while Bern opened the wine. He said that now was the perfect time to be out in the park. Most of the best areas to stop were crowded at morning tea. All of the daytrips out of lodges had to be in town by lunchtime. The larger companies that camped out for a few days, went to their sites for lunch and quiet time, to wait for the afternoon game-drive.

Except for a lone jackal keeping to the shade under a bush, they had the whole park to themselves on such a steamy afternoon. Bern then told Bella in detail about his recent trip to the Kalahari.

'I'm so sorry, Bern, how awful for you. I'm thankful you're all right, but now I'll worry about you each time you go on a safari.'

Bern gave her a perplexed look, and Bella feared she may have said too much. 'All the guides are on alert now, and please don't do anything to endanger your life, I couldn't live in a world without you in it.'

Bella shook her head to free it from notions of falling in love with Bern. He was too enmeshed with Lan at the moment, and things were happening way too fast for her.

Bern wrapped his arms around Bella. 'I've never enjoyed a game-drive as much as this one, unless you count the one we did in Moremi Game Reserve.'

His ardent kisses took her by surprise, and if a small troop of baboons waited another minute to scramble past, she might have surrendered to the moment of passion. 'Please, Bern, I fell for your charms ages ago. You're living with Lan, and I imagine your house exploding with Lan and me sharing you. I've experienced her darker side over the last week or so. I don't think she's the sharing kind, if her right hook is anything to go by.'

'Trust me, Bella, you're the love of my life; the only one I dream of being with.'

Bella shook her head. 'Sorry, Bern. I think it's too soon for comments like this. My divorce is still raw, and I'm not ready to fall under your spell.'

They packed up the remains of their lunch, stowing it in the back seat before climbing into the front. Their kisses sizzled in the tight confines of the vehicle. Bella pulled herself away, straightening her shirt and fizzing with desire. Bern groaned under his breath, clearly reluctant to start the vehicle to drive out of the park.

For Bella, the day turned out to be more perfect than any other day in her entire life. She would never forget the magic weaving through her, drawing Bern closer to her.

When Bern stopped at the Chobe Safari Lodge, he took Bella's hand to help her out of the vehicle. Inside the lodge, a cooling breeze from the river chased away the heat of the sun. They stopped at the curio shop where Bern bought Bella a solid gold bangle with lions etched into the smooth surface.

'Now, you'll always have lions close to you. To protect you.' He kissed her as he slid the bangle onto her bare arm.

The touch sent shivers through her.

They wandered into the open bar area, searching for a vacant table, soon spotting one on the edge of the deck where the views overlooking the water dazzled them in the afternoon slush of heat. Several boats ferried tourists along the slow-moving flow of the tide.

The waiter appeared to take their orders.

While they waited, Bern leant across the table to kiss Bella on the lips. 'Thank you for the third-best day of my life. The first was the day I found you with that damn cat, the second was the day I spent with you in Moremi. The third day is most definitely today.'

'You're welcome.' Bella's fingers caressed the bangle, letting the heat of it curl into her soul. 'I agree with you; they were special days for me also, except for the first day I saw you. I thought you were the most arrogant, overbearing man I'd ever met. Thank you for the other two days, though.'

'At last, my sweet Bella, you realise I'm not such a bad person. I'm making a bit of progress with you.'

They were on their second round of drinks when Bella saw Steven ambling in.

Steven paused awkwardly, talking on his mobile, a scowl etched on his face.

Bern waved to him, and Steven ambled over.

'Howzit, man?' Bern greeted him. 'You look like a honey badger cornered by a lion. What's up, can I help in any way?'

'Dumela, Bern, Bella, I didn't know you two were so cosy. Seagal never mentioned that you two had ever met each other.' His voice was edged with sarcasm.

The waiter came over to ask if Steven wanted a drink. He ordered a scotch on the rocks.

'So, you're onto the heavy stuff, you must be in trouble. I've never seen you drink anything stronger than beer,' Bern joked.

Steven took a big gulp of his scotch. 'It's been a rough couple of days, but I'm starting to find the light at the end of the tunnel. So, tell me about this?' He said, pointing to Bern's hand on Bella's. 'I spoke to Seagal yesterday, and he told me you came up here to do a safari. Is it a private safari with the two of you, or is it something I should mention to Lan?' There was sourness in his voice.

Bern sighed. 'Lan's being shitty at the moment. I'm on

eggshells all the time trying to navigate her moods. The only way I stay sane is getting away from her for a bit. She's been spooked ever since the Chobe safari. Bella and I met on her first day in Botswana, and she told me about her love for lions. Seagal told me Bella moved here a few days ago, so with some free time, I came up here to take her into the park to look for lions.'

'And did you find any?' Steven asked.

'Ja, we saw a mating pair.' Bern's eyes lit up.

'Great, eh.' When his drink arrived, Steven reached for the glass with shaky fingers.

Bella got a premonition something bad festered close to the surface as she watched Steven. She shivered a little, despite the fact the temperature in the bar area nudged thirty. Maybe it was nothing, and she was imagining shadows that weren't there.

'So, man, don't mention this to Lan?' Bern asked.

Bella felt annoyed that Bern was so dismissive of Lan. If he cared so little for her, why didn't he kick her out of his home? He could still keep an eye on her if he thought she was involved in the poaching.

'Of course not. You can buy me another drink to seal the deal, if you like, eh.' Steven smiled, but Bella noticed his eyes flicker with something nefarious.

'Bella, do you want another glass of wine?' Bern raised his hand to get the waiter's attention.

'No, thank you, I'm fine.' Her breath caught in her throat. What was she getting into by confusing Bern's life? She had to get away from Bern and Steven.

'Everything okay?' Bern whispered to her after the waiter left.

'Yes, of course. But I might go now, to let you and Steven catch up. I have to go home to feed the cat anyway. Thanks again for

the game-drive, perhaps I'll see you again someday. Bye, Steven.'
Bella flew out of the lodge in her haste to get away from them. The
unease she felt still lingered.

Dingo

I saw her coming towards me. Her soul was troubled, so I ran to her, to rub my warm body against the chill that had settled in her. My eyes bored into her. I detected danger crowding near. A darkness fluttered beside her. My paw touched her arm, in an attempt to warn her to take care. She seemed to startle when my claw touched the softness of her palm. She sat with me until her breathing returned to normal.

CHAPTER 48

Bella let the warmth of Dingo soothe her nerves. She went inside, hoping the familiarity of her home would chase these doubts from her mind. She poured herself a large glass of brandy before heading to take it out onto the verandah.

The front door suddenly banged open.

Bella screamed and dropped her glass.

Bern flew into the room. 'For God's sake, what's the matter with you, liefie? You're quivering.' He enfolded Bella in his arms.

She rested her head on his shoulder.

'You're safe now, nothing's going to hurt you while I'm here. Please tell me what happened. Did Steven say anything inappropriate to you, because if he did, I'm in the right frame of mind to punch his fucking face in?'

'No, of course not. Steven holds a resentment; I've never felt before. I fear his mind is troubled. Something bad is about to happen, I simply know it. You and Seagal consider him as your friend, and I've tried to like him. But I'm convinced there's more to Steven than he lets on. Even Dingo is warning me of a danger to come,' she blurted out.

Bern held her tighter. 'I'm sure it's nothing. Steven's one of the good guys; it's probably all the excitement of the drive putting you on edge.'

Bella looked up at him. 'Maybe, but I'm watching him like a hawk from now on.' She detangled herself from his arms. 'Also, you seemed so dismissive of Lan. Why don't you ask her to leave, if she means nothing to you.' She stood her ground.

Bern's eyes darkened. 'That, my sweet Bella, is complicated … for the moment. I still believe she's involved somehow in the poaching, but Steven, Seagal and I have to find out who she's dealing with in Botswana. Please trust me, for a bit longer.'

'I'm not sure I can do that.' Bella needed another drink. 'I'm so confused.' She shook her head.

Bern lightly cradled her chin. 'Never doubt my feelings for you.' His eyes implored her.

He then bent down to clean up the mess from Bella's broken glass. He poured her another brandy as he led her out to the verandah.

They lay close together, and over time, Bella felt the reassuring heat of his body enveloping her. She rested her head on Bern's chest; the beat of his heart helped soothe away the shadows from her troubled mind. Bern's arm was protectively around Bella, his fingers knotting through her hair. When Bella's breathing slowed to a more even rhythm, she sat up, tucking her legs under her, to reach for her drink.

'Better now, my sweet? Please, you have nothing to worry about with Lan,' he whispered in Bella's ear.

Bella smiled. 'Yes, you do possess a charismatic side sitting in harmony next to your arrogance. Thank you, Mr de Villiers, I'm calmer now.'

'My pleasure, liefie, any excuse to get close to you.'

The house was more tranquil with Bern occupying it. Bella knew she had to let go of her insecurities and memories of her ex-husband. When she was with Bern, she felt safe, and that had never happened to her ever before. She tried to get Steven out of her mind; she hated the way he clouded her thoughts. She told herself to forget all about Steven, her ex-husband and Lan.

Bern stayed another night with Bella, in her bed and now in her heart.

Bern took a long time to say goodbye the following morning. His flight to Maun left in an hour. Bella saw his reluctance about leaving burning in his eyes. He obviously didn't want her to dwell on any negative attitudes towards Steven or Lan.

'I love you, Bella, please stay safe … and remember, call me if you're worried or want to talk to me.'

The beep from his taxi broke into their quiet moment together.

'Bye, Bern, take care and safe travels.'

Bern gave her one final kiss and then hopped in the taxi.

After she waved him off, Bella went inside, the air, which Bern no longer occupied, pulsed dull and heavy again. Bella picked up her phone to text Karyn, hoping they could meet for lunch.

The phone beeped a few seconds later.

Sure, meet you at the Safari Lodge at twelve. You have a lot of explaining to do. I hear Bern never slept at the Old House. Wonder where he spent his time?

Bella ignored her inquisitiveness and replied: *See you at twelve.*

Karyn sat smiling from a table by the edge of the deck where two full glasses of wine sat on the table.

'Cheers,' she and Bella said, clinking glasses.

Karyn then leant in closer. 'Now give. I want to hear all the details, and I do mean, all the details. What are you doing with the drop-dead gorgeous Bern, and what's he like without his clothes on? I can always dream about his tanned, taut, muscled body next to mine. Mind you, I'm not complaining about Mike. I love him to bits, but my God a girl can dream, can't she?' She laughed.

'I've no idea what you mean, Karyn.' Bella browsed the lunch menu. 'What are you having to eat? I might try the roast vegetable salad with feta.'

'Yeah, me too. Now details, please.' Karyn's eyes were wide and imploring.

They finished off the bottle of wine during lunch, while Bella gave as many details as she was willing.

'I think you may be right about him. He's a charming, caring guy, if you scrape away all the arrogance. It's such a shame Lan's always in the background. It's getting harder for me not to surrender to him, though this is all I dream of doing. Lan's scary ... and getting her jealous again may stir up more trouble,' Bella admitted, retreating back to her insecurities.

Karyn grinned. 'I guessed you two were perfect for each other. The other night at dinner, I saw how nuts he is about you. Forget Lan; now Bern's shown you how much he cares about you, he'll dump her. With Lan out of the picture, you, my friend, can bask in the love Bern showers over you.'

Bella wasn't quite as sure. 'I wish I shared your optimism. I have a tight knot of dread that bad things are about to happen, and I don't want anyone I care about getting hurt.'

'Nothing's about to happen, Bella. Be happy and embrace the fact you found love and harmony again, in such an amazing country.'

Bella smiled brightly. 'You may be right … now I'd better let you return to work. I'm going to visit Steven, to see if I can't shake off this feeling of dread when I look at him. I'll give you a call later. Say hello to Mike for me.'

Bella arrived at Steven's office a bit before three-thirty. He sat at his oversized desk talking on the phone and motioned for her to wait outside.

Once he was off his call, he beckoned her into his office. 'Sorry about that, Bella, please come in. It's much cooler. Did you enjoy your game-drive yesterday?' Steven's words were full of sarcasm.

'Yes, I did, I'll never forget the amazing lion sighting.'

'Great, do you reckon you might be able to locate them again?'

'I'm not sure … I guess. We saw a mating pair, and Bern says they usually stay in the same area. They were close to the Serondela Picnic Ground. Why are you asking?' Bella felt prickles up her spine.

'I'd love to see them. I never get the chance to go sightseeing. I know I own the safari company P.A.W. Safaris, but I leave it up to my manager and safari guides to run things. I'm tied to my office chair and don't venture far. It's hard to believe that in the almost three years I've lived here, I've visited the Chobe National Park only once. Coming from the urban jungle of Gaborone, it became my duty to familiarise myself with the park. That seems a lifetime ago now, so I should return there.'

Each word Steven spoke fell out of his mouth to pool inside

Bella. She feigned an interest in what he said. 'All right, I can drive you there. How about we go tomorrow?' She hesitated for a moment, hoping Steven didn't catch the tremor in her voice. Steven frightened her, and she wished Bern lived somewhere close enough for him to protect her. Bella began to question Steven's motives for asking her to take him into Chobe. She stalled for time, trying to get rid of the tight wrinkle of terror that had coiled in her stomach. 'Why don't you get one of your guides to take you? They're more experienced with locating lions.'

'They're all busy at the moment, and I want to go now.' He jostled Bella out of the office, his hand a hot poker to her back.

'What's the hurry, the lions will be there tomorrow, and it's getting late. I'm not confident about finding them again.'

'You'll be fine, now get moving.' His voice sounded threatening, nesting in the air like the twisted branches of a baobab. He then gripped Bella's arm, ushering her to the vehicle, his fingers bruising the soft flesh above her elbow.

Her body flinched, waiting for a punch she thought Steven was about to inflict on her. And then she climbed into the driver's seat.

Steven had picked up a small heavy bag, which he threw into the rear seat. There was a clanging noise as it settled on the seat then silence. He climbed into the front, slamming the door with so much force the vehicle shuddered.

Bella panicking took a while for her shaky fingers to start the engine.

She drove towards the entrance gates to the park.

'Stay here and don't do anything stupid.' Steven climbed out of the vehicle to go inside to pay the park fees.

Bella knew she had to get the hell away from him now, but fright had paralysed her. So, she tried to hold onto the fact both Bern and Seagal held Steven in high regard. Perhaps she had been imagining Steven's callous side. She wanted to phone Bern regarding her trepidations, and also to hear his calming voice. She reached into her bag to search for the mobile. Shit, she forgot to charge the battery in her rush to meet Karyn for lunch.

Finally, Steven strode back to the vehicle, his face a stony mask. He told Bella the park gates closed at six and the time now nudged four o'clock.

All the sandy paths looked the same to her, and what signage that used to be there was almost illegible or broken off by elephants. She remembered Bern telling her about the one-way road from the entrance gates down to the river. She hoped she was on the right track, and not the loop track that returned to the gate.

Steven's edginess spilled over; his sighs spiralled in the confines of her vehicle.

Bella then remembered the warning Mike told her about not taking her vehicle off-road. She lurched from one pothole to another, berating the elephants and warthogs who spent their days destroying the tracks. Sand clutched at the wheels holding them firm. Bella pressed hard on the accelerator, swerving at an awkward angle in an attempt to regain control of the vehicle.

Steven swore loud enough to entangle the vultures from their perch each time Bella became stuck. It set her nerves on edge. She made it, though, without too much trouble, down to the river. The friction between them had started to coat the windscreen. Steven's eyes tore through Bella, and his hatred floated over the hippos. The ground firmed up a bit closer to the water, so she followed the river's gentle flow for a few kilometres.

Bella stopped the vehicle to let a herd of well over twenty elephants make their way to the river.

'Drive through them. I'm in a hurry.' Steven's voice was low and menacing.

'No, I better let them pass. There are a lot of females with babies, and I don't want an outraged elephant charging at my car. We should wait till they get nearer to the water. I think we're close to where I have to turn inland.' Bella's voice wavered with her nervousness.

The sun dipped low in the sky. The shadows along the ground scratched east. It took Bella longer to pinpoint the exact turning point Bern used, to drive up the steep bank where the lions sheltered.

Steven spat at her, 'You think you're so much better than the rest of us, fucking rich bitch. With your looks and money, you worm your way in here and take whatever you fancy. To hell with the rest of us.'

Bella gasped with shock. 'What do you mean? What did I take from you?' Her foot slipped off the accelerator, and she swerved in the wrong direction before regaining control of her vehicle.

'Lan's in love with Bern, and do you care? You waltz in here, batting your long eyelashes, expecting men to fall all over you. You better not come between them. They were happy with their life until you showed up.' Steven snorted. 'Messing with those two is not a good idea, believe me. Leave them alone. Lan can be dangerous, even more so where Bern is concerned.'

'You don't have to keep reminding me about Lan's temper; I tasted her violent side first-hand,' Bella countered.

Steven started getting twitchy; his hands were shaking uncontrollably. 'Get out of the fucking car.'

'No! Why are you doing this to me?' she demanded, her heart battering in her chest.

'I'm up to my neck with these fucking poachers. They're giving me nothing but trouble. The head man in Vietnam is threatening to use my blood to paint his office. If I don't give him lion bones in the next day or so, it's over for me and Lan. So … princess, rest assured I'm doing everything in my power to prevent that from happening. I had to think of a good reason for Bern to come here to search for the bloody lions.' Steven was rambling; he didn't make sense.

'Why Bern?' Bella tried to calm her trembling voice. 'Don't you have guides that work for you?'

He glowered. 'Fucking bastards. One's in hospital with appendicitis. Not expected home for a bloody week. The other prick took his family on vacation to Kruger. I have to act NOW, there isn't time to waste. My life depends on getting lion bones to Vietnam pronto. So you and Bern are my last hope. I can't think straight. I haven't slept for days. This has to work … Shit … Fuck!' Steven wiped his brow with a white handkerchief. His hands were shaking.

'Steven, you're a mess. Surely this guy in Vietnam understands tha—'

'Shut up! Shut up! I have to do this before he kil … fuck,' Steven shrilled.

Bella had had enough. 'This is crazy. It won't work,' she warned.

'Shut up! Let me think. I want you wandering about in the bush. Bern's sure to come up here and save you. He has to. Shit. You're smart … you should be able to survive the night. The predators won't be looking for a skinny human. You could hide at that picnic ground. Fuck, I don't care. With any luck, all you'll get is a couple of scratches.' The last sentence was more of a whisper.

'But why?' Bella felt her face pale. 'You're scaring me.'

'I want Bern here, and I needed a reason. Bern wouldn't fucking come here for nothing. I can't do this on my own … Like I said, I've only been in Chobe once before. How could I find a bloody lion? The park gives me the creeps ….'

'What if Bern doesn't come to Chobe?' Bella challenged.

'Trust me, princess. He will. When we find you tomorrow, all Bern has to do is take me to the lions. I'll handle the rest. Now get out of the fucking car.' He reached into the back seat to get his bag. Inside a Glock pistol glinted in the late afternoon sunshine.

'Steven, what are you doing? Calm down and think this through. This will never work. It's too ridiculous. Please, Steven, let's go back.' Bella's words echoed off the river.

He pointed the gun at her. 'Get out of the fucking car, bitch.'

The terrifying words sliced through Bella. He then punched her across the face and shoved the gun against her ribs. He leant across her to open her door; his fingers fumbling with the door handle. When the door was open, he pushed Bella out of the vehicle.

She landed in a heap on the ground, and a sharp ache pierced into her shoulder. She tried to get up.

Steven jumped out of the vehicle in less time than it took for a moth to sneeze. He ran to where she lay.

Bella held up her hands to shield herself, but he kicked her in the ribs. The force took the breath from her, allowing him the freedom to kick her repeatedly. His boot kept pummelling into her sides.

Steven then bent over her, breathing hard from the exertion. 'Sorry … shit … sorry,' He straightened up and went back to the vehicle, glancing at Bella before jumping into the driver's seat.

'Please, Steven, help me,' Bella pleaded. His insults crashed over her as she tried to claw her way out of this hellish dream.

The tyres twisted and squealed in the soft sand.

All Bella saw from the cold angle of the ground where she lay gasping for fresh air were the taillights of her vehicle being driven in the opposite direction, from where the red ball of the sun sizzled towards the horizon. She watched in horror as the vehicle was swallowed by the dust and sand. It disappeared into the grit, settling over the trees. Then a deathly hush coated the land.

Bella lay broken in the sand for about ten minutes, staring at the elephants silhouetted against the setting sun. A searing pain coursed through her shoulder, and it felt like some of her ribs were cracked, because breathing in sent a knife to pierce her chest. Bella tasted blood from the cut on her lip. Another bruise chased a stain across her face. The night began confusing the clear blue of the sky. The sun streaked crimson and golden lights on the surface of the river. Bella intended to move, but for the moment, she let the terror consume her.

Bella felt her world had coalesced into a labyrinth. She understood the dangers if she stayed out in the open on the flood plains beside the river. The forest or the picnic grounds were her only options, but they remained an agonising climb up a steep bank away from her. The elephants loomed large, their shadows disappearing into the twilight. Bella listened to the rumble of their tummies and smelt the sweet earthy tang of their urine. Bern had explained to her about elephants, mentioning their poor eyesight. She clutched onto this fact; also she was downwind from them. Nevertheless, they sent a tremor to her heart.

She didn't want to stand up and spook them for fear they may charge, so she crawled away from them, pain thrumming through her. She inched up the steep bank, clutching onto tufts of grass to stop herself from sliding backwards. Her thoughts were erratic. She wondered where the hell it would be safe, alone, out in the park with all the predators starting to stir.

Bella's logic frayed with the dwindling light, to hover out of reach. Her mind was stung with a million wasps. She counted on the fact that if she reached the Serondela Picnic area that Bern drove through on their way to lunch, she might be able to hide in the toilet blocks there. Bella worked out her plan, at least for the moment. She tunnelled all of her concentration into getting to the toilets.

Night fell too fast for Bella. She wanted to hold onto the last rays of the dusk. Bella's eyes tried to pierce through the blackness. All she saw were ghostly shapes in varying shades of charcoal.

The sand sucked the breath from her; thorns snatched at her hands and legs. Bella knew she had to keep moving. She found small achievements with each step, although she sensed the picnic area to be a frighteningly long way from her. If only everything didn't look blacker than the inside of a hornbill's yawn, she might be able to see something familiar in the landscape. An unusual tree shape or maybe a termite mound would help her get some bearings. Bella tried to recollect all that Bern told her yesterday. *Immerse yourself in the surroundings, look beyond what you see, and open your ears to the sounds of life.*

She tried to take in a deep breath until a wave of dizziness caused her to stumble. She cursed Bern for telling her what all the sounds were – they terrified her now, so much so that she couldn't think properly. A rustle through the bushes startled her, it might be impalas trotting close, or the wind teasing the leaves now the sun dipped lower. She listened to the elephants; soft footfalls crinkling over leaves. Hyenas whooped, an eerie noise floating through the night. She knew they lingered a long way from her because their muffled sound wasn't much stronger than a cat's mewing.

Bella stood shaking from fright, more fragile than an old lady. The elephants had retreated into the forest. She fumbled her hands out in front of her and shuffled along, her fingers scratching the bark off trees. She let ants crawl along her arms until their bites pricked her.

She turned west, wishing the picnic ground lay in that direction, and waited for the moonbeams to glitter on the treetops. She kept stopping to regain her breath; a fire wrinkled through her.

Her eyes soon adjusted to the opaque gloom. Instead of it being a blessing, it meant Bella saw things becoming way too frightening. Two honey badgers left their burrow for a night of feeding and fun. They reminded her of judges rushing to the courthouse. She waited until they wove a path out of sight before moving on.

She staggered along, tripping over tree roots and furrows in the ground. She found a small herd of impala, tiptoeing in the sand, feeding on the short grasses tufting out of the ground. She stayed close to them, thinking they would alert her to any danger. All of a sudden, their nostrils flared, their flanks quivered, and in a millisecond they darted away from her, kicking and snorting a warning to anyone within earshot.

Bella crouched low behind a tree. When she peeked out, she saw the reason for their flight. A leopard stood ten metres from her, and in the murky shadows of night, she could tell the leopard hadn't experienced a lot in her young life. This little one showed no fear as she wandered alone through the bush. Bella stood as still as the night air, hoping the leopard kept her interest in the impalas, not her. After a minute or two, the leopard turned from Bella to follow them.

Bella glanced up at the stars; the Milky Way bright and dazzling in the sky failed to reach her all alone and scared. Her watch gave up telling her how much time had elapsed, its little luminescent dots wilted into the inky night. Thorns tugged at her dress and snagged down her legs in painful scratches. Bella's fingers laced around the gold bangle Bern had given her. She needed to gather strength from Bern's words. And she knew she had to find somewhere to shelter; she became too exposed staying out in the open. Time ceased to exist for her, seconds scraped into minutes and minutes dragged into hours.

Bella then saw – or thought she saw – Dingo's eyes searching for her. He seemed to be floating above the treetops willing her to follow him. Bella kept Dingo in her sight. She drew strength from him, even though pain seeped into her soul. Finally, she staggered into the picnic area.

The noise of lions roaring cascaded into her. They sounded close enough for her to reach out and touch them, although she saw nothing when clouds scudded across the sky, blocking out the pale moon. Bella guessed them to be the mating pair they saw yesterday. She let their roars reverberate through her, to calm the erratic beat of her heart. Their nearness flowed over her; deep down, Bella knew they meant her no harm.

She crept over to one of the toilet blocks, trying to push open the door, but the rangers had bolted them shut. Why did they have to lock the doors, she questioned before screaming silently into the night. She didn't imagine the baboons or monkeys having the wherewithal to be interested in using the facilities.

Bella crept towards the other toilet block. The first door she pushed on remained shut. Holding her breath and staring into the piercing eyes of Dingo, she pushed on the second door. The padlock lay broken on the ground, allowing the door to creak ajar with little effort. It swung with ease on its heavy hinges, allowing Bella to fall inside. She looked up to thank Dingo, but he had disappeared into the mist. Maybe she had imagined him.

The smell of excrement and urine assailed her. She eased into the stench, thankful to be in relative safety, and then she propped her aching back against the door, closing it to the night. Only then did she allow herself to cry, great heaving sobs that tormented her body.

What was the matter with Steven, she pondered. *And does Bern know what he's really up to.* Bella guessed at his indifference, although his ingrained violence shocked her. What possessed him to own a gun? At first, Bella imagined he would use it to intimidate her, until the vitriol of his speech. With hatred clouded over him, she figured he would be crazy enough to kill someone. Why then did Seagal and Bern always hold him in great esteem. She just couldn't get her head around this.

Bern was right – Lan was clearly there with the murderous attempt to kill lions. She and Steven had evidently been scheming together for some time and no one guessed what they were doing.

How did they all get it so wrong?

Bella was almost positive Steven intended to tell Bern about what he did to her. She hoped Bern didn't give in to Steven and that he stayed in Maun. She couldn't stand it if he endangered his life to come here to rescue her. She felt safe for the moment, and by tomorrow morning, tourists and guides should be flocking through the picnic area. They could rescue Bella and drive her to the hospital. Her main goal now became surviving the night. 'Please, Bern, stay in Maun, Bella pleaded into the wind.

Finally, she fell into a fitful sleep, full of nightmares from the bush.

CHAPTER 49

Bern was standing on his back deck; dusk had coated the Thamalakane River a dusty grey. Lan was in the kitchen, making a cup of coffee. His mind was on Bella. After their few nights together, he sensed a shift in her feelings for him.

His phone beeped, bringing him back to the present. Steven's name flashed on the tiny screen. 'Howzit, man?' Bern greeted him warmly.

'Shit … Sorry, Bern. I didn't know what to do. Fuck! This is all my fault,' he stuttered out.

'Slow down. Start at the beginning,' Bern said calmly.

'Bella and I went into the park this afternoon. Everything was going well until Bella jumped out to pee. I waited and waited. Fuck. Why didn't I go with her? Isn't she bush-wise? I'm not. How was I to know? Shit.'

'What do you mean? Where's Bella?' Bern blanched.

Steven's voice went up a few decibels. 'I don't know. I couldn't find her. Sorry, Bern, I searched for hours. I couldn't find her.'

Bern raked his hands through his hair. 'Shit, are you fucking crazy?' His blood boiled. 'Abandoning Bella out in the bush … she could get killed! Didn't you think about the consequences of your actions? Why didn't you tell the rangers?'

'I did. I'm so sorry. They said they'd look, but not until tom … Shit.' Steven whimpered, but Bern wasn't listening to him anymore.

'I'm on my way to Kasane. Christ, Steven.' Bern ended the call and shoved his phone in his pocket, his heart in his throat.

'What is it, honey?' Lan almost purred from their kitchen; for once she didn't sound like a buzz-saw. She tripped over to Bern.

'Fucking Steven lost Bella somewhere in Chobe.' Bern's voice, like storm clouds, gathered on the horizon.

'Your little piece of trash in trouble? No wild animal will find her appetising. Bit of luck all she gets is broken fingernail.' She sounded pleased with herself.

'How can you be so cold?' Bern yelled, gripping her by the shoulders.

'Let go, you're hurting me. It's not my fault. Steven lost her.' She tried to free herself from his grip.

Bern raced out of the house, slamming the door with such force the breeze fell silent.

'Not so fast, I'm coming with you. I'll help you look for her.' Lan ran after him, climbing into the vehicle.

Bern, too furious to care by now, slammed his foot hard on the accelerator, spinning the tyres on the loose gravel of his driveway.

Bern's mind, already in Chobe, clouded his thoughts. He kept swerving to avoid hitting cars, people and dogs as he tried to get to the airport. He screeched to a stop, centimetres from the glass entry doors, flinging Lan into the dashboard.

'Shit,' she yelled at him.

Bern stormed into the terminal; anxiety filling his soul.

Lan scrambled out, scurrying unsteadily behind in her flimsy sandals.

'Get me any available plane, pronto. I must get to Kasane ASAP,' he yelled at the poor guy standing in front of the Delta Air counter.

'Hey, Bern, why the hurry, there are no pilots available at such a late hour. All of the flights have shut down. I'm about to finish up. How about I book you on the first flight out tomorrow though?' The guy behind the counter said, evidently in his most cordial voice.

'Tomorrow's too late, I have to be there immediately. Rent me a plane; I can fly the damn thing up there myself?'

'You're full of surprises; I didn't know you were a pilot. Where did you learn to fly?'

'I learnt years ago in South Africa. Get me the bloody plane, whatever it costs.'

'Give me a few minutes to make a couple of phone calls.' He reached for his mobile, punching in some numbers.

Bern filled in the time by pacing the floor and glaring at Lan.

A torturous hour and a half ticked by before Bern secured his plane.

He strode out onto the tarmac and did all the necessary safety inspections. Bern checked the wing flaps and tyres before climbing into the cockpit to settle into the seat. Lan struggled up into the passenger seat of the small Cessna 152. Bern hadn't flown for a while, although he remained confident in his ability to remember the basics.

He adjusted the seatbelt and familiarised himself with the

instruments, so he could do his pre-flight checks. Taxiing out onto the tarmac, Bern reminisced about the last time he had sat in a cockpit ready to fly. It seemed years ago that he took a group of Americans to one of the posh lodges in the Sabie Sands Game Reserve in South Africa. Now he was in Botswana on a completely different mission. Bern spoke to the air traffic controller before whirring down the runway.

Once airborne, he banked a little to point the aircraft in a north-easterly direction. He reached his optimum cruising height of 3000 feet, levelling out the plane. The night breathed clear air; the sun having left hours ago. A bleakness descended over the land; it was as though one was soaring through the ocean at midnight. There didn't appear to be any major wind disturbances showing up on the radar screen, so he figured on a smooth flight through the heavens tonight. Bern estimated the flying time to be about 120 minutes.

It felt good to be flying again, he almost forgot how much he enjoyed it; he only wished for a better reason to take to the air. Bern's mind was too consumed with Bella out there, alone in the bush. He knew she carried a deep empathy and an uncanny gift for reading the mindset of the animals.

The seconds marched way too slow for Bern's racing mind. Neither of them spoke, Lan busy texting, and Bern too worried about Bella.

Ninety-five minutes later, he began his descent into Kasane International Airport. He was a little rusty with his landing. The small plane bucked in a slight crosswind when it lost altitude approaching the runway. It forced the aircraft to bounce heavily on the runway. Bern used his skill and strength to regain control. He slowed the plane down to a manageable speed. Bern veered sideways, straightening up a few metres from the end of the runway.

Breathing a sigh of relief, Bern taxied towards the airport terminal. He brought the plane to a stop and finished with his post-flight duties before he jumped down from the plane to race into the terminal. Lan struggled behind him. He didn't look at her or try to help. He had almost forgotten about her.

Steven was already at the airport, leaning against his vehicle with a worried look on his face.

Bern strode over to him, tightening his fist into a ball before smashing Steven on the nose.

Steven stumbled from the shock of being punched. 'You fucking broke my nose. I told you I'm sorry. It's not my fault Bella wandered off,' he slurred; blood spurted down his gaudy green shirt depicting palm trees, hoopoes and sunsets.

'A broken nose is the least of your worries, every bone in your flabby body will be snapped in two if one hair on Bella's head is damaged. What's the matter with you, are you insane? Why didn't you take care of Bella? Leaving her alone. Fuck, Steven, what's wrong with you?' Bern's rage had now boiled over. He tried to remain calm; getting frustrated with Steven wasn't going to help him locate Bella.

Steven put a hand on Bern's arm. 'Sorry, mate. Let's go to my house. We can go and search at first light tomorrow. Maybe she's with the rangers and safe.'

'You better hope she is.' Bern recognised with a sinking sensation in his stomach it wouldn't be safe to search for Bella until dawn. Bella held such gentleness and compassion for the bush and animals. He recognised that quality in the first instant he saw her.

After his speech about 'become your surroundings,' he hoped she listened to him and stayed safe. He would go out in the dove-mist colour of pre-dawn before the sun coloured the sky, and God help Steven if he couldn't find her.

Steven climbed into the front passenger seat. He clutched his broken nose with one hand, and a grimy bag with the other. Bern crawled into the back seat, and Lan jumped into the driver's seat.

When she took off, she swerved wildly, gripping the steering wheel.

Steven reached for a rag he found lying on the floor and pressed it to his nose to try and staunch the flow of blood. 'My nose is throbbing like hell. I know you're anxious about Bella. She'll be okay. You have to calm down, mate.'

'I won't be calm until we find Bella.'

Lan drove them to his home. Steven lived in a modest guest house in Tholo Crescent, around the corner from his office. When Lan approached his house, she bounced the vehicle over the kerb, skidding in the loose gravel. She came to a sudden stop in the dirt beside the front gates.

Steven's house resembled him: small and a little untidy around the edges. The two rooms smelt of stale body odour, day-old coffee and loneliness. In the larger of the two rooms, the kitchen backed up along two sides. The countertops were thick with grime, full of dirty dishes, left-over food, dusty pizza boxes and scrunched-up beer cans. The table in the middle of the room groaned under the filth, papers and laptops covered every grubby centimetre of it.

On the other side of the room, a bed scraped along the wall under a window. Bern doubted the bed linen had ever seen the inside of a washing machine. It crinkled with stiffness, and the odour coming off it clung to the stale air. A broken couch with tattered blankets covered with stains so ingrained they became a smudged pattern was squashed against the remaining wall.

The other neglected room in the house was the bathroom, it looked to be in a shambles also. The glass door of the shower hung limply off its hinges. Mould and old soap flaked off the grimy tiles. The sink crumpled in despair. A distinct shade of grey crusted over it. The toilet bowl stank; its smell permeated the entire house.

The three of them filled the small rooms. Bern's bulk overpowered the space. He paced Steven's home, fifteen strides long. Nowhere near enough for him to vent his growing irritation.

Bern knew that Steven had spent his childhood roaming the streets of Gaborone. He knew the man had grown up in poverty; his father broke stones at a pit to be used for building blocks in the fancy hotels, while his mum took in laundry. He had always admired Steven for running away from the slums and making a better life for himself. He hadn't realised Steven still lived in squalid conditions. Right now, he didn't care.

Steven fumbled inside his bag. And then he pulled out his Glock pistol, aiming it at Bern.

Bern's heart dropped. 'What the fuck? Where did you get the gun from, and *WHY* the hell are you pointing it at me?'

'Where do you think I could get a gun like this? For a smart guy, you're sounding a bit slow.'

'What do you mean?' Bern was confused.

'Do you want me to spell it out for you? I'm the *low-life* you've been wanting to meet.'

'What the fuck?' Bern said again. He was dumfounded.

'Yeah. I've been up to my neck with the poachers for years now. I lost a hell of a lot of money gambling. I borrowed from the wrong people. I don't have to bore you with all the details. I met this guy called Johan. He dragged me out of the gutter. I owed him. Johan introduced me to the head guy in Vietnam, Nguyen. That was a long time ago. Then the trade in illegal ivory kept us in money. Things changed the minute Nguyen found out about the benefits of lion bones. He believed it to be the answer to his flagging libido. Fucking lion bones are a pain in the side for all of us. If they were easier to acquire, I could fucking retire in luxury, and not in this God-awful town,' he admitted.

'Are you insane? Getting mixed up with the thugs who peddle in illegal poaching! You're a dead man walking, mark my words.' Bern held onto the table, reeling from what Steven had told him. He and all the other guides believed Steven to be one of them. He had an abhorrence to violence and was always at pains to show how much he hated the poachers. How did they all remain so blind to Steven's criminal side? Living a double life couldn't have been easy. Bern admonished himself for assuming Steven was their friend.

Steven pressed the Glock into Bern's ribs, forcing him into the chair. 'Don't try to act a hero. I'm in the right mood to shoot you now.'

'Man, I don't think you're stupid enough to shoot me after all the trouble you went to, to get me up here. Did you ask a fucking troop of baboons to help with your plans? I doubt you could've come up with this on your own.' Bern fumed; his inactivity chafed across him. He longed to disappear into the night, to get away from Steven and Lan. Being held at gunpoint, Bern knew he must play the game at least until he found Bella.

Lan stood unusually quiet for once.

Then it dawned on Bern that she knew the way to Steven's house without Steven telling her. 'You know about this?'

'Course, lover, I know. Steven and I planned this,' she admitted smugly.

Bern shook her as though she were a rag doll. A rage surged through his body. 'You stupid bitch, what have you and Steven done?'

'Nothing, lover, not yet anyway. We needed you to help us find a lion. The bitch was your bait, and you fell for it. Not so stupid now, am I?' Lan spat at him; glee twirling around her words.

Bern couldn't control his anger any longer. 'I want to snap your worthless head off. God, how did I ever get involved with you? Why didn't I throw you out from the start? I'm in the right mood to strangle your scrawny neck with pleasure. So, how did you two idiots come up with this plan? It sounds like you are becoming desperate.'

'Lan's flawed strategy of using her three brothers showed weakness from the start. Nguyen's pissed with us. Shit, you don't know how sadistic this man is. Lan, to her credit, tried to keep her end of the bargain. Her unreliable brothers disappeared at the first opportunity.'

'I don't miss them. I can shoot the lion now. I already killed two worthless men.'

'What! You say that like you just bought a pair of shoes.' Bern was shocked at the coldness of Lan.

Lan giggled.

'But where do Bella and I fit in all this?'

'We need a guide to find the lions. I haven't a clue where to look.'

'There are other guides. Why me?'

'Yeah, but when I saw you with that bitch, I knew I had found my guide. It was so easy to lure you up here,' Steven's voice slurred over the words.

'Not that easy. You still don't have a lion to shoot.'

'Tomorrow we will,' Lan added.

'This job will set both Lan and me up with enough money to get the hell out of Botswana.'

Why do the few ghostly hours of pre-dawn always last a lifetime? Bern hated inaction; he wanted to be out in Chobe looking for Bella. Whenever Bern closed his eyes, he saw Bella's face. He knew from the first moment he laid eyes on her, that she was the one he'd searched for, his entire life. Bella was his kindred spirit, the one he intended to marry and share a life with.

Steven propped himself on the bed, leaning his head against the wall. His pistol was at the ready on his lap. His glassy eyes remained open as he stared into the room.

Bern went to sit on the floor, he pushed his back against the door, his long-muscled legs stretched in front of him. He was too furious, too much on edge to contemplate sleep. He waited for daylight to tint the bleakness from the sky, so he could get the fuck out of there to search for Bella.

Lan sashayed over to him, having tossed her bag on the table. 'One last fuck for old time's sake, lover,' her razor-blade voice bit into him.

Bern didn't bother to reply. He pushed her across the room.

She fell onto the table, knocking over a chair. 'Shit,' she yelped before trotting over to the bed to cosy up beside Steven.

Bern reckoned there remained about three hours until dawn crept into their world. Three hours to think about the bizarre predicament Steven forced them all into.

CHAPTER 50

The noise of the baboons leaving the safety of the trees shook Bella awake. Their chattering, a jarring sound first thing in the morning. It took her a few minutes to comprehend that the nightmare she was living refused to let her go.

The lions had kept entering her sporadic attempts at sleep. But Bella welcomed their closeness. For some uncanny reason, she knew they were there to protect her. The strong smell of urine didn't worry her anymore, although she craved the sweet scent of dawn.

She tried cleaning her hands and face, giving up the futile effort. The baboons wouldn't care if her face showed traces of grime. Her hair became an intricate mess of curls, so she twisted it into a knot and let it trail down her back.

She then breathed in the dew-filled air, which swirled through the remnants of night. Her body burnt with pain as though fire licked at it, bringing tears to her eyes. The landscape looked shrouded in a sheer grey curtain. Bella vaguely made out the tree shapes, their leaves shaking once the first blast of dawn hit them. She shivered, waiting for the sun to warm the earth. The baboons chattered about their dreams; their sound broke the quietness of dawn.

Her fingers fluttered on the cold concrete blocks of the toilet, hesitant about what to do next. She hoped that Steven hadn't phoned Bern, although she guessed this had been his intention all along. She again fervently wished for Bern to stay in Maun, so Steven's ridiculous scheming didn't stand a chance of seeing the daylight.

Bella limped towards a picnic table. She hoped to watch the Chobe River blush with the first rays of sunshine. It lay iridescent in the dawn light; a few pods of hippos made a splash on the smooth surface of the water. A small herd of zebras trotted to the water's edge. Bella guessed they chose to be the first to sip the water on a brand-new day before the heat tugged at their hides. Africa began waking up, and if she hadn't been so anxious and alone, she might have enjoyed the sunrise.

Bella watched the tops of the trees flush crimson once the sun hit them. A herd of impala skittered past. They snorted a warning to everyone close that danger lurked in the shadows. Their flanks quivered from the nip in the air that clung low to the ground. Bella turned in the direction they came from and saw what spurred them into flight.

The mating pair of lions sat twenty metres from her. They spent the bite of a spring night under a thick bush not far from the toilet block. The male stood; his mouth wide as a yawn tumbled off his tongue. A few scars scratched below his right eye, tiny streets on a road map. His thick mane, flattened from sleep, managed to fall in golden strands on his chest. His amber eyes held Bella in an intense stare. She stood motionless, except for the drumming of her heart. She held her breath, staring into his eyes.

The lion moved towards Bella, evidently more out of curiosity than anything else. Maybe he had never seen a human so close before. His mate lay on her back beside him. The chill air teased over her thick coat. The lioness rolled over, and with the elegance of all cats, she stood up and stretched her claws into the sand. She glanced at the rear of the male. She looked to be tiring of the mating business, as she too yawned in the crisp dewy air. Her muscles rippled under her fur, and her golden eyes held a strip of pale cream under them. The lioness' compassion seeped into Bella, filling her with tranquillity. The lioness wasn't there to harm Bella but to protect her. She remembered what Bern said about the rituals of mating lions.

Bella trusted this pair remained in the early glow of their love-making and kept other things in their mind apart from breakfast. If this turned out to be the case, they might forget all about the human who stood so close to them.

The female padded to the front of the male; she held Bella in a curious stare and then all of a sudden appeared to forget all about the human standing near her. She clearly yearned for her mate and didn't care who watched them.

It lasted mere seconds, and growls resounded across the sand.

The female purred as she rolled away, waving her legs in the air, satisfied at least for the next fourteen minutes or so. The male sniffed her arse before he plopped on the ground. He licked her coat, his long tongue pink against her fur. The sun-drenched them in gold. All recollections of the human seemed to float away on the sunbeams.

Bella knew not to make any sudden movements towards them. She didn't want to frighten them, even though they seemed relaxed with her closeness.

Bella watched them mate again before starting to worry. *What if Bern comes to Chobe to rescue me*, she worried. And with Steven having the damn pistol, it didn't bode well for the lions. Bella knew this pair wouldn't be moving far from their bush, so she had to leave them.

She backed away, one agonising step after another. She had to get herself down to the edge of the river, where Steven threw her from the vehicle. She reached the edge of the steep bank before glancing at the lions. They looked in her direction, and Bella experienced a swirl of tenderness permeate through her. She realised the lions knew she meant to save them. She crept a few hundred metres to where the curve of the river left the incline. The bank angled steeply there, but she had no energy left to go further upstream. She turned and tried to crawl backwards down the slope, only to fall most of the way, trying to clutch onto the tree roots to break her fall. Thorns caught in her dress, scratching at her arms and legs. She tried to ignore the stinging pain.

Once Bella reached the level ground, she sat winded in the sand gasping for breath, the ache in her ribs and shoulder a relentless reminder of her vulnerability. She turned east, facing the sun and traced her footsteps towards it. If Steven or Bern did happen to locate her, she had to be as far away from the lions as her aching body allowed. The lions protected Bella last night, and so now it became her turn to protect them. She picked up a tree branch lying broken on the ground, thanking the elephant who ripped it off a tree. It was the right height and sturdy enough to use for a crutch.

Bella pulled herself up, trembling from the effort, but sheer determination urged her on. Blood dripped down her arms and legs from the thorns. Bits of twigs and grass matted through her hair. Bella continued east towards the rising sun, and away from the lions. If Bern drove into the park, he would in all likelihood follow the flow of the river. Bella knew with a clarity clearer than the sky, that with each step she took, Bern was getting closer to her.

Lion

I took the oldest female with me because she produced the strongest cubs. We found a secluded spot, high above the river. Our shelter became a thick bush. I lay beside her, watching the evening fall. I became perplexed at the sight of the human. I had seen this human not too long ago and knew her to be a gentle soul. She appeared from nowhere. One minute we were staring off towards the riverbank, the next she crouched low on all fours like an impala. She didn't see us. She carried an injury. She stood with care, limping towards the building not far from where we lay.

I didn't feel alarmed at having this human so close. My mind was too full of the scent of my mate. I wasn't interested in hunting. However, I watched over the human to make sure she came to no harm. With dawn starting to crease the sky, I heard her movements. She crept towards us, grubby and smelling of human urine, not all of which belonged to her. She also seemed coated in the chill of pre-dawn while we waited for the sun's warmth.

She limped towards the riverbank, standing gazing into memories long forgotten. She turned to watch the antics of the baboons, and I saw a smile etch across her face. Her bright-blue eyes radiated kindness. A small herd of impala wandered close. We weren't interested in a meal, but our presence spooked them. At that exact moment, she spied us. Her eyes bored into mine, and I saw she showed no fear. She looked contented, as if she needed us to be near her.

All of a sudden, a change crept into her attitude; she knew danger hovered close. She blinked a farewell in our direction before she backed away to continue her painful hobble along the riverbank.

CHAPTER 51

Bern figured no one slept at all, although they may have dozed intermittently during the long hours until dawn. He focused his eyes on the window facing east. He watched the night sky through the dirty windowpane. Once the darkness faded into streaks of grey, he jumped up, stamping the cramps from his legs. His movements galvanised both Steven and Lan, who cuddled together on the bed. He raced out of the door to Steven's vehicle.

'These might help.' Steven held up his car keys and pointed his gun at Bern. His nose was swollen to almost double its size, and a deep-purple bruise seeped across his cheek. His voice sounded sticky; the words slushed in his throat.

Bern caught the keys Steven threw to him before getting into the driver's seat.

Lan tripped over the gravel in the front yard. 'Shit.' She struggled to get to the vehicle.

Steven jumped into the passenger seat.

'Fuck you. My feet hurt,' Lan swore at Bern. She collapsed into the back seat, slamming the door. She took off her sandals to shake the pebbles from them.

Bern drove along the tar road towards the park, bypassing the main entrance gates where a gloomy silence coated them in the pre-dawn. Seventeen kilometres from the Sedudu Gate, he turned off the tar road onto the Nantanga track, taking them deep into the park.

The sun, already yawning, began its trek across another day. It chased away the shadows of night, and a golden glow sifted down to them. The Nantanga track, thick with sand, made driving difficult and way too slow for Bern's liking. He tried to urge the vehicle through the worst parts, speeding up once the track flattened out. Bern braked hard, gripping the steering wheel tightly. He spun down hard, bringing the vehicle to a sudden stop. A small herd of kudu careened out of nowhere right in front of them. They were spooked by the noise of the vehicle and looked to be on alert.

Bern waited until they moved off. He then drove with more care, not wanting to have an accident. His mind floundered with images of Bella alone and frightened. He bypassed the picnic ground, not sure if the mating pair of lions still lingered there.

The sun dazzled in bright sparks off the water. Facing east, Bern knew he ought to do a U-turn to follow the river in a westerly direction. Stalling for time, his gaze stretched across the flat plains. His mind frizzed with the knowledge of Steven's involvement in poaching, but he had to remain calm if he was to find Bella.

Both Steven and Lan held their pistols ready to use. Steven's lay across his lap, with his right hand resting on the trigger. His left hand held a bloody rag against his face. Lan tucked her gun beside her, she stroked it in a perverse sexual way.

What sort of sick bitch was she, Bern thought as he glanced at her.

'Why are you stopping? You better get moving; I want this over with. I can't afford to be surrounded by huge hordes of tourists traipsing through the park.' Steven's swollen face made it difficult to understand him.

'I appreciate all you carry is peanuts growing mouldy in your fuddled brain. I'm only interested in finding Bella and getting the hell away from the two of you fucking idiots.'

'I'll tell you the plan again, this time a bit slower. You look smart enough to understand what we're doing out in this desolate shit of a park. I shoved Bella out here; God knows where. I wanted to use her for bait to get you to drive us into the park. We figured you to be the big macho guy, swooping in to rescue Bella. I've bad news for you, because even if the bitch survives, you can bet your last pula she'll be dead by a bullet if you don't get us a lion.'

Bern's head felt on fire with rage. 'Are you both lunatics? There's no way in heaven I'm about to let either Bella get shot, or a lion butchered to save your sorry arses.'

Steven shoved the barrel of his pistol into Bern's side. 'I've got the gun, you fucking smart prick, now get moving, or I'm in the right frame of mind to shoot you now.'

'Kill me, man. It won't take long for someone to hear the shot,' Bern threatened.

'Move!' Steven screamed.

Reluctantly, Bern drove west. He weaved in time to the curves of the river; he had to locate Bella before deciding how to deal with these two.

The land flattened out; elephants and buffalo meandered towards the river. Bern kept stopping every few metres to let them pass. The knowledge he learnt about reading the bush and the animals became second nature to him.

It seemed to take forever on this slow-moving morning. His eyes scanned away from the water towards the thickets.

Finally, Bern spotted Bella. She staggered along, close to the edge of the steep bank. Bella struggled with each step, and straightaway he knew she was in a lot of pain. She leant on a thick branch. Her footsteps eventually slowed to a stop, and she held up her hand to shield her eyes against the sun. She seemed to have spotted the vehicle. Bern's heart filled with love for Bella the closer he drove towards her.

At last, Steven spotted her. 'There she is. That's a relief. How she survived all night alone is a fucking miracle. The odds of this succeeding are tipped in our favour now. Bern, it's up to you now to find a lion, any mangy one will do. Lan, get your gun ready.' Steven almost smiled.

Bern kept his eyes fixed on Bella's. She stared straight at him, and he recognised her fear. She appeared wary, almost like she didn't expect him to be the one to search for her. He skidded to a stop in the soft sand, jumping out of the vehicle to rush towards her. The tears in her eyes conveyed more to him than words. She shivered from clear fright, wincing when his fingers touched her shoulder. A rage surged deep inside him. There was blood on her arms and legs, and on her swollen face, a bruise blushed her cheek. She smelt of fear and urine; her thick hair hung in a tousled matted mess down her back.

'Glad you got all spruced up for me, liefie.' Bern's voice caressed over her. 'But we have a bit of a problem to sort out first.'

'Please, Bern, stay away from the picnic area.' Bella's ragged whisper barely reached him.

Bern's wink told her he understood.

Steven struggled out of the vehicle to run towards them. His steps were staggered and clumsy. He pointed the gun at Bella. 'Stop fucking chatting. Bella, get in the vehicle with Lan. And you, Bern, get into the driver's seat. Start driving, and you better not try anything heroic, Lan's gun is trained on Bella. She's itching for any excuse to shoot your girlfriend.'

'That's right, lover boy.' Lan's smile failed to take the acidity out of her words.

Bella crawled into the seat, grimacing from the effort, beads of sweat forming on her upper lip and between her shoulder blades. She sat behind Bern, staring at his black curls.

'You smell like the inside of a sewer.' Lan screwed her nose up. 'It suits you, bitch. Say goodbye to lover boy, 'cause you'll never touch him again.'

Bella grimaced at her. 'Shut up, Lan, I'm not in the mood for your irritating babble. It's too early in the morning for me to be civil to you.'

'Stop talking. I'm the one holding the gun, and I kill for pleasure not necessity.' Lan sounded cocky, and because pain tortured Bella's body, she fell silent. She hoped Bern understood her urgent plea about the mating lions and stayed away from the picnic ground.

She guessed all of Bern's tracking skills were going to be channelled into not looking for any lions today.

Bern jumped into the driver's seat before turning around. He winked at Bella again, without anyone else seeing. And then he turned to face the front. He made a show of pulling out his seatbelt to click it in.

Bella guessed he meant for her to do the same. She slipped on the seatbelt, clipping it in. She pulled it away because the slightest pressure on her body caused waves of nausea to spill into her throat.

'Don't forget that Lan has a gun pointed at Bella, so if you don't find any lions, her brains are going to be spread all over the windows.' Steven's voice kept a touch of mania about it. It became obvious he was getting desperate in his hunt for lions, and a desperate man sometimes slipped up.

Bella tried without success to sift her muddled brain into a coherent order. She couldn't fathom why it took so long to acknowledge Bern's love for her. He risked his own life to rescue her. Bella longed to get the chance to tell him how sorry she was for doubting him. The instant Bella stared at Bern driving towards her, a bolt of lightning pierced through her. Bella had, at last, let go of a past too painful to recall. She was now free to fall in love with Bern.

Steven and Lan terrified her, because they nursed a hysteria of madness about them, and Bern and Bella were in danger of not surviving this hellish day.

The friction in the vehicle thickened. It scraped off the windows to pool beside them. Bella glanced towards Lan. The way she held her gun, stroking it, made Bella's blood curdle. Steven, on the other hand, looked jumpier than a kitten left outside at night. He shook uncontrollably, and she imagined his teeth jangling to the floor one by one. Her one desire was for Bern and the lions to stay safe today.

CHAPTER 52

Bern knew the slower he drove, the more likely it became for other safari vehicles to start coming into the park. His one motivation revolved around keeping Bella safe. He scanned the banks of the river, not looking for lions but stalling for time. From what Bella whispered to him, he knew not to go near the picnic area. However, he had no clue about the whereabouts of the rest of the Kabulabula pride.

Huge herds of buffalo meandered from the forest to the water's edge. If Bern drove into the herd, he might be able to gain valuable time. Soon, the buffalo surrounded the vehicle, pushing and shoving each other like opinionated protestors at a riot. The buffalo sniffed the air, shifting their gaze from grazing to the vehicle moving towards them.

'Keep moving,' Steven yelled above the noise.

'Sorry, man, these buffalo are sometimes called black death, and for a good reason. Look over there, the females with young ones at their heels. A herd of this size can inflict serious damage to a vehicle. There are many sad stories about stampeding buffalo overturning vehicles larger than the safari trucks. If you don't mind, I'll wait a bit, till they're more at ease with us being so close to them. I don't want to spook them.'

'You better not be playing with us, or I'll kill your bitch girl-friend myself.'

'Call her "bitch" again and I'll rip your tongue out with my bare hands and make a bow of it, gun or no gun.' Bern fumed with an anger he'd never experienced. He would do anything in the world to protect Bella. He inched his way through the herd; the buffalo parted when he drove close to them. They left the buffalo in their dust whipping from the tyres. Bern continued driving in a westerly direction.

'What the fuck. Turn inland, now! You're smart. No lions on flat ground near water.' Lan's jarring voice ruffled over the currents that swirled in the river.

'I'm looking for lion spoor in the sand,' Bern countered, although he was doing no such thing.

Steven pushed his pistol hard into Bern's ribs, the metallic touch of the barrel filtered under his shirt. 'Turn inland.' His deadly words cut through the vehicle.

With reluctance, Bern drove up the next steep track away from the river. From all his years of game-driving, Bern knew lions were the hardest cats to find. They were the exact colour of the long grass they lay in. If you didn't catch sight of a tail flick, or a sudden movement in the grass, you could drive within millimetres of them, without realising they were close. Bern counted on this as he steered the vehicle along the sandy tracks.

Well over an hour dragged by, and Bern observed the body language of Steven and Lan showed signs of irritation. The hostility in the vehicle boiled over. He had to do something fast, or it could end badly for Bella and him. He had worked out a sort of plan that he hoped didn't kill the lot of them. Bern had never in his life cornered an animal into a situation where there was a potential for it to be injured. Unfortunately, he was planning to do that now to stop Steven and Lan and save another lion from slaughter.

He turned the vehicle around, pretending to be searching in a particular area. His sketchy idea involved driving towards the river. He could always count on elephants to use their ancient paths from the river into the shadows of the forest.

He then drove off the track, having located one of the paths the elephants always used. He hoped a lone bull would start to amble up the path from the river to feast in the forest. A breeding herd could make the situation even more dangerous. He soon spotted an old bull trudging towards them. The elephant showed no signs of being in musth, which meant his temper should stay at a more mellow level.

Bern took a deep breath. He accelerated towards the elephant, beeping the horn. He didn't stop or swerve away. The big bull got the fright of his life at the jarring sound. He shook his head at the approaching vehicle, trumpeting loud enough to startle a flock of vultures from their perch high in the trees. Bern skidded to a stop fifteen metres from the elephant.

'What the fuck. Bloody drive away.'

Steven sounded nervous, but Bern pretended he didn't hear him. His eyes never wavered from the elephant. The huge male stood firm, getting into his aggression mode. He swung one enormous foot up and down, kicking up the dust. His ears, which always flapped to cool his body, stood straight out from his head, strangely still.

Bern read the signs to perfection, and when the male lowered his head, trumpeting again, he pressed his foot hard on the accelerator. The tyres spun, trying to gain traction in the soft sand. Bern drove towards the elephant, and at the last possible moment, he turned the vehicle sharply to the right, exposing Steven and Lan to the full force of the elephant's wrath.

Steven groped for his pistol, and with shaking hands, he aimed it at the elephant. But it was to be of no use to him. The elephant charged the few steps to the vehicle, pushing his long tusks through the side windows. One of his tusks pierced Steven's head, breaking it open like the fruit of a marula tree. Lan screamed hysterically. Steven's blood and bits of his brain spurted over her. The other tusk missed her by a few millimetres. The force of the elephant's weight upturned the vehicle. The crash caused her to hit her head hard on the roof. Bella shuddered from the impact of Lan crashing into her, pinning her against the door.

When Lan slammed into Bella, she dropped her pistol. Lan lay winded for a moment, giving Bella the chance to retrieve the gun from the floor. She clutched it against her chest.

The elephant edged away from the vehicle; his bad mood disappeared in a beam of sunlight. He shook his head again to scatter the reasons for his interrupted stroll, then continued on his way.

Bern pushed the dead body of Steven away from himself. 'Are you all right, Bella?' He held his breath until she spoke.

'I've had better days, but I think I'm okay.' Her breath sounded ragged, and Bern caught the tremor in her voice.

Lan had passed out; blood trickled from a cut above her right eye. Bella tried to push her off but collapsed against the door. She almost fainted; her cries of agony filled the vehicle. The front windscreen had exploded from the force of the elephant's fury, giving Bern a narrow gap to escape from.

He climbed onto the overturned vehicle; the rear passenger door gave way on his third attempt. Bern reached in to drag Lan out of the vehicle. He tossed her on the ground, thankful she weighed less than a sack of maize. She lay on the ground, next to the broken windscreen, moaning softly. He didn't give her another thought. He crawled in the upturned vehicle to lift Bella out. 'You're safe now, my love.' Bern whispered. He laid Bella on the ground, cradling her while he tried to reassure her.

Bella lay in Bern's arms, struggling with every breath.

'It's going to be all right, Bella,' he whispered against her tangled hair.

She held Lan's gun clutched in her hands, having forgotten all about it until Bern prised it from her fingers. She then breathed a sigh of relief to be free of its jarring metallic touch. Bern could deal with Lan now.

Lan moaned; her eyelids flicked open. She shook uncontrollably, her eyes darting around the scene.

Bern held her pistol in his firm grip and aimed it at her.

Lan rolled her eyes. 'Fucking shoot me, I'm dead anyway if Nguyen knows we have no lions.'

'Not on your life, I'm eager to see you rot in jail for what you did. You better start learning some manners. They'll come in handy in the jails here.'

'I'll not go to jail. I won't survive in a cell,' she yelled at them before she sprang to her feet to start running away from them.

'Stop her.' Bella begged. She glanced up at Bern; his face was etched with sorrow.

'It may be too late to save her now.' He said, nodding across the ground to a small thicket of bushes seventy-five metres away. 'Lan, stop don't move. There's a lion not far away. I'll come and get you.' Bern's determined tone tried to warn Lan of the danger. He stood. 'Lan, please stay still, don't move.' He took a few paces towards her.

She ignored him in her haste to get away. 'I cannot go to jail!' she shouted.

'Lan, please listen to me. Stand still and shut up. I'm almost with you.' Bern's words were clearly lost on Lan.

Bella saw one of the Ihaha pride males. His majestic head rested on his front paws. He seemed perplexed by all the commotion. 'Oh my God, Bern. You have to help her. Lan, listen to Bern, please.' Bella tried to stand.

'Stay still, Bella.' Bern turned back to Lan. 'Lan, please DON'T MOVE!' he yelled. 'I'm coming to help, don't move.' Bern started to approach Lan.

Lan ran straight towards the bush, shouting obscenities, tossing them behind her to twirl in and out of the trees. She wavered when she saw the lion standing up in full attack mode. Unsure of what to do, she stopped for a moment; her breath caught in her throat. The lion's fluffy ears were at half-mast as his eyes bored into Lan. She shivered without realising why.

Lan stood on the edge of life and wondered if all her scraping and scheming to survive had been worth it. She glanced at Bern and Bella. *Why couldn't I have had a love as intense as theirs*, she pondered.

'Don't move,' Bern cautioned again. He had about ten metres to go before he reached Lan, but it was too late.

Lan suspected her miserable life was about to end, yet flinty instincts to survive urged her on. She stared at the lion, locking her eyes with his. Lan naïvely figured she could run faster than an impala and outrun the lion. Her false bravado proved to be her second and final mistake. Lan didn't know the golden rule of never to run away from a lion, because if you did, he thought you were food and would chase you.

Lan began to sprint past him. 'Fuck you!' she screamed to no one in particular. Unfortunately, those words were the last she ever uttered. The lion had her in the blink of an eye, his powerful front paw reached out when Lan went by. His long claws ripped into the soft flesh of Lan's waist. Lan, horrified, watched her blood start to squelch from her body. Bile bubbled into her throat, to gurgle down her chin. She crumpled to the ground.

The lion sprang on top of her; still, Lan clung to life. Her eyes bulged staring up into the sky. The sun used to dazzle her with a bright-blue sheen, now an opaque fug covered her. The lion's powerful jaws slipped around the slim throat of Lan, his long fangs biting down hard, breaking the bones in her neck and piercing her carotid artery. Blood spurted over his mane as he greedily tore into Lan's flesh. She twitched with a life already starting to flow into the atmosphere.

Finally, Lan gasped, her life trickling into the ether of time. Pictures of Mai blinked like a faulty light in front of her eye – the one person in her miserable life who loved her. Johan and her boss crowded her last memories in this mortal world. Apart from the frenzied eating, a deathly calm coated the air as Lan's spirit floated above the bushes.

Vultures, soaring high on the thermals, had already started circling the kill. Their penetrating eyes picked out the scene from far above.

Bern retrieved a two-way radio Steven kept in the glove compartment of his vehicle. He tuned it to a station, sending out a mayday call, telling anyone in range, his name and his exact whereabouts, hoping somebody was listening.

A few attempts later, a crackling voice answered, 'Hey, Bern, I'm about a kilometre from you, I'll be there in a jiffy, hold tight, over.'

'Thank you, Justin, we're waiting for you. If you have guests, you better park a bit away. It's a gruesome sight here and there are lions in the vicinity. Also, there's an injured female to go to the hospital ASAP, over and out.'

'Righto, over and out.'

In no time at all, the sound of an engine chugged up the rise. Justin parked several metres from the top of the bank. He wandered over to them and said, 'Hey, man, you're in a bit of trouble out here this morning. What did you do, upset a bull elephant and some lions?'

'Something like that, Justin,' Bern answered. 'I'll fill you in on all the details later. This dirty, smelly female by the name of Bella could do with a shower and a trip to the hospital. She has somehow managed to survive her first night alone in the bush.'

'Thanks for the compliment.' Bella stood, wincing from the pain.

Bern supported her as she limped towards Justin's vehicle.

'I sent a message to Andy, who was close. He has no guests at the moment, so he's going to meet us down by the river. He can take your friend into town, straight to the hospital. You stay with me to explain things. I'll take my guests to the campsite. Once I make sure they're all right, we'll return here to sort out your mess.'

'Thank you, Justin. My only concern is that Bella gets to the hospital.'

Andy already waited for them by the river. He came over to Justin, and they spoke for a few minutes in Setswana. Finishing their conversation, Andy went to help Bella struggle into the front seat of his vehicle. He made sure she was comfortable before turning to wave to Justin.

Both vehicles drove off in opposite directions. Bella and Andy going east towards the main gates and the hospital. Bern and Justin turning west to the public camping ground at Ihaha.

Andy wallowed over the sandy tracks. Every hole and twist stabbed into Bella's aching body. She breathed a small sigh of relief at the entrance gate. Thankfully, Andy didn't mention her unkempt appearance or ask any questions about how she got her injuries. She found him to be typical of all the men from Botswana: quiet, confident and caring.

Bella almost smiled at the entrance doors to the hospital. She saw a stretcher being wheeled out. 'Thank you, Andy.'

'You get good help now, mma.' He climbed into his vehicle, waving goodbye.

The hospital staff soon whisked Bella into the waiting room where a doctor was on standby to look at her. Before they took Bella for an x-ray, the doctor ordered her to have a shower and clean up.

A nurse helped Bella undress. There were bruises on her rib cage and shoulder, but the nurse refrained from mentioning anything. Bella welcomed the pure indulgence of a hot shower because she could smell her body odour. The nurse stayed with her, washing out the thorns and dirt from her hair, before getting a clean hospital gown and colourful mule slippers for Bella to wear.

An orderly took Bella in for an x-ray. The doctor confirmed that she had five cracked ribs and torn ligaments in her shoulder. He gave the nurse instructions about what medication to give, then left to attend to another patient.

Bella crawled into a spotless hospital bed. The crisp white sheets smelt of lemon swirled with peppermint. A nurse stopped by to bring a hot cup of Rooibos and a couple of Eet-sum-mor biscuits. With the strong medication the doctor prescribed, her shower and something to eat, the terrifying events of last night trickled out into the steamy heat of Kasane. However, the horrors of this morning, watching the gruesome deaths of both Steven and Lan were going to stay with Bella forever to haunt her nightmares.

CHAPTER 53

Bern continued with Justin to the Ihaha public campsite. Blessing, Justin's cook, jumped from the vehicle to settle his guests. He set up brunch on the long trestle table, where views of the Chobe River swept in front of them.

Justin went over to his guests. 'I have a few things to sort out with Bern. Blessing is more than capable of looking after you until I get back. I promise to be back in time for the afternoon game drive.' He then spoke a few words to Blessing in Setswana before he left them.

Justin and Bern climbed into the vehicle to drive to where Steven's wrecked vehicle lay scrunched in the sand.

'Something bad has happened here, mate.' Justin said. 'It's apparent an elephant attacked your vehicle, and over there, lions slaughtered someone.'

The vultures Bern and Bella saw circling high in the sky now scrabbled and clawed over the upturned vehicle. They flapped over the coiled body of Steven; the smell of death caught in their nostrils. A few of them persisted in fighting over the remains of

Lan, their wings flapping as though they were stuck in a jackalberry tree. Justin drove his vehicle right at the vultures. He scared them into flying to a nearby tree where they sat waiting for another opportunity to return to their scavenging.

Both men jumped out of the vehicle to go to the remains of Steven.

Justin winced. The vultures had already pecked out Steven's eyes in what remained of his face. 'Christ, Bern, I've been doing this job for fifteen years. I know what elephants are capable of. It's clear Steven's been gored by an elephant tusk. I want to know why the elephant charged. They don't go out of their way to charge, unless it is a last resort.'

Steven's eye sockets, bloody and raw, stared vacantly into the interior of the vehicle

'And over there in the flattened grass.' Justin pointed. 'Those scattered bones and bright-red blood once belonged to a human.'

They saw no sign of the lion. He had wandered off deeper into the thickets. The sun climbed higher in the sky, bringing with it a zing of heat. The lion would now be sheltering out of its reach.

'My mind's buzzing with a million questions,' Justin admitted. 'About Steven and the scattered bones … but first let me get a tarp from my vehicle. I want to cover Steven.' He dragged out a tarp from behind the front seats.

Both men strapped it over the broken front windscreen, in an attempt to keep off the circling vultures.

'What's gone down here, man? How could you let this happen? You're one of the most respected guides in all of Botswana, but something horrific happened here today.' Justin's eyes pleaded for the truth.

Bern sighed before replying, 'You know we're trying to stop the illegal poaching of lion bones in Botswana?'

'Yeah, I'm always on the lookout every time I go out. What the hell does the poaching have to do with Steven?'

'It's hard to believe, mate, but our friend, Steven, has been living a double life. On one side, he was all for the conservation of lions and our best friend. On the other side, he was the number one guy in Botswana. His immediate boss used to be a low-life South African hitman called Johan. The blood over there belongs to Johan's assistant and my so-called girlfriend Lan. I was keeping her close because I figured her to be involved in such a heinous crime, and now I've been proved right. Seagal and I guessed the Vietnamese were involved. We had to find out how, and who the mongrel in Botswana turned out to be who fed Lan the information.' He paused, allowing all that he had shared to settle with Justin. 'Lan wriggled into my life, thinking I'd lead her to the lions. I never met a tougher bitch, or one with a harder heart. Ag, man, she boasted to Steven about how she shot and killed Johan. She shot the man through the heart while he slept, how's that for ruthlessness? She bragged about it last night to Steven. She even dared to laugh.'

'Wow! Bloody hell, this is doing my head in. Lan a murderer and Steven the bastard, into poaching.' Justin shook his head. 'They must have been working for someone. Poor bloody sod, Steven, getting mixed up in all this shit.'

'Yeah, bloody fool. He was working for some big honcho in Vietnam called Nguyen. He's responsible for the death of countless numbers of rhinos and elephants but has spread his web wider into the slaughter of lions. You can bet your last pula I wasn't about to let another lion be slaughtered if I could help it,' Bern admitted adamantly.

Justin frowned. I'm having trouble getting my head around what you're telling me. I can't believe Steven's mixed up in such a shady business. I sometimes reckoned he cared about the money, not the wildlife. I kept ignoring his shadier side. I should've listened to my misgivings about him and stopped this from happening.'

'We've all made mistakes about Steven, the poor sorry bastard. Steven lived his life in the pursuit of money, and it led him down a dangerous path towards death. He abused his friendship with Seagal and the other guides to feed his ego. Hell, how do I break this to Seagal? He always regarded Steven as one of his best mates.'

'So, tell me, man, how did you end up here? How does an experienced guide get himself into a position where a bull elephant attacks him, and two people are killed? Also, how did an Aussie get mixed up in all of this? She looked and smelt as though she spent the night at the bottom of a toilet. How she survived on her own out here all night is a miracle.' Justin leant against his vehicle, digging stones out of his boots with a stick he found on the ground.

Bern put his hands in his pockets. He glanced at the overturned vehicle, then brought his gaze back to Justin. 'I'm not sure how she managed that either, given her injuries. I haven't had a chance to question her yet. All I know is she's one of a kind. She feels your country more than anyone I know. It seems she exists purely because of our African earth.' Bern had a smile on his face. 'When I found her struggling and in pain this morning, she didn't care at all about her injuries. Bella's first concern seemed to be warning me not to go near the picnic area. I'm guessing the lions stayed close to her all night; and with Bella's gentle empathy for cats, I sense they kept watch over her, keeping her safe.' Bern continued telling Justin about Steven's phone call and the events that had transpired.

Justin remained silent, only interrupting Bern with the occasional, 'fuck' or 'I don't believe this.'

Bern rubbed his eyes; they were stinging from the glare and dust. 'I'm amazed I found her, given the vastness of the park, although I'm guessing she knew I'd start looking for her beside the river. But the ordeal had only started for us. Steven jammed his gun into my ribs, while Lan aimed her pistol at Bella. Steven said if I didn't find a lion they could slaughter, Lan would shoot Bella.' Bern shuddered at the memory. He scratched his chin. 'My mind raced with a million things I ought to be doing to protect Bella and the lions, and this was all I could think of to do.' He shifted his weight from one foot to the other. He stretched his back trying to straighten out the kinks from spending the night at Steven's house.

'As for Steven, the poor guy didn't deserve this, although he turned out to be a criminal; dying by an elephant's wrath is not a nice way to go. The stupid bitch Lan ran straight into the path of one of the Ihaha pride males. I tried to save her, but she kept ignoring me. Bit of poetic justice if you ask me.' Bern stopped speaking.

Justin clenched his hands into fists. 'Geez, man, that's quite a tale, and you did the right thing from what you are telling me. If Steven was mixed up in the illegal poaching of animals, he deserved to meet his maker. I always wondered what you saw in that freaky bitch, though. She made my skin crawl. Not your type at all, but that Aussie; man I'd love to get to know her a bit better.' Justin pulled out his mobile phone. He made a quick call to the garage, in Kasane, to arrange a truck to come and remove Steven's smashed vehicle. He gave the guys detailed instructions about the exact location. These men were used to driving into the park to tow away vehicles stuck in the soft sand.

With Justin busy on the phone, Bern took a spade out of the vehicle. He began digging a grave next to where Lan's remains lay discarded in the sand. He filled in the hole, smoothing it out, placing a few stones in a little pile on top, a final tribute to Lan.

Next, both men struggled to free Steven from where he lay twisted in death. They wrapped him in the tarp, before lying him in the back of Justin's vehicle. The vultures persisted in circling, but with Lan buried and now Steven stowed away, they flew off to the thermals to seek out another carcass.

With Steven's vehicle now the only lasting crumpled reminder of a tragedy, Justin and Bern drove out of the park. Justin picked up speed on the tar road. Bern phoned Karyn to fill her in with a few sketchy details about Bella. He asked her to go to the hospital to sit with her until he got there.

The heat sizzled along the tight maze of streets in Kasane. The sun arced high and sent waves of steam to bounce off the parched earth. Forlorn weeds at the side of the road lay prone, too exhausted to stand to attention. Justin nosed his vehicle into a space in front of the police station. A warthog wandered in from the bush, and ignoring bystanders, it grunted in the short grass at the entrance.

The police station looked to be disorganised chaos for the police so late into the muggy heat of morning. People gathered in small groups, gossiping about the steamy atmosphere. Most of them sauntered in to stand in the welcoming shade of the ancient baobab trees. In dusty memories of long ago, one of the trees used to house the prisoners. Justin stood by his car while Bern went into the office.

It wasn't every day that someone got killed by an elephant, although it did happen. Two muscular detectives wandered over to the vehicle; one twirled a toothpick around his tongue. They lifted the tarp, flinching when they recognised the gory remains of the body. Even a rooky knew Steven met a sudden violent death, and no man was capable of inflicting those wounds. The detectives finished photographing the body and writing copious notes in tiny notebooks.

Bern followed them indoors out of the heat. Sergeant Baruti led Bern to his small untidy office towards the rear of the building. Bern refused the kind offer of coffee and ginger crisp biscuits, aware that Justin was in a hurry. Sergeant Baruti, after getting the pleasantries out of the way, questioned Bern for almost an hour. He looked at the notes from Constables' Akanyang and Ditiro, and once satisfied, Steven's body was released into police custody. They would handle it from now on.

Justin dropped Bern off at Bella's house. 'I won't stay, I'm anxious to return to the Ihaha public camp to take my guests on their afternoon game drive. You owe me a beer, man,' he said, waving a farewell to Bern.

'Ja, anytime, thanks for all your help.'

'Not a problem … what are friends for, eh?' Justin disappeared into the twisted maze of Kasane.

CHAPTER 54

Bella woke up when she sensed someone in her room.

Karyn stood beside Bella's bed. 'I'm so sorry, Bella love. Bern phoned to tell me you were in the hospital. How are you? Bern also said you spent last night alone in Chobe. I can't begin to comprehend how awful that must have been for you.' Karyn took Bella's hand.

Bella scratched over the surface of her nightmarish experience. She didn't intend for Karyn to be traumatised by the tale.

'I'm stunned to learn of Steven's involvement in the poaching of animals. I always pictured him to be a kind and generous man. How wrong was I about a person I once called a friend? No wonder his demeanour was wound tighter than a spring. I'm not surprised by Lan's involvement, though. I always suspected something fishy chased after her.' Karyn paused for a moment.

'So, how did Bern know about you being left adrift in the bush? Wasn't he in Maun yesterday, if I'm not mistaken?'

'Yes, I think so. I'm guessing Steven phoned him, in the likelihood of luring him into coming up here to rescue me. Bern could have ignored Steven's request and stayed in Maun, leaving me to fend for myself.'

'That would never happen, the man's besotted with you, he'd do everything in his power to rescue you. Trust me when I say Bern's in love with you.' Karyn smiled mischievously.

'I hope you're right, because I think I'm falling in love with him. My divorce wrinkles inside me, and I'd be devastated if Bern wandered off to his next conquest, forgetting I existed.'

'Bella, that's never going to happen.'

Bella yawned, fighting away tiredness.

'Sorry, I better leave you now and let you get some well-deserved rest. I can pop in for a visit tomorrow.' Karyn bent to kiss Bella's cheek before leaving her to sleep.

Bern turned towards Bella's house. He wanted to check up on the cat; he knew Bella would fret about Dingo. He used the spare set of house keys Bella had given him. The empty house remained icy without Bella to warm it. His footsteps sounded hollow on the polished concrete floors. Going straight to the fridge, he pulled out a few pieces of chicken from a plastic container.

Bella kept the gate to Dingo's enclosure open, to give Dingo his independence. She had installed a flap on the back door, where he could come inside whenever he fancied.

Dingo paced along the fence line; his tail swished against the slight breeze. He ignored the chicken. His amber eyes burnt into every corner of the enclosure, clearly searching for Bella.

'Bella's going to be all right, little one.'

Dingo purred at the mention of Bella's name, as though he understood every word Bern said. It then seemed to Bern that once

Dingo was certain Bella wasn't in danger anymore, he commenced eating the chicken.

Bern phoned for a taxi, though it was a short distance to the hospital. He felt bone-tired and worn out, but he wouldn't sleep until he knew the extent of Bella's injuries. The taxi arrived a few minutes later, skidding to a stop in the gravel driveway. Bern jumped into the passenger seat telling the driver to take him to the hospital.

He went into the reception area, going straight to the desk.

The attractive nurse glanced up at Bern.

'Can you please tell me Bella Winter's room number.' He smiled.

'I'm sorry, visiting hours are over for the day. You can come back tomorrow morning at nine.' The nurse shuffled papers on her desk.

'Please, I'll stay five minutes, no longer.' Bern used his most charming voice.

She pointed him in the right direction. 'Room 24. You can stay one minute and no longer.'

'Thanks.' Bern strode down the corridor into Bella's room.

Bella was fast asleep, her long hair cascaded across the pillow in ripples of liquified onyx. He bent to kiss her on the lips. They must have given her something to help her sleep, because he doubted lions' roaring beside her bed would disturb her dreams. He leant over to kiss Bella again. 'I love you. Don't worry about Dingo. Once I told him you were safe, he started purring.' He then left the hospital; the cooling evening air surrounded him.

Bern held himself entirely responsible for the dangers Bella had endured over the recent days. He wouldn't rest until she recovered from her injuries; the idea of losing Bella was something he refused to contemplate.

After checking to make sure Dingo had eaten his meal, Bern met up with Karyn and Mike for dinner at the Old House. The emptiness of Bella's house rattled him; it seemed too stark without her in it. Also, Bern hoped that talking about the dramas of the last couple of days might lessen the guilt he held about putting Bella's life in danger.

Bella didn't wake up until the sun streamed through the window. She had a premonition someone sat beside her, to keep her safe. She opened her eyes to see Bern staring at her. She could tell he had spent a troubled night.

He winked, leaning over to kiss her, and the smile on his face caused Bella's heart to flutter. 'Hallo, sleeping beauty, I visited you last night. You were dreaming romantic dreams about me, so I didn't want to disturb you. How are you, my gorgeous one?'

'I didn't dream about you; in fact, I didn't dream at all. I expect the doctor will let me go home today. I ought to be there to keep an eye on Dingo.'

'Leave the cat to me, the little scrap and I are bonding since I'm now taking care of him. He likes me now, although he's missing you.'

Bern stayed an hour, holding Bella's hand while he filled her in with the details about how he flew up and the sleepless few hours at Steven's house.

'I phoned Seagal. The poor sod is in shock about the news of Steven's involvement in the poaching. I'm sorry for not listening to you when you said Steven carried a remoteness about him. I'll let you rest now and visit later this afternoon.' Bern lingered, his hand touching her arm. He seemed so reluctant to leave. 'Sergeant

Baruti asked me to go to the police station to tie up a few loose ends. I have an inkling he'll want me to join him for coffee and a *nice* slice of malva pudding.'

'Lucky you.' Bella laughed.

The doctor visited Bella at lunchtime, saying she was now free to go home, if there was someone to take care of her. It would take time for her wounds, both physical and mental to heal. Bella lied to him, saying she had a live-in housekeeper. She craved privacy. Bern had to return to Maun for work, and she still carried some doubt about whether to ask him to stay.

The nurse arranged for a taxi to take her home. With all the tumult of the last couple of days over, the serenity of her surroundings sounded wonderful. Bella couldn't keep imposing on Karyn's friendship when she was at work. Bella also carried a niggling belief, somewhere deep inside her, that she had inadvertently caused Bern's life to be in danger. Bella blamed herself, believing that her visit to Steven had become the catalyst that caused the horrific events in Chobe to balloon out of control. Not trusting Bern's love was her first mistake.

Dingo

I refused to go too far to hunt for food. I wanted to be close to her to make sure she was safe. I slept on her bed during the day, to surround myself with her love. I sensed her presence getting closer to me. I went outside. The heat of the afternoon fell heavy on my coat. I retreated to a small bush beside the fence. When she arrived home, I ran up to her. She struggled to sit on the ground. An ache gripped her shoulder and chest. I sat on her lap, letting my purrs erase the guilt she carried. I stared deep into her bright-blue eyes; her mind seemed clouded, but she would recover, and I was happy she was home with me.

CHAPTER 55

Having reconnected with Dingo, Bella opened the front door. The emptiness of her house skulked off the walls. Dingo was close on her heels. The memories of the last few days bubbled to the surface, washing over her. She had arrived in Botswana a little over two weeks ago and felt she had been living her life on fast-forward. No wonder depression had sought her out again.

Bern stormed into the house. 'Why the hell didn't you tell me the doctor allowed you to go home? I picked up your vehicle from Steven's office then phoned the hospital to find out if you had any news about leaving.'

'Don't worry about it, Bern, you said Sergeant Baruti asked you to go to the police station … and I've imposed on everyone's friendship a lot lately.'

'You, liefie, can impose all you like, but what's with the tears?' He enveloped Bella in his strong arms.

Bella longed for Bern's gentle touch and to taste the sweetness of his lips, but she stepped one pace away from him. 'I'm sorry; a lot has happened to me in the last few weeks, and I'm struggling a bit at the moment. I came to Botswana to free myself of the guilt I carry about my marriage break-up. I'm so confused. I want to believe you and surrender into your embrace. I tremble each time you're near me and ache for you if you're gone. I've never known such an intense passion for another person, yet there's that other persistent voice in my head, asking if your love for me is about to end. You, my gorgeous man, ought to turn away and without a backward glance, leave me alone. Go look for some agreeable lady who doesn't come with demons.'

'Too late, liefie.' Bern took that step towards Bella; his arms curled around her. 'Now I'm positive you love me Miss Bella, there's no way I'm ever letting you go. I adore you.' He picked Bella up to carry her into the bedroom.

Her ribs ached, and she winced, sinking into the softness of the bed as he tucked her in.

Bella then fell asleep almost instantly, listening to the rhythmic beat of Bern's heart.

Dingo rarely left Bella's side. He was always lying on the bed touching her or curled up on her lap. His purrs melted away the grey clouds that surrounded her.

Bern stayed with Bella for two days, keeping track of her medication. He also chased away the black dogs of depression that followed her everywhere. Bern surrounded Bella with a tenderness she had spent her entire life searching for. She loved him to distraction, if only she had the courage to tell him.

The day Bern left to return to work, Bella told him she might be ready to meet his parents.

His smile lit up the room. 'I'll arrange it, but first I'm planning something special for us, following my ten-day safari to the Central Kalahari I couldn't get out of.'

They stood outside, Dingo at Bella's heels until Bern's taxi arrived.

'I love you,' he said, hugging her tight and then kissing her gently on the lips.

Bella ached to tell him she loved him too, but in the blink of an eye, he strode towards the taxi and soon became swallowed up by the brightness of the sun.

Bern returned to his house to get ready for his safari. The tranquillity of his house washed over him. The house smelt of Lan – her spirit lingered in all the corners floating off the walls. It seemed too soon for her journey into the afterlife to begin. Her personal belongings lay dotted across the lounge room. In the bedroom, Lan's dirty dresses and bras were strewn across the floor awaiting her return. A return now lost in the rhythms of eternity.

Funny how her untidiness never bothered him. The bathroom cabinet overflowed with all of her lotions, potions, make-up and hair crap. It seemed weird how when a life was gone, pieces remained to remind us that once a person lived and breathed in these spaces.

Bern never cared for Lan. He wouldn't miss the scratchy voice or the cheap sex, but he paused to give a final farewell to someone he briefly shared a life with. He took some garbage bags out of the cupboard and began shovelling in all of Lan's possessions. Those three meagre bags, full of junk and fragments of life, were all she possessed in the world. He tossed them into the dumpster in the front yard. They would be gone by tomorrow, carrying with them the memory of Lan.

Bern sat in his favourite chair on the deck, sipping a Lion Lager. The view of the river stretched in front of him. Letting his gaze fall across the water, Bern realised Bella might be starting to let go of her past. There was a lightness to her memories of Australia. The heavy clouds that scatter around her disappear if he stared into her incredible eyes. He sensed Bella's love for him now, even if she was reluctant to admit it to herself. He had arranged a romantic weekend away. He already purchased a ring. All he hoped to do was propose and pray her answer would be yes.

Two weeks later, Bern returned. The evening had started to reach the windows. The sun's rays trailed off the river, to send golden streaks to frolic in the cooling air. They hadn't seen each other for two weeks. Bern phoned every night, to make sure Bella was all right. She tried not to dwell on how much she missed him. Bella took extra care with her appearance, untangling the curls in her thick hair and applying make-up.

The minute Bern came into the house, Bella stood so still her breath caught against the walls. She had ached for this moment to be alone with him, but for some reason, her feet weighed heavy on the concrete floor.

'Hey, Bella, you showered and are wearing a clean shirt, does this mean you're starting to fall for me?' Bern teased.

Bella felt herself light up with his joy. 'Possibly, but … I might keep you guessing for a bit longer. I only showered and changed so I didn't have to hear your smart-arse comments about my appearance.'

'No matter, come here and kiss me,' he demanded with a wink. 'It seems months since I touched you, and how I have missed your bewitching smile, and those sapphire eyes I get lost in whenever I look at you.' He picked Bella up.

She flinched when her legs straddled his waist.

'Sorry, liefie,' he said.

Bella's hands curled in his hair; her kisses grazed his cheeks before her lips sought the softness of his mouth.

He pulled away. 'At last the lioness in you crawls out.'

Bella slipped down to the floor and took a few paces away. His eyes seared through her, making her tremble. Now that he stood centimetres away, all her misgivings surfaced again. This infuriatingly good-looking man could have any woman. Why did he persist in trying to chase her demons? Bella waivered on the edge of something incredible, unsure of her next move.

Without saying a word, Bern held out his arms, and as the last shreds of indecision floated away, Bella went to him. His love closed around her; his kisses burnt through her.

After they made love, Bern eased himself off the bed. 'I love you and could show you how much again, except we're due at the Old House in fifteen minutes for dinner with Karyn and Mike.'

Bern and Bella woke to another pristine day, the sun dazzled on the river. Bella reached across the bed, her fingers on Bern's bare chest. She wanted to touch the heat of his body against hers. A nervous sigh tingled through him. To lessen the tightness that stretched across his shoulders, she crawled out of bed, reaching for his hand.

'Ag, honey, what's so urgent, come to bed.'

'No, please greet this incredible dawn with me.'

The first rays of morning sunshine bathed the verandah in a golden glow. On the far side of the river, elephants played in the water. Hippo pods grunted in the shallows. Fish eagles floated on the first thermals of the morning. She wanted Bern to witness the magical start to the day.

Bella commenced dancing, swaying to the rhythm of a favourite John Lennon song. She tried to forget about the nightmares crowding through her since the horror of Chobe.

Bern encircled Bella in his arms, and together they danced around the verandah, in and out of the furniture.

'Mr de Villiers, I think I may be falling in love with you.'

'It's about time, because we're about to embark on the most romantic two days anyone could ever imagine.'

They retraced their dusty footsteps inside to finish packing.

'Did I mention you need to bring your passport with you?' Bern asked.

'Yes, of course.' Bella picked up her bag to take it outside. 'Where are we going?'

'It's a secret, liefie. Show a bit of patience, we'll be there soon enough.' He kissed her cheek.

They threaded a path beside the untidy gardenias to say goodbye to Dingo. Even though the gate remains open, Dingo still roamed and stayed in his enclosure.

Dingo

I ran up to them, sensing they were going away. She sat on the ground, so I crawled onto her lap to let my purrs trace through her. I felt a tragedy about to unfold. He bent to pat me. I touched my paw to his hand. My eyes tried to warn him. She trembled, and I realised she too sensed heartache about to cloud him.

CHAPTER 56

The shuttle bus arrived fifteen minutes later. Bern tossed the bags into the back of the vehicle. Their driver continued along President Avenue until he came to the A33. He picked up speed on the main road leading to the border into Zambia.

There were long queues of vehicles, and people meandered in the lazy heat towards the Kazungula ferry. The ride across the Zambezi River into Zambia took about ten minutes.

Bella and Bern stood on the deck of the ferry, watching the waves skip against the bow.

The transfer shuttle handled all the necessary passport and visa details. The whole procedure took well over one hour and seemed to be a game of disappearing in and out of several tired-looking buildings to pay fees and chase paperwork. The tangle of the border crossing soon faded in the rear-view mirror.

They drove along the M10 towards Livingstone. Several kilometres before the town, the driver turned off the main road towards the river. He stopped in front of the exquisite Tongabezi Lodge. It looked divine, designed in the true African style of concrete, timber and with thatched roofs draped low. The interior was infused with a golden glow. The Zambezi River sparkled in the sunshine, as it flowed to a gentle rhythm along the edge of the lodge.

To Bella, it oozed luxury, yet Bern persisted in fidgeting about something, which unsettled her. He spoke to the owner; someone he knew well from South Africa. He ushered them through the lodge, down to a small landing hovering above the river. Bern helped Bella into a canoe that wobbled alarmingly against the small jetty. She collapsed into a seat, clutching the side of the canoe.

Bern climbed in with the suppleness of a cat to slip into the seat behind Bella. The driver motored out into the middle of the river. He wove between hippo pods and manoeuvred through frothing waters similar to a washing machine. He pulled to a stop, bumping up a slippery bank. With the grace of a hungry vulture, Bella managed to stumble out.

Bern jumped from the canoe, coming over to where she stood. His kiss lingered over her lips, and his arms curled around her. Bella didn't believe there could be such a magical island. The owners named the island Sindabezi. It sat full of pride in the middle of the Zambezi River. Four private chalets were hidden from view between the trees. Bern had booked the entire island. He told Bella this was their own romantic time together. One of the welcoming staff members, Jemmy, led the way to where the room sat overlooking the river.

A timber walkway folded along one side, ending at the edge of the riverbank. Their room consisted of only one sturdy wall. It was built high above the river on a timber platform supported by heavy posts. The one wall turned its back to the rest of the island.

Stepping inside, they entered an enchanted fairy tale. A huge king-size bed was nudged against the wall. This meant the room opened out to views across the river. The timber deck floated lighter than a waterlily above the river. A claw-foot bath perched close to the edge. It boasted a bit of luxury on the crude timber floor. Beside it, a canvas wall tugged between three posts, where the outdoor shower opened out to the elements. On a rough wooden table, on the other side of the bath, sat a basin adorned with paintings of flamingos. Sheer white curtains struggled to free themselves in the light breeze, where jute ropes tied them against timber poles along the edge of the room. These poles held the thatch roof at bay. The thatch spanned the entire structure, a perfect spot for spiders to build their webs. Bern outdid himself by picking such a bewitching romantic lodge.

When the staff left, Bern swept Bella into his arms. He told Bella of the deep love he had for her. She had almost started to believe him, if only she could learn to trust him enough, to step away from her past life and begin to love him the way her heart was telling her to.

The next morning dazzled with the promise of romance. The sun glistened off the river. It sent sparks of light to dance with the currents. Bern went to stand on the edge of the deck, and Bella sensed a nervousness clouding him. She reached out to him. She felt the stiffness across his muscled back ripple away at her touch. He snuggled Bella in his warm embrace, kissing her.

They had breakfast out in the open on a timber platform overlooking the river. The air smelt sweeter than freesias, and Bella breathed it in, savouring every second. She couldn't get enough of

Africa. A smile etched across her face as she watched Bern eat his breakfast.

'Hurry up and eat, woman. Stop staring at me, I've a big day planned for us.'

'I'm not staring. I was miles away, thinking about how relaxed I am here.'

'Are you starting to be more relaxed with me also?'

'Yes, I'm beginning to lose my past to the desert winds blowing across Australia.' Bella held a speck of hesitation in her voice.

With the sun starting to bite, they scrambled into the fragile canoe for the short ride to the main lodge. Bern organised a private tour, and their guide, Thomas, waited by the reception desk. He drove them to Victoria Falls, or Mosi-Oa-Tunya, as the locals called it. The falls were carved into a landscape so quintessentially African; Bern watched Bella fall under its spell.

Bern didn't seek to be anywhere else in the world except here with Bella. He watched the laughter crease across Bella as she looked upon wall upon wall of water cascading over the rocky outcrops. She didn't seem to care about her hair or clothes when the mist of water sizzled over her softer than summer rain. She giggled with glee as Bern hugged her, much to the surprise of other tourists and Thomas. He had never seen her this happy.

He knew that he should ask her to marry him now, with the falls as a backdrop. He could tell his nervousness had made Bella fidgety, but for some reason, he chose not to.

'You look worried. Please tell me what's wrong. Are you about to confess you have found someone else to share your life with?' Bella's voice had an edge of doubt.

'Never.' He shook his head. 'I'm sorry. A twinge of anxiety, that's all. Come, Bella, let's see what's next on the itinerary.'

They retraced their steps along the path to the waiting vehicle.

They had a lazy lunch at the Royal Livingstone Hotel, overlooking the river, before returning to Sindabezi in the middle of the afternoon. A hazy light trailed over the washed-out African rugs that hid bare patches on the polished timber floor. It brought a romantic ambience to the room. Bern stood beside the claw-foot tub, gazing out across the river.

Bella wrapped her arms around his slim waist, resting her head against his muscled back. 'Thank you for such a perfect day. You outdid yourself, Bern.'

He turned in her arms, putting both hands on her cheeks to pull her closer. He kissed her passionately and felt sparks of heat throughout his body. 'I'll spend my life giving you special days like this, Bella.'

They didn't leave the fluffy pillows and crisp white doona until the sun dipped low to the river.

Bern had ditched his safari clothes for a smart pair of chinos and a crisp white linen shirt. He stood on the edge of the deck, waiting for Bella to get dressed. Tension flew about him as he kept rehearsing his proposal.

He stopped breathing for a moment when he saw Bella. Her dress, the colour of dawn, billowed around her body. Her sturdy black boots were polished, gone were the scuff marks that always etched them. Bella had combed out the tangles in her long hair.

She scrunched most of it into an untidy bun, fastening it with a gold clasp. Wisps of hair fell down her back and across her face. She had taken extra care putting on make-up, using kohl eyeliner to enhance her deep-blue eyes and lashings of mascara to coat her long eyelashes. Bella finished the look with a lip gloss. It made her lips glisten as though kissed by dew.

'*Sjoe*, you polish up nice. You are stunning, Bella. I can't believe how lucky I am to be here with you. Come, I'm more nervous than a baby springbok. Let's go eat.'

They sat in comfortable timber chairs close to a huge fire burning bright in the evening air. Bern ordered champagne, and they sat sipping it while gazing into the fire. Licks of flame danced in the night air.

Stars glimmered in the sky; dots of white jade sprinkled over a cover of black silk. Their table sat waiting on the timber platform with spectacular views over the river to the forest where Bern pointed out hippos foraging.

'Why are you so jumpy tonight? You are the most arrogant, confident man I've ever met. Please don't tell me you are leaving me.' A slight tremor snatched at her voice.

'I'm never going to leave you. I love you too much.' He knelt in front of Bella, seeming to hesitate when his phone beeped. 'Shit, I forgot to turn it off … Never mind, it can go to voicemail.'

'No, it might be important. I remember Dingo warning me about something. You better answer it.'

Bern took out his phone. 'It's Mama, I better see what's up, sorry, my love.'

'Hallo, Mama.' Bern listened. There was a slight pause before he replied, '*God nee, Mama. Hoe kan dit gebeur?*' Bern then fell to the ground, dropping his phone. His anguish pierced into Bella. He sobbed for a full ten minutes.

Bella had no idea what had happened, but she cried with Bern; her arms circling him in comfort.

They stayed huddled together beside the table while Bern sobbed as though his life had split in two. Their romantic night had turned colder than snow on Mount Kilimanjaro.

'Whatever is the matter? Please tell me so I can help you,' Bella implored.

Bern sighed deeply; his pain etched across his face. 'Papa is dead. Someone shot him. Murdered. How does this happen? I must go be with Mama. She sounds broken. God, I'm broken.' Each word Bern uttered fell from his mouth to pool on the ground.

Bella too collapsed. She seemed uncertain about how to console someone who had learnt of the sudden death of a loved one. 'Bern, I'm so sorry; what happened?'

'I'm not sure; Mama sounded too distraught to talk. I'm phoning my brother to find out if he has any additional information.'

Bern stayed on the phone for about five minutes with his brother before he ended the call.

'Let's get away from here, there's a bitter smog hovering.' Bella supported Bern back to the room. She pulled the doona away, and Bern collapsed into the bed. Bella lay close to him, pulling up the doona. Although the night air carried the heat of the sun with it, Bern shivered uncontrollably, eventually falling asleep due to sheer emotional exhaustion.

CHAPTER 57

All of a sudden, Bern jumped up, throwing his clothes into his bag. 'I have to get to Cape Town immediately,' he sobbed.

Bella gathered up her clothes. He had only slept for a few hours, and now wasn't the time to do anything. 'It's too late now, Bern, we should wait until morning.'

'Fuck it, I'm leaving now, I'm about to explode if I stay here another minute. I've got to keep busy so my mind doesn't keep snapping back to Mama's phone call.'

'Fine, we'll leave now, I'm off to tell Jemmy to organise a boat.'

The helpful staff soon organised everything, and in minutes, they were motoring towards the main lodge. The manager met them at the dock. He arranged for a taxi to take them to Livingstone Airport.

Bern strode into the terminal straight up to the counter where he demanded to charter whatever plane might be available at the moment.

Two hours later, they permitted Bern to charter a Cessna 401. It sat on the tarmac waiting to be refuelled. Another hour dragged by while the ground crew refuelled the aircraft and positioned it ready for take-off.

Bella turned to glance at Bern as they taxied down the runway. His face was etched with sorrow, but she also saw a steely determination clouding his eyes. He would clearly do whatever it took to be with his loved ones. Soon, they were airborne slicing through the black sky, a quiver of light in an otherwise bottomless night. The plane banked when Bern changed direction towards Maun.

They landed in Maun about two and a half hours later. The time nudged two o'clock in the morning. Bern began preparing to fly out again until Bella cautioned him not to. He was in no state to continue. Bern looked worn out and way too stressed to be in charge of an aircraft.

'Ja, you're right, Bella, but what do I do now? I should be with Mama.'

'Of course. Let's get you home first. I'll organise the flights to Cape Town. Please, Bern you must rest.'

'I won't rest until I'm with my family, but you're right. Let's go home.'

A solitary taxi waited at the airport. The tired driver yawned and scratched at his shaved head before belching loudly. He opened the door; it creaked against the hinges. It was a short drive to where Bern lived on the banks of the river. The journey seemed to take forever on this sombre morning.

When they entered the house, the walls sighed with sorrow. Grief clung to the air. Bella opened the windows to bring the warmth inside. The atmosphere crinkled as brittle as glass. Bern threw his bag onto his bed, too distraught to begin the arduous task of repacking it. Bella busied herself on her laptop, organising the flights to Cape Town. While he waited for her to finish, he sat in his favourite chair on the deck, where the view of the river did not calm his tattered nerves.

Bella came up to Bern, pressing her head against his chest; stress hummed through his body. She saw the hurt in his eyes when he bent to kiss her. Tears etched a furrowed path down his cheeks. They clung together, sharing the sorrow. Bella told him she managed to book two seats on the Air Botswana flight to Cape Town, which left at eight o'clock.

She held Bern until six in the morning, listening to his stories about his father. Bern was in shock, reeling from the devastating news his mother had told him. He felt a desperate longing to talk about the man he had loved all his life. The man who made Bern the person he was today.

'Christ, Bella, I phoned Papa a couple of days ago. He sounded in fine-form, telling me how he beat his mates in a game of tennis. He seemed chuffed that at his age he still had the power to smash his opponents all over the court. I told him all about you, and he said Christmas this year was going to be a true family celebration. What do we all do now?'

Bella could find no words to answer such a grave question. She pressed her body even closer to Bern, trying to take away some of the hurt that knitted through him. Bella kissed him. 'I love you, Bern, now and forever. We'll get through this together.'

Bern told Bella his parents moved from Durban to Cape Town following his father's retirement from the University of Kwazulu-Natal. They purchased a grand house with sweeping views across the Atlantic Ocean. It was happy times for his folks, the two of them enjoying retirement with visits from their grandchildren, little Arno the second, and his sister Gracious.

His brother Hans married a Zulu woman by the name of Petal. Bern told Bella that Petal embodied the true Zulu, proud and tall; the two of them made a stunning couple. Their son and daughter, in no time at all, became treasured members of the family.

Now what were they all supposed to do, Bern questioned her. Their father lived his life an honourable strong man, so full of energy he overpowered all the spaces he occupied. His fierce, stubborn nature meant he ruled their house with a strong arm. Arno also had nurtured a softer side and loved his wife and sons with an all-consuming passion. It felt too sudden for such a great man to be taken. No one found the time to prepare, no one thought his life would end in the blink of an eye.

At six-thirty, they crawled out of bed. Bella went into the bathroom while Bern packed his bag. The clothes she went away with would have to do. Hopefully, her dress would be suitable enough to wear for the funeral. Bella's soul clutched at how awful the word funeral sounded.

She phoned Karyn, telling her of the sudden death of Bern's father. Karyn's voice cracked with the suddenness and the violence of it. She promised to take care of Dingo. 'Try not to worry about anything here, Bell, concentrate on Bern and pass on our condolences and our love.'

'Thanks, Karyn, I will.' Ending the call, Bella went to check on Bern.

He tossed his clothes into his suitcase without care. She watched him sob as he took his suit out of the wardrobe to fold it on top of all his other clothes.

'Christ, Bella, I wore this suit not long ago for Papa's birthday celebrations. Laughter and happy memories flowed freely that night.' He shook his head in clear disbelief.

Bella joined him on the deck.

Bern enveloped her in his arms, almost crushing her. 'God, Bella, how do I cope with such a tragedy without you by my side? Promise you won't leave me alone please, not now anyway.'

'Never, Bern. I love you, and we'll walk through this tragedy together.' Bella kissed Bern, tasting the saltiness of his tears.

The flight left at eight in the morning, arriving in Cape Town at two-fifteen in the afternoon after a short stopover in Gaborone. His parent's house sparkled in Camps Bay, south of Cape Town. The grandness of it took Bella's breath away. It portrayed luxury from the concrete and timber structure to the stone walls and atriums filled with exotic plants from all over the world. The balconies featured sweeping views over the windswept Atlantic coastline.

But the most heartbreaking sight of all became Arno's bakkie parked forlornly in the front drive. No one found the courage or the resolve to shift it into the garage out of sight. It held the essence of a father, grandfather and husband, whose life ended way too soon.

Bern knocked on the front door, almost setting it free of its hinges.

An attractive older woman opened the door. She hesitated on the threshold, as though she had forgotten why she stood in the doorway. Sorrow surrounded her like a desolate fog. Bella could tell straight away it was Bern's mother. He had her eyes, but now his mother's carried the haunting look of loss. It was a sadness Bella recognised all too well. 'I'm deeply sorry for your loss,' Bella said before moving aside to allow Bern to hug his mother.

He encased her in his strong arms, shrinking her small frame. She disappeared into him, and Bella listened to the heart-wrenching sobs coming from both of them but stood back. Now was their private moment to share in the horror of such a sudden death.

With grief hovering in the air, Bern peeled himself off his mother. He held out his hand. 'This is Bella, Mama,' he said with tears glistening in his eyes.

Chiara waved a shaky hand, her fingers fluttered like a breeze had caught them.

Bella wrapped Bern's mama in her arms. Tears rolled out of her eyes as she clung to Bella. Their tears joined together in grief. Bella wasn't quite sure how long they stood, clutching each other in a tight knot of sorrow she knew would stay with them forever.

Chiara stepped away but refused to let go of Bella's hands. 'So, you're the one he daydreams of.' Her voice cracked and broken. 'He keeps a lot to himself, but a mother always knows her son's heart.'

Bella smiled warmly at her. 'I'm sorry to intrude on you at such a harrowing time. I couldn't stay away without offering my deepest sympathies. I can book into a hotel, though, if you prefer this private time to be with your family. You should be surrounded by their love, not worried about a stranger in your home.'

'No, stay, Bern needs you now, and my dear, you are no stranger. You are Bern's other half.' She enfolded Bella in her warm embrace.

Their footsteps were hollow in the still house. They stepped out onto the balcony where the light dazzled off the ocean, bouncing off the brilliant white tiles. Two people already there sat talking in hushed tones; whispers echoed off the tiles. They refused to allow the harshness of their voices to shatter the sorrow. Bella guessed them to be Bern's brother and sister-in-law. Bella stood close to Chiara, her arms around her waist.

Bern went across to Hans and Petal. The three of them embraced while tears of melancholy flowed again.

They stepped away from each other, but somehow they managed to stay connected.

Bern reached out for Bella's hand.

'I'm so sorry for your loss, please accept my sincere sympathies,' she said to Hans and Petal with a quiet serenity because she thought the harshness of her voice might snap their fragile hold on sanity. Bern then introduced Bella to Hans and Petal. Bern had black wavy hair and chocolate eyes, while Hans was fair with deep-cerulean-blue eyes. The brothers were as opposite as a starless midnight and a clear blue sky, each striking in different ways, but both undeniably handsome.

Petal exuded a warm caring nature, and when they hugged, she sighed. 'I knew Bern was keeping a secret from us, I'm guessing it's you. Bern is a good man, almost as good as my Hans.'

They sat on the verandah, fingers touching each other, their shadows blended on the tiles.

A maid brought out a bottle of wine, coffee, and a cup of tea for Bella. The family's heartache was visible for all to see. Bella was poignantly aware that no one knew how to manage without their husband or father. Death was always too final, no one ever prepared for the suddenness of it. In an instant, your life changed, and the loss stayed with you forever.

Chiara gulped down the last of her wine. She appeared ready

to tell the horrific story of her husband's death. Her voice wrinkled with emotion during her tale, but she held onto a steely determination to tell the brutality of the day Arno ceased to be in the mortal world.

CHAPTER 58

Arno, fresh from another game of tennis at the club, boomed into his house. 'Chiara, my love, I beat those bastards again,' he yelled smugly into the silent rooms. 'Where are you?' For someone so self-centred, even Arno tweaked that something smelt wrong. The air inside his house held its breath, the perfume from the roses clung to the petals refusing to let go.

He strode through the entry and turned right to go into the open-plan lounge, dining and kitchen areas. He opened the door; light leapt off the Atlantic, flooding the room. His wife sat on the sofa, fidgeting with her hands. She didn't smile that gorgeous smile he loved. He glimpsed terror in her eyes. During their forty blissful years of married life, they never quarrelled or disagreed on anything. Even now, her beauty staggered him. Arno had loved her from the moment they met. She became his calming rudder. He domineered everyone, but his wife saw all the good that was inside him.

They had a perfect marriage. Their two sons seemed settled. Hans was happy with his life in Umhlanga, and from what Bern told them, he too had found his mate, and about time too. Both he and Chiara were looking forward to meeting Bella at Christmas.

'What's wrong, honey, come and give me a kiss. I beat those pricks at tennis again.' He saw her eyes flicker towards the entry. When he turned, he caught an arc of something bright before he crumbled to the floor. The barrel of the gun grazed him above his left temple. 'What the fuck?' he yelled, trying to stand.

Two foreigners stood in his house. They looked Asian, although he couldn't be certain.

The two intruders appeared almost identical. They must have spent every waking hour in gyms lifting weights. Their muscles bulged across their heavy chests and ballooned down their thick arms. One nursed a scar across his ugly face. It made his mouth twist into a permanent grotesque grin. The other was bald, his shiny great head beading with sweat, and his nose lay flat across his bland face. It caused him to wheeze continuously. Both carried Beretta 92 pistols.

'What the fuck are you two goons doing in my house, threatening my wife?'

'Shut up, we talk, you listen, wife stay alive.' One of the goons reached for a chair, pulling it out. He strolled brazenly to Chiara. He scrunched his bear-sized hands in her luxuriant black hair, in an attempt to pull it from her scalp.

She cried out from the pain, and Arno saw the terror mesh into her. He tried to go to her, until the other thug, Baldy, man-handled him in a vice-like grip. Chiara fell awkwardly, wincing when her hip struck the back of the chair. Scarface taped her ankles to the harshness of the timber. Her hands were pulled behind her back, and she shivered, but he ignored her. He taped her hands together.

Arno winced feeling her pain, and it was a blowtorch to his heart.

'Please, please why are you here?' she cried.

Scarface hit her hard across the mouth to shut her up. Drops of blood slid down her chin until he stretched a tape across her mouth from ear to ear. 'Shut the fuck up, bitch.'

Arno tried to reach her, but the thug holding him had youth and strength on his side. *God, what is happening to us?* Arno kept a gun in the drawer of his office, but it would be of little use to him there.

'Where is that son of yours?' Scarface, the one clearly in charge, yelled at Arno.

'Which one, I've got two sons?'

'He called Bern, where is he?'

'How do I know? I don't hear from him every day. The last I heard he was in Chobe in Botswana. What's your interest in him?'

'He kill lion for boss, we threaten you, he kill lion, all live. You ring him now, tell him Mama gets shot in six hours if lion not killed.'

'I'll do no such thing, I refuse to be intimidated in my own home, untie my wife NOW and get the fuck out of here or I'm calling the police.' Arno reached into the pocket of his baggy white tennis shorts to get his phone. He prided himself on being invincible, most people feared him, but not these two. Arno reached for his phone; a sharp pain caught him on the mouth. Scarface had clubbed him in the head again. He fell awkwardly to the floor, his hand twisted painfully. Arno tasted his blood from the cut to his lip. '*Verdomde hel,* I can't tell Bern what to do, he's never in his life listened to me. Why should he start now.' While Arno struggled to stand, he recalled an old rugby tackle. He crouched low, springing forward to grapple Baldy by the waist. He pushed him into the wall.

They both fell hard, sending a family photo crashing to the floor. Glass shattered across the tiles.

His attempt at bravery might well have been Arno's biggest blunder.

Both thugs pulled him to his feet, pushing him hard into a chair.

His face hurt from where the gun hit him. Arno ignored his suffering. He glanced at his wife; tears streamed down her face to catch in the tape. 'I'm sorry, I love you,' he said to her.

Baldy threw a phone to Arno. 'Phone Bern NOW!'

'NO!' Arno yelled. *Why do I always insist on being so stubborn*, he questioned.

A gunshot rang out, breaking the deathly silence seeping into the room. The noise was deafening. The bullet went straight through his knee; Arno screamed so loudly that it seemed to peel the paint off the walls. The strong stench of gunpowder filled the room.

Chiara's heartfelt sob became trapped in the tape across her mouth.

Arno collapsed to the floor. He writhed in agony as he clutched at his knee; blood bubbled through his fingers to drip onto the tiles.

Both Scarface and Baldy manhandled him onto the chair. They ran the tape around his thick waist, fastening him to the chair, tighter than a chicken ready for the braai.

'Now phone Bern,' Scarface said. He handed Arno his phone.

Arno continued to be pig-headed; he spat at Scarface, sending droplets of blood and spittle to sprinkle over the fat face of his aggressor.

Baldy went over to Chiara. He pulled her hair in a painful grip, exposing her throat.

Arno yelled, 'Leave her alone, you brute.'

The knife pricked at Chiara's throat. Blood trickled from a slight cut under her chin.

'Give me the damn phone, do *not* touch her again.'

Scarface threw the phone to him.

Arno's hands shook as though a stiff breeze caught at his fingers. Never in his life had he been so helpless. He punched in Bern's number, but it went to voicemail. 'He's not answering, please leave us alone, I can't get in touch with him.' For the first time in his life, Arno tasted fear. He flinched from the agony of his wife's pain, not the pain in his knee. He hardly felt the throbbing ache, his mind filled with the agony on his wife's face.

'Not believe you, try again or we shoot wife.' Scarface held the gun to Chiara's temple.

She began to cry; tears fell on her slim-fitting floral dress.

'He's not there; he must be working. Bern sometimes turns his phone off if he's on a game-drive. I'll try later, please leave my wife alone. I'm begging you.'

The two stood uncomfortably glancing at each other with sweat beading on their faces. Baldy's wheeze shuffled about the room. They were all brawn and had no brains, and they stared at each other, their expressions blank. They seemingly understood Arno told the truth about not being able to talk to Bern, and the orders from their boss appeared to be unravelling. Arno thought that their thick brains refused to process what to do if he didn't contact Bern.

Both men went into a huddle, talking in a language Arno failed to understand.

Scarface then took out his phone and yelled into it. 'Nguyen?' he yelled, but Arno couldn't make out any words after that. Scarface flinched at the shouts that came back down the line at him. When he hung up, his face was grim. The two thugs began talking again in their native language. Arno couldn't understand a word of it, but when one of them drew a finger across his throat, his intentions became clear.

Scarface sneered his lopsided grin at Arno. It chased a groove across his cheek. He raised his Beretta 92 pistol like he was about to swat a fly, pointed the barrel between Arno's eyes, pulling the trigger.

In the split second before his life ebbed away, Arno felt his piss warm on his legs as he stared down the barrel of the gun. Flashes of his life spun uncontrollably, a dandelion flailing in a windstorm. His eyes bulged; he yearned for one last look at the love of his life, but a chubby finger squeezing the trigger blurred his vision. Then he saw only the blackness of death. He never got the chance to hear his wife's agonising gasp that caught in her throat. She had witnessed the violent murder of her beloved.

The two smiled, pleased with themselves. They turned towards Chiara. She welcomed the fact death faced her. The vision of seeing her husband's brains spill over the floor became a hideous dream she could not live with. She loved Arno from the first day she saw him, and now she didn't know how to live without him. Her grief swallowed her. She sought death as a way to end her suffering. Baldy raised his gun, pointing it towards her head.

He started to squeeze the trigger, clearly savouring the moment. All of a sudden, loud footsteps resonated up the driveway, crashing through the afternoon vapour off the ocean. The front door to the house exploded into the room. Three policemen rushed in to assess the situation with their guns drawn. Baldy turned slightly; the shot hit him right through his heart. His life snuffed out before he hit the floor. It took mere seconds for the other two policemen to overpower Scarface.

One nightmare ended, and another one began for Chiara. Once the policeman freed her from the chair, she threw herself over Arno, sobbing uncontrollably. Her heart clutched into a tight knot; her breaths ragged.

Her neighbours had been relaxing on their verandah finishing off the bottle of wine from lunch. The jarring sound of a gunshot broke into their silence. They ran inside to call the police. The officers left Chiara to grieve for her husband while they completed their work. They handcuffed Scarface, putting him in a police car for the short ride to the station and jail.

With practised gentleness, they lifted Chiara off the dead body.

'Is there anyone we can call to come and be with you?' one officer said as he bent over Chiara, holding her hand.

But Chiara made those private calls herself. She breathed in trying to compose her erratic thoughts before making two heart-breakingly shaky calls to her sons.

CHAPTER 59

Bern swore under his breath. He needed fresh air; he stumbled out onto the verandah, and Bella followed. The touch of Bella's hand on Bern's arm startled him into the present. 'This is all my fault, Bella.' Bern tried to make sense of the tragedy. 'They should shoot me, not Papa. Why didn't I stay a vet? I had to be the arrogant selfish one, putting my desires first by becoming a bloody guide. Those fucking poachers kill anyone who gets in their way.'

'Please don't blame yourself … it's not your fault. How were you to know anything like this would happen?'

Hans, Petal and Chiara wandered out of the splintered house to come and stand beside Bern.

'Darling boy, you're not to blame, come here.' Chiara enfolded her youngest son in her arms.

'I'm so sorry, Mama, please forgive me.' Bern's anguish was visible in the mist blowing off the ocean.

Hans and Petal expressed to Bern that they refused to let him take the blame. The blame for such a tragedy lay at the feet of Steven and Lan, and the two thugs. They were the ones to take full responsibility for their heinous crimes. Arno's blood stained their hands, not Bern's. They were the ones with greed glinting in their eyes, trying to get rich by killing endangered animals. Their involvement caused the death of a loving caring man.

'Please, I need a moment alone,' Bern said.

Chiara, Hans and Petal wandered into the study; no one went into the lounge room where the ghost of Arno lingered.

Bella stood a little away from Bern, looking lost in the grief surrounding this peaceful family.

Bern realised with a sinking heart that the lion-poaching racket in Botswana wasn't over by a long shot. His father's violent death brought even more resolve to those determined to kill for their selfish greed. The deadly fight against such an evil crime was only beginning. It didn't matter to the ones in charge how many people died, there would always be a never-ending parade of thugs. Bern vowed to do everything in his power to end the gruesome slaughter of his beloved lions. He also pledged to do whatever it took to protect the ones he loved.

He punched Seagal's number in his phone, knowing full well he should be awake at this late hour.

Seagal answered on the second ring, 'How are you, my friend?'

'Not good at the moment ... I'm a bit shell-shocked.' Bern then spent a few tortured minutes catching Seagal up with the suddenness of his father's murder. 'I'm in Cape Town at the moment, with my family and Bella. It's hard to say how long we'll be here. Please ask Justin to fill in for my next Chobe safari. Let's see what happens next. I can't think straight at the moment, but Hans and I have arrangements to make here.'

'Sure, man. Don't worry about anything here, eh? I'm sorry for your loss. Take care of your family.'

They finished off their conversation.

Bern went to Bella standing against the railing. He encircled her with his arms, kissing the nape of her neck.

Bella turned slightly. 'I'm so sorry about your papa. Please, Bern, believe me, this horror isn't your fault.'

'You're right, deep down I know I'm not to blame, but God I miss him. Papa was too full of life to be taken like this.'

They left the blue mist to hover across the tiles.

Bern led Bella to his bedroom. 'I love you, Bella, please never leave me.' His whispered words caught in his throat as though they were too precious to leave him.

Bella spent all of those days with Bern's family. The five of them echoed against the empty walls. Chiara seemed to barely come to terms with why her family and not Arno were in her house. The funeral passed in a quagmire of sorrow. Chiara became lost in her grief but somehow managed to surround her family with warmth and compassion. It took Bella no time at all to love her. And Chiara welcomed Bella into the family like she was one of her own. The suddenness of losing her husband clearly haunted her and always would. A loneliness appeared to crowd her; a veil settled over her eyes, and Bella doubted it would ever leave her.

Hans and Petal teased Bern mercilessly about Bella.

'We gave up the dream of Bern finding someone to love and settle down with,' Petal said, holding onto Bern's hand.

'You do know he is arrogant and has a persistence bordering on mania,' Hans added with a wide smile.

'I knew all about his arrogance the first second I laid eyes on him, but after a time, I realised Bern carries a softer, caring nature and that is what I fell in love with,' Bella shared with them.

'Bella made it hard for me at first, though I think with dogged persistence, I'm winning her over.' Bern beamed at her.

'I'm already yours, Bern.' Bella winked.

Over time, the family allowed themselves to laugh again, and Bella felt honoured to be a part of it. She was now free to allow herself to believe in the love Bern professed for her, because it was the same love she felt for him. Bella's insecurities and past had started to trickle out of her. The intensity of Bern's passion sent a tremor through Bella's body each time he looked at her or held her in his arms.

Exactly one month after they had arrived in Cape Town, Bern and Bella flew back to Kasane. Hans and Petal left mere hours after them, for their flight to Durban. Bern's mama had booked a one-way ticket to Italy for the following day. She was going to stay for an extended period with her brother and his family in a villa near Lake Como. She said it was time to return to her roots; time to heal.

When the plane touched down, Bella breathed a sigh of relief. She was at last home. Dorset was her only connection with Australia, and now his spirit soared in Dingo.

Bern went inside to make a few calls, leaving Bella to sit with Dingo. His paw rested on her arm. She stroked his soft fur and felt a lightness enter her heart.

Bern found them an hour later. He sat beside Bella, encasing her in his arms. His tears fell to blend with Dingo's and Bella's. He let his hand rest on Dingo's head. 'Come, my love, we must go now. Dingo will find us later.' He then lifted Dingo off Bella's lap. '*Dankie. Tot* later, my little *maatjie. Bly veilig.*'

Bella smiled. Dingo would come inside when he was ready.

She couldn't quite believe how much she had changed since moving to Botswana and meeting Bern. And while she still didn't understand why Bern chose her, she was so grateful for his love and support.

Bradley had never treated her with respect during their marriage. She was his accessory not his partner. Bern included her in everything he did. After witnessing first-hand the devastating effects of poaching, Bella was determined to help Bern, Seagal and the other guides in their fight to stop this insidious crime. She couldn't imagine a world without lions roaming free.

She put her arm around Bern, and together they walked inside; they would tackle their future challenges *together* – as they were always meant to do.

Dingo

I sat with patience and a bit of anxiety, waiting for them to come home. Before going to her, I went to him and rubbed my body against his leg. He had experienced a great loss, and I wanted to erase the suffering from his heart. She sat on the ground waiting for me. After he stroked my head to reassure me that time would heal his loss, I went to her. I climbed onto her lap. He sat beside her with his hand on my coat. My purrs sifted through both of them as we watched the changing colours of dusk streak across the sky. When they left me to go inside, I stretched. It was time to begin my night-time hunt. I would return to them later, to sleep on their bed.

ACKNOWLEDGEMENTS

I started writing *The Hunted* sitting around our campsites in Botswana. Watching elephants, painted dogs and giraffes wandering by, filled me with inspiration. When I had finished the first draft, it spent a lot of time idling on my computer. I had started another manuscript when I decided it was time to do something about *The Hunted*.

Letting go of my words was a nervous time for me, but I have so many people who made the journey more bearable.

I want to thank Jane Smith for assessing the manuscript. She pulled many threads together and helped me streamline my work. A big thank you to Michele Perry for editing *The Hunted*. Michele was gentle and constructive with her feedback, and I learnt so much from her.

I'm also grateful for the support I received from Ann Dettori at Dettori Publishing. She helped me navigate the complexities of self-publishing with professionalism and warmth, making *The Hunted* shine.

In 2022 I did a writing safari in Zimbabwe. The hosts were

Jo-Anne Richards and Tony Park and I thank both of them for their support. I took my manuscript of *The Hunted* with me. Jo-Anne and Tony were complimentary during our one-on-one sessions. Jo-Anne has a PhD in Creative Writing and is from South Africa. Tony is a best-selling author from Australia, who also loves writing about Africa. Penny, Merle L, Trevor, Merle G, Elinor, Leslie and Jane were on the writing safari with me and all of them were warm and welcoming and helped me realise that maybe I could do this.

The first time Peter and I went camping in Botswana, our guide was Seagal Tembwe. Seagal quickly became our friend and after that our camping adventures with him began. Peter, Seagal and I would immerse ourselves in the Game Reserves and National Parks. Seagal's natural ability and patience in finding my favourite cats (lions) never ceased to amaze me. I thank him for instilling in me an appreciation for the wildlife. His stories and humour are forever stitched into my heart. I know he won't mind that I have made him a character in my book.

And last of all I could not have written a single word if it wasn't for the support I receive from Peter. He makes it possible for me to chase my dreams.

Colleen Flanagan was born in Brisbane Queensland and now resides in Redcliffe on Moreton Bay.

Colleen and her husband Peter ran an architectural Practice in Redcliffe for many years. In 2019 they spent ten months camping in the southern African countries. This is when Colleen started to devote her time to writing. She is constantly inspired by the people, landscapes and wildlife in Africa.

Her wandering spirit has taken her to many countries around the world but Botswana holds a special place in her heart.

www.colleenflanagan.com.au